I have no reputation to speak of, she thought.

It won't matter what I do, and I only know to do one thing.

He obliged her by kneeling. He closed his eyes and rested his head in her lap. She put her hand lightly on his head. After a moment of tension at her touch, he relaxed completely. Her heart went out to him, and she wondered when the last time was anyone had touched him. Never mind. She would comfort him the only way she knew how.

His arms went around her, circling her hips and waist. She closed her eyes against the pleasure of it all. I may be comforting you, Mr. Trevenen, but I am finding this entirely agreeable.

She opened her eyes quickly with another thought: I am enjoying this too much. And then she thought, how long has it been since a man touched *me*?

* * *

Beau Crusoe
Harlequin® Historical #839—March 2007

Praise for Carla Kelly

Carla Kelly
Beau Crusoe

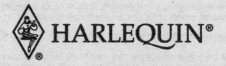

HARLEQUIN®

TORONTO • NEW YORK • LONDON
AMSTERDAM • PARIS • SYDNEY • HAMBURG
STOCKHOLM • ATHENS • TOKYO • MILAN • MADRID
PRAGUE • WARSAW • BUDAPEST • AUCKLAND

ISBN-13: 978-0-373-29439-8
ISBN-10:   0-373-29439-5

BEAU CRUSOE

"The discomposure of the mind must necessarily be as great a disability as that of the body."
—*Robinson Crusoe* by Daniel Defoe

For my agent, Ruth Cohen

Prologue

"I declare my blood flows in chunks when I get a letter like this from Sir Joseph," Lord Watchmere pronounced over breakfast.

He peered at his wife, two daughters and grandson, then glared at the note. "There is always trouble when Sir Joseph begins, 'My dear Watchmere, I forgot to tell you.'"

"He must know how busy we are," Lady Watchmere said.

Busy with what? Susannah Park wondered. *We are more idle than most of the population.* She glanced at her small son, who seemed unconcerned about the conversation. He needed a haircut but she always waited, because his curls reminded her of David, late a clerk of the East India Company and now only a two-by-three-inch miniature beside her bed.

Mama weighed into the conversation. "Husband, I do not care that Sir Joseph is your relative and Susannah's godfather. He is a trial."

"Heaven knows we have enough of those in this family," Loisa commented.

Noah looked at Susannah then, and edged himself closer. She touched his head, well aware that Loisa watched every movement. *How long do you mean to punish me, Loie?* Susannah asked herself. *Did I really ruin all your chances by eloping with David? Really?*

Papa shared the rest of the letter. The winner of this year's Copley medal was due in London this week and Sir Joseph Banks, head of the Royal Society, needed a favor. "It says here, Agatha, 'He is a navy man shipwrecked and five years cast upon a deserted island'—Hmm, careless to be so long stranded—'Rescued by missionaries'—Lord, what penance for carelessness—'and eight months in returning.'"

Watchmere stabbed the letter with his fork. "Here it comes, Aggie: 'I call his survival a triumph and so is his treatise, but my gout is troubling me and I would be a terrible host.'"

He kept reading. "We are to harbor this curious man until the Copley is awarded. Then we can put him back on the mail coach to Cornwall. God help us, Cornwall." He contemplated the vast desert of Cornwall for a moment, then looked at Susannah. "I will add the post script, my dear. I request that you take charge of him."

"Me?"

"Clarence! The propriety!" Mama exclaimed. "Susannah is… not received. You know that."

"I owe my ruin to Susannah," Loisa snapped. "You would have her peacock about town with a bumpkin from Cornwall?"

Noah edged closer to Susannah.

"You do it, then, Loisa," Papa said. "He's probably broken in health after such an ordeal and won't require much except a sedate drive in Hyde Park and bread and milk before bedtime."

"I will do nothing of the sort!" Loisa shouted, then looked around at the footman, who had studiously ignored her outburst, even as he edged away, too.

Watchmere smiled at Susannah. "Then it is your lot, dear. You've seldom wanted for sense." He coughed into his napkin. "Since your sad lapse, at any rate."

"Clarence, Susannah is but twenty-five," Mama reminded him.

"And has more sense than a roomful of ladies twice her age," Lord Watchmere concluded. "You can probably take him walking in the Royal Gardens, if the weather is nice. Besides, you know how I hate to exert myself."

She did, remembering something David had told her after

their elopement when they were sailing to Bombay. "Dearest, let us be honest. You don't really think your father dictated all those letters of business to me, do you? I had to follow him into the bird blind for his signature, so it became easier to do it all myself. I think that was why he paid me so well."

She tried again. "Papa, this Mr...."

Watchmere looked down again. "James Trevenen."

"...Mr. Trevenen is an elderly man?"

He shrugged. "First mates of His Poor Majesty's navy tend toward youth, but who can be sure? Mr. Trevenen's treatise on crabs speaks of mature years."

"Crabs?" Mama asked, investing a treatise of her own in the single word.

"What can I say?" Watchmere replied, holding up his hands in self-defense. "As a Royal Fellow, I read the whole thing. It is a mature work of great genius."

Mama and Loisa laughed then, and Susannah and Noah made their escape, pausing for nothing except bonnet, short cape and Noah's nankeen jacket. As always, they left by a side door, avoiding the main entrance and her father's toucans, who reigned supreme there. They frightened Noah and disgusted everyone else.

The day was warm for late September. Noah skipped ahead, pausing for her at the stile that separated the estate of Clarence Alderson, Viscount Watchmere, from the Royal Gardens of Kew—royal land, but largely unoccupied since Poor George's current descent into madness.

She went first to the rose glass house, already opened for her by the gardeners. Today she would finish pruning the roses and preparing the beds for winter. As she deadheaded the flowers, Noah gathered the faded blooms into a burlap sack. Eventually, they would end up with the piles of leaves the gardeners were beginning to rake together, preparing to burn them.

The smell of smoke would be pleasant enough, but even seven years was not enough to drive from her mind and heart the columns of smoke all over Bombay during that season of cholera, when nearly everyone in the East India compound had died.

David had been an early victim, waking one morning with a slight headache and dead by nightfall. Before the sun had set, his linen-wrapped corpse had joined others on the funeral pyre in the courtyard.

It was not surprising that she did not care for autumn at Kew Gardens.

Instead of going to the Botanica Exotica glass house when the roses were done, she pointed Noah toward Spring Grove instead.

"No painting, Mama?" he asked.

"Not today. I need a word with Sir Joe." She smiled at him. "And you're probably desperate for a macaroon."

He hurried ahead again and she smiled to watch him. She didn't like to miss a day of painting, especially since the Royal Society paid her a shilling each for her renderings of the plants and flowers brought back to British shores on research vessels and ordinary ships of His Majesty's navy. Sir Joseph had easily persuaded his fellows in the Royal Society to let her continue where others had left off, notably Sydney Parkinson, the artist who had accompanied a much younger Sir Joseph on that voyage to the South Pacific with Captain James Cook. After she painted each bloom or shrub, a secretary at Sir Joseph's residence in Soho would apply a brief description to the back, all in the name of science.

At Spring Grove, she quickly learned that Sir Joseph had not been fooling. In a whisper, Lady Dorothea diverted Noah to the sitting room for macaroons and sent Susannah down the hall.

"It's bad?" Susannah whispered back.

Lady Dorothea nodded. "So much pain." Her eyes filled with tears. "Seeing you will help. You know it will."

She did. As she followed Barmley, the footman, down the hall, she contemplated again the injustice in an unjust world, where kind men and women sometimes are not blessed with progeny of their own. So it was with Sir Joseph and Lady Dorothea.

In the library, Sir Joseph could barely turn his head to acknowledge her. Barmley quickly went to his wheeled chair and turned it just enough so his master could see her.

She smiled at the footman, grateful he seemed to love his employer as much as she did, to think of such a little kindness.

He blushed and fled the room, murmuring something about tea.

"You'll have to cease charming my help so blatantly," Sir Joseph said, resting his hands in his lap. "I think you should turn your attentions to one more eligible."

"I barely glanced at Barmley!" she protested, then blushed to see his smile.

"Just quizzing you," he said and shook his head, careful to make no sudden movement. "I suppose Clarence never thinks to tote home any young gentlemen."

"He would if one of them came with a…a…cloth-brained towhee perched on his shoulder."

Sir Joseph laughed, a gentle hiss that caused no movement to his body. "Life with a birdwatcher must be a trial."

The footman returned with tea, bowed and left, after a proprietary look at his master. Susannah poured, then held the cup directly to her godfather's lips. He gave her a look one part gratitude and one part embarrassment, then drank.

You dear man, she thought, then sipped her own tea. "It seems I am to get out more, Sir Joe," she said. "Papa has decreed I am to escort old broken-down James Trevenen when he arrives."

"Old? Broken down?" her godfather repeated. "How did my cousin arrive at that conclusion?"

"Papa decided anyone five years alone on an island must have suffered a complete breakdown. He also insists no young pup could have written such a treatise."

"It is a fine paper," Sir Joseph agreed. He looked at her, and she held her breath in hope. "Perhaps you would like to read it. Go ahead, dear. It's on my desk."

Without a word, she leaped up and found the manuscript. "The Gloriosa Jubilate: Creatures at Play in a Tidal Pool on a Deserted Island in the Tuamotu Archipelago," she read. She couldn't help but smile at the crab on the cover. Obviously Mr. Trevenen's talents lay with the pen and not the brush.

The dedication touched her: *To my dear mother, who was*

ever near me, though far away. The opening paragraph took her breath away:

> Owing to the workings of Divine Providence and none of my own exertions, since I was far gone, my small boat found a gap in the coral reef and grounded me on the sandy beach of my exile. I alone survived.

"Sir Joe." She breathed. "Do you mind…"

"Go ahead. Noah will eat macaroons all afternoon and I will just rest my eyes."

She took off her shoes, made herself comfortable on the sofa and continued.

> The Tuamotu Archipelago contains uncharted reefs. The *Orion,* which had survived typhoon and Maoris in New Zealand, found herself split wide-open by a coral reef, and sank in less than ten minutes. Captain Sir Hugo Marsh tossed me the ship's log as my crew launched the dinghy.

Susannah took the treatise with her when she and Noah left Spring Grove in late afternoon. After dinner and an impatient time in the sitting room listening to Mama and Loisa argue about next spring's Season, she hurried Noah to bed.

She took a moment to observe the day's work of the servants, who had taken the Holland covers off the furniture in the chamber across from her own. The bed was made, but the curtains around it not rehung yet. Soon, all would be ready for Mr. Trevenen.

She got in her own bed then and continued reading.

> I discovered that the Gloriosa Jubilate is a gregarious creature, relishing the society of other kindred crabs. Who knew how long I might live in this place? I had no companions. I resolved to become more closely acquainted with these small companions of my exile.

Susannah rested the manuscript on her stomach, thinking of her own circumscribed life at Alderson House. "Exile, indeed! I could dream of a tropical island," she murmured out loud. "Warm Pacific waters, fruit for the plucking, fish in the lagoon."

She pinched out the candle, careful to keep hold of the treatise as she arranged her pillow. "Be you young or old, you simply must tell me of your life in paradise."

The *Gloriosa Jubilate* seemed to glow at her, courtesy of the full moon outside her window.

Chapter One

~~~~~~~~~~~~~~~~

The *Orion* might have sunk six years ago, but James Trevenen felt the hairs rise on his neck when the innkeep's wife snapped open a tablecloth on the table in a private parlor by the public room, the sound remarkably similar to the ripping hiss of coral on a ship's underbelly.

He looked around, hoping no one had noticed his sudden intake of breath. He wondered how long the ordinary noises of life in England would startle him. The inn was crowded, and everyone was too busy to bother with one average-looking fellow.

He had no problem waiting; Lord knows, he was patient. According to the coachman, the district had suffered from heavy rains recently, which had loosened the bridge footings between Lovell and the next village. The result was an unexpected stop at an inn not used to such heavy trade.

No matter. He had listened to the complaints of others ahead of him in line, demanding this room or that convenience, serene in the knowledge that no matter how uncomfortable he was likely to be for the night, it would never be as bad as five years marooned, alone and hungry on a tropical island.

He had felt some pity for the governess with the two children who had sat across from him for hours on the mail coach. Her dickering with the innkeep sounded particularly desperate. She kept peering into her reticule, as though hoping the few coins might have reproduced since her last inspection. He suspected this sudden stop had forced the governess to rely on her own means, which were shabby, indeed, if her threadbare cloak was any indication. Her employer must be a stingy bastard, James decided. He wanted to pull out his own stuffed wallet and help, but he knew better.

He had signed for his own room—after arguing the keep out of a private parlor for dinner because, of all things, he hated to be alone—when a fop strolled into the inn and demanded lodging.

The much-tried keep had assured the man there was nothing left, that Mr. Trevenen had the last room.

The fop turned to James. "I will relieve you of it."

You're a cheeky fellow, James thought, amused. He didn't care one way or the other but, for argument's sake, had to ask. "Suppose I say no?"

The fop had buggy eyes, which popped out even more at his quiet response. Unruffled, James watched his complexion turn an unhealthy mottled hue. Not used to an argument, eh? he thought.

When the skinny fellow attempted to draw himself up, it occurred to James that this was probably the worst setback he had ever encountered. Will he try to bully me, or play the sympathy card? James asked himself.

It was the sympathy card. Maybe something firm in James's expression had sparked a change in tactics.

The fop whisked out a scented handkerchief and delicately touched his eyes. "You cannot imagine what this day was like," he said.

"I'm sure I cannot," James agreed, trying not to smile when an Englishman smelling of lavender chronicled his misery. You can't imagine misery, James thought.

Still, the man looked put-upon, with drooping collar points and limp lace awash over wrists as delicate as a female's. James tried not to stare at the odd lumps in the fop's pantaloons. Whatever padding he had applied to his calves to make them shapely must have broken loose from their moorings and drifted.

This is not a man who travels well, James decided, as he turned to the innkeeper.

"I have no problem relinquishing my room," he said.

"It's the last room," the keep reminded him. "I have nothing else for you, sir."

James shrugged and glanced into the public room. "I can sleep on that settle, if you can spare a blanket and pillow."

"Sir, it's…"

"Done then!" exclaimed the fop. His pleasure vanished when the keep described the room's location. "It overlooks the cattle yard and the necessary?"

"Aye."

The fop put his handkerchief to his nose, as though he already smelled the horses in their stalls. "I suppose nothing can be done about the view."

"Not unless we turn the building around," James said. He winked at the innkeep, who could do no more than shrug. "I can leave my luggage behind that counter."

"Certainly, sir," the keep replied, relieved and embarrassed at the same time. He would have said more, but the fop, who announced himself as Sir Percival Pettibone, demanded his attention with another wave of his handkerchief.

Better you than I, James thought as he put his luggage behind the counter. He took out the leather satchel containing his treatise and walked into the inn yard. I hope I was never like that. His family had land and money enough but no titles, and his mother had sent him to sea well-mannered. Since his return, James had observed many of his countrymen who would have profited from a few years' solitary confinement on his island. It had the wondrous effect of teaching survival *and* humility.

He sat in the inn yard until the sun started to set, doing nothing more than ruffling through the pages of his treatise, even though he knew it by heart. Indeed, after he ran out of ink on his island, and before he figured out how to make ink from an octopus, he had memorized blocks of it.

There was the *Gloriosa* itself on the title page. Before he had left London last year, he had asked an apothecary to blend the colors he remembered. He was no artist, but that night as he shivered in the cold English summer, he painted *Gloriosa* to the best of his memory.

He turned several pages, relishing the story of his daily observations. He had even named the crabs he came to recognize: Boney, who was a little smaller than the others but aggressive; Lord Nelson, missing one eyestalk; Marie Antoinette, whose colors, while in the mating act, glowed even brighter. They were his companions even now.

He looked up quickly, thinking of his other companion. "All right, Tim, where are you?" he asked softly. He held his breath, but he saw no familiar faces in the inn yard. It was too much to hope that Tim had finally decided to leave. Perhaps he had decided, in that perverse way of ghosts, to bother Sir Percival Pettibone for an evening's entertainment. Specters were hard to reason with, James had discovered.

Before he went inside, he stared at the night sky, out of habit expecting to see the Southern Cross. *I really need to quit looking for it*, he told himself.

The public room was already deserted. The innkeep had put a blanket and pillow on the settle and what looked like a bottle of beer close by on the floor.

And there was the keep, polishing the last of the glassware. He glanced overhead, and James could tell his embarrassment had not abated.

"Don't worry about Sir Percival," James said. "I really don't mind."

"You should," the man said, casting a dark glance toward the stairs this time. "I think Robespierre was right." He made a chopping motion. "Zip!"

James winced. The innkeep smiled and turned back to his work. James placed the *Gloriosa* on the settle, then walked through to the cattle yard behind, where he had noticed the necessary.

He had buttoned up and left the privy when he smelled smoke. Alert, he glanced along the upper row of windows. Smoke billowed out of the room he thought had been appropriated by Sir Percival Pettibone. He hurried toward the building as the fop, clad in a nightshirt, darted from one open window to the next, back and forth, indecisive.

James might have resigned his commission, but nothing could ever sever him from a lifetime of training. In his best quarter-deck voice, he roared for the innkeep.

Sir Percival stuck one skinny leg out of the window.

"No! Don't!" James ordered.

"Save me!"

The innkeeper ran into the yard. He took one look and turned in the doorway, calling for his wife to get the guests out. Sir Percival continued to teeter on the window ledge.

James gave the drainpipe a shake, pleased it was anchored firmly to the building. Pretend it's a palm tree, he told himself. He pulled off his boots and stockings, shinnying quickly up the pipe as the yard filled with people in nightclothes.

"Pull your leg in," James demanded. "Do it now."

Despite his terror, Sir Percival made his mouth small in the expression James already knew too well.

"I don't care who you are!" James roared. "Do as I say!"

The leg vanished to the sound of a high-pitched shriek. James pulled himself into the room, turning his face away from the smoke. His audience in the yard cheered.

He stayed on his hands and knees with his head low to the floor, even as Sir Percival clutched him. "For the Lord's sake, buck up a little," James muttered. "I don't even see any flames."

There weren't any; the smoke began to lift. His eyes watering, James looked around and spotted smoke coming in smaller puffs from the end of the bed. He looked closer. Someone—probably the pitiful specimen huddled on the floor, weeping into a handkerchief now—had flung a robe over the warming pan, which must have been filled with too many coals. As the smoke began to dissipate, James saw the long handle. Gingerly he picked up the smoldering robe, and tossed it out the window, following it with the smoking blanket underneath.

He leaned out of the window. "It's over. We'll just have to air out this room."

He laughed at the applause from the little group below. Clasping his hands over his head, he bowed, amused at what passed for entertainment among the inn's guests. He knew he should say something to Sir Percival, who was alternately sniffing and blowing his nose, but the door opened and the innkeeper came in.

The sight of him seemed to revitalize Sir Percival, who pointed a bony finger at the keep. "You have dangerous warming pans!" he declared. "I will have this…this infamous heap you call an inn pulled down and…and plowed under…and sown with salt!"

James grinned. Man milliner though he was, Sir Percival seemed to have read his Roman philosophers.

The innkeeper stared at Sir Percival. "*You* started the fire!" He pointed to James. "Thanks to Mr. Trevenen here, nobody died, and you will live to irritate other innkeepers!"

"I hardly think the fire was that serious." James stopped. Neither man was listening to him.

Sir Percival blinked and his lower lip quivered. The innkeeper sighed. James tried not to smile. "I will get some more bedding," the keep said at last. He pointed at Sir Percival. "But I'm *not* bringing up another warming pan!"

"Heartless brute!" Sir Percival blew his nose, and then shrieked to see so much sooty residue on his handkerchief. He pointed to it. "I am dying, and all he can think about is his precious warming pan!"

I am in the land of the barely coherent, James thought. I was safer from freaks on my South Sea island. "I believe you will live," he said, proud of the control in his voice when he wanted to laugh until he ached.

Sir Percival's eyes were still on his handkerchief. He looked up and asked what was certainly his first non-self-absorbed question of the day, possibly the year. "What is your name?"

"James Trevenen," he said. "I'm from near St. Ives, and I am…"

"'Kits, cats, sacks, wives?'" Sir Percival said.

"I was asked that a lot when I was in the Navy," he said. Silly

man, he thought, but there was something endearing about a
fellow who could sit collapsed in the corner of a room and still
maintain some sort of presence. "Let me call your valet, sir." He
looked around. "Do you have one?"

Sir Percival waved his hand. "I believe he is dead drunk in the
adjoining parlor."

James blinked, but Sir Percival offered no explanation. In
fact, the magnitude of what had just happened seemed to pene-
trate his mind. "I owe you my life," the fop declared.

James stifled a groan. For the Lord's sake, it was only a warming pan and a smoldering robe! Any reasonably bright seven-
year-old would have known what to do. He almost said as much,
then stopped. Years ago, his fellow midshipmen had agreed he
had a wicked sense of humor. He made an elaborate bow and
placed his hand over his heart. "I am only too glad to have saved
you from a fiery death, Sir Percival."

Such simplicity was too graphic for Sir Percival, who shuddered and drew his legs up close to his body. Gradually, the romantic appeal of the whole adventure took over his mind. He
shook his head. "My loss would have been catastrophic to the
world of style and good manners," he said, as James looked
away to control himself.

Sir Percival was recovering rapidly. He held up his arm to
James, who understood the implied command and helped him
to his feet. "That is a regrettable waistcoat you are wearing. Is
there no fashion in Cornwall?"

"Precious little, I fear," James told him. "I'm only just back
from five years on a deserted island in the South Pacific, so it
seems unfair to cast the whole blame upon Cornwall."

He doubted a more inane sentence had ever come out of
his mouth, but he couldn't resist. Besides, his casual reference
to the South Pacific had the desired effect. Sir Percival's eyes—
already somewhat prominent—seemed to bulge from his face.
"Marooned! Cast away! And what do you do but come to England to save my life!"

That wasn't the total sequence, James thought with amusement. Having spent his life in the company of men with little time to think of themselves, he found this monument to preening esteem before him hilarious. "I am happy to have been of service," he replied. And then he couldn't help himself. "Death by fire would have been excruciating."

Sir Percival shuddered again, but, surprise of surprises, he had another thought for someone beside himself. "Let us not discuss the matter anymore! Are you bound for London to seek your fortune?"

I don't need a fortune, James thought. "Not precisely. While on my deserted island, I wrote a treatise on crabs." He sighed inwardly at Sir Percival's uncomprehending stare. "There wasn't much to do."

To his further amazement, Sir Percival nodded, his expression serious. "I know what it is like to spend a desolate weekend at a country estate when it is raining. Go on. I am intrigued."

James tried not to stare. "I suppose that is one way to look at it. At any rate, when I was rescued by missionaries…"

"Good Lord, that sounds even worse than a country weekend," Sir Percival murmured.

"Well, yes…I…I suppose." How can I tell you of *1,825 days* of solitude, each one spent wondering how I would die the next day, or in a week, or in fifty years without seeing another face? James asked himself. Even missionaries had looked good, but someone like Sir Percival would never understand. "We eventually returned to England, and I submitted my paper to the Royal Society for the annual Copley medal. What do you know, it won," he concluded.

"The Royal Society." Sir Percival leaned closer and patted his arm. "They aren't so totally bent upon style, either, so your waistcoat probably will not offend."

He is making this difficult, James thought, amused again. "I am relieved to hear it," he managed.

"Think nothing of it." Sir Percival blew his nose again and shuddered. "Where are you staying in town? Can you afford lodgings?"

"I have been invited by Sir Joseph Banks to stay with a cousin of his, a Lord Watchmere."

Sir Percival gasped. "Watchmere? Lord, help us! This will

never do for someone who spared me from a horrible fate! Watchmere spends all his time birdwatching and has even less style than you do!" He sniffed. "I know. This is hard to imagine. You will have to trust me on the matter."

James strode to the window and leaned his head out, hoping that he turned his laugh into a successful cough. He waited until he could face Sir Percival again. "Smoke plays such merry hell with the lungs," he said, unable to look the fop in the eye.

He saw no reason to remain in the room. The smoke had dissipated, and the innkeep stood in the doorway with more blankets and a pillow.

"Good night, Sir Percival," James said.

"I will not forget your kindness in saving my life," Sir Percival said.

Please do, James thought, repentant already. I should never have led you to believe you were in the slightest danger. He went down the stairs slowly, smiling to see that the keep had made up his bed.

The smile left his face. Someone sat at the table, half-shrouded in darkness. "Go away, Tim," he said softly. "Don't follow me to London."

Chapter Two

James woke to the aroma of sausages. He lay on the narrow settle, hands folded across his chest. There had hardly been a morning on his sea island when he had not woken up dreaming of food. He knew where he was, but the idea lingered.

He opened his eyes, surprised to see the table in front of him spread with sausages and eggs. And there was toast, all soft in the center with butter oozing. He sniffed. He just knew that earthenware pot contained quince jelly. He closed his eyes against the carnality of it all.

He looked around to see the innkeeper bringing out a roast of beef, all steaming and cunningly sliced so the tender, moist pink interior winked at him like… Oh, God, and now he was thinking of Artemisia, Lady Audley with her legs spread wide, eager to seduce him after they left the miserable fever harbor of Batavia, prepared to cross the Indian Ocean.

She had succeeded with neither a gasp nor a whimper from him, starved as he had been after five years of abstinence from the delights of both bed and table. The only thing that could have made that first climax more piquant would have been to clutch a chicken leg in one hand as he rode Lady Audley to the finish line.

Food and fornication, a sailor's delights. "What is all this?" he asked, trying to elevate his mind.

The keep turned the roast beef around until it was practically leering at him. "Mr. Trevenen, this is compliments of Sir Percival Pettibone who…continues to be convinced that you saved his life last night." He winked at James.

"I should be ashamed of myself for taking such advantage of his credulity, but I could not resist."

"I can well understand that, sir!" the innkeep declared. "What an ass he is."

"Yes, indeed," James agreed, "but I must tell him the truth about last night."

"You're too late, Mr. Trevenen," the keep said. "I doubt he would believe you. Now he means to feed you well."

"With any luck, this meal will end his gratitude." James raised himself up on one elbow and stared at the breakfast before him. "I cannot begin to do justice to all this, and there's nothing worse than wasting food." If you only knew, he thought. If you only knew how I bloodied my hands starting that first fire using friction and a piece of wood, so I could cook a fish. He had only cooked it for a few minutes before grabbing it from his puny fire and eating it all from lips to tail, blood and sea water gushing from his mouth as he chewed and gulped.

"I have an idea," he said suddenly. "Remember that governess? Invite her and her two charges in here for breakfast. I had the feeling she didn't have much money for this unexpected stop."

"My feeling, too," the keep said. "She only ordered two bowls of soup for dinner, so we can guess who went without."

James looked at the table, unable to lift his heavy mood. This feast would have kept his entire boat of shipwrecked sailors alive until they all reached the island. "And please, bring me a bowl of cooked oats with butter and clotted cream. It's what I fancy even more," he said quietly.

"As you wish, sir," the keep said, and left the public room.

James folded the blankets and took himself off to the necessary. By the time he returned, the governess and her charges were seated around the table.

"We didn't expect this kindness, sir," she told him, her plain face red.

He joined her at the table. "It was a surprise to me, as well, Miss…uh…"

"Haverstock, sir," she said. She managed a slight smile.

"Let us begin," he replied. When the children were engaged in eating the eggs and sausage, he looked at her, a woman past her middle age who probably had never been shown such attention before. "When I helped Sir Percival last night, he apparently decided to make sure that I did not starve before the mail coach left."

Miss Haverstock looked around her, amusement in her eyes. "I would say he has succeeded admirably, Mr.…."

"Trevenen. James Trevenen. Bound for London," he added.

She was too polite to question him, but merely nodded and returned to her raspberries and clotted cream. From the way she ate them, relishing each bite, they must have been an unheard-of luxury. James had cause to contemplate the plight of governesses.

"Your employer won't be upset you were late?"

"I suspect he will," she said. "He is Lord Eberly of Maines, and he loathes tardiness."

"Surely you can explain the delay and he will reimburse you," James said. "I have a feeling you spent your own money."

"I did."

Disquieted, he finished his oatmeal and was eyeing the remaining sausages when Sir Percival came into the public room. James wondered if it was his first venture into such a common place. He carried a lace handkerchief, as though ready to put it to his nose should any rude odors come his way.

James rose, wiping his lips, and bowed. "Good morning, Sir Percival," he said cheerfully. "Thank you for keeping my hunger pangs away. Won't you join us?"

"Thank you, no, dear boy," he replied. "I had tea upstairs, and a piece of bread lightly toasted with the merest sprinkling of cinnamon sugar."

"That will hardly maintain a sparrow, Sir Percival," James

said, "and yet you have been so generous to me that I was able to share. May I introduce you to Miss Haverstock?"

"Bless you, Sir Percival," Miss Haverstock said, and her voice trembled a little with emotion as she curtsied to their benefactor.

James decided that being thanked for a good deed was a novel experience for Sir Percival. The fop's little chest seemed to swell with pride. He smiled at the gathering, as though he had fed five thousand with loaves and fishes, and not merely James, a hungry governess and two children.

Is benevolence so new to you? James thought. Lord, soon *I* will be thinking I did something of real courage yesterday, when it was all a humbug.

He had a sudden thought, as though yesterday's imps had returned. "Sir Percival, I wonder…" he began, then shook his head. "Oh, no, it is too much to ask."

The bloom of philanthropy obviously still sprouted around Sir Percival. "Only ask, dear boy," he said. "I owe you everything."

James winced, then indicated Miss Haverstock. "This lady tells me she could be in jeopardy of losing her position. Her employer is a stickler for punctuality, and here she is, a day late, because of that demmed bridge."

"Hmm," was all that Sir Percival could work up.

Better hurry, James thought, before the bloom vanishes. "His name is Lord Eberly of Maines."

Sir Percival glanced at the children, who were finishing off the sausage, and whispered, "Eberly is a stingy ass, Miss Haverstock, to force his children to ride the mail coach. He also has dreadful taste in waistcoats. I hope you realize that."

The governess blinked. "All the same, Sir Percival, I need the employment."

The baronet's eyes grew bright. "I have a brilliant plan! Let me escort you and the children to Maines. I will explain the situation to Eberly. He looks up to me in matters of good taste. When I have finished, he will never dream of sacking you."

I am amazed, James thought. "You are too kind," he murmured, well aware that he was in far too deep now to explain away last night to Sir Percival.

"I shall smooth over the whole matter," Sir Percival declared. He looked at James with real apology then. "Dear boy, there will not be room for you in my conveyance, too. I regret you must continue your own journey on the mail coach."

"Have no fear," James said promptly, ashamed of his own mischief. With any luck, Sir Percival would forget where he was staying in London.

In less than an hour, the mail coach from the opposite side of the river passed through, signaling the way was clear. Before he boarded, James returned to the inn to say goodbye to Miss Haverstock.

He bowed to her. "I know you will pull through this little difficulty in good shape."

She blushed. "Thank you."

He glanced toward the stairs, where Sir Percival was descending, pulling on an eye-popping pair of lavender kid gloves. His valet, looking none the worse for a night of drunkenness, came behind, bearing a jewel box.

Sir Percival indicated that Miss Haverstock and her charges should follow his valet. When they were gone, he patted his neckcloth. "I didn't dare leave the inn until my valet was sober enough to tie this."

"You could get another valet," James suggested.

Sir Percival sighed. "That is my dilemma. No one ties a neckcloth as well as he does." He sighed again. "Was ever a fellow so put-upon?"

"I doubt it," James said, discarding five years of shipwreck, terror, hunger and despair in one short sentence. "Thank you for your kindness to Miss Haverstock."

"It is nothing to your kindness to me," Sir Percival said. "I will not forget."

"I wish you would," James said.

Through the open door, James saw the coachman climbing onto his box on the mail coach. "I must go," he said.

"I, too." Sir Percival leaned toward James and whispered, "Don't be troubled by Lord Watchmere, my boy. He is a fanatical birdwatcher and will scarcely know you are there. Lady Watchmere can only manage one thought at a time. The daughters? One is red-faced with thin hair—regrettable—and the other trails the odor of scandal, or so I have been told."

He minced into the inn yard then, allowing his valet to hand him into his carriage. James crossed to the mail coach and settled himself in the corner. As they bowled along toward London, James put Sir Percival far from his mind.

James arrived in London in early afternoon, tired of travel and still disgusted with himself for toying with Sir Percival's sense of obligation. To divert his mind, he thought of Sam Higgins, one of his rescuers from his South Sea paradise prison.

A year ago, in what he still considered an odd reversal of obligation, he had deposited Sam Higgins in London at the Missionary Society in Aldergate Street. As soon as the door swung open to James's knock and his companion announced himself, there had been no opportunity to say farewell.

James smiled ruefully at the memory of standing on the doorsill, forgotten, as Sam was borne away. He had closed the door himself and made his way to Admiralty House, where he dropped his own bombshell concerning the long-sunk *Orion,* and resigned his commission.

He had been tempted to return to the Missionary Society to say a proper goodbye to Sam, but decided against it. The Society was more interested in exotic heathen sinners than in an enthusiastic fornicator late of the Royal Navy, a species more common than petunias. So had ended his stewardship over Sam Higgins.

But as London came into view, James thought of his rescue from the island. The first two years, he had lived in anticipation of rescue. By the third year, he had given up hope. Fear had yielded to resignation and a certain acceptance of his plight. No ships came; he was doomed to remain king forever of his island roughly one mile by three miles, surrounded by coral, washed by warm Pacific waves. All he had to do each day was find food and observe his *Gloriosa* friends.

He did one thing more. He kept meticulous record of the days, weeks, months and years. Each Sunday, he recited the Articles of War from memory, as he would have done on any Sunday on any quarterdeck in His Majesty's fleet. In the evening, if he had enough wood, he touched off a bonfire. His Sunday ritual reminded him that although he was naked, brown and bearded, he remained an Englishman.

After five years, he was ready to discontinue his ritual, which was beginning to mock him. Since his woodpile was large, he decided on one last bonfire. For a few minutes, he was fiercely proud to be a son of England, even though it was a land he had seldom seen since his eighth birthday.

As he touched off the blaze, he noticed a low cloud to the west. By morning, the previous day's low cloud had turned into a ship under sail. He woke to see a longboat shooting through the gap in the coral reef, making its way into his placid inlet directly toward him.

To his disgust, instead of running to meet them, he turned into the foliage and hid himself. Later he told his rescuers he was ashamed of his nakedness, but that was a lie. He had panicked at the sight of men as if he had been a wild animal.

The ship was the *Odyssey,* sent from the Missionary Society with more evangelists for Tonga, but fleeing now from that island and bearing the missionaries—Sam among them—who had survived. Only five of the original ten were alive, having suffered through several years of servitude to a king of enormous dimensions but little patience with pale men who smelled bad and disapproved of everything he did.

So the *Odyssey* found him. Naked as the day he was born, Lieutenant James Trevenen, first mate of His Majesty's *Orion,* found himself on the deck of the missionary ship, covering his privates with the pouch bearing the *Orion's* log and his notes on the *Gloriosa.*

The coachman blew on his yard of tin, and James opened his

eyes, looking down involuntarily to make sure his loins were covered. It vexed him to be thinking of the South Seas again. Here he was, on his way to accept a most prestigious prize, and all he seemed to think of was the island, Sam Higgins and even, God help him, Lady Artemisia Audley.

The coach was emptying fast, but still he sat there in a panic, jolted by the knowledge that once he received the medal, he had no plans. Not one. He thought about his Cornwall estate, left in the excellent hands of a distant cousin and happily relinquished to James on his return from the grave. His bailiff was nearing retirement but superb, and required no assistance from him. James had no wife or child who would be looking out windows, waiting for his return. There was no one and nothing. He had survived shipwreck, starvation, despair and solitude, and it made no difference to anyone.

He managed to get his luggage from the mail coach and tucked the smaller leather case containing the *Gloriosa* manuscript under his arm. Unnerved, he found a corner in the nearest public house and sat there, after ordering a pork pie to keep the proprietor at bay.

He watched the pork pie congeal and willed himself to breathe calmly. The terror passed. As his mind began to settle, he realized that in the middle of the comforting humanity swirling around him, he was homesick for his South Sea island.

He found a jarvey to drive him to Richmond, a pleasant spot some seven miles upriver.

Since James had admitted to being from Cornwall, the jarvey pointed out several landmarks on their journey. One landmark made him sit up straight. He leaned forward.

"'Pon my word, a pagoda?"

The jarvey pointed with his whip. "Tis a heathenish sight, eh? Ten stories. Do you think the royals run up and down in there and cavort?"

James laughed and shook his head. "Is this the Royal Gardens?"

"'Tis."

A bare quarter mile later, they turned into an estate's grounds through handsome brick pillars and a wrought iron arch that bore the name Alderson. James couldn't help but notice the mortar was crumbling around some of the bricks. Perhaps the Aldersons—Lord and Lady Watchmere, according to his letter—could have used a wallet as well tended as his own.

James paid the jarvey well, went up the front steps and knocked. He knocked again when no one answered, and was raising his hand for another knock when he heard a voice on the other side of the door.

"When I open this, come inside quickly."

Well trained from his midshipman years to do what he was told, James darted inside when the door opened. He had barely pulled in his satchel before it closed again.

He looked up in surprise to see a large tropical bird perched on a bust. Across the hall, a similar bird—he thought it was a toucan—perched on a similar bust. Both watched him with dark, calculating eyes.

The butler bowed and kindly inquired if perhaps he should have taken the servant's entrance.

I am definitely too shabby, James concluded. "I am James Trevenen from St. Ives, and I think I am expected."

The butler blinked. James was struck by his resemblance to the toucans, who were also blinking and bobbing.

"Beg pardon, sir. We were expecting someone older."

"Hmm, singular," James said. He raised his hand slowly to remove his hat, trying to ignore the intense interest of the toucan sitting on what looked like a bust of a Roman statesman. "Julius Caesar?" he asked.

"Lord Watchmere calls him Don Carlos, and that one is Dona Isabel." The butler smiled then. "You mean the busts, do you not, Mr. Trevenen? Yes, that is the unfortunate Julius Caesar and the other is Octavian."

Unfortunate indeed, James thought, as Don Carlos clacked his long beak against the Roman's neck. One day you rule Rome, and the next day you're a rubbing post in a menagerie.

"Mr. Trevenen, Mrs. Park mentioned to me that you would be arriving soon."

"Mrs. Park?"

"Lord Watchmere's younger daughter. She is the relict of the late Mr. Park, who perished of cholera in India."

Such a chatty butler, James marveled. If you were ever to meet Orm, my nosy butler, you would get along like dowagers at a garden party. With toucans.

The butler must have realized he was revealing more family news than was strictly necessary. "Sir, you have been put in Mrs. Park's care for the duration of your visit."

"Lord Watchmere is not in town?"

"He is here, sir," the butler assured him. "You will meet him this evening. He generally secretes himself in a bird blind each morning and seldom emerges until he has observed a number of our feathered friends."

The man spoke in such round tones that James had to turn his head and convert his laughter into a cough that made Don Carlos ruffle his feathers and unloose an indignity upon poor Julius Caesar. James could only close his eyes and concentrate mightily on the inside of his eyelids. He patted his chest. "Tropical ailment. Comes on me suddenly."

The butler smiled. "Mr. Trevenen, we know we are an eccentric household."

"He's in a bird blind *all day?*"

"Quite, sir. I take him luncheon, of course."

"Up the tree?" James asked, fascinated now, and trying to imagine the tall butler shinnying up a tree with a tray in one hand.

"I will have a footman take your effects to your room, sir. Mrs. Park told me that if you don't mind a little walk, you can find her in the exotic blooms glass house at the Royal Gardens."

And probably with a toucan on each shoulder, he thought, dazed by the Alderson household. "Come again?"

"Every day, she and her son walk to Kew to tend the flowers. In the afternoon, she usually paints blossoms brought back from naval voyages."

This he did understand. "I've served on a ship or two where we potted plants and returned them to England," he said.

"She does it for her godfather, Sir Joseph Banks," the butler informed him. He lowered his voice, as though the toucans were foreign agents. "She is *not* an eccentric."

He nodded, and the butler gave him precise directions to the glass house. "Thank you." He looked at the toucans. "I'll open the door quickly."

"Excellent, sir."

James yanked the door closed behind him, but not before he heard a jungle chorus from the toucans. It dawned on him that they must fly toward the door every time someone knocked, ever hopeful of escape. I know I would, he told himself.

He enjoyed the walk. Lord Watchmere may have been careless about his entrance, but the gardens were magnificent and full of birds. No wonder the toucans were so eager to fly away.

As he crossed the stile to the Royal Botanic Gardens side of the fence, he noticed footprints of a child—the butler had mentioned a son—and a woman. Her stride told him she was not tall. The depth of them indicated she trod the ground in a middling way.

He reminded himself he was no longer on the prowl on his sea island, and he focused his attention on the row of glass houses directly ahead of him.

He admitted to faint disappointment, having thought he would see airy chambers reaching toward the sky, somewhat on the order of the Chinese pagoda over his left shoulder. These glass houses were squat and wood-framed, with glass panels on the sides and a substantial skylight in the middle of each building.

He found the Rose House, but it was locked. Two houses over, a boy was playing by the door with what looked like a miniature horse and cart. He noticed James and stood up.

I am a stranger, James thought. I wonder if he will hurry inside. What happened next touched him. Instead of retreating, the boy moved in front of the door, tossing his little toy from hand to hand. James didn't think him more than five or six, and yet there he stood.

"Good for you," James said, still out of the child's earshot. He raised his hand and called, "Are you Master Park?"

The boy nodded and seemed to relax as James came closer. "Noah Park. My mother is inside." He still did not step away from the door.

"I am James Trevenen. The butler said I would find your mother here."

Noah tucked the toy under his arm, a little boy now and not a protector. He grinned at James. "Did you have to slam the door really fast to keep the birds inside?"

James nodded.

"I don't like them. I wish they could escape someday, but Mama says I am not to…to foment revolution."

James hid his smile at Noah's use of big words, equally aware of the wistfulness behind them. "I had the same thought," he admitted.

After another long appraisal, the boy opened the door slowly, careful to make no noise. "I try not to startle Mama when she is painting. She gets cross if her hand jerks and she has to begin again."

"I can imagine," James whispered back. "Is she a good artist?"

He knew it was an unfair question to ask a small boy, but Noah intrigued him.

"She is the best in the world, sir," Noah replied, with no hesitation.

They stood in the open doorway. James closed his eyes for a moment, relishing the fragrance of tropical plants and imagining himself back on his island, if only briefly.

Noah cleared his throat. "Mama is watching us," he whispered.

The lady sitting under the skylight was doing precisely that, her brush raised. She smiled, and James felt his heart turn over.

Chapter Three

He had not been right about her size. Even though she was seated, he could tell she was taller than her stride had indicated. She must have been matching her paces to those of her much smaller son. The skylight provided perfect painter's light and her lovely face was turned in his direction. She sat casually, her legs crossed at the ankles, her slipper dangling off the end of her toes. She wore a dark dress, covered with a big apron.

"I am James Trevenen," he said simply.

There was no disguising her surprise. Quickly, she pushed her foot back into her shoe, stood up and took off her apron.

She was slim enough, with comfortable breasts that had suckled a child. Every man had his tastes. His interest ran to women with deep bosoms.

Her lively eyes held his attention. They were brown and large, brimming with good humor, even though she did not know him. Her eyes dominated her face because of their handsome contrast to her blond hair and light complexion.

He bowed and she curtsied. "I'm delighted to meet the Parks," he told them both. "Your butler said you were expecting me?"

She nodded, then spoke to her son. Noah darted down one aisle of plants and returned with a stool. His mother indicated where it should go and then gestured for James to sit down.

He looked at the easel. She had finished the stem and leaf of a flowering plant. He noticed another easel beside the one she worked on, with the actual plant pinned to a board. He recognized the plant, although he had no idea of its name.

"I know this plant. I remember it from my island." He laughed softly. "I can tell you it tastes most awful and gave me a two-day grippe!"

Mrs. Park laughed and leaned toward him. "Sir, *why* on earth would you eat it in the first place?"

"Mrs. Park, I tried every plant on that island."

Her marvelous eyes regarded him with sympathy. "You must have been so hungry."

"I was hungry all the time."

He watched her expression then, wondering if she would do what most people did when he tried to talk about his experiences. Some changed the subject; others fell silent.

"What did it taste like?" she asked.

"Something perilously close to boiled cabbage left out too long," he told her, pleased at her interest. "Slimy."

She looked at her son. "Noah, you'd best not complain when I ask you to eat rice pudding."

James laughed. "There were moments I would have swapped my best friends for rice pudding!"

"I think I will stay away from ocean voyages," Noah said.

"You are wiser than I, lad."

Noah considered that, catching his hand in his mother's dress and winding his fist in the material. "I do not suppose when you started your trip, you thought it would end badly, did you?"

You're a bright lad, James thought, impressed. He glanced at the boy's mother, who smiled back at him and then lifted her shoulders in a little shrug, as if to say, "That's my son."

"You're correct, Noah," he said. "Perhaps it's just as well we don't know the end at the beginning, or we would never try anything."

Mrs. Park gently unwound her son's fist from her dress. "I must disagree with you, Mr. Trevenen," she told him. "There are some things I would still have done, even had I known the future."

He considered the *Gloriosa Jubilate* and its effect on him. "You may be right, madam. Without a shipwreck and my little crab, I wouldn't be here in Richmond."

"And you wouldn't be meeting us," Noah spoke up.

"Really, Noah. I don't know that we are anyone's cause for rejoicing," she said.

The look they exchanged told him volumes about their relationship and made James miss his own mother all the more.

"I am glad you have come," she said. "We were about to stroll over to Spring Grove, where my godfather resides." She leaned forward, including him. "He most particularly wants to meet you."

"I doubt there is anyone here who knows me," he said, puzzled.

"He is Sir Joseph Banks, who would have been your host, but for his illness."

He recalled the letter. "Of course. How dense you must think me."

"I think nothing of the kind," she replied. "After all, sir, I have read your treatise and must agree with my father, who calls it a 'mature work of genius.'" She smiled. "Forgive us for imagining you much older than you are."

"Just twenty-eight, Mrs. Park," he said cheerfully. "No genius involved; just a man with time on his hands."

Mrs. Park put her paints back in their box, which must have been Noah's signal to leave. "Speaking of works of mature genius, how old is your son?" James asked, after Noah left the glass house.

"Six," she replied. "He *is* a bright lad, isn't he?"

He wanted to smile at her mother's pride, but he didn't wish her to think he was teasing. "He is. Do you know, when I was trying to find the glass house, he stayed between me and your door? You have a valiant champion, Mrs. Park."

"We are all we have," she said simply. She reached for her shawl. "Let us go now. Spring Grove is not far from here, Mr. Trevenen."

Struck by his own shyness, James followed her from the glass house. He could think of nothing to say until he recalled her words. "Mrs. Park, you said you read my treatise. Why?"

"You think I cannot understand a treatise, sir?" She didn't say it with indignation but more in mild reproach, as though she would have teased him, had she known him better.

"No, indeed, ma'am," he assured her. "I only hope that my poor efforts to understand a crustacean did not sink you into profound slumber."

"It did not put me to sleep. You have a way with words, sir."

He felt his face flame, even as her soft-spoken praise thrilled every part of him. "I'm blushing like a maiden," he joked. "I'm not a man used to praise, Mrs. Park."

"I doubt you are even a man much used to company," she said. "What did you miss the most? Was it other people, or was it food?"

There it was. He had told himself only a few hours ago in the pub that he would never speak of his exile, and here was someone already wanting to know. She even looked interested.

"Sometimes it was the sound of another human voice. At other times, it was something as common as porridge." He felt his face grow even redder. "You must think I am an idiot."

"Hardly," she said. "Here is the stile. Noah, lend me a hand."

He waited as her son scampered over the stile and held out a hand for his mother. James's view allowed him a glimpse of her ankle. He ignored the stile and vaulted the fence.

Noah watched him with admiration. "When I am older, I will do it that way," he said.

"I am certain you will," James replied. He looked ahead. "Is that Spring Grove?"

As he watched, a large dog with considerable white on his muzzle lumbered toward them across the lawn that sloped down from the handsome manor. Noah skipped ahead to meet the animal. Mrs. Park watched her son a moment.

"Nearly everyone at Spring Grove is ancient, including Neptune there," she told him. "Barmley the footman is the only servant younger than fifty."

She watched her son as he meandered with the dog. "I do not think Noah knows anything about straight lines."

He thought of his own childhood. "Then put him to sea, ma'am," he told her. "I remember a ten-year-old midshipman learning the parts of a sextant and figuring the distance between Tenerife and Lisbon."

"You, sir?" she asked.

"Me."

The horror on her face disturbed him, and reminded him of lengthy letters from his mother that had caught up with him in ports around the world. He had read them and cried himself to sleep. The midshipmen who had fared best in those early years had been the orphans among them. After three or four years, the matter had equalized itself.

"Perhaps he will be a scientist like your godfather, Mrs. Park," he stammered, hoping to recover himself. "Look how Noah stops at every rabbit hole and spider web."

She stood still. "You went to sea at ten years old?"

"I was eight, actually," he replied, wary of her expressive face now and not wanting to horrify her further. "It happens all the time. Don't you know that?" He hurried to fill the space. "Trevenens are seafarers. I had an older brother then to inherit the family property. As it turned out, I was leading the healthier life on my weevily biscuit and dirty water."

"Oh, my," she replied, understanding him perfectly. "And your parents did not retrieve you from the sea then?"

He shook his head. "By then I was ten and used to the life, and so were they, I think."

"I could never..." she began, then stopped. "I do not mean to sound critical of your parents, Mr. Trevenen. Dear me, you will think I have rag manners."

"I think nothing of the sort, Mrs. Park," he said, and he meant it. "The sea is not for everyone. I liked it, actually."

They were approaching the mansion from the back, working their way now through a formal garden where gardeners were preparing the beds for winter. He noticed they all waved to Mrs. Park. So you and your boy are universal favorites, he thought. I have known you but thirty minutes, and you are already a favorite of mine.

A question that had troubled him on the journey from Cornwall surfaced in his mind. "Mrs. Park, have you any idea why your godfather invited me here two weeks before the Copley ceremony? I think at one point he intended to be my host."

"He did," she assured him.

"Why?"

She wrinkled her brow. "I'm not certain, Mr. Trevenen, unless he wanted to talk of the South Seas."

He stepped aside as a gardener hurried by with a wheelbarrow. "I fear my stories would be more desperate than diverting. We could probably cover the subject in a night or two." He inclined his head toward hers, hoping he was not being too forward. "I can tell him of all the plants I chewed and spit out and five hundred ways to fix coconut." He raised his hands. "Navy men have no conversation, Mrs. Park."

"Nonsense."

"You are kind." He paused, wondering if he was going to sound like an awestruck child. "No one worships your godfather and our own Captain Cook more than seafarers. I admit to some trepidation."

"If you can survive all those years alone on an island, you are equal to my godfather."

So it proved. He did not know what he expected, but it was not a fleshy man confined to a wheeled chair, looking supremely uncomfortable, except for the energizing gleam in his eyes.

Mrs. Park introduced her godfather, and James found himself touched by the esteem in her voice. He stepped forward and bowed.

"Sir Joseph, this is a pleasure far beyond even a medal. I have long been an admirer."

The old man inclined his head ever so slightly toward a nearby chair. "Do be seated, Lieutenant." He glanced at his goddaughter. "My dear, let Dorothea know that we would like some refreshment, if you please."

Mrs. Park blew a kiss in Sir Joseph's direction—James wanted to sigh with pleasure—and left the room.

The scientist was silent for a moment, and James felt too shy to break the stillness in the sunny room. Then his host remarked, "Lieutenant Trevenen—oh, Mr. Trevenen—isn't she a fine one?"

James hoped he did not appear surprised. "Why…yes, indeed, Sir Joseph." When Banks said nothing, only looked at him with amusement in his eyes, James stumbled on. "I have to wonder why so fair a lady has not remarried."

What am I saying? James asked himself in sudden desperation.

Sir Joseph was kind enough not to remark upon his embarrassment. "Perhaps she will tell you, Mr. Trevenen. May I call you James?"

"James or Jem, if you please, sir," he replied in a small voice, feeling younger than a midshipman again.

"James then, and we will not be formal at all. You wrote an excellent paper."

"Thank you."

Again the silence, as though the old man were measuring him. "I suspect you began it to keep yourself from madness."

James stared at him. "How did you know, sir?"

"I remember those islands, James, beautiful to look upon but deadly to endure. After several weeks on Otaheite, I began to ask myself, 'Can one have too much paradise?'"

They looked at each other with complete understanding.

"Sir Joseph, is it the South Seas that you wish to reminisce on for these next few weeks?"

"Partly," Sir Joseph replied. "My voyage with Captain Cook was the hardest exertion of my life, and yet I have always wanted to return. I want to know all about that voyage of yours, and…" He stopped, and again James felt himself being measured and scrutinized. "I want you to do something else for me."

"Anything within my power, sir."

"I want you to marry my goddaughter."

"What?" He could not possibly have heard the old man correctly. "S-s-sir?"

"I have too few years left to stand much upon ceremony," Sir Joseph answered, unperturbed. He peered kindly at James down his long nose. "I trust I do not shake you to the core of your being, James. You seem to be a flexible man."

"A...flexible man?" There was no way he could hide the incredulity in his voice. "Sir, although I am no expert—far from it—I think that marriage requires more than...flexibility."

"Not really, and by the time it does, you won't want out, anyway," the old fellow replied. "Love helps, but are you even aware of that look you gave my goddaughter when she left the room?"

"Who wouldn't admire Mrs. Park?" he pleaded in his own defense.

"Alas, too many," Sir Joseph said. "You have no idea how many nincompoops there are in England."

You can't be serious, James thought. Hmm, how to reason with a madman? He began cautiously. "Sir Joseph, Mrs. Park told me that her father considered my paper to be a 'mature work of genius.'"

"So it is," was the serene reply. "Even Watchmere is right, on occasion."

"'Mature' implies age to me. For all you knew, I was fifty years old! You wouldn't have wished a...a...Methuselah on your goddaughter!"

"Calm down, James. Take a deep breath." Sir Joseph managed to lace his plump fingers across his paunch. "After I read your paper, it was an easy matter to consult with the Lords Admiral and get a copy of your service record. If I recall, you'll be twenty-eight this coming May."

"Twenty-nine. I'll be twenty-nine."

"But a youth."

"For all you know, I am a murderer!" The words had hardly left his mouth before he knew how monumentally silly they sounded. He heard footsteps coming down the corridor. "You don't know anything about me!"

"On the contrary, after reading your treatise on the *Gloriosa Jubilate*, I know *everything* about you. You're brave, intelligent, witty, resourceful and perhaps even wise, although I cannot be completely sure about that particular virtue." Sir Joseph gave him a kind look. "It's only a suggestion, lad."

James couldn't understand why he was arguing. The steps got nearer and louder, and he lowered his voice. "Her father seems to think I am a Methuselah, and he has commanded her to be my escort," he whispered. "He will change his mind when he sees me. I'll have no opportunity to get to know her well." He blushed, caught and trapped. "Providing I decide to have anything to do with this!"

"You do not know Lord Watchmere. I never met a sillier human being. He will not change his plans." The old man sighed. "You have two weeks. See what you can do about Susannah's sister Loisa, too. And get rid of those toucans. They frighten Noah."

The door opened. "Oh, my dear! You have returned with refreshments. Have Barmley open a window for our guest here. I think he is overwarm."

Two weeks, he thought, in panic as he looked at Mrs. Park's lovely face. Something about her demeanor calmed him.

Genesis would have us believe the Lord God Almighty created the earth in six days, he told himself. I suppose stranger things happen than people falling in love in a fortnight.

He thought about his ever-present phantom. He didn't dare fall in love.

Chapter Four

Mr. Trevenen looked more than overwarm to Susannah. He looked positively distracted.

"Certainly," she said, and nodded to Barmley, who opened the window. "Mr. Trevenen, you are certainly flushed. You may loosen your neckcloth, if it's too tight. We've never stood on ceremony when strangulation threatens."

He loosened his neckcloth without a word. Susannah glanced at her godfather. "Sir Joe, have you been quizzing our guest?"

What *can* my godfather have said? Susannah asked herself. She set Sir Joseph's tea on the table beside his chair and took the other cup to Trevenen at the window.

She thought to put him at ease. "Mr. Trevenen, you should be grateful that you are only a recent acquaintance. Two years ago, my godfather decided that I had been a widow long enough. There was a shy gentleman who had been coming 'round to visit me on occasion. Can you imagine—Sir Joe told him to hurry up and propose!" She laughed. "Scared him right off!"

"You two would never have suited," Sir Joseph said. "Anyone that fussy would have driven you to distraction inside of a week. No, my dear, you need a man with some flexibility."

Susannah heard Mr. Trevenen's teacup rattle in its saucer, and decided that it was hardly fair to subject a man unused to her family to such bantering. "Dearest godfather, do let us not air our eccentricities to a new acquaintance who might still think we are rational beings!" Mr. Trevenen had clamped his hand over the cup to stop the rattling. "Sir, don't regard anything he said!"

"Certainly not," Mr. Trevenen replied. He took several breaths, which relieved Susannah.

I wonder, she thought, if Papa was right. Maybe Mr. Trevenen is not used to society. Perhaps his lengthy island sojourn did cause some disorder of mind. She had to admit that he looked sane enough. He had turned his attention to something her godfather was saying now. In fact, he appeared to be giving Sir Joseph all his attention, as though he did not wish to consider her presence. She could hardly blame him.

She stood by as the men carried on their conversation. In the years after her return from India in disgrace with her late husband's child, she had learned to blend into the wallpaper. Now it was nice to do exactly that and observe Mr. Trevenen.

She knew he was no longer connected with the navy, but he could never have been mistaken for anyone but a seafarer. He stood with his legs slightly farther apart than landfarers stood, one leg back of the other, as though ready to brace himself in an instant, should Spring Grove suddenly shift on its foundation.

He was of medium height and solidly built. He must have been eating steadily since his return from his island to have achieved that pleasant sort of mass, but there was still something starved-looking about his face. His cheeks had a lean cast to them, which emphasized the prominent lines of his face. Mr. Trevenen's eyes were green, that deep sea green she remembered from the crossing to India. His hair looked recently cut, as if his valet—supposing he possessed such a servant—had prepared him for this trip to London. His brown hair had not been teased into any fashionable style.

Nothing about James Trevenen could be described as remarkable, if one overlooked his eyes. But as he stood there, she had the distinct impression of Trevenen's capability. In no way that she could put her finger on, he looked like a man who could do anything, say anything, perhaps even *be* anything.

She knew she was not mistaken in James Trevenen's capability, even though their acquaintance was of less than one hour's duration. Most navy men had that air of invincibility. Perhaps a fool could buy his way into an army commission; she suspected many did. It was different with the navy, Susannah reasoned, where the margin of error was so thin. Navy officers faking nautical experience probably did not live long.

Her godfather fell silent. Susannah touched Mr. Trevenen lightly on the arm. "We had better save more conversation for another day."

Mr. Trevenen jumped as though she had jabbed him in the back. "I didn't mean to startle you," she said.

"It's not you," he said. He took several breaths, as though to calm himself again. "I remember one time on the island—I think I had been there about three years—when a branch nicked me in the back of the neck when I walked by."

"Did you make water, lad?" Sir Joseph teased.

"I fainted," he replied. He looked at her with an apologetic air. "I knew that island was uninhabited, Mrs. Park, but I wish I had a shilling for every time I looked over my shoulder."

"And here you are," she said, for want of anything cleverer.

"That, too, gives me pause," he told her. He bowed to her godfather. "Very well, Sir Joseph, only tell me when you wish to discuss the South Seas, and I will be here."

She kissed her godfather's cheek and let Barmley hold open the door for them both. "I must retrieve my son," she said, as they walked down the hall. "You can meet Lady Dorothea and Sir Joe's sister, Lady Sophia. They would feed Noah sweets until he foundered, except he invariably dozes off before that danger."

Noah slept in the wing chair, telltale macaroon crumbs upon his face. Quite filling the settee opposite him were the ladies of Spring Grove, tatting as usual. She had long been tempted to ask what they did with their yards and yards of fine trim. Perhaps they gave it to the parish vicar, who sent it to heathens in Africa.

"Mr. Trevenen, may I introduce Lady Dorothea Banks, my godmother, and her sister-in-law, Lady Sophia Banks. Dears, this is Mr. James Trevenen, winner of this year's Copley medal."

She was immensely gratified by her companion's sharp bow and his attention to the ladies while she woke Noah and brushed off his nankeen jacket. "Time to go, my love, since you have eaten all the macaroons."

"Only three, Mama," he told her with a yawn.

Playfully, she put her hand against his forehead. "You don't appear to be ill. Why such restraint?"

He merely shrugged, then rubbed his stockinged feet against the old dog that had flopped at his feet. "I fed one to Neptune."

"He doesn't appear to be in need of sweets," she reminded him. She glanced at Mr. Trevenen, who was accepting a macaroon from his hostesses. To her amusement, she noticed that he quickly put two more into his pocket.

She chatted with the old dears, admired their endless tatting and waited until the footman announced that the barouche had pulled around to the front. She nodded to Mr. Trevenen. "The Bankses always give us a ride back to Alderson House."

"Of course we do," Lady Dorothea said, without the slightest pause of her flashing shuttle. "It's getting late. Soon it will be dark." She shifted her bright glance to Mr. Trevenen. "And you sir, are probably still exhausted from all those years in the sole company of…of crabs."

To his credit, Mr. Trevenen did not even blink at such curious logic. He bowed and thanked them for their hospitality. Susannah thought his lips twitched, but obviously it took a great deal to surprise him.

They took their leave of the ladies, but Neptune followed them to the front steps, as though it were his office to be the perfect host. She was amused to see Neptune drop down on Mr. Trevenen's boots. The gentleman obligingly tickled the old dog, who heaved a generous sigh and rolled onto his back.

"You have a friend, sir," she said.

Mr. Trevenen laughed and squatted down to rub Neptune's stomach. "Good thing you weren't marooned with me, sir," he murmured. "I'd probably have eaten you in that first week."

"But not later?" Susannah teased.

"No. It's better to be hungry than lonely."

I must agree, she thought. After a few more words to Neptune, Mr. Trevenen rose to his feet, stepped over the rotund dog, and helped Susannah into the barouche.

He seemed on the verge of conversation, but she bided her time. Noah usually took this carriage ride home as another signal for a nap.

He did not fail her. Noah's eyes drooped, and then with a sigh, he rested his head in her lap.

She looked at Mr. Trevenen, who gazed out the window with a slight frown, sitting very still. Perhaps such stillness was required of a man hunting for food, she considered, then thought about the macaroons he had slipped into his pocket. At least the hunt was easier now.

She determined to set him at ease. "Mr. Trevenen, I do not know what my uncle asked you to do, but please be assured that whatever it is…" She stopped, unsure.

He glanced down at Noah and spoke softly. "He suggested that I do something about the toucans. He said they frighten Noah."

"They do," she agreed. "They frighten all of us. Thank goodness we can close off the foyer from the rest of the house." She brushed her hand across her son's forehead. "My son used to tell me that he was afraid he would wake up and find them perching at the foot of his bed."

"That would frighten any little boy," Mr. Trevenen said. He looked out the window again at the gathering dusk.

From the way his jaw tightened, she thought he was thinking of something else. Was he seeing something else? Surely not, and yet the idea persisted. "Do go on, Mr. Trevenen," she told him.

"He also wanted me to do something about Loisa." He leaned forward. "Your sister?"

"Yes. Loisa is twenty-seven and there is not a suitor in sight. She blames me for her misfortune."

"How on earth—" he began, then closed his lips.

"…am I to blame?" she asked, finishing his sentence. "That's a long story, Mr. Trevenen."

"Two weeks won't be enough time to tell it all?" he questioned.

She could not meet his eyes, which looked at her with such honesty. She had kept her own counsel for so long that it was second nature. In that tiny moment before she caught herself, she wanted to drop the whole load at this stranger's feet.

"It's a family quarrel," she managed to say. "I suppose she is justified, in many ways."

To her relief, he did not pry, but murmured "Families."

Noah stirred and sat up when the horses made the turn into her father's estate. "Will we return tomorrow?" he asked.

"That will depend on what Mr. Trevenen requires of us, son," she told him. "We have been commissioned as his escorts while he is in London."

Noah looked at Mr. Trevenen. "Lady Dorothea and Lady Sophia tell me that the macaroons stack up something fierce, if I am not there to eat them."

"Noah!" she declared with a laugh. "They were quizzing you."

He shook his head. "They would never do that, Mama."

She couldn't resist a quick rub of his head. "You goose! They used to tell me the very same thing!"

Noah's eyes widened farther. "Mama, only think how they have been stacking up since then!"

Mr. Trevenen laughed out loud, a hearty, comfortable sound that she was powerless to resist.

They approached the half-moon drive in front of the house. "I hope your parents do not mind too much that I am here," Mr. Trevenen said. "I could have stayed in a hotel, but after my island, I like company."

She hated to be disloyal to her own flesh and blood, but this seemed a good time to educate him. "Sir, they will be so involved in their own little worlds and squabbles that it will never occur to them that you are any trouble."

He seemed surprised, or perhaps disappointed. "Is that how families are?"

"Mine, anyway," she said dryly. "Perhaps your family has an occasional eccentric?"

He shrugged. "I wouldn't know. I was young when I went to sea. I thought all families were wonderful."

Instantly she felt ashamed of herself for her cynicism. You ninny, she told herself, at least you have a family, even if they are fit only for Bedlam much of the time. "I'm sorry."

He waved away her apology. "No need. It's hard to miss what you never had, eh?"

Noah looked at the front steps. "We don't have to go in the front, do we, Mama?"

"Certainly not," she told him. "Mr. Trevenen, we usually walk around the house to the side door, where there are no toucans. You may wish to store up this bit of information for future use during your stay."

"No need," he replied cheerfully as Noah hurried ahead. "Sir Joseph requested I get rid of the birds, and I shall. Mrs. Park, one lesson I learned on my deserted island was never to put off anything. Give me a day, and the toucans will be but a memory."

"How…"

He shook his head. "The less you know, the less you have to account for."

"Very well, then," she said, mystified.

"Good! No argument. You make my life simple. I trust you will eventually tell me a little about Loisa, if I am to work some sort of miracle there."

Her smile went away. "I've been in her black books for some years now. She blames me for all her misfortune. I doubt even you can help."

"Trust me," he said. "Mrs. Park, I am adept at solving problems. Say goodbye to the toucans."

"My sister will require the services of a diplomat," she said. He stood close, and she did not mind.

Noah had reached the side door and stood there waiting for them. To her surprise, Mr. Trevenen waved him in.

"We'll join you in a moment, lad," he called. He waited a moment too long to speak, and then she knew what he was going to say. Sir Joe, she thought in horror, why did you *do* that?

"My godfather wants you to marry me," she stated, before he could speak.

He nodded. "He said it as calmly as though he was asking me to water the plants in the corridor. You know, just toss it in before Trevenen has a moment to think."

"I'm sorry," Susannah said.

There was no serenity on his face now, just a puzzled look. "I'm certain you're a fine lady, but I'm only going to be here two weeks. I could be wrong, but I think attraction that leads to matrimony must require more time."

"Sir, sometimes people fall in love instantly," she replied without thinking.

"Only in novels," he said quickly.

Well, then, she thought, you and I have nothing to fear from each other. There was no need to dread her association with this quiet genius. She would escort him around London to whatever degree he required, then send him back to Cornwall.

Impulsively, she put out her hand. He took it without hesitation. "Very well, sir," she told him. "Let's not disturb my godfather by acquainting him with this conversation! Let him have his fun."

Mr. Trevenen lifted her hand, and almost—but not quite— brushed it with his lips. "Done, Madam."

They walked to the side door where Noah still waited for them. She smiled at her son, and he opened the door.

"The toucans first, Mr. Trevenen," she said, "then Loisa."

Chapter Five

The toucans were gone before dinner.

"The toucans it is," he had told his pretty hostess with as much confidence as he could muster. For all he knew, Lord Watchmere was a sparring partner of Gentleman Jackson and would toss James out a window if he touched his precious toucans.

James had no use for birds. The ones on his island had been too smart to fall prey to his clumsy traps, thus condemning him to a numbing diet of fish and crab.

He and Mrs. Park walked toward the stairs. The closed door to his right must have led into the foyer, where the toucans reigned. He stopped.

"Right now?" Mrs. Park asked, surprised.

"I'm not one to wait around for the perfect moment," he told her. "If you want to solve a problem, do it."

"Did you learn that on your island?"

"Earlier. When you are up to your…um, buttocks…in seawater and your ship is sinking, my, how you can make decisions."

She considered the matter, pursing her lips in a way he found attractive. "Mr. Trevenen, I am the Duchess of Hem and Haw, and here you are ready to do, I know not what, to rid my son of toucans. Lead on, sir."

He admired her courage, but he shook his head. "No, Mrs. Park. I suggest you and Noah continue upstairs. This is my task."

"Very well," she said after a moment's hesitation. "We dine at six. Absurdly early, but Papa is set in his ways. Noah eats with us, which is my choice."

She glanced at the closed door again, and he knew she still wanted to help. "When you have finished whatever it is you plan to do, you might wish to adjourn to your room and dress for dinner."

"I don't really have much in the way of fancy dress," he admitted.

"You may do whatever you wish, Mr. Trevenen. Why do I have the funniest feeling that you would, anyway?"

She took Noah's hand and went upstairs, pausing once to look back at him. He knew she was dying to ask what his plan was, but since he hadn't formulated one yet, he was grateful she did not.

When they were out of sight, James stood a moment, listening for the birds. He had heard them a moment or two ago, drawn to the door by his conversation with Mrs. Park, and probably poised to fly out if someone opened the door. He waited.

To his amusement, he found himself standing absolutely still, scarcely breathing, as he had done so many times on his island. In his never-ending quest to find food, utter silence had become his ally, although he had not expected to revert to his island ways in London.

He heard that familiar clacking, and then the almost noiseless sound of wings as the birds flew away. He yanked open the door, leaped in, then closed it behind him. The birds in flight didn't have a chance to change direction.

"Good Lord," he muttered, as he looked at the droppings on the parquet floor. Lord Watchmere must be a great eccentric to tolerate such filthy birds. James could understand a genteel canary in a cage, but who on earth would let birds fly free and ruin an otherwise handsome foyer?

The birds perched on their Caesar busts, eyeing him with what he thought was considerable rancor. He surveyed the spattered room, the bowls of rotting fruit and beetles.

"Gentlemen, I know what it is like to be trapped," he told them. "No wonder you try to escape at every opportunity."

He knew what to do then, and he did it, striding to the front door and flinging it open. Without a fare-thee-well, the birds spread their wings and ghosted past him.

He watched them go, feeling a small lift to his heart. For a moment he was in the longboat with the missionaries again, making his own escape across the reef to the ship anchored in open water. He had not looked back at his island prison. The toucans did not look back, either. Perhaps they would perch on the pagoda tonight. On the whole, he didn't really care.

"Sir!"

He turned around to see the butler. "I let them go," he said simply.

Then it happened again, just as it had in the inn: some little imp slapped the back of his head to get his attention, then nestled onto his shoulder to whisper in his ear. He moved closer to the butler, whose face was white.

"I have done this household an enormous favor," James said, his voice filled with resolution. He led the butler to a chair. James noted that the man was not so far gone that he did not check for toucan droppings before he sat.

"I cannot imagine what Lord Watchmere will do," the butler said. His voice shook.

"He will thank me," James said. The imp on his shoulder jumped up and down and applauded in his ear. "I will go to my room now. When Lord Watchmere appears, please tell him that I wish to speak to him immediately. It is a matter of some urgency."

James closed the front door and looked around. A thorough cleaning would have the place in shape in no time, although it might be prudent to retire Julius Caesar and Octavian, who had suffered indignities even a good cleaning could not remedy. He turned back to the butler. "Can you tell me which room is mine for the duration of my visit?"

The butler gave him a bleak look, then seemed to recall himself. He stood up. "The third door on your right, at the top of the first floor landing."

"Very good. I trust I will hear from Lord Watchmere soon." He will probably pitch me headfirst out of the window, James thought. I should have requested a room on the ground floor.

He changed his mind about that at the top of the stairs, where he noticed the portrait of a smallish man with a dreamy expression and thinning hair. A brass plaque under the portrait identified it as the current Lord Watchmere.

"Better and better," he said out loud. Humming, James located his room.

He hadn't long to wait. He was standing in the dressing room off his chamber, where a servant had taken out the rumpled clothing from his bag, when he heard a bloodcurdling scream from the approximate location of the foyer. "Impressive," James murmured.

He heard doors open all along the corridor, but thought it wise not to open his. You'll find me soon enough, he told himself, and this is a conversation we need to have in private. You have no idea what a lucky man you are. He stood back from the door and listened to someone pounding up the stairs. I wonder, will you knock or just plunge in?

The door banged open. Lord Watchmere stood before him, the image of the painting, but with a complexion of a hue not normally found in nature. He wore a curious cap of leaves and twigs that he yanked off his head and slapped against his leg until the leaves settled around the room like autumn indoors. His green cape was covered with cloth leaves.

I am in the presence of a lunatic, James thought, as he bowed and smiled. "Good day to you. Lord Watchmere, I presume?"

The man opened and closed his mouth several times as his color deepened. He finally extended a shaking finger. "You! You! I did not know a houseguest would treat me so abominably! Where have my *ramphastos tucani* gone?"

James put his finger to his lips and closed the door quietly. "I had to act quickly, my lord," he said, pitching his voice deliberately low so his furious host would be forced to listen. "You were in real danger."

His words had the desired effect. Lord Watchmere lowered his hand and frowned. "Come again, you upstart?" he growled.

James observed that Mrs. Park probably stood a foot taller than her father. "They weren't *ramphastos tucani* but *ramphastos tucani incogniti,* quite a different bird," James said, perjuring himself without a qualm. "I saw this particular toucan in Guiana during a port of call." James felt the imp on his shoulder again and heaved a sigh that sounded almost genuine to his ears. "My lord, I am so glad I arrived in time."

Whatever anger had propelled Lord Watchmere upstairs vanished, to be replaced by a look of concern. "There is a subspecies of that toucan?" he asked. "Tell me, man, what made you so concerned that you let my birds out?"

James looked around. "Let us come away from the door," he suggested, motioning his host toward two armchairs by the fireplace. "I wouldn't want to be overheard. This is a sensitive subject."

Lord Watchmere needed no urging. He took off his peculiar cape and dropped it to the floor, obviously a man used to having servants trailing in his wake. "Speak up, man," he demanded.

All solicitude, James slid a hassock under the man's legs. "Are you feeling all right?" he asked.

"I had a slight cough this morning," Lord Watchmere said, the anger in his eyes replaced now by fear.

James leaned back in relief. "I was in time," he said, keeping his voice low. "Thank God." He leaned forward until only a little space separated them. "Have you been experiencing hair loss lately?"

Lord Watchmere nodded. "These two or three years and more." His hand went to his head and his eyes seemed to widen farther. "Surely not...."

"I'm afraid so," James said. How far do I dare go? he asked himself. "There is something worse, my lord, much worse." He looked around again and lowered his voice another notch. "Have you...oh, I cannot ask this of someone I have not even been introduced to yet...."

Impatiently, Lord Watchmere gestured with his hand. "Lord Watchmere, and I am pleased to make your acquaintance, Mr. Trevenen! Now. Tell me!"

James choked down the urge to collapse in fits of laughter. "My lord, have you had trouble refreshing Lady Watchmere lately?"

Lord Watchmere stared. "Not that!" he croaked.

James nodded. "When *tucani incogniti* are confined in a small area, the atmosphere becomes permeated with foul humors from their droppings. You will never see any people of Guiana with toucans as pets." He looked away. "Roman Catholics take no chances on stifling their, uh…" James coughed politely "…reproductive powers."

He closed his eyes, considered his massive lie, and waited for lightning to strike. Nothing happened. He dared a look at his host, who was frowning. "How does it happen that Chumley has a full head of hair?"

"Chumley?"

"My butler."

Think fast, James commanded himself, but his imp did not fail. "The people of Panama have a theory that only the upper orders—those with titles such as you have, my lord—are afflicted by this curious phenomenon." He held out his hands. "I have no title, so toucans would probably never bother me." He leaned forward again. "My lord, I was only thinking of you, when I carried out that rash act. I trust you will forgive me. I simply couldn't delay."

To James's relief, the frown left his companion's face. "I should have Chumley and the footmen clean out that foyer immediately, shouldn't I?"

"As soon as is humanly possible."

Lord Watchmere stood up quickly. "I'll tell them right now before dinner." He turned back, and motioned James closer. "This…problem. Is the damage reversible?" He put his hand to his balding head. "Tell me the truth. I will steel myself."

"I think so, my lord, because I believe we have nipped the matter in the bud." He came closer to his host. "My lord, typically it takes about four weeks for things to right themselves."

"The other matter, too?" Watchmere asked in a low voice.

"I believe so," James replied. Let me be on the mail coach in two weeks, he thought. "In both instances, the improvements seem to be gradual."

"Mr. Trevenen, you are a wonder," Lord Watchmere said fervently. "And to think I was irritated with Sir Joseph for foisting you on us!" He picked up his cape and left, trailing the ugly thing behind him.

Then Mrs. Park stood in the doorway of the chamber opposite his. One eye on her father at the other end of the corridor now, she started to say something. James put his finger to his lips. Her eyes merry, she tiptoed across the corridor to his room.

"I was about to fear for your life," she told him in a whisper, her eyes still on her father. "I've never heard him so upset. Whatever did you do?"

Told him a whopping great lie, James thought. As pleased as he was with the outcome of the toucan episode, he felt unease similar to the night before, when he had assured Sir Percival Pettibone that he had saved the fop's life. I trust I will not have to tell any more lies to accomplish my purposes in London, he told himself.

But Mrs. Park was eyeing him now. "Come, sir, confess."

He shook his head. "You'd never believe me."

"Try me," she teased.

"Maybe later," he told her, suddenly embarrassed.

"Very well, sir, we will credit this to an extraordinary set of circumstances." Her face grew serious. "It will take a miracle for you to sweeten up my sister Loisa." She returned to her side of the corridor and closed her door.

Ah, yes, Loisa, he thought. He knew little enough about women, but he already knew Loisa would be more trouble than toucans.

With a sigh, he removed his boots, lay down on the bed and closed his eyes.

* * *

He woke with a start as he always did, never quite sure of his surroundings, even though the bed was soft. It was a far cry from his hut made of palm fronds and the remnants of the longboat.

He looked around quickly, then closed his eyes again, wondering if he would ever wake up and not feel hungry. Not a morning on the island had he wakened peacefully. No, he had scrabbled about for food like an animal. The damned thing was, he still did.

I will not look in my suit coat, he told himself, even as he reached for the garment he had placed at the end of the bed. A quick pat reassured him, but still he felt inside the interior pocket until his fingers touched the macaroons he had appropriated from Lady Dorothea's tea table. I can wait for dinner, he thought, even as he took out a macaroon, stared at it in huge relief and ate it.

He lay on his back staring at the ceiling then, thinking absurdly of Lady Audley, and that first morning of the Indian Ocean crossing, after he had spent half the night tupping her. Naked and thin, he had crawled right over her body to reach a battered tin pitcher of water and gulp it down. She had laughed at him, even as she tugged him back to straddle her.

The memory was not one he was proud of. His face went hot from the embarrassment of those seven weeks of almost endless fornication. It had taken sharp words from Sam Higgins to make him see the shame of his conduct with a married woman, no matter how imprecise her own morals.

As much as he had been at sea for most of his life, or incarcerated on an island, James knew the society he came from. Men could sow and plow indiscriminately. Most of his acquaintance did—he among them—when they came to a port after a long voyage. So what if he felt vaguely ashamed after he pried a whore's legs off his back and tossed a handful of coins on her? No one cared.

He needed reassurance, so he glanced at the bureau, where he had left his leather case containing his *Gloriosa* treatise. He knew it was in there, so he did not feel the urge to rise. Not this time, anyway. "Life was less complicated on our island, wasn't it?" he said. And now I am talking out loud to a crab, he thought.

Soon, he heard the footman's gong in the hall. And now it is time for dinner with these strange people, he thought. Then he reminded himself that he was the one who spoke to crabs thousands of miles away and told whoppers to gullible men, two by his count now.

Still, he smiled at the image of Lord Watchmere in that curious cape of green leaves. Quite possibly, I have stumbled into Bedlam, he told himself. I should feel quite at home.

He prepared himself for dinner, which didn't take long, considering that he had only acquired the barest wardrobe since returning from the island. His neckcloth took only a minute to tie and looked it. Even a baboon could do better than this, he thought as he stared into the mirror. "At least you are not skin and bones anymore," he said as he buttoned his waistcoat and picked up his coat.

Suddenly shy, he waited until he had heard all the doors open and close and people walking. He went to the stairs finally, and looked down to see the whole family assembled below, waiting for him. He glanced at Lord Watchmere's face and was relieved to see peace. I suppose my prevarication there was not a total loss, he thought.

Mrs. Park was lovely in a gray gown. Across from her stood an equally lovely older woman, who—he could tell even from the top of the stairs—was taking his shabby measure. He gulped, and looked at the other woman, who could only be Loisa. His heart sank.

The only attribute she shared with her mother was the look of disdain. In all other ways, she resembled her father: short, red-faced, pop-eyed. He tried to look without looking, but he thought her hair might even be thinning on top. I do not think two weeks will be enough, he told himself in sudden panic.

He sighed, thought about the tranquility of his deserted island, and started descending, feeling with each step that he was walking deeper and deeper into quicksand of his own making. Smile,

James, you lying meddler, he ordered himself. He stopped at the foot of the stairs, his heart pounding in his chest.

"Delighted to meet you all," he said.

Chapter Six

Oh, dear. Mr. Trevenen is looking as though he wishes he had engaged a hotel, Susannah thought. Are we so odd?

She knew the answer. It made her heart sink a little, but only a little. Family was what they were, with all their imperfections. They're all I have, she thought.

Her mother was staring at Mr. Trevenen. Susannah sighed inwardly. Mr. Trevenen's neckcloth was being weighed in the balance and found wanting. Her father appeared to be gazing at him with relief, making her wonder all over again what on earth James had told him about toucans. She could put what she knew about James Trevenen into a thimble, but one thing was already clear: he was expeditious.

She hated to call attention to herself, because it only roused Loisa to unreasonable ire, but she had to rescue him from all those prying eyes. She stepped forward. "Mr. Trevenen, may I present my family. Papa, Viscount Watchmere, I believe you know. This is my mother, Lady Watchmere, and my sister, Miss Loisa Alderson."

"Delighted to make your acquaintance," he said. He bowed in that brusque way of military men; Loisa curtsied, while her mother inclined her head.

"I can't remember when I have seen a more common-looking man," Lady Watchmere murmured. "Above stairs, at least."

Her voice was low, but Susannah could only cross her fingers and pray Mr. Trevenen's hearing was not acute. "Do join us, Mr. Trevenen."

"Do, lad, do," her father said. "Nothing's worse than cold mutton."

Her mother drew herself up. "Lord Watchmere," she exclaimed, "I never serve mutton, only spring lamb."

Her father took her rebuke in good spirits. "My dear, it is nearly October now and spring is far away." He winked at James. "We just give mutton a fancy name, lad, and no one's the wiser."

Mr. Trevenen laughed. "Lady Watchmere, I know I am common."

Susannah winced.

Their guest continued, "I've had many a cold mutton sandwich on watch, and I can assure you I've eaten things you'd never dream of serving at what I am certain is an excellent table here. Thank you for letting me be your guest."

He couldn't have done it better, balancing praise with simplicity. It was an excellent response, and even her mother was flattered, likely in spite of herself.

"Very well, sir, shall we go in?" Lady Watchmere asked, and put her hand out to her husband.

Susannah took Noah's hand and he smiled up at her. She looked at Mr. Trevenen, silently willing him to do the right thing.

He did. With a bow in front of Loisa, he offered her his arm. Excellent, Susannah thought.

Loisa stood there a moment, collecting herself, and Susannah felt her heart go out to her elder sister, destined always to be awkward.

The matter was resolved when Loisa shyly tucked her arm in Mr. Trevenen's and preceded Susannah and Noah down the hall. To Susannah's confusion, before he turned to converse with Loisa, he winked at her.

It was highly improper, but she couldn't help but feel flattered—at least until Noah nudged her. "Mama, Mr. Trevenen winked at me."

Silly me, Susannah thought. "I think he likes you," she whispered to her son.

There was nothing unusual about dinner, to Susannah's way of thinking, except that everything was different. The food was excellent, as always, so that wasn't it. Papa carried on his usual conversation about birds with Mama, who talked to him about fashion and the next season. She knew what the difference was, and thanked Mr. Trevenen from the bottom of her heart.

He was a quick study. It had taken only one of Loisa's barbed remarks when Noah accidentally spilled soup on the tablecloth. Mr. Trevenen stepped in to keep Loisa distracted with conversation, asking her questions about London. Even Lady Watchmere unbent enough to contribute responses, when her advice was applied for.

Susannah could feel Noah relax beside her. When her son pushed a little food off his plate by mistake, no one said anything. She almost felt rather than heard his small sigh of relief.

When the dinner was nearly done, Susannah noticed Mr. Trevenen deftly pocketing several slices of cheese and a handful of nuts. Does he fear being without food? she asked herself. The thought sobered her. She could not imagine being that hungry.

The men assembled with the ladies in the sitting room directly after dinner, Papa to read his books in one corner, Mama to work on her embroidery and Loisa to sit and fume over some slight or injury. This was Susannah's cue to take Noah upstairs and away from an aunt so willing to find fault, but she remained in the sitting room this time, mainly because she did not think it sporting to abandon Mr. Trevenen.

Besides, Noah had already found the jackstraws and he and Mr. Trevenen were sitting cross-legged on the floor. They played quietly. Noah was always subdued in the sitting room, and Mr. Trevenen seemed adept at taking his cues from precious few signals. Susannah was sewing a button on one of Noah's shirts when Chumley came into the room with a silver tray bearing a letter. He went to Mr. Trevenen and bowed.

Surprised, Mr. Trevenen took the letter. "Mrs. Park, it's from Sir Percival Pettibone."

He suddenly had Lady Watchmere's attention. "Sir Percival? He's the first stare of fashion. How did *you* meet him?"

Susannah could have cried at her mother's tactlessness, but to her relief, beyond a twitching around his mouth, Mr. Trevenen seemed willing to overlook it.

"I did him a trifling favor last night." He opened the letter, read it and looked up at Chumley. "Is he expecting a reply?"

"He is, sir. Or rather, his footman is."

Lady Watchmere cleared her throat, and Susannah felt her face go hot with embarrassment. "Whatever it is, tell him yes, Mr. Trevenen," her mother commanded. "You will be the most successful man in London, I vow."

"Then I suppose it is yes, Chumley. Tell the footman I…I," he paused and looked at Susannah, "Mrs. Park and I will pay a morning call."

"Surely not I," Susannah said quickly.

"But didn't your father say…"

"That Susannah would be your escort?" Loisa spoke up, making no attempt to disguise her irritation. "Susannah is hardly received in anyone's house, and most certainly not in the first circles that Sir Percival represents."

Humiliated, Susannah glanced at Noah, who had risen now to stand beside her in childlike defense. She could feel him trembling. Susannah rested her hand on his shoulder, reassuring him. There was no overlooking the question in Mr. Trevenen's eyes, but this was no time to satisfy his curiosity. Her heart thundered against her ribcage. "Loisa's right," she said. "I am a liability."

She glanced at her father, who was deep in his books, ignoring them all, then at her mother, whose lips were pressed tight. Seven years and still so much disapproval! She could not bring herself to look at Loisa, because she knew she would see only triumph. Noah was leaning harder now against her leg. She took his hand and rose.

"I will do whatever I have promised to do, Mr. Trevenen," she replied, wishing her voice didn't sound so weak, wishing she weren't so spineless. "If you will excuse us, it is past Noah's bedtime."

Mr. Trevenen bowed to her, his eyes troubled. He was likely having second thoughts. "We can sort this out in the morning, sir," she said quietly.

"Certainly," he replied. He touched Noah's head. "I'll put away the jackstraws, lad," he told her son. "The interruption worked in my favor, because I do believe you were about to thrash me."

Noah mumbled something, and Susannah walked with him to the door. To her discomfort, Mr. Trevenen strolled along beside her. At the door, he held out the folded note for her to see.

"Mrs. Park, he has addressed it to 'Beau Crusoe.'"

"W-well, you are rather an exotic hero, are you not?" she stammered.

"Far from it."

She looked at the note in his hand. "Sir Percival seems to think so."

"The more fool he."

This is strange, she thought. Or perhaps you are just saying that to distract me. She managed a smile. "I doubt Sir Percival is ready for two black sheep to visit him, sir."

"We'll find out," he said, and bowed again.

The door to the sitting room closed behind her, and she felt nothing but relief. She and Noah walked down the corridor toward the stairs, Noah stopping to look at the open door leading to the foyer.

"Are the birds really gone, Mama?" he asked, holding back.

"It appears so," she replied.

"Is Mr. Trevenen a magician?"

She smiled. "I'm not quite sure what he is."

James escaped to his room when Lord Watchmere began to snore, and Lady Watchmere and Loisa started to argue the merits of silk over muslin for the lady who was approaching yet another season with no hopeful entanglements and—as far as he could tell—no prospects of any. He made his escape when Chumley and the footman came into the room with tea and cakes.

He grabbed a petit four on his way out the door, eating it in the corridor as he looked at the note with Beau Crusoe written across it with a flourish. He sighed. There was no point in regretting his foolishness at the inn, when he had assured Sir Percival that he owed his life to James Trevenen's timely intervention. He had done it and had now to live with the consequences.

Still, if Sir Percival, in all his silliness could recommend a good tailor, then he could use the man's services, drift quietly into anonymity, mark time until the Copley award presentation and leave.

He went to his room. He hadn't meant to eat them, but the handful of nuts he had swiped at dinner was gone even before he changed into his nightshirt. *There is still the cheese,* he reminded himself, as a clammy mantle of fear tried to settle around his shoulders. *It's there on your bureau top. Just relax and go to sleep.*

He hated having the door shut. He had always left it open at home, so he could hear the servants moving about late at night, and catch their first footsteps in the morning before the sun rose. The noisy public room last night had proved no problem.

He slept, but not for long. He thought he heard something in the room. *So you have followed me here?* he thought as he moved from slumber to a wary wakefulness. *I thought I saw you last night.* Sweat started to prickle his forehead.

"I wish you would go away," he said. He hoped he did not shout out loud. That had happened in Cornwall, until Orm had moved into his master's dressing room. Finally, after many months, the butler had returned to his usual quarters.

"Please, go away," he begged, keeping his eyes shut. "Take the cheese if you want; it's on the bureau. You should know by now that I always leave food for you."

The sound continued and James shuddered. "I know you're not there," he said again. His voice was rising, but he could not help himself. He took a deep breath and opened his eyes.

The man was sitting in the chair between the bed and the door, so James could not flee the room. Ragged shirt, ripped pants, his face red, blistered and swollen from nineteen days in an open boat. James's eyes went immediately to the man's legs, and there was only one because Tim Rowe had a wooden leg. He was chewing on Walter Shepherd's arm, making quiet, smacking noises, interspersed with low murmurs of satisfaction.

He seemed to notice James then. The man took the arm from his mouth, smiled with shreds of flesh hanging from his teeth and held it out to James.

James couldn't help himself. He ran from the room.

Chapter Seven

Susannah hadn't meant to stay away so late, especially since motherhood dictated she be an early riser, but she lay in her bed, thinking how nice it would be to paint Mr. Trevenen's face.

He had such bright eyes, and there was something about the way he leaned forward and listened so intently that captured her interest.

Of course, sometimes he seemed just to stare across the room, making her turn and look, too, even though she knew nothing of interest was there. His inattention never lasted long; she wasn't even sure anyone noticed but her.

Botheration, Susannah, she told herself. Go to sleep.

And she would have, if she hadn't heard Mr. Trevenen noising about in the corridor. Or someone, at any rate, had stumbled into something and uttered a word not normally heard in Alderson House.

She grabbed up her robe and hurried into the corridor in time to see Mr. Trevenen, clad in his nightshirt, staring hard at the stairs, his thin lips set in a firm line. A vase was teetering on a small table. He didn't seem to be aware of it, so she darted across the corridor and steadied it.

She had his attention now. He managed a self-conscious smile.

"Is there something you need?" she asked.

"Oh, yes…yes," he began and it seemed to her ears that he was temporizing.

She thought of the food he had been tucking away when he thought no one was watching. "Are you hungry, Mr. Trevenen? We can certainly go downstairs and find some food."

He seemed to jump at her suggestion. "That is it. I'm used to having some extra food in my room at night. It helps keep away…the hunger pangs."

She knew he meant to say something else, but couldn't imagine what. Just then he noticed his spare attire and the thin nightshirt that barely grazed his knees.

"I'll go put on my trousers," he said.

She watched him, noticing his hesitation before he entered his room.

And here I stand with my robe in hand, she thought in amusement. She put it on and buttoned it as Mr. Trevenen came into the corridor again, stuffing his nightshirt into his trousers. Like her, he was barefooted, but something in the comfortable way he stood made her suspect he preferred it that way.

"Mr. Trevenen, did you climb date palms in your bare feet?"

"Coconut trees," he corrected. He smiled at her. "There's a skill not much in demand in London, I suppose. I doubt Sir Percival would ever recommend climbing a tree."

"True," she agreed. "It's a skill hardly called upon at all. Come sir, let us go below stairs."

A light burned in the servants' hall, as they descended the stairs. "If we are really quiet, we will find some food in the pantry and not disturb Chumley or Mrs. Baggs, the housekeeper."

"Mrs. Park, how may I help you?"

She sighed, and looked at the door to Chumley's chamber, where the butler stood, managing to look dignified even in a nightshirt and robe. "I had hoped not to bother you, Chumley," she said. "Mr. Trevenen needs some food. Just some bread and cheese, I think."

The butler bowed, as though they had just requested tea on the veranda. "Do be seated," he told them, and gestured to the servants' table. "I have some excellent cinnamon bread. It is only half a loaf."

"Which we all know is better than none," Mr. Trevenen said.

"Chumley can butter some slices for you," Susannah said.

He shook his head. "I don't need that. Chumley, if you could add some cheese—nothing fancy, mind—that would be enough. And…" He stopped.

"Chumley, I think if you have something like that every night in Mr. Trevenen's room, then he will not be waking up at three," she said.

Mr. Trevenen nodded. "That's right. There just needs to be something there for—"

"For you?" she asked. "No need to be embarrassed about the matter, sir. I've never had to go without anything, so I cannot fathom what it must have been like to starve."

"That's part of it," he said. She thought he might say more, but he did not. She could hear Chumley in the pantry, humming as he prepared a tray. This was probably as good a time as any to explain her own situation. She was about to speak, when the butler came into the servants' hall carrying a tray with bread under a cloth and cheese in a glass container.

"Can I get you anything else, sir?" Chumley asked.

"No, thank you."

"Shall I take it upstairs for you?"

Mr. Trevenen took the tray from the butler. "Your kindness is greatly appreciated." He nodded to Susannah. "And yours." He shook his head. "This is a pretty poor showing for someone Sir Percival calls Beau Crusoe. I am not a particularly brave man."

She didn't know what to say to this frank statement, but Chumley came to her rescue. The butler bowed to them both. "Sir, who of us knows how he will act, given a set of circumstances?"

She glanced at Mr. Trevenen, pleased to see the embarrassment leave his face. "Come, sir," she said. "I am feeling a great need to locate my pillow and attach my head to it again."

They retraced their steps in the dark. Halfway up the stairs, he surprised her by sitting down. He carefully rested the tray on the steps above him, then patted the tread. "Mrs. Park, I really do need to know what is going on in your family," he said, then stammered, "I…I mean, why is Loisa so bent on hurting you?"

She sat down beside him, relieved that he had brought up the subject, but embarrassed all the same.

"Why would you not wish to accompany me to see Sir Percival tomorrow? I'll grant he is the silliest man I ever met, but he is harmless. And what does Sir Joseph want me to *do* about Loisa?" He was silent, then, waiting for her to speak.

"They're all tied together," she said finally. Her bare feet were getting cold now, so she drew her knees up and wrapped her robe tighter around her legs. "Loisa is two years older than I am," she began, keeping her voice low. "Papa and Mama decided to postpone her come out. Strange, isn't it? Did they think she would turn into a beauty?"

"That's hardly your fault," Mr. Trevenen said. He reached for a piece of cinnamon bread. "Want some?"

"Yes, thank you. Can you spare a slice of cheese?"

"Certainly. I only need a little bit of food at night. Just enough to…" He stopped again. "Just enough."

They ate in companionable silence, and Susannah felt herself relaxing in his company. "When Loisa turned nineteen, my father hired a new secretary." She tugged her robe tighter, wondering how to say this. "His name was David Park and I fell in love with him." That didn't begin to cover the experience, but it was good enough for now.

"I take it he wasn't from…"

"…the *ton?* No, indeed. His late father was a vicar and David the oldest of seven. He attended Jesus at Cambridge on one of the poor scholarships. Mama was preparing me for my come out, which bothered Loisa to no end."

"Did Loisa seriously have any prospects?" he asked.

"No, but she thought I would be a distraction to any suitors who might materialize."

"A reasonable fear," was all he said, and she felt her face grow warm. She realized with a start that it had been years since she had thought of herself as anyone but Noah's mother.

"It was hopeless, Mr. Trevenen. My parents would have… have…let me deal faro in a gaming hell before they would have consented to such a marriage. Mama had plans," she said simply. "I was to be the season's reigning beauty, only…" She stopped. How could she tell him what she barely understood herself?

He surprised her. "The whole thing wasn't quite to your taste?"

"You have hit upon it, Mr. Trevenen." She sighed. "I just wasn't interested."

"Susannah the late bloomer. Would you want to dance now?" He laughed softly. "Not precisely right now, but you know what I mean."

"The time is past. Mr. Trevenen. Surely you see that."

"I suppose I do," he agreed. She heard him shift on the stairs. "Funny about time, isn't it? I was six years away, all told, and somehow in my brain, I thought all would be the same when I returned. But we are at war with France and my mother is dead."

My woes are small, Susannah thought. She touched what she thought was his shoulder, but which turned out to be his chest. "I'm sorry," she murmured.

"No fears, m'dear."

"To get back to the matter at hand," she continued after a moment, "I never came out. David and I eloped to Scotland and were married over the anvil. We returned here to a dreadful row, and then fled to Bombay on the next East India ship."

He was silent for what felt like an uncomfortably long time, then said, "That must have been a stunning bit of news for the *ton,* to put it mildly."

"Oh, my, yes," was all she said.

"It's probably safer at sea in wartime."

He was treating the whole matter so lightly that she felt a pebble or two of the whole burden roll from her back. "It was scandalous, and you know it!" she said, amused.

"I suppose," he agreed. "Forgive me if I can't quite grasp the total horror of it."

"Sir, I ruined my family." There wasn't any other way to say it.

He did a surprising thing then, leaning over to nudge her. "I'm sorry."

"This must seem awfully silly to you, but it isn't." She took a deep breath. "Mr. Trevenen, every door in London closed to my family, and we are an old name in this part of England. Loisa never had a chance to find anyone."

"Are people's memories so strong?" he asked. "Noah is six. Has it been seven years?"

"Yes. Matters have changed in the past year or two. Mama goes into society occasionally. Papa never cared for it."

"Ah, yes," he interrupted. "The feathered friends."

"Indeed. And Loisa is twenty-seven and on the shelf, and she is convinced I put her there."

He was silent for a long time. "This is awfully rude of me, Mrs. Park, but does Loisa ever look in a mirror?"

"I'm sure she must," Susannah said quietly. "I suppose when there is nothing to be done about the hand nature dealt, it is less painful to blame someone else."

"It needs to stop," he told her. "You and your son should not have to make yourselves small in your own house. But I'm not really sure what to do."

"You don't have an instant plan already?" she teased, trying to turn the conversation away from her. "I'm still perfectly astounded about the toucans."

"That was the easy task," he told her. "As for Sir Joseph's first request, we know two weeks is not time enough for us to fall in love and get married, even if he demands it."

She laughed softly. "Certainly not." She couldn't resist adding, "Besides, Mr. Trevenen, I couldn't possibly give my heart to a man who said what you said earlier in the corridor when you stubbed your toe on the table!"

"I'm chagrined," he declared, "especially since I know so many other worse words. Some in several languages. There are tables like that one all around the world."

After a moment, he brought the conversation back to her. "I

hope you will go with me tomorrow morning. Surely Sir Percival will never slam a door in your face."

"I don't know what he'll do," she said frankly. "I have hardly been beyond these gates in years, except to visit the Royal Gardens and Spring Grove."

He rose to his feet and held out his hand to her. "Come with me to Sir Percival's. If he wants to receive a visit from Beau Crusoe, then he'd better be willing to entertain Mrs. Park, too."

She didn't reply, but grasped his hand. He pulled her to her feet and then retrieved the nearly empty tray. She followed him the rest of the way up the stairs. He stopped on the landing, as if reluctant to go into his room again.

"Come to Sir Percival's with me, Mrs. Park?" he asked again, his voice gentle.

She took a deep breath. "I'm afraid."

"Me, too. Desert islands are safer."

How shallow I am, she thought. This is just a visit to an older lady and her son. Mr. Trevenen must be wondering if I have any backbone at all.

"Very well."

He touched her arm. "I'll protect you, Mrs. P, and maybe we can think of something to do about Loisa."

"Protect me?" she teased, wishing her heart did not feel so heavy.

He opened his door. "Of course. You think I can't?"

On the contrary, she knew he could. It was a pleasant sensation, and reminded her of her brief marriage, when she knew that David would do anything to keep her safe.

But he couldn't, she reminded herself, closing the door. David had been helpless before cholera, dying almost without a murmur, after the most awful cramps and convulsions. It was she who had tended him, and then others like him as the disease swept through their compound in Bombay.

Why she had never contracted the disease she had no idea. She had wanted to, at first, until the baby stirred in her womb. She had known then, despite her great grief, that she would do everything in her power to stay alive and birth this child who would never know his father. If there had been some grand cosmic design in events, it had escaped her.

She sat on her bed, looking at her closed door. Mr. Trevenen really had no idea how much shame she had heaped on her family. "No, not even if I actually decided I could fall in love with you in two weeks, Mr. T.," she said, her voice a whisper. "I have embarrassed enough people I love. I wouldn't dare marry you."

She got under the covers. Perhaps Mr. Trevenen really could do something about her sister. She had long thought that if Loisa were busy, she would have less reason to pine about the state of affairs that kept her firmly fixed upon the shelf. And who is to say that marriage would solve any problems? She sighed. Loisa would still be plain, and probably disagreeable, as well.

Susannah yawned. Perhaps she could get a little more sleep before Noah woke up. Or maybe she would just lie here with her hands behind her head and think about what fun it had been to sit with Mr. Trevenen on the stairs. She hadn't sat alone with a man since David. She smiled in the dark, feeling a little giddy. Perhaps it was a good thing Mr. Trevenen had declared he could never fall in love in two weeks' time. Of course, she had known right away with David.

She closed her eyes. That could never happen twice.

With food to appease his ghoul or without it—considering that he and Mrs. Park had consumed most of the bread and cheese—James hadn't thought he would return to sleep, but he did. Maybe it was because the room was too light now for any ghosts. Maybe it was because the servants were already about.

He woke when he heard someone stop outside his door. His stomach tensed as he remembered the night he had dreamed just such a thing, and when he opened the door, there was the carpenter's mate again, offering a shin bone this time. After a moment, the quiet footsteps receded.

A knock, low on the door, woke him later. He put on his robe, then opened the door to see Noah. He also noticed the note pinned to the door. That explained the footsteps, he thought with relief.

"Good morning," he said, aware of his rusty voice and un-shaven face.

"Good morning, Mr. Trevenen," the boy replied. He pointed to the note. "I wish you would read that, because I am hungry."

James took off the note and read it. "It appears that your mother began her day much earlier," he told the boy.

Making sure his robe was adequately cinched, he squatted on his haunches to be on eye level with Noah. "You and I are to breakfast together and meet her at Sir Joseph's house." He glanced at the note again. "You have dog-tending duties today."

Noah nodded. "I have been waiting and waiting for you, sir," he said. "My stomach is starting to growl."

James wondered why Noah didn't just go down to breakfast by himself, but perhaps Mrs. Park wanted her son to be the perfect host. Still, he was curious. "What is your mother doing so early?"

"Maybe she wanted to finish that flower she was painting yesterday," Noah replied. "Sir Joe pays her a shilling for each painting. We need it."

And that, I am certain, is more than your mother wishes a stranger to know, James thought. Perhaps the Aldersons were not as plump in the pocket as he had first thought.

Noah cleared his throat softly, and James rose to his feet, having been politely reminded that the little boy was peckish. "Very well, Master Park," he said. "Come in. I should shave and dress before I go downstairs."

Noah came in and James closed the door behind him. "You may sit in that chair if you wish, or on the end of the bed, if you like," he said over his shoulder as he went into his dressing room. When he came out minus his nightshirt and with a towel around his waist, Noah had perched himself on the end of the bed.

The water in the can was still hot. James prepared to shave himself. The mirror was small, but he watched Noah seated behind him, and the child's interest in his every movement. You would think he had never seen this before, James thought, then chided himself. Of course he had never seen this tedious ritual. His father had died before he was born.

"How did you shave on your island?" Noah asked, after quiet observation.

"I didn't shave," he replied. "Didn't cut my hair, either."

"You probably didn't have to wash your hands before every meal or after you petted a dog, did you?" Noah asked, sounding more than a little wistful.

"Does she make you do all that?"

"That and more, sir," Noah told him. "Sometimes she is a trial."

James stifled his laughter. He wiped the lather off his face and sat down in the chair beside the bed. "I wouldn't complain overmuch, Noah," he told the boy. "She is only trying to civilize you. That is what they do. Ask your questions."

"What did you wear on your island?"

"Very little," James began, then changed his mind. "Actually, nothing."

"Nothing?"

"Not one stitch. I was alone. Material rots in that climate." He chuckled. "My leather belt did hang on a little longer than my trousers and shirt, but I'd have looked foolish wearing only that, eh?"

Noah nodded. "Were you ever cold?"

"It wasn't like England, lad," he replied. "Now and then when it rained, I might have wanted a shirt, but hardly ever." James glanced at his bare legs and arms, pale now. "After a few weeks I was as brown as an African. My beard grew so much I braided it to keep it out of the fire." He leaned forward. "You wouldn't have recognized me."

"I think I might have liked it for a while," Noah said. He considered the matter. "Then I would have wanted to leave."

"So did I," James said. They looked at each other with perfect understanding.

Noah spoke first, his tone polite. "I'm still hungry."

James stood up. "I'll be only a minute. I promise." He hurried into the dressing room, calling over his shoulder. "If you can't wait, go ahead. I'll be there soon."

"I can wait."

When they finally came down the stairs and opened the

door to the breakfast room, James understood Noah's reluctance to go alone.

Loisa sat by herself at the table, sipping tea. At the sight of her, Noah stepped back, leaning slightly against him.

James glanced at Loisa, disquieted to see a flash of triumph in her eyes. She *likes* to terrify him, he thought.

"It's all right, lad," he said in an undertone, then gave him a little prod toward the sideboard. "I'm right behind you."

Sir Joseph expected him to do something about Loisa? Telling her good morning should be unexceptionable. "Good morning, Miss Alderson," he said with a small bow. "Lovely day, isn't it?"

She turned and looked out the window. "It appears cloudy to me, sir," she replied, each word rimed with frost.

Noah looked back at him as they stood at the sideboard, his eyes troubled. James rested his hand on the boy's shoulder and was dismayed to feel the tension in his small body.

"At least it's not raining," he said, then wanted to kick himself because he sounded so impotent. "Eggs, Noah?"

The boy just stood there, afraid to move. James spooned eggs onto Noah's plate, adding bacon and toast, feeling his own stomach contract under Loisa's odd scrutiny. This was almost as bad as the shipwreck and bad dreams. No wonder Noah was so willing to wait for me, he thought. I'm not positive I could come in here by myself. Gently he moved Noah along, helped him seat himself, then pulled his own chair close.

Noah's hunger won out over fear. After tucking his napkin carefully under his chin, he started to eat. James rested his arm along the back of Noah's chair and picked up his fork, too, wondering how many breakfasts Noah skipped when his mother went early to the glass house.

"You're taking that boy with you to see Sir Percival?" Loisa asked.

"His name is Noah," James said evenly, before he could stop himself. He felt Noah tense beside him again. "No. I believe this is the day he is to brush Sir Joseph's old dog." He tried to smile, but it felt as though he was just baring his teeth. "We are under direct orders to report to Spring Grove, are we not, Noah?"

The boy nodded and kept eating. Loisa said nothing, although she looked as though she wanted to. She stared out the window.

James observed her profile. Despite an amazing proficiency with Lady Audley that still made him blush when he thought about it, he knew that his experience with women was limited. However, he had been in enough ports in South America—when Britain wasn't at war with Spain—to know the world was filled with lovely women.

Loisa was not one of them. She had none of her mother's height and grace, which Mrs. Park seemed to have inherited. Her fingers grasping the teacup were stubby like her father's, and she had his same regrettable profile with that bump near the bridge of her nose. Her complexion was florid and her eyes were prominent in their sockets.

There must be something redeeming, he thought. No one is hopeless. He didn't notice anything particularly unpleasant about her figure, except it lacked the comfortable grace of her sister's deep bosom. He thought of Sir Joseph's words and felt a certain desperation. In two weeks he was supposed to "do something about Loisa." What, he had no idea.

Something must have captured her attention through the window. As he watched, her face lost some of its rigidity. She didn't smile, but she came perilously close. In that moment, he noticed Loisa Alderson's lovely lips. He could have sighed with relief; any woman with one nice feature had possibilities.

Filled with a thimbleful of hope, he finished breakfast. Noah was eating his toast and glancing at the sideboard. "Do you want some more?" James whispered.

"I daren't," Noah whispered back.

"I do," James replied. He returned to the sideboard for more eggs and bacon, sat down again and slid half onto Noah's plate.

Loisa watched the whole thing. She started to speak, appeared to change her mind then reversed herself. "That boy is inclined to gluttony and should not be encouraged, Mr. Trevenen."

Noah froze beside him, and the fork halfway to his lips. James touched his shoulder, "It's all right, lad," he whispered. "Eat your breakfast. That's what it's here for, and so are you."

James directed what he hoped was his best first mate's gaze at Loisa Alderson. "He's hungry, Miss Alderson," he said. "That is all. When he's full, he will stop. I promise to make sure he walks briskly to Spring Grove with me, to ward off any possibility of fat accumulating." He hoped she would say no more; he was finding her unnerving.

To his relief, she was silent. Noah finished breakfast, then sighed. Perhaps taking a cue from James, he took a deep breath. "I hope you have a very pleasant day today, Aunt Loisa."

The silence was deafening, but Noah didn't appear to mind. He smiled at James. "I think Mama will be done with that painting by now, and Neptune really does need to be brushed."

Bravo to you, lad, James thought. You're braver than I am right now. "Very well, Noah," he replied. "Start out if you wish. I'll finish my tea and join you."

Why he wanted to remain behind one second longer, he couldn't have explained. He knew he didn't have the nerve—or the reason, really—to confront that prickly woman about anything. These were family problems of long standing, and he was here only for a few weeks.

Noah left the room and James finished his tea, unable to think of a single thing to say. He didn't have to; Loisa looked at him and spoke.

"Are you really taking my sister to Sir Percival Pettibone's house?"

"Yes, I am," he replied, deliberately pitching his voice lower than usual, so great was his fear that he would squeak.

"What will you do when the door is slammed in her face?"

He was alert for triumph in her voice, but she surprised him. As he listened, he thought he heard just the tiniest bit of concern.

"I don't know what I will do," he told her frankly, then surprised himself. "Miss Alderson, would you like to come along, too? If Percival's mother can't tolerate sinners—I speak of myself more than your sister—I suppose we'll just take a ride in a park. You're welcome to join us."

He had startled her. She had obviously never expected to be invited anywhere. She even hesitated before she said no.

James shrugged. "I suppose you have a myriad of duties to occupy your time here," he told her as he rose.

She wasn't much of an actress, he decided, as a flicker of real discomfort crossed her face. Quite the contrary, he thought. Miss Alderson, you have nothing to do, do you? Your sister has a boy to rear and flora to paint for her godfather, and you have nothing to occupy your hours. How sad.

"If you change your mind, we would enjoy your company," he said, and hoped it sounded truthful. Hmm, he thought, fibs to Sir Percival, outright lies to Lord Watchmere about toucans, and now another whopper to his daughter, Miss Loisa Alderson. Where do you get your nerve, James Trevenen?

He went to the door and stood there a moment, his hand on the knob. "Miss Alderson, you appear to be an extraordinarily capable lady. Good day now."

He left her there in the breakfast room, her mouth open like a grouper. Still, she did have finely chiseled lips. He hadn't been wrong about that.

Chapter Eight

⚜

The relief he felt in getting away from Loisa was succeeded by mild disappointment that Noah hadn't waited for him in the corridor. He had been alone so much in past years that he did not relish it now.

But here was Chumley. "This way, sir, if you please," he said.

The butler opened the door to the foyer. James stood in the doorway and watched Noah twirling about in the entryway. Drop cloths were everywhere, but Susannah's little boy spun about between them, happy to be free of the toucans.

"You're painting today?"

"We are, sir," Chumley replied. "Lord Watchmere informed me this morning there would be no more shitting birds."

It came out of the butler's mouth with such aplomb that James was helpless to hold back his laughter.

"Forgive that, sir," Chumley said, his dignity unruffled. "Let me add that you have the thanks of the entire staff."

"You're welcome," was all he said, even though he could tell that the butler, like Mrs. Park, would have probably traded a year's wages to know what he had said to Lord Watchmere. He went to the door then looked back. "Chumley, has Mrs. Park left the estate much since her return from India?"

"No, sir," the man replied, his voice slightly wary. "Scarcely at all."

His guarded tone told James everything he needed to know about how the wind blew. Susannah Park had her champions here, even if they consisted only of people as powerless as she was.

He nodded to the butler, and strolled across the foyer and into a beautiful morning, beckoning Noah to join him. The little boy soon ran ahead of him, only to stop and squat on the grass just beyond the curving gravel driveway, intent upon something. James caught up to him, and they peered together at a spiderweb still obvious with dew. The web was much smaller than the gargantuan ones of his island, which were purgatory to brush against and had frightened him on more than one occasion. Even now, the only dream worse than the cannibal sailor was one about running through a field of webs, each larger than the one before. He shuddered and returned his gaze to the boy.

"They're like diamonds, aren't they?" he said.

Noah nodded. "Mama would want to draw it."

"Would you?"

"Mama said she will get me my own sketch pad soon."

He should have one now, James thought, and wondered if it was a matter of expense. He looked over his shoulder. The sun was coming around the house now, and time was getting on. "We had best find your mother," he told Noah. "She has promised to accompany me into London."

"I would like to come, too," Noah said, "but I am to take care of Neptune today."

"We all have our tasks," James replied, touched by something in the boy's eyes that told him he wasn't separated much from his mother. "I will bring her back to you as soon as possible. I don't have much business with Sir Percival Pettibone."

Perhaps there would be none at all. He really shouldn't be holding Susannah Park to her eccentric father's command that she accompany him during his London visit. It wasn't proper; even he knew that.

Still, he wanted her with him. At some point between sitting on the stairs with her and having breakfast with her son, he knew he wanted to become better acquainted with Susannah Park. Too bad he wouldn't be here beyond a few weeks.

Noah looked back at the house. "Sometimes when Mama goes ahead of me to the glass house, I do not eat breakfast."

James winced. He had been afraid of that. Noah skipped on ahead of him as they walked toward Spring Grove. I would like a son someday, James thought as he watched him. Maybe two or three, and a daughter to provide the leavening. Maybe two daughters. Some instinct told him he would be an excellent father, perhaps because he was a patient man.

He walked slowly. James had no wish to put himself in the hands of Sir Percival Pettibone any sooner than necessary. He couldn't have explained to anyone why he had encouraged the silly fop to believe he had actually saved his life. Hardly anything could have been further from the truth.

But as he ambled after Noah, James reconsidered the matter. Yes, the man was a fool, but if all went well this morning with Sir Percival and his mother, possibly Susannah Park could be eased into society. Surely stranger things had happened in the history of the world. He could return to Cornwall and know he had set that sweet-faced lady on a path that might find her a husband.

Noah waited for him, and they walked together. He could tell the boy wanted to ask him something.

"Do you have a question?"

Noah nodded. "A lot. Mama might think I am prying, and I would not do that."

"Of course you would not, lad. But then, you have never known anyone who was stranded on a deserted island, have you?"

Noah flashed him a grateful smile. "That is it, sir. Mama made me promise I would not pester you with questions, but how could someone not have questions?"

"How, indeed," James agreed.

"It's this, sir. How did you know what time it was?"

"Time didn't matter. Time is something we use to accommodate others. I had no one to account to."

"So you just ate when you were hungry?" Noah asked.

Little boys think through their stomachs, James thought with amusement. "At first I was hungry all the time." No sense in lying to the boy, who had asked an honest question. "Then later, when I learned how to fish, and discovered which plants would not kill me, it was not so bad."

Noah stopped then, his hands spread out. "But how did you know which plants wouldn't kill you?"

"You try them all, lad."

"Did any of them make you sick?"

"Oh, yes." It was enough said. Noah needn't know how sick some of the plants had made him. "I learned how to climb a coconut tree. Once I did that, I managed."

The matter of time seemed to interest Noah. "But you didn't know Tuesday from Friday? How did you know when it was Christmas?"

"I kept a record of the days," he told the boy. "I had the ship's log with me, and I marked each day in the longboat until we found land." He paused then, holding his breath, hoping that the boy would not notice what he had said.

Too late. Noah stopped. "You said you were alone. Were you not?"

"There were five of us in the longboat, but I alone survived."

Noah thought it over. "My father died before I was born."

"I know. I'm sorry," James said.

They continued in silence, but Noah wasn't through with his questions. "Did you keep a calendar for your whole time on the island?"

"I marked each day on a tree with a little slash and was doing well enough, until I got sick," he said. "Really sick. I lost track of nearly a week, as far as I can tell."

"When you felt better, you didn't know what day it was?"

"Hadn't a clue. I thought I should continue my calendar, though, so I added two or three slashes and called it Wednesday, January 10." He grinned at the expression on Noah's face. "Lad, you can do anything you want, when you are the only one on an island."

After they crossed the next stile that took them onto Spring Grove property, James saw Susannah Park ahead, ambling along much as they were, her sketchbook tucked against her side. "There's your mama," he said.

Noah smiled, but he did not hurry ahead right away, and James was glad of that, enjoying as he did the pleasant sway of Mrs. Park's hips. He felt his loins grow heavy. Rather than shrug off the sensation—as he should, good Lord, for here was her young son beside him—he let the pleasure infuse him. He was a man, after all. He admired her; who wouldn't?

Noah watched her, too. "She's teaching me to draw and paint. In a few years, she said she will let me paint stems on her flowers."

"That's a good start. I'm certain you will do well."

"I want to," he replied gravely. He slipped behind his mother then, reaching out to yank on the tie at the back of her dress.

She spun around before Noah could quite accomplish the devilment. "Lad, I could tell you they have eyes in the back of their heads," James said out loud, but out of earshot.

He watched in appreciation as she grabbed her son and tickled him, then dropped down beside him in the grass as he shrieked with laughter. She kissed the top of his head, set down the sketchbook on the path, and wrapped both arms around him as he leaned comfortably against her belly, claiming ownership that James could only envy.

She waved to James then, and he joined her, conscious that she was watching him approach. Since she did not rise when he came to them, he squatted on his heels. Did this woman never look out of place? Her blond hair was again knotted high on her head, with stray wisps escaping. Her cheeks were bright with the exercise of walking. In that moment, he could only pity poor, dead David Park, entering the employment of a man with such a beautiful daughter. Park had probably been distracted from day one.

James decided he didn't like thinking about David Park. He rose and offered Mrs. Park his hand, which she accepted. He pulled her to her feet, enjoying the brief warmth of her palm before she let go and retrieved her sketchbook. She watched her son as he moved ahead now as he had yesterday, completely at home on the grounds of Spring Grove.

To his gratification, she wasn't in any more of a hurry than he was. "I trust he did not wake you too early," she said after a moment.

"Not at all," he assured her.

"Sometimes I go early to the glass house. He's old enough to join me when he finishes breakfast."

James hesitated, wondering about the delicacy of involving himself in this family. "Mrs. Park, he told me that when he is alone, he does not go into the breakfast room."

Her face reddened, and she uttered a low murmur of disapproval, probably directed against herself. "Please believe that I didn't know," she said finally.

"I was certain you did not," he assured her. "Today he had seconds and wished his Aunt Loisa a good day."

"To which she replied nothing," Susannah said, her tone matter-of-fact.

"Does she never acknowledge him?" James asked. This was so decidedly not his business that he wondered at his own temerity.

"Never. If she could, she would look through both of us."

"It's been seven years, has it not?" James asked.

"And a little more." Mrs. Park lowered her voice. "I wonder what possible pleasure she derives from tormenting us, and then I wonder how I could ever have been so thoughtless, to elope with Mr. Park and ruin my family." She started walking again. "But what is done, is done."

She looked at him then, sympathy in her eyes. "And here all you thought to do was spend a few weeks here and pick up a medal."

"And so I shall, Mrs. Park," he murmured. "If you do not mind, we will answer Sir Percival's summons and I will quit myself of him. Then, I will spend the next few weeks chatting with Sir Joseph about the South Seas, if that is what he wishes."

"But you do not," she said suddenly.

He wondered how she could know, but had not the courage to ask. He had to say something, though, or she would think him rude. "No, I do not," he agreed, his voice frank.

She startled him by leaning against him briefly. Or so he thought. The path was narrow and the stones uneven; maybe she lost her balance. One touch and she was walking steadily again, but it had been enough. Again he felt that heaviness in his loins. It passed as quickly as her touch, but left him smiling.

Chapter Nine

Lady Dorothea apologized, but Sir Joseph was too ill to see them. "One day he is better, and the next he is in such pain that we place a basket over his legs so not even a sheet will brush against them."

They were walking quietly along the corridor, far away from Sir Joseph Banks upstairs, but everyone tiptoed, even Lady Dorothea, who weighed as much as both James and Mrs. Park put together.

"In all of his pain, he thought to lend us his barouche," Mrs. Park said. "When he feels better, do tell him how thankful we are."

"He insisted on doing that," Lady Dorothea said. "'How is Susannah to make an impression on that frivolous man milliner if she arrives in a smelly hackney, Dottie?' he asked me."

"I would like to have known him twenty years ago," James said.

"I expect you would have found him much the same in temperament, at least," Lady Dorothea replied. She stopped. "Do excuse me, you two. I promised Joseph I would lend you a monograph he wrote about the shipwreck on the Great Barrier Reef. I will be back directly."

Spare me, not a shipwreck, James thought. But Lady Dorothea was looking at him with that eager expression of hers, so he bowed. "I would enjoy that." He watched her retreat down the corridor.

"I'm not so certain I believe you," Mrs. Park said when Lady Dorothea was out of earshot.

"You would be right," he agreed. "No man wants to suffer through more than one shipwreck, even one in document form."

She hesitated, but her curiosity was as lively as her son's. "Did you…did you know what was happening? Was there any warning?"

"You read my treatise," he said quickly.

"You wrote nothing about the shipwreck. I just wondered."

"I thought I had," he temporized. He looked around the corridor, feeling the heat rise up from under his neckcloth, at a loss as to how to change the subject.

It was then he noticed the watercolors on the walls. He knew nothing about art, but he could tell these were not of recent origin, nor works Mrs. Park might have painted and given to her godparents. He crossed the corridor for a closer look, and found himself smiling in familiarity at the one that had caught his eye with its nearly opaque petals like droplets coming from the center of a lacy fern.

"'Baby's tears,'" he read. The sailors on the *Orion*, starved for females, had called it Virgin's Bush, reckoning (as one of them had told him) that this virgin was primed like a pump and already moist. There was a Latin name, too, something dignified. He smiled. Here was the virgin with her bush spread so invitingly, on the wall of one of England's most proper households. Amusing.

"You must have called it something else," Mrs. Park commented.

He looked at her in surprise. Had any woman the right to be so blasted observant? "We called it something different." He put his hands behind his back. "Even bamboo slivers under my fingernails will not induce me to reveal it."

He strolled to another picture, admiring it. "Who did these?" he asked.

"My godpapa's chief illustrator on the *Endeavour*," she told him. "Sydney Parkinson."

He did not try to hide his awe. He had heard of Parkinson's illustrations, and assumed they were all squirreled away in the British Museum. Poor Parkinson, dead of a fever caught in

Batavia, where the *Endeavour* had remained for fatal weeks to refit and repair for the return voyage. He remembered his own stop at that cursed port.

Mrs. Park joined him in gazing at the pictures. "Sir Joe says he knows these belong in the Museum, and every few years or so, he assures me they will go there, but still they hang here."

"They are his old friends, Mrs. P," he replied.

He walked a few more feet admiring the gentle colors, then started to breathe more rapidly. It was as though he was surrounded by the South Seas again, marking off each day and wondering how it would end, even as he made his study of the tidal pool crabs, so alone.

Suddenly he was too far away from Susannah Park. He was rational enough to know had it been Loisa standing there, or even a servant, he still would have hurried back. There were moments when any distance from a fellow creature was too much distance.

When he took Mrs. Park by the hand, she did not start, nor try to back away.

"Can you even imagine five years without another human in sight?"

He knew he should not be clutching her hand so tightly, but she did not flinch. To his surprise, she raised her free hand and rested it, warm and soft, against his cheek, almost as though she could sense he needed to *feel* another human being. It was indescribably comforting.

She continued to press her hand against his face until he felt his heart stop racing. He began to breathe normally again, and his face did not feel hot. Only then did she take her hand away.

"Sorry," he mumbled.

"You owe me no apology, Mr. Trevenen," she told him, her voice gentle. "If I were five years alone, I would never let anyone out of my sight again."

"That is it," he said. "You understand."

She did step away from him then, and he became painfully aware that he had practically been leaning up against her. Not quite, but close enough to feel her leg through layers of fabric.

He managed a shaky laugh. "And your father thought the worst guest of all would be a doddering old fellow quite destroyed by his tropical paradise? He wasn't far wrong, Mrs. Park, was he?"

"No, he wasn't," she said, her voice matter-of-fact, "but knowing my father, I can only credit such perspicacity to blind good luck."

Lady Dorothea came into the corridor then. She held out the bound document. "There, Mr. Trevenen. Do take it with you. When Joseph is feeling better, he will send for you."

The footman appeared in the corridor. "Madam, the barouche is ready."

"Then you should be off," Lady Dorothea said, shooing them with her plump fingers. "Noah is brushing Neptune in the library now. Sophia and I will see to him. Go now."

James noted how Susannah Park paused, as if reluctant to leave, her assurance gone. He doubted she ever left Noah for any length of time.

Lady Dorothea was already making her way back down the corridor again, so he stepped forward quickly and put his hand against Mrs. Park's cheek this time, pressing as she had done. "Buck up," he whispered. "We'll be done with this visit soon, and you'll be home again." Her face was so soft, he couldn't help himself; he rubbed her cheek gently with his thumb. He could hardly imagine anything more improper, but she seemed to accept the gesture in precisely the way he intended it: returning favor for favor, courage for courage.

"Very well, Mr. Trevenen," she said, and stepped gracefully away from his hand. "Let us pay that visit to Sir Percival."

She did insist upon stopping at the door to the library, to peer in for a moment and watch Noah, who was brushing Neptune. The big dog lolled shamelessly on his back, feet splayed.

"Pitiful sybarite," James murmured. "Doesn't he know he's a dog?"

"Not in this household," she whispered back, her eyes on her son. "We won't be gone long, will we?"

James knew she was thinking of her son. He itched to slip his arm around her waist and pull her close to reassure her, but did not think his credit extended that far. "He will be fine, Mrs. Park. I cannot imagine Sir Percival's interest in me lasting beyond a short visit. But to find out, we must leave the house, Mrs. P."

They followed the footman to the side door with its porte cochere, where the barouche waited. The footman was ready to help her in, but James did so instead. He would have sat opposite her, except that when she got in, she pulled her dress closer to her legs, a clear invitation that there was room for him beside her. He settled back against the leather cushion, prepared to enjoy the ride.

To his amusement, Mrs. Park seemed suddenly shy, all the more surprising after her firm touch. He doubted she went around touching men she hardly knew. He only wished the barouche had been a little smaller, so they would be touching now.

He noticed the sketch book on her lap, and thought to relieve her unease. "Are you planning to sketch Sir Percival? I hope you brought along some vivid pencils. The last time I saw him, he had on a breathtaking pair of lavender kid gloves."

"He is what my mother would call 'an exquisite,'" she replied. "I am depending upon you to sufficiently awe Sir Percival, as you seem to have done already. Mama assures me that an early morning invitation to his home is a signal honor. She says he does not generally rise before noon."

James pondered that bit of information. "I kept hours like that on my island, but I wasn't much troubled about what to wear, or which of the evening's invitations to choose."

She opened the sketchbook. "I went to the rose house this morning to paint this. It was the one rose still blooming, and I did not deadhead it yesterday." She moved the book closer to his lap. "I thought I would give it to Sir Percival's mother."

He looked at the watercolor, to his eye as fine as anything Parkinson ever painted. She had captured the color of the bloom, but somehow invested it with the slightly tired air of a rose past its prime.

"No one is going to think ill of you, Mrs. Park," he said, not knowing if he was speaking the truth, or only hoping. He knew so little of English customs, except that people of their station wishing to remain in respectable standing never fled to Scotland for a wedding across the anvil.

"Are the *ton* such sticklers?" he asked.

She carefully creased the page and tore out the rose. "I think life must be far less complicated on a deserted island."

"I am certain of it," he agreed. He admired the rose, wishing he could frame it for himself. It would be something to remember her by.

He thought of what she had just said about sufficiently awing Sir Percival, and felt a twinge. Better to confess the matter to this lady. He turned slightly to face her. "Mrs. Park…" he began.

"I like it better when you call me Mrs. P," she interrupted.

He couldn't help smiling at that. "Mrs. P. it is, then," he amended. "I should confess." He looked down at his hands. "Sir Percival labors under the misapprehension that I rescued him from a raging fire at the inn where we both stayed."

"And you did nothing of the sort?" she asked.

"I threw a smoldering blanket off a bedwarmer. Noah would have done the same. So would you." He thought about the matter. "I had been standing in the inn yard and noticed the smoke, so I climbed the downspout into his room."

Her eyes opened even wider. "Good heavens, sir."

"I only climbed one story," he added weakly. "I wish you wouldn't look at me that way. I told you it was silly."

"It is not," she replied, emphasizing each word.

"You should have seen some of the coconut trees I climbed on my island," he said, trying to make her see how tiny was his contribution to Sir Percival's well-being in a universe that circled around the fop.

"Mr. Trevenen, you must seem to Sir Percival as someone from another planet! Don't you see? If he is as big a gossip as his mama is reputed to be, he has probably told this tale to others and magnified it."

That sobered him. "You're serious?"

"Never more so."

He thought about that, unable to wrap his mind around that

much silliness, and forgot where he was. "I'll be buggered," he murmured.

Mrs. Park sighed and he felt his face go red again.

"Mr. Trevenen, no matter how much the fribbles of the *ton* are going to want to imitate you, the matter will not extend to your language," she told him, mincing no words.

He apologized, not wanting to look at her for a moment. If he could have sunk down in the barouche, then slithered out into the road, he would have. "Blame it on the Royal Navy," he told her.

"To which you are no longer attached!" she reminded him crisply. Then her tone softened. "You really don't see it yet, do you?"

"No, I do not," he agreed. "Anyone would have helped Sir Percival. I just happened to be there."

She sank back into the cushions of the barouche in what looked remarkably like a slouch. "It's more than that, sir. Let me see if I can make you understand."

He smiled, happy to be in her good graces again. "Say on, lady," he told her.

"Tell me something, sir. You have passed it several times now in the Royal Gardens. Could you climb the Chinese pagoda?"

"Mrs. Park, there are stairs. Anyone can climb it."

"No! I mean, could you scale the outside?"

He tried not to laugh at the absurdity of the question. "Of course."

"But you have never done it."

"True, but I could."

"That's it," she told him, and he could tell she was pleased with herself. "Most people, when asked that, would immediately say no. I would, but not you. Was it desperation that drove you to lengths the rest of us have not considered, making you so…so confident now? Or is it something innate, the likes of which none of us have ever seen?"

If you only knew the depths of my desperation, he thought, suddenly fearing the night again, and worrying that there might not be enough food in his room. With an effort, he considered what she was saying.

"I've never thought of it that way," he said at last. "You could be right. I know I could climb the pagoda simply because it is there." He looked at her. "But how does this…this talent of mine exhibit itself to the average observer?"

She frowned "I'm not sure. You're not overpowering in any way. It's something indescribable. Somehow, you simply know there isn't a thing you cannot do. Your survival on that island is ample proof of that, sir, you know it is."

"And somehow this translates to my very demeanor?" he asked, still skeptical, but not a little flattered.

"I suppose that's your burden," she teased.

"I suppose it is," he replied, after a long silence. He leaned back, too, then, thinking of the implications of what she was telling him. "What will he do with me?" he asked her finally.

"It sounds strange, put that way," she said. "I suspect, Mr. T, that Sir Percival's own life is boring to him. You are a nine-day wonder, and he will want to bring you into society."

Bring me into society, he thought. I never wished for that. I do not wish for it now. And yet, Mrs. Park needs to be brought back into society.

He thought of what Sir Joseph had told him. You have it wrong, sir. It is Loisa who needs the husband and Susannah Park whom I need to "do something about." Susannah merely needs the opportunity.

"He already calls me Beau Crusoe," he said crossly, embarrassed. "You saw his note." He sat up straight again and in his frustration, held his hands out in front of him in a grandiose gesture. "Look at me! Beau Crusoe? Horrors!"

Her lips twitched. "P'raps this is a punishment for telling him a whopper that night, when the simple truth would have sufficed."

"Go ahead and laugh," he retorted. "I should write on a wall somewhere, 'I will always tell the truth, no matter how painful or obvious.'"

"That would be a start," she replied, her voice serene.

. He could only be grateful that it was last September, when London was thin of society. James took a deep breath. "Mrs. P, if I am about to become the toast of what *ton* is here, I won't do it by myself. You, my dear, are going to toddle along with me."

He knew he had startled her. "I do not think many doors will open to me."

"I believe all will," he told her, taking both her hands in his for emphasis. "Who on earth will take any of my actions amiss, should you accompany me to an occasional dinner, perhaps a lecture? What happens in London in September? And when people are reminded how charming you are, and how much a lady…"

"The *ton* has a long memory."

He tightened his grip on her, sensing that this was the moment when she would go along with his plan, or remain in the barouche. "I disagree. From what I see of Sir Percival, this is a frivolous bunch, chasing after whatever tempts them out of boredom."

"Well…"

He persisted. "There is no reason why two…yes, two!… interesting people cannot shine in such society."

She did smile then, even as she protested. "Mr. Trevenen, I am just a mother with a small son. If you want interesting, take my father along!"

He knew he had her, because she had smiled and made no attempt to pull away from his grip. He released her then. "Mrs. P, with a very little effort, the Beau can grease the wheels of society for you. Don't look so dubious! You can meet some worthy gentleman when the Season begins and we can still make Sir Joseph happy. What could be simpler?"

"I can't imagine," she murmured.

Her reply sounded a little dry to him, but he wasn't about to quibble. "Any minute now, I'll think of something to occupy Loisa's time. You'll see."

"I suppose." It was her turn to take a deep breath. "Soon we shall be there, Mr. Trevenen." She looked at the rose watercolor she had set on the seat opposite them. "It's too puny. Sir Percival's mother will throw it in my face," she said, and he could hear the fear in her voice.

"She'll do nothing of the kind," he retorted.

"You still do not comprehend the enormity of my sins," she said.

And you cannot possibly comprehend mine, he thought. He took her hands, knowing how improper it was. She looked ready to bolt from the moving barouche. "Do you regret a minute of your marriage, Mrs. Park?"

"No," she said, but it was as though she had spoken volumes with one quiet word.

"We can do this! You're with Beau Crusoe now. Just remember that."

Chapter Ten

Sir Percival's residence was one of the beautiful row houses lining Half Moon Street. Mrs. Park was silent now; in fact, she was so quiet James could not hear her breathing. Her face was pale as she looked up at the house before them.

He helped her down from the barouche. She wore gloves, but he thought he could feel the cold through them. He knew he didn't imagine the trembling. "No matter what happens, I will stand by you," he told her.

"Even if she sees me and slams the door?"

"She will never do that. No London lady opens her own door."

He could tell from her expression that was cold comfort. He was about to knock when the door opened. "I am Beau Crusoe," he announced. "I believe Sir Percival is expecting me and Mrs. Park."

It slipped out effortlessly, as though Mrs. Park had been part of the invitation all along. I can't believe I actually called myself Beau Crusoe, he thought. If I have a brain in my head, I will turn on my heel, go directly back to Cornwall and have the Royal Society send me that medal by post.

Instead, he effected what he hoped was a bored air, afraid, under all his subterfuge, the butler would see him as the counterfeit he really was.

It didn't happen. The butler bowed. "Do come in. Sir Percival is expecting you."

James stood where he was until Mrs. Park joined him. Her reluctance to move one step farther was so great that he thought he might have to tug her along.

His fear lasted only a moment, and then they were inside. The butler showed them to a pleasant sitting room and bowed himself out. James turned to look at Mrs. Park, and saw she was frowning at him.

"What's the matter?" he said.

"You look dyspeptic," she replied. "If you were Noah's age, I would give you a dose of cod liver oil."

He grimaced. "Mrs. P, that is Beau's languid expression."

"You have it all wrong, Mr. Trevenen," she informed him, with a hint of a smile. "Someone named Beau Crusoe should appear as though he has just committed some act of derring-do. Or is it derring-did, since the act is past?"

He laughed. "Very well, I'll discard the languid visage and try to look more...piratical?"

She shook her head. "No. The best thing you can do is simply stand there and look capable of nearly anything."

"I don't know how to do that."

"On the contrary, Mr. Trevenen," she said softly, "in our short acquaintance, I've noticed it's what you do all the time."

Her mild compliment made him feel pleasantly warm in all the right places. *What a dear thing you are*, he thought. *Only show your approval and I am ready to loll about like a puppy and dribble on the floor.* "Thank you," he told her. "If only it were so."

"Beau! And is this the charming Mrs. Park?"

Sir Percival didn't so much stand as pose in the doorway. He wore a dressing gown of vivid red and yellow, reminding James forcefully of toucans. Sir Percival was a specimen.

James managed a bow. "You wanted to see me, sir; here I am." He indicated Mrs. Park. "And I have a fair companion, who is determined I will not get lost in London. Sir Percival, may I present Mrs. Susannah Park, Lord Watchmere's younger daughter?"

Mrs. Park curtsied. "I am pleased to meet you, Sir Percival."

James watched Sir Percival for some sign of revulsion, some turning away from the lovely lady at his side, but he saw nothing of the kind.

"You were wise to accompany the Beau," he was telling her. "I do not think he knows his way around London. And how is Lord Watchmere?"

"As barmy as ever," she replied with a straight face. "How kind of you to ask."

Sir Percival threw back his coiffed head and laughed carefully. Before she could react, he took Mrs. Park's hand and planted a firm kiss upon it. "Beau, how clever of you to bring along this charming lady," he said. "We three will enliven many a salon this winter."

"I'm only here for a few weeks," James said in mild protest only, since Mrs. Park had pinked up nicely. He was relieved to see her relaxing. There obviously were worse men on earth than silly Sir Percival.

"A few weeks?" Percival repeated in what sounded like genuine dismay. "Surely we can change that."

"I doubt it," James replied, hoping he sounded properly regretful. "I am staying with the Aldersons and would not wish to exhaust my welcome."

Sir Percival stood silently, as though at a loss. James cleared his throat. "Sir Percival, you requested my attendance upon you this morning?" he asked finally.

Sir Percival gestured toward an armchair. "My dear Mrs. Park, do be seated. You, too, James, if I may call you that."

"Indeed you may, sir. It's my name and I have never been formal."

When they were all seated, Sir Percival addressed Mrs. Park. "I have a mission, my dear. James is too shabby for London, and I intend to remedy that."

"How kind of you," she replied. "He is rather a ragbag."

"Sir Percival, I was going to find a tailor," James protested.

"How, sir? By walking through the streets and calling out, 'I say, can someone show me the way to a tailor?' It will never do. You might end up with last season's waistcoat, and then who would receive you?" Sir Percival gave James a pitying look. "It will never do for Beau Crusoe. After all, I owe you my life."

Here it is, James thought in a panic. Every fiber in his body wanted to protest, but there was Mrs. Park, brave enough to walk into what could still be a lion's den. The least he could do was follow her example.

"Very well, Sir Percival," he said. "I am in your hands."

"And they are clean hands. I always make sure that Percy washes in a solution of rose and glycerin water at least three times a day," came a female voice from the corridor.

Startled, James looked toward the door and then at Mrs. Park, whose face appeared to be draining of all color. He looked back at the door. So this was Lady Pettibone.

She was small but carried herself in that dignified way of the petite. Lady Pettibone appeared dressed to venture outdoors, clad in a spencer of subdued color and boasting a hat of moderate height. Everything about her seemed to say "à la mode." No wonder you're pale as pudding, Mrs. P, he thought. Don't fail now.

She didn't. He was close enough to Mrs. Park to hear her careful intake of breath, which was followed by as deep and graceful a curtsy as he had ever seen.

As he watched, he realized what she was doing. A glance at Sir Percival told him that gentleman had no clue. On the other hand, Lady Pettibone did. It was as though with that beautiful gesture, Mrs. Park was apologizing for scandal and ruin. He could only stand there and marvel at her wisdom.

The response lay with Lady Pettibone. A curt nod of the head, a quick turn on the heel would seal Mrs. Park's fate. He felt his own breath rising and falling in relief as the lady at the door executed her own curtsy, just a slight one, but fitting for her age and rank. "Mrs. Park," she said, "it has been too many years, has it not?"

"It has, Lady Pettibone," she said.

"Your mother is well?" Lady Pettibone asked.

"She is. Perhaps you have seen her about."

"I have," Lady Pettibone said. The look she gave Susannah was kindly. "She has been too long away from society."

"We thought it best." With a bobbing curtsy that was charmingly childlike, Mrs. Park held her watercolor out to Lady Pettibone. "I wanted to give you this," she said.

Lady Pettibone took the picture and studied it for some moments. As she did so, Mrs. Park glanced at him, as if for reassurance. He wanted to hug her, but he substituted a feeble wink. She returned her attention to Lady Pettibone, who was going through an odd transformation.

"That's it!" the lady exclaimed, stabbing the painting with her finger. "Percy, dear, come take a look!"

James looked at Mrs. Park. "Oh, dear," she said, her voice barely audible.

Sir Percival was hovering beside his mother, looking mystified. James watched as the fop gazed at the picture, some sort of light flickering in his tiny brain. "Mama," he declared. "This is most assuredly it!"

James came closer, because Mrs. Park seemed to be summoning him with desperation in her eyes. He looked at the painting, still just a rose drooping in the last gasp of summer.

"Lady Pettibone, it is but a rose," Mrs. Park said.

"Most certainly, my dear," Lady Pettibone replied, all indulgence. "It's the color. We have been wondering for three months what color dear Percy should bring into fashion next season." She gave Mrs. Park's cheek a pat. "We have lost sleep over the matter."

"What a relief this is, Mrs. Park," Percival said, echoing his mother. "Were ever two people more put-upon?"

James felt a huge laugh rising in his throat. He didn't dare look at anyone right then, certainly not Mrs. Park. I will walk away for a moment, he told himself. No one will notice, because the nincompoops who live here are in raptures over, God-help-us, pink.

He moved away, finding that while he could stifle the laugh, there was no way he could keep his shoulders from shaking. He rested his forehead against the window glass and closed his eyes.

Then Susannah was standing beside him. She avoided his

eyes. "If I look at you, I will throw myself on the floor in a riot of mirth," she whispered.

"Susannah Park! Only you can help me now!" Lady Petti-bone declared.

Susannah clutched him. "Take me home," she whispered.

"Too late," he murmured back. "No telling what will happen, when you keep low company with Beau Crusoe."

She didn't release her grip on him, so he covered her hand with his and gave it a little squeeze. "Don't worry," he told her. "You're going to come about."

Lady Pettibone dabbed at her eyes. "Mrs. Park, we must go immediately to the Pantheon Bazaar and track down every bolt of cloth this shade of pink." She appeared to be thinking, if such a thing were possible. "Perhaps all bolts of pink cloth."

"Surely you don't need me."

James released Susannah's hand. "She'll be delighted to help you, Lady Pettibone," he said. "Mrs. Park, this is a lovely oppor-tunity for you."

Then Susannah seemed to see it. "Yes, I think it is," she replied in a calm voice. "It will be my pleasure to help you, Lady Pettibone."

"I will be in your debt, my dear," the woman said. "I am de-pending upon your artist's eye."

"Then I shall not fail you," Susannah replied. "But I must ask—why do we need to buy all the pink fabric? Surely only a waistcoat or two will be sufficient to establish Sir Percival in the first stare of fashion. Perhaps a…a…cloak lining, as well?"

Lady Pettibone gave an indulgent laugh. "My dear! Surely you understand that once we have chosen pink—and just that marvelous faded rose hue—we need to make sure that no one else will be able to buy any." She looked at her son, her eyes soft. "My son will be next season's Original."

Lady Pettibone had Susannah by the arm now and was pulling her across the room. Susannah glanced at James in alarm. She needs me, he thought, and it was a pleasant sensation, a welcome antidote to his thoughts. No one else needed him.

He was beside her in a moment, but only to open the door.

"Mrs. Park, only think how nice it will be for you to go with Lady Pettibone to the Great Pantheon!"

"But…"

"And to see so many of your mother's friends there," he continued, then addressed himself to Lady Pettibone. "Mrs. Park has been somewhat out of circulation. She has a small son who requires her attention. And this and that," he concluded, sweeping away a half dozen years of scandal in a nonchalant fashion quite in keeping with what—hopefully—Beau Crusoe would do.

Susannah's look of alarm made him wonder whether he had been wise to test the social waters so blatantly, but Lady Pettibone did not fail him. The dowager took Susannah even more firmly in tow.

"You must tell me all about your son. Dear me, you have been out of circulation too long! What on earth were we all thinking? Come along, dear. This is serious business."

Susannah gave him one last glance before the door closed on them. James had a sudden thought then, and reopened the door.

For an older woman, Lady Pettibone was propelling Susannah down the hall at great speed. "One moment," he called.

Susannah seemed so relieved to see him so soon that he felt like a perfect churl. But only briefly.

"Mrs. Park, please get some hair ribbons for your sister."

She raised her eyebrows.

"I need to impress her and will grasp at whatever straw I can," he murmured.

It scarcely mattered that he lowered his voice. Lady Pettibone appeared to be residing upon another planet. Perhaps she always did.

"I don't think hair ribbons will do," Susannah said dubiously. "Besides, I don't have any money."

He took a coin from his coat pocket and pressed it into her palm. "Then I will go through a process of elimination until I find something. Start with her ribbons."

Lady Pettibone cleared her throat. "Mr. Trevenen…or should I just call you Beau?"

James forced himself not to sigh. "Whatever you please, Lady Pettibone."

"Susannah and I must hurry to the Pantheon. Suppose someone else should steal our idea and buy all that fabric?"

There's not a chance, he thought. "Oh, yes," he assured her. "Beg pardon."

The lady glanced past him toward the stairs and exclaimed, "And here is dear Percy's tailor."

A footman was ushering a nervous little fellow with ferret eyes down the corridor. "Him?" James exclaimed.

"The very one."

I'm not going to like this, he told himself. Why didn't I just tell the truth at the inn, and then get a room at a hotel in London? He thought of his *Gloria Jubilate* treatise back at Alderson House and sighed. All for a damned medal.

Then he steeled himself. If Susannah can face dragons, I can strip for a tailor.

He bowed to the ladies. "Good luck on your errand," he said. To Susannah he added, "I'll see you back at your godfather's place."

She nodded, then was whisked away by Lady Pettibone. It took all his willpower to go back into the sitting room, where Sir Percival was still staring at Susannah's watercolor rose. Perhaps he was already thinking about what awaited him in the next Season. And I won't be here to see it, James thought. Praise God from whom all blessings flow.

The tailor came into the room and looked hopefully at Sir Percival, who shook his head.

"Not until the quarter, Redfern," Percival said. "I haven't a sou."

The little fellow seemed to deflate visibly with the unwelcome news.

"I have money now," James assured him, which brought about an immediate transformation. Redfern whipped out a tape measure, tablet and pencil.

"Strip, sir," he declared.

"Everything?"

"Pantaloons are quite tight this season, sir. We want a good fit, don't we?"

"Oh, we do," James said dryly. He draped his coat over a chair, took off his neckcloth and shirt and dropped his trousers with a sigh.

Sir Percival stared. So did Redfern. The baronet even put his quizzing glass to his eye. "'Pon my word, Beau," he said when he could speak. "I say, do all seamen get tattoos when they are drunk?"

"Would I do this sober?" James countered.

"Then you weren't in your right mind when you… Good God, sir, is that an arrow pointing down toward your…well, you know."

"Yes, my you know. I was young and drunk and we were in Rio de Janeiro during Carnival, when such things happen."

"Singular," Sir Percival said. He looked at James's face this time. "I don't think we can bring this into popularity, no matter how remarkable you are."

"If you repeat this to anyone, I will call you out and shoot you," James said calmly.

"I will be as silent as the tomb."

Chapter Eleven

James smiled as the baronet hurried to lock the door. I think I've embarrassed him, he thought.

As the tailor measured him, James felt hopeful about his tattoo. Perhaps this Royal Navy crudity would discourage Sir Percival from bringing him to anyone's notice. Maybe the Beau could go away before he even came to anyone's notice.

"Did you mean what you said, sir?" the tailor asked him. "Hold out your arm, if you please. Now bend it and put your hand on your waist. Just so."

James did as he commanded. "You mean, would I pay you? Of course I meant it. Don't your clients pay?"

Redfern took his measure from neck to wrist and then shoulder to wrist. He lowered his voice. "They pay only if they have to." Unperturbed at the intimacy, he ran the tape around James's thigh at its widest, and then across his hips and from waist to knee and then to ankle.

He stood up, scribbled some more notes, then asked, as though he were inquiring about the weather, "Mr. Trevenen, does your private organ lapse to the left or to the right when you sit?"

James stared. "I don't think I ever gave the matter any thought before. Does it matter?"

The tailor ordered him to sit. "To the left," he murmured.

James looked down. "So it does. Is this something I should be relieved or chagrined about?"

Redfern permitted himself the smile of a man proud of his work. "Left or right doesn't matter. Have you never had a really good pair of trousers made just for you?"

James considered his years with the Royal Navy. "Certainly, but no one ever measured me with your thoroughness. I don't think the navy has any hard and fast rules about where my dong lies."

"It is simply this: When I cut out your trousers, I will allow a little more room in the crotch on the left side. You will never have a more comfortable fit."

"I say," Sir Percival interrupted from a seat by the door, where he was studiously avoiding a glance in James's direction. "Do you do that for me, too?"

"I would, if you paid your bills on time," the tailor whispered under his breath. He bowed to the baronet. "Have you even felt any discomfort, Sir Percival?"

"Well, no…"

"That is your answer, sir." He whispered to James, "Actually, his is so small he would never notice."

"What do you recommend for my wardrobe, Redfern?" James asked, when his urge to laugh passed. "I'm only going to be here two weeks for an event that I suspect…" he glanced at Sir Percival "…requires knee breeches?"

"It does indeed, Beau," Sir Percival said. The fop addressed the tailor. "Make him at least one other grand set for special events; a cape, too. Leathers, as well, maybe two coats of superfine and at least a half dozen linen shirts. Neckcloths, of course."

"No. It is only two weeks," James said.

"Don't you dress in Cornwall?" the tailor asked.

"Of course," he replied, exasperated. "Just one set of evening wear. I insist." He shivered. "Would anyone object if I put on my clothing again?"

No one objected. He dressed quickly, wondering at the absurdity of the whole business. He reached into the inside pocket of his coat for his notebook and wrote out his orders to his counting house. He held it out to Redfern. "Take this round to Golden and Durfee and they will pay you fifty pounds. I am at Alderson House in Richmond. Let me know if you have any trouble with my banker."

Redfern gasped.

"That is enough for at least half, isn't it?" James asked, uneasy.

Redfern took the paper and folded it reverently. "More than sufficient for the entire amount, Mr. Trevenen," he said. "My tailors will drop everything else and have all ready by the end of the week." He leaned close. "Actually you have overpaid me."

James grinned. "Feels good, doesn't it?"

"You never worked so quickly for me, Redfern!" Sir Percival declared, wounded.

"You never paid me in advance, Sir Percival," Redfern said, his voice respectful, but no longer a whisper. "Mr. Trevenen, I forgot to inquire about waistcoats."

"Black only," James said, then added, "Well, perhaps a dark green with the leathers."

The tailor bowed. "Would you object to one with narrow stripes on a watered silk?"

"Not if you approve," James said. "I trust you, Redfern. You're worth every shilling."

Redfern beamed. He turned to Sir Percival. "If there is nothing you require, Sir Percival, I will leave now."

"My mother will send round some pink material for waistcoats," Sir Percival said.

"Oh," was all Redfern said. Only the tiniest sigh escaped him as he left.

James turned around to face his host.

"James, James, such betrayal," Sir Percival said with a sigh.

"Because I pay my tailor?"

"Your actions will give us all a bad name. What a sad state of affairs it will be if all of London's tailors demand payment, because of Beau Crusoe."

"It seems only fair."

He could tell from the expression on the baronet's face that this was a new concept. Maybe the French revolutionaries were right, James thought. Quite possibly there wasn't a more useless set of people than aristos. He imagined that the road to the Place de la Concorde, with its dripping guillotine, must have been lined with cheerful tailors, seamstresses and housemaids, happily sending their former employers to untidy ruin. Perhaps they had even pushed the tumbrels along, and no wonder.

James glanced at Sir Percival, grateful that years of hard service in the Royal Navy had given him an expressionless face, when it was needed. I was bored in Cornwall, he thought, and now I am repelled in London. Who *are* these people?

"Thank you for all your help, Sir Percival," he said, and let himself out of the room. That should do it, he told himself. He started down the stairs. Since he was to meet Mrs. Park back at Sir Joseph's house, there was no reason to stay another minute. He was halfway down the stairs when he heard the door open.

"Mr. Trevenen!"

James sighed and leaned against the railing.

The baronet peered down at him. "In thinking over the matter, I doubt Redfern will tell any of his other customers—my friends, you know—about your paying him so much."

Of course he will not, you simpleton, James thought, but he will tell other tailors and all the powerless people he knows and your punishment will get back to you.

"You're quite safe from ridicule, Mr. Trevenen," Sir Percival concluded.

Ah, but you are not, James told himself as he bowed. "I'm relieved to hear it."

"I thought you would be," Sir Percival said. "There is one more thing I wanted to tell you. It is about Lord Eberly."

"Who?"

"You've forgotten already? He is the regrettable employer of that mousy little governess I so kindly escorted home. I told him of your services to us…"

"Just to you, Sir Percival, just to you," James reminded him, but not without a warning bell going off in his mind.

"Alas, James, I did enlarge upon the tale, so he would grasp the gravity of the situation and understand why his children and their governess were a day late."

"All he needed to know was that the bridge was out," James began. He started up the stairs again. To his growing discomfort, Sir Percival backed away. "What did you tell him?"

"That you had also rescued Miss Haverstock and his children from fiery death," the baronet said in a rush. "Carried them all out on your back and down the drainpipe."

"What?" James shouted. "What I did originally was fantastic enough, and now you must add to it? Sir Percival, what were you *thinking?*"

"Poor Miss Haverstock was so afraid Eberly would cut up stiff that she gave me the headache," Sir Percival said, venturing closer to him. "I knew such a statement would end any protestations on Eberly's part, and do you know, it did. All the man could do was clutch his children to his bosom and sing your praises."

James sat down on the top step. "Oh, Lord," he groaned. "Please, please, tell me I will never see the man."

The words tumbled out of Sir Percival. "Not until the Copley award. He is coming to town specifically to thank you." He must have felt on firmer ground. "He never leaves his estate, so this is a signal honor."

"But I didn't *do* anything!"

"Perhaps I did go a little astray, James," he replied, with no particular concern in his voice. "It's amazing how one little prevarication likes to leap upon the back of another."

Yes, isn't it? James thought wearily. I have discovered that myself. He stood up, choosing his words carefully. "Sir Percival, there must be no more falsehood. I am here to receive a medal, after which I will retreat…er…return to Cornwall, and you will never hear of me again."

"No harm will be done then, will it?"

"Let us pray. Good day."

James was too irritated to sit still in Sir Joseph's barouche, but he knew the walk to Richmond was a long one. To the coachman's questions, he merely said, "Follow me." James strode along, perfectly unhappy and prepared to walk off his frustrations, as he had done innumerable times on his narrow island. Three miles this way, one mile that way.

Half Moon Street turned into Curzon, and then, a few blocks later, he found himself facing a welcome stretch of green. He gestured to the coachman, who obligingly pulled his vehicle to the side of the street.

"Where are we?" he asked.

"Sir, this is Hyde Park." He gestured with his whip, and then coughed politely. "It is an excellent place to…ah…walk."

"Good."

It was shortly after midday and the park was empty of carriages and hacks. "Has this a name?" he asked his coachman, who drove beside him.

The man pointed with his whip again. "Broad Walk, I believe." He gestured behind him. "Rotten Row is that way, sir. It's where the toffs preen."

James nodded. He was probably destined to ride there soon. "Ahead?"

"More Broad Walk, sir, and then there is something diverting. It's a place where troublemakers and religionists sometimes gather to speak their piece."

"I shouldn't wonder it is full of London's tailors," James murmured.

"Sir?"

"Nothing. You may drive there and park. I will be along."

The open expanse of green calmed him. He slowed his steps. He had saved a piece of toast from breakfast, and he munched it idly, careful not to finish it. Why he should husband scraps in broad daylight he could not understand. Surely the flesh-eating sailor would not appear in this civilized place. He looked around, though, just to be sure.

He sat for a while on a stone bench and stretched his legs out in front of him. The sun broke out from clouds and he raised his face to it. Soon all the warmth would be gone and another winter would begin. He found even the thought of winter distasteful. Much of his naval career had been spent in warm waters, even discounting his five-year island exile.

As he continued walking, he noticed a gathering of men ahead. He heard laughter now and then. Coming closer, he saw the crowd was grouped into separate circles, with taller men in the center of each. No, they weren't taller—they stood on boxes or maybe benches. Then he noticed Sir Joseph's barouche to one side, with the coachman standing by the horses. This must be the speakers' corner.

As James came closer, he realized the various crowds were generally bent upon heckling the speakers. He nodded to his coachman, then stood on the fringes of one group and then another, finding amusement in the cacophony of speakers and hecklers. One orator, an old rabble-rouser from the look of him, waxed on about the Irish question. After listening to his argument, James decided the Irish would always be a question.

He found another speaker also circled by hecklers, but the man was only reading from one of the Gospels, something about "Go ye into the world" to do thus and so. As he rambled on, he took sideways looks at a man leaning upon another fellow, both of them with their backs to James. The speaker and his friends were all dressed in sober, ill-cut clothing. James thought of his tailor and his pledge to give James's crotch room to relax. What a sybarite I am becoming, he thought. Maybe evangels would look less dour if they had comfortable trousers. Even missionaries have dongs, after all.

"And now, sirs, if you will permit…" The orator stopped and glared at the hecklers before him, who obviously liked to leap in whenever they could. "If you would permit," he began again, then glanced down, with noticeable concern in his eyes. "Can you?"

He wasn't speaking to the crowd, but to the man leaning against the other. James moved closer. The man nodded and held his hand up so the orator could assist him. Even before the man turned around, James murmured, "I know you." He came closer, and found himself starring into the face of Sam Higgins, the missionary he had shepherded home from Batavia to Portsmouth.

James shouldered aside protesting hecklers, until he stood right below the park bench where Sam wobbled, his eyes pained, his face sallow and his cheeks hollow with the same disease that had nearly killed him in Tonga. You should be in bed, Sam, James thought.

He could only stand there and watch as Sam began to speak. His voice was low as he spoke to the restless crowd about the South Seas and the Missionary Society's need for more people to voyage there.

"If it's so grand, what's keeping you from going back, eh, mate?" someone jeered.

"Ye ain't much of a h-orator," another heckler declared. He cupped his hand to his mouth so the sound would carry farther. "Too scrawny for a savage's stewpot?" Everyone laughed.

You dolt, James thought, then watched Sam. The other missionary had stepped down from the bench, leaving Sam there alone. James's stomach tightened as Sam swayed, opened and closed his eyes rapidly, then righted himself. Two patches of fever burned in his cheeks.

"What are you doing here?" he said quietly, even though he knew Sam could not hear him. "Does nobody know anything?"

Sam tried to begin again, but he had lost his audience. The other two missionaries looked at each other and frowned. James spoke to them. "Don't you think you should do something?" he said. "This is a sick man."

One of the men shrugged. "He insisted. We all have to work this corner now and then, and you can well imagine how useless he is at going door to door to solicit funds."

"My God," James said. He looked back at Sam, who was swaying again. As James braced his legs, Sam Higgins fell into his arms. James staggered under the weight of the man, who, though thin, was still full grown. James felt the fever through the missionary's clothes.

There was no question as to what he would do, and he expected no trouble from the other missionaries, who just stared. Maybe Mrs. Park is right, James thought, as he strengthened his hold on Sam. I am capable.

To his relief, Sir Joseph's coachman also appeared to be no stranger to quick action. The coachman had already swung himself into the box and was coaxing the horses closer. Hecklers scattered, and even the other missionaries gave him a wide berth. Sam opened his eyes and tried to speak.

"Save your breath, Sam," James said.

Sam closed his eyes. He sighed, as though relieved to know someone of sense was finally in charge.

"He's coming with me," James announced to the missionaries. The coachman had opened the door and stood beside him now, his hands steadying Sam's legs.

"We protest!" one of the men said, but he made no move to stop James.

"Do you?" James asked as the coachman climbed backward into the barouche and took Sam's weight into his arms when James transferred him. "Cover him," he said, then climbed in and took Sam in his arms again.

The coachman did, then hurried out of the barouche and back onto his box. He picked up his whip, then pointed it at the missionaries. "Back off, gents," he ordered. "To Alderson House?"

"No. To Spring Grove. But, we must find a pharmacy first," James said. He looked at the missionaries. "We will be at Spring Grove in Richmond, but I will not relinquish him to you until he is over this relapse."

"The Lord might punish you for kidnapping," one of the men said.

"The Lord punishes me every day," James replied. "You need to take better care of your practitioners or He might punish you, too."

James settled Sam's head into his lap and looked around. The commotion had caused a larger crowd to gather. There were other carriages now, some with crests on the door, and onlookers of more ordinary means, as well. One well-dressed man went so far as to rise up in his own open carriage. "I say, you cannot swipe people from the streets of London, sir!"

"Well, I have." He managed a brief bow, thought of Mrs.

Park and tipped his hat to the fellow. "Beau Crusoe at your service, sir."

As the coach bowled along, James looked down at Sam, whose eyes were open now. "Old boy, you still seem to need looking after, eh?" He touched the missionary's forehead with the back of his hand. "I didn't do a very good job of it on that voyage from Batavia, did I?"

Sam said nothing for a long moment. "You're a fornicator and a wretched sinner, James," he managed finally. "It's good to see you. Where are we going?"

"Where a lady I know will find herself with something to do," James replied. "She's going to nurse you through this relapse and then you're going to do me the favor of staying infirm for at least two weeks."

Sam's eyes were closing, but he opened them again. "A week is all I need," he protested feebly. "You know that."

"Loisa Alderson doesn't."

Chapter Twelve

The coachman found an apothecary, sandwiched between a to-bacconist and a perfumery. Once he had secured the horses, he clambered into the barouche and took Sam from James. "Gor, he's shivering," he said. "Tell me this ain't contagious."

"It's not," James assured him. "It's caused by bad air. I'll hurry."

The apothecary had ground cinchona bark. In fact, it was even in the same stoppered, dark blue bottle James was familiar with from seagoing medicine chests. "I'll take one of those," James said. "Sell me a spoon and cup, too, and put water in it."

He hurried from the shop, chagrined to see a small crowd gathering. Ignoring them, James gave Sam three sips of the ground bark. Sam made a face against the bark's bitterness, but he swallowed anyway. Two more sips and then he shook his head. The coachman climbed back onto his box. One of the men in the crowd on the pavement loosed the reins from the post and handed them to him, and they edged out into traffic again.

It was eight miles to Richmond, with the man in his lap alternating between shivering and sweating. Sam had a few lucid moments on the drive to Spring Grove. "Where… going?" he mumbled.

"Spring Grove," James replied. "It's the home of Sir Joseph Banks."

The name didn't appear to register with Higgins. He murmured something about "letting them know at Aldergate Street," then drifted off.

"Why are you here?" Higgins asked when they approached Sir Joseph's estate.

"Trying to do a better job of taking care of you than I did on that voyage from Batavia."

Higgins nodded. "Too preoccupied with Lady Audley. Not wise."

"So you told me," James replied. "At least I never contracted any diseases of an embarrassing nature." Just a mountain's load of regret, he added to himself.

It was easier than he thought to get Sam Higgins into Spring Grove. He didn't even have to knock on the door. Mrs. Park must have heard the horses. "We've been wondering where you—" She stopped. "What's wrong? Who is this?" she asked, looking in the barouche.

"His name is Sam Higgins. You remember my treatise. I know I mentioned my rescue by missionaries fleeing Tonga."

"I remember." She reached into the carriage to touch Sam's hair. "He's sweating."

She paled suddenly and stepped back. "Please, let him not be contagious."

He understood her fear because of what little she had told him about her husband's death in India. "He's suffering a malarial relapse," he assured her. "I just happened upon him in Hyde Park. He practically fell into my arms."

"John, go get Barmley," she told the coachman. "He will help you carry Mr. Higgins."

"What will Lady Dorothea and Sir Joseph think?" James said, even as he was grateful for her speedy grasp of the situation.

"They will never be discomforted or bothered," she said. "I will find someone from Alderson House to tend him."

"I have someone in mind," he told her, wondering if his hasty plan had even the slightest chance of success. "Your sister."

Mrs. Park gasped. "She will never!"

"I believe she will, because I intend to appeal to her better nature," James said, hoping he sounded more capable than he felt. "Your godfather told me to do something about Loisa. I intend to put her to work."

She frowned. This is not promising, James thought. She was only prevented from saying something pithy, he was certain, by the arrival of Barmley and the coachman. They carried Sam up the front steps. Mrs. Park followed, then regained her power of speech.

"Sir, I do not care if you are as capable as…Hercules, with those…those seven labors…"

"Twelve," he murmured.

She glared at him, then hurried ahead of the men carrying Sam. Lady Dorothea and Lady Sophia stood in the hall clutching their tatting. James explained the situation quickly as the men waited at the foot of the stairs. Mrs. Park looked in the sitting room and went in.

"You were right to bring him here," Lady Dorothea exclaimed. She looked at Barmley. "Upstairs and to the left, Barmley, then summon the physician."

"I will come up shortly. Thank you, Lady Dorothea," James said. "You needn't call a physician right now. I can begin to care for him, and then I will find help at Alderson House."

Lady Dorothea shook her head at the mention of Alderson. "The only sensible person at Alderson is already here, and Noah needs her." She looked around, but Mrs. Park was not in sight. She leaned her ponderous bulk closer and whispered in his ear. "She suffered so when her husband died in India. It would be painful for her to have sickroom duties. Surely we can engage a nurse."

"I think Miss Loisa Alderson is sensible, too," he said firmly. "I will ask her."

"Loisa?"

"I do believe she will surprise all of us," James said, hoping he sounded more convincing than he felt. "I only hope Mr. Higgins will not disturb Sir Joseph."

"You can ask him yourself," Lady Dorothea said. She gestured toward the sitting room. "He is feeling much better."

Mrs. Park was there already, talking to her godfather quietly. James hoped she was explaining the situation. Noah was lying on the floor, his head on Neptune's great bulk, reading a picture book. All these people, James thought. How can I return to the solitude of Cornwall?

"Sir Joseph, are you feeling better?" James asked.

"Well enough to declare you are a rascal," the old man said, but there was no sting to his words. "You honestly think Loisa Alderson will tend this man?"

"I do. What's more, I think she will jump at the chance. She needs an occupation."

Sir Joseph shook his head. "I admit to considerable skepticism."

"You asked me to do something about her."

"Indeed I did," Sir Joseph agreed. "This is your solution?" He was silent a moment. "Very well. Sam Higgins may stay here, as long as he does not preach at us."

"Done, sir."

"Now you have to convince my sister," Mrs. Park said.

That's all, he thought, as he climbed the stairs to the bedchamber. He helped Barmley divest Sam of his clothing. The footman found one of Sir Joseph's night shirts. It was big enough to wrap twice around Sam.

Mrs. Park came into the room with a canister of hot water, which she set on the washstand. Noah peered around the door before he brought in a pitcher of cool water, holding it carefully in front of him.

"Excellent, son," Mrs. Park said as she took it from him.

Barmley gathered up Sam's clothes and left the room. Mrs. Park stood beside the bed, unease visible in every line of her body. She hesitated a moment, then rested the back of her hand on Sam's forehead. "Noah," she said, her voice soft. "Gather up our things, for we are leaving soon."

She waited until her son left the room. "When my husband died, I had to pull a sheet over his face, leave him on our bed and go tend others who were sick. He was thrown upon a funeral pyre and burned." She looked at James, and his heart lurched to see tears on her cheeks. "Please, tell me this man is not near death."

"I won't tease you," James said. He ran a damp cloth around the missionary's face. "He is ill, but he will be better."

He took the quinine from his coat pocket and set it beside the bed. "Don't worry, Mrs. P."

To his surprise, she leaned against him. "This is a hard thing," she murmured.

He enveloped her in his arms, enjoying the moment. "I wish I had a better way to keep Loisa busy, but here it is. His companions were inept. I couldn't just leave him."

"Certainly not," she said. She left his embrace and sat on the edge of the bed. "Take Noah home. I will stay here with Mr. Higgins until you return with Loisa."

"Barmley could do this," he protested. He wanted to hold her longer. How soft women were.

Mrs. Park shook her head. "He needs to be available for Sir Joseph." She smiled at him. "Hurry, before I change my mind!"

"Very well." He went to the door. "Do you think I can convince her?"

"You said you would."

His imp flew into the room then, plopped down on his shoulder and made itself comfortable. "Would you care to wager, Mrs. P?" he asked.

She did not throw him out of the room, so he took that as a signal to proceed. "If I convince your sister—and I will—to come to Spring Grove, I want you to paint another *Gloriosa Jubilate* for me, a large one. You've seen the drawing in my treatise. You know I'm no artist."

"True. And if I win?"

"Anything. Only name it."

"You will tell me your whole story of life on that island."

The imp staggered off his shoulder and flopped onto the floor. "You want that?" James asked, wishing his voice didn't suddenly sound so strangled. "Why, in God's name?"

"You need to tell it," she told him. "I want to hear it."

She had cornered him. "Then I had better convince Loisa, eh?"

He went downstairs and into the sitting room, where Lady Dorothea waited. "Mr. Higgins is resting quietly, and Susannah—Mrs. Park—is with him."

"I wish you had not done that," Lady Dorothea said. "Surely Barmley…"

"Barmley is here to help you and Sir Joseph," he reminded her. "I won't be long, and I will return with Loisa. Noah, your mother wants you to come with me."

Seated in the barouche again, he wasn't sure what he expected from Noah. To his surprise, the boy moved close to him and leaned against his arm. In another moment, James put his arm around Noah.

"Mama isn't staying there tonight, is she?"

"Oh, no," James assured him. "I'm going to convince your Aunt Loisa to go to Spring Grove with me and tend Mr. Higgins. Your mother will come back with me."

Noah nodded, and James could tell he was thinking over the matter. "Will Aunt Loisa stay at Spring Grove a very long time?"

James chuckled to himself. "Two weeks at least. That's my plan."

"That is a long time."

Not really, James thought. A long time is five years. He held Noah close, enjoying his warmth. "Are you cold?" he asked the boy.

"Not when you're here. I forgot." Noah took a small box from the cloth bag he had carried to Spring Grove that morning. "Mama wanted me to give you this. The change is inside."

James opened the box and looked at the gloves within, kidskin carefully dyed to a soft pink. He thought of Sir Percival and his stupid waistcoats, and wondered if Lady Pettibone had convinced Mrs. Park to buy them instead of ribbons for Loisa.

"Mama thinks Aunt Loisa will have more use for these than for ribbons."

"She is undoubtedly right," James said. To him, pink hardly seemed the proper color for someone as red-faced as Miss Alderson. Still, Susannah and Loisa were sisters, even though estranged. Surely Susannah would know. He held up the gloves to the afternoon sun, suddenly convinced that nothing he would say would ever induce Loisa to help. He crumpled the dainty gloves in his fist. He could imagine her scorn, if he were to hand these to her and then beg a favor.

He closed his eyes, thinking of every impossible task he had accomplished on his island, simply because he had no choice. He remembered Loisa's look of concern for her sister that morning, if he had read her right. It wasn't much to build upon, but it was all he had, a glimmer of something besides disdain in Loisa's eyes.

He told himself it must be a frightful thing for a woman to contemplate living on the sufferance of relatives. I belong to no one, he thought, but I have an income. Women have so little, and Loisa less than most. Susannah at least has Noah. Has no one ever really *needed* Loisa before?

"Lady, I need you now," he murmured. When Noah looked at him, a question in his eyes, James just pulled him closer.

When they arrived at Alderson House, he asked the coachman to wait. Noah hopped down from the barouche, skipped up the steps and knocked on the front door. James followed, amused at the small boy's bravado, now that the toucans were gone. One of the footmen opened the door, and grinned broadly when he saw who it was. He opened the door wider, with a real flourish, to show off the newly painted hallway and the impeccable parquet flooring.

Noah skipped on ahead, then looked back. "Mama said I was to go below stairs and help out where I could," he told James.

"Then you had better do as she said."

Noah hurried down the hall, leaving James alone to face the dragon. First, he had to find her.

"Where is Miss Alderson?" he asked the footman.

The footman started in surprise. "Miss *Alderson?*" he repeated, as though no one ever asked for her.

Perhaps no one ever has, James thought, shaking his head. I wonder if life isn't harder on *this* island. "Yes, Miss Alderson."

"The green room, Mr. Trevenen. She often sits there in the afternoons."

The footman led the way, then eased the door open, almost as though he was afraid to ruffle the sensibilities of the inmate within. Does everyone walk upon eggshells around the formidable Miss Alderson? James asked himself.

She sat facing the window, apparently unaware the door had been opened. James had thought the footman might announce him, but the servant backed away and was soon retreating down the hall.

James stood where he was, not out of fear but curiosity now. As he watched her, he realized she was doing nothing except sitting with her hands folded in her lap. How sad, he thought. Other ladies her age were occupied with children, or at least a household to run or calls to make in the neighborhood. Here she sat, waiting for nothing because there was nothing.

He went back out the open door, closed it silently behind him, then opened it after a brief knock. She tensed, turning to look at him, and then beyond him. He thought she must be looking for Susannah, and it gave him hope.

"I'm sorry to interrupt you, Miss Alderson."

She favored him with a curt nod, glancing at the empty doorway again.

"Your sister is still at Spring Grove, but Noah went to the kitchen," he said. "May I sit down?"

She indicated he could. "They feed him too many sweets," she said. To his ears, it seemed more of a statement than a complaint.

"I imagine they do."

She said nothing in return, so he plunged ahead. No sense in reaping her disdain by hemming and hawing.

"I am in real need, Miss Alderson," he said. "In fact, I don't know anyone else who could help me more."

She moved her hand in a dismissive gesture, and his heart sank. Then she spoke. "First I must know how my…sister…fared?"

She seemed to find the word *sister* hard to speak, not so much from anger now, but from some well of emotion he had not thought existed. "I thought you disliked your sister," he blurted.

Miss Alderson resumed her quiet contemplation of the view outside the window. "Let us say, I have had ample reason for displeasure. Monumental reason, perhaps." She shrugged. "I am no longer sure what I think. How did she fare?"

He realized that in all the sudden concern for Sam Higgins, he had not taken the time to ask Mrs. Park. "I don't know," he said honestly. "Something came up that quite moved it from my mind."

Loisa sat forward and looked at him then, her breath coming faster. "She isn't hurt, is she?"

Well, bless my soul, he thought. "No, she's fine." He smiled then. "She went to the rose glass house early this morning and painted a wonderful rose which she presented to Lady Pettibone. I think it quite charmed the old biddy."

"Suze has that knack."

He strained his ears for any nuance of sympathy, but all he heard was a definite dryness of tone. Still, Loisa had called her Suze. Perhaps it was a childhood name. Lord, I am a disgusting optimist, he thought.

"The matter concerns another."

He told her about Sam Higgins, talking faster in the face of her silence.

"Mrs. Park is watching him," he finished. "We daren't throw him on Sir Joseph's or Lady Dorothea's shoulders. The youngest servant in the whole house is Barmley, and maybe a scullery maid somewhere below stairs."

"You left Suze there alone?" There was no mistaking the anxiety in her voice. "After the way her husband died?"

He nodded. "I don't want to leave her there alone much longer. That is why I need your help." He knew he was pleading now. "Will you help, Miss Alderson?"

He knew she was going to say no. He must have been wrong about any glimmer of feeling, because her face was solemn again, unreadable.

"This is going to inconvenience me mightily, but I will do it," she said, after another long look out the window. She shook her finger at him. "Don't you dare for one minute think it is because you are persuasive, Mr. Trevenen! I think you are a scoundrel."

"The worst," he agreed cheerfully. He wanted to throw himself on his knees and kiss her feet. He knew that would earn him a well-deserved kick, so he refrained.

She stood up. "Hurry," she demanded. "I might change my mind!"

Chapter Thirteen

Miss Alderson was quicker than most females in preparing herself for a visit of indeterminate length. She scrawled a note for her mother, who was playing cards with her cronies, and threw some clothes into a satchel, which she thrust at James to carry.

"Your father?" James asked.

"He is sitting in his bird blind," Loisa said. "I doubt he will know I am gone." She started for the entrance at such a rapid pace he had to hurry to keep up.

In the foyer, she stopped so suddenly that he nearly ran into her. "Thank you for ridding us of those disgusting birds," she said.

"My pleasure."

"This used to be such a fine entrance. Let us pray my father does not develop an attraction to polar bears or baboons."

It was so droll James was momentarily stunned into silence. Then he burst out laughing. He was still chuckling when he helped her into the barouche.

She didn't say much, but looked around at autumn in progress. Then, "My mother will be shocked I am attending to an unknown man. I shouldn't, you know."

"If I had thought someone else could help me, I would never have presumed," James said. "Barmley has already agreed to tend to his bodily needs. I can tell you this: Mr. Higgins—Sam—will sweat and stink, and then shiver and freeze for the next few days. If you can keep him warm with blankets and a hot water bottle when he shivers, and then cool him off when he burns, he'll manage."

"A few days?"

Tactical error. James was going to fib about several weeks of agony and then a slow recovery that would see him safely away. He glanced at her. Behind that forbidding exterior lurked a superior brain he could probably not bamboozle. Well, not too much. "He'll be weak and exhausted for another week, I imagine," he said. I will instruct Sam to be weak, he thought.

"I can manage that," she told him. "We cannot pretend that I am too occupied at Alderson House, can we?"

"No," he said honestly. "Of course, I suppose you have dress fittings and such to prepare for the next season."

"There isn't going to be another season," she murmured.

He didn't know what to say. The little that Mrs. Park had said about her sister's Marriage Mart doldrums had led him to think Miss Alderson was oblivious to her own scant charms. He wondered how he could convince the sisters to talk to each other. No sense in beating about the bush, when he had so little time in London. He took a deep breath.

"I think you and Mrs. Park should talk," he said.

"That would require that I forgive her," Miss Alderson said, looking straight ahead now.

"I believe it would."

"Have *you* ever begged forgiveness?"

Where would I start? he thought. Should I forgive my parents for not rescuing me from the ocean when my brother died? Should I forgive the half-wit who ground us onto a shoal and then ran around screaming? Should I beg forgiveness of Lady Audley for humping her through several longitudes and then dropping her like an anchor? There was a worse one. He couldn't bear to think of it.

He glanced at Miss Alderson, who wrinkled her nose in distaste. "I thought you hadn't," she murmured. "Not easy, is it?"

He shook his head. Then he took the easy way out, considering that if he stayed healthy and avoided small islands, the final judgment was probably a long way off. "I will have to start at the top and ask God to forgive all those terrible things I said about Him during my exile."

He couldn't fool Miss Alderson. "How useful for you, calling upon a deity you needn't face, like a sister," she said, not disguising her contempt.

And then she was silent. He wanted to stop the barouche, leap out and keep running until he found a mail coach heading toward Cornwall. At the very least, he wanted to hurry back to Alderson House, grab his treatise on the *Gloriosa*—the only constant in his life—and just hold it.

He did neither. "I'm making a muddle of this."

She surprised him again. "I'm not so certain about that, Mr. Trevenen," she said. "You *are* making things more interesting. Let us leave it at that for the moment and concentrate on Mr. Higgins."

"You're kind, Miss Alderson."

"Not noticeably."

He laughed then, surprised how much he was enjoying the prickly Miss Alderson. *I wish I had had a sister like this,* he thought. "If you're not kind, you're at least tolerable," he told her.

It was her turn to laugh, and there was no hard edge to the sound. "Since we are being somewhat honest, tell me this: if you had my face, would *you* attempt another London Season?"

He had not expected this, either. "I should think not, Miss Alderson, but maybe not for the reason you imagine," he ventured. "I doubt the people you meet at Almack's would appreciate you. At least, not if Sir Percival Pettibone is a good representative. He wouldn't know wit if it smacked him across the chops."

But *I* know someone who does, he thought suddenly. And you're about to meet him. Another thought intrigued him.

"Miss Alderson, our acquaintance has been short and frosty, up to now. Why are we suddenly being honest with each other?"

"Simple," she said promptly. "You will be leaving in a few weeks and I will never see you again. We can tell each other things we would never tell others."

They were on the elm-shaded lane to Spring Grove now. In contrast to his earlier wish to run away, he now felt a greater desire to ask the coachman to slow down. "Miss Alderson, I have to know—this morning you were forbidding, and now you are not. What has happened?"

"I have been thinking about you and those stupid toucans," she said. "Here not even a day, you managed to get rid of nasty birds that have been plaguing the rest of us for years. You just... you just did it!" She touched his arm. "It was enlightening to see what happens when someone *acts.*"

She looked away, and James sensed a great struggle. "Go on," he urged.

"As much as I thought I hated her for it, Suze acted seven years ago. She did not pine or droop, she *acted.*" Miss Alderson pinched the bridge of her nose with her fingers, as though warding off tears. "Things have not turned out to her liking, but I don't think she has regrets."

He spoke to the coachman. "John, a little slower, if you please. We have a conversation to finish." He returned his attention to Miss Alderson. "When I first met Sir Joseph, he told me to get rid of the toucans, do something about you and marry your sister."

Miss Alderson let out a whoop of undignified laughter. "He is a meddling old rascal," she said, when she could speak.

"Decidedly. I got rid of the toucans..."

"...and now you're doing something about me."

"Yes. I got lucky there. Sam needs help."

"Are you going to marry my sister?" she teased.

He shook his head. "I told her about that conversation with Sir Joseph, and we both agreed that no one falls in love in two weeks."

"You're wrong there, sir," Miss Alderson contradicted. "I think Suze loved David Park the moment she latched eyes on him."

"Then it probably won't happen again," he said. "I'm not a very good man, Miss Alderson. If I were to propose to your sister, she would turn me down flatter than a French-made bed." He hesitated a moment, considered the one other thing bothering him and decided to push ahead. "About Noah..."

She sighed, and he knew the matter had been weighing on her mind, too, perhaps more than her treatment of Mrs. Park. "I was resolved to dislike him forever," she said, and he could only marvel at her honesty. "It's hard to change a course once committed."

Ask Beau Crusoe, James thought sourly. "I think I have a glimmer of what that means," he said. Beau Crusoe had not only saved Sir Percival Pettibone from death, but now an inn full of lodgers, too, as flames engulfed the building. He thought of the crowd that had gathered outside the apothecary's. And let us add a poor stranger in Hyde Park who keeled over. Next thing you know, Beau Crusoe will be rescuing kittens from tall trees, perhaps even swinging from a chandelier in a Drury Lane theater to help an actor suffering a fit on stage.

"I don't know anything about little boys," she told him, as the barouche stopped in the circular driveway.

"They're entertaining and vastly loyal, if you appeal to their sense of fair play. Try a small compliment, Miss Alderson."

"He avoids me," she countered.

"You frighten him. He skips meals when his mother isn't there to be his champion."

"So he does," Miss Alderson said. She looked him square in the eye. "I have a long way to go, haven't I?"

Not as far as I have, he thought. "Noah will surprise you. Do something kind for his mother, and he will be your friend for life."

She stood up. The coachman opened the door and helped her down. She looked up at the manor with a grimace. He was preparing to follow her when he noticed the small box still on the seat. He handed it to her.

"I meant to give you this," he said.

She opened the box and saw the pale pink kid gloves. She picked up one by thumb and forefinger. "What were you thinking?"

He shrugged. "I have no idea. I gave Mrs. Park some shillings to buy you a present at the Pantheon. Lady Pettibone took her there."

"Pink," Miss Alderson said, investing the word with all the disdain he knew she was capable of.

"Sir Percival is determined to wrench it into fashion next season."

"The more fool he," she replied, but put the gloves in her reticule. She gave him another long look. He was becoming used to those now. "Tell me, Mr. Trevenen. When you embark upon a scheme, do you ever give it much thought?"

"I wouldn't dare," he said, and she laughed.

To say that Mrs. Park appeared startled to see her sister in his company was an understatement of the grossest proportion. As they entered the sickroom, she stood up, as though the seat was hot.

Miss Alderson gave her an amused look and took off her bonnet. "You need to have more faith in Mr. Trevenen, Suze," she said. "He is a thorough-going rascal but amazingly persuasive. Yes, I will tend Mr. Higgins." She peered down at the sleeping man. "He doesn't look promising." She glanced at her sister, then at James, who was hard-pressed not to smile. "Susannah, has the cat got your tongue?"

"Yes, as a matter of fact," Mrs. Park said. "I had not thought you would be disposed to help." She put down the damp cloth she had been using to wipe Sam's forehead. "Now this means I must paint a crab."

It was Miss Alderson's turn to look startled, but only for a moment. James knew how quick she was. "That was the wager?"

"It was."

"What did you wager in the more likely event I would turn him down?"

"I was going to force him to tell me everything that happened to him on his South Seas island."

"I think you should demand that anyway," Miss Alderson said, in her no-nonsense way. "Mr. Trevenen, tell me what to do for this disgusting specimen. I will do my utmost to not send him into a coma from which he will never awaken." She sniffed the air. "Although from the stench, I doubt he would be missed."

Still amused, James showed her how to measure the precise dosage of quinine. "Keep him cool, keep him warm and summon Barmley when he needs to use the urinal."

"How will I know that?" she asked.

"He will probably tug at his member," he told her with an absolutely straight face, even as he marveled at having such a conversation with two refined ladies in the room.

Mrs. Park put her hand over her mouth and turned away, which caused Miss Alderson to remark, "Susannah, you are too easily amused. Mr. Trevenen, if he should wake up, what should I tell him?"

"Your name, Miss Alderson," he teased. "If he asks how he got here, do fill him in, for I doubt he remembers anything."

"You plucked him out of Hyde Park?"

"That will do. I'll be by tomorrow."

"I will, too, Loisa, if you think you need me," Mrs. Park said.

"I think not," Miss Alderson replied, and James's heart sank. It rose quickly, though, as she continued. "You've been through enough of this, haven't you?"

Mrs. Park's lips trembled, and her eyes seemed to bore a hole into her sister. "It was a lonely vigil, Loie," was all she could manage.

"I imagine it was," Miss Alderson said, her voice soft. "You were so far away, too."

Mrs. Park hesitated for only a second, then rested her hand on her sister's shoulder. "Thank you."

Miss Alderson looked at Mrs. Park's hand, and then into her sister's face with such an expression of regret that James had to turn away.

He turned back, curious as to what Mrs. Park would do about this silent apology for years of misery and discomfort. He doubted it could be so easily forgiven, but as he watched the two sisters, he wondered.

The lump in his throat grew larger as Susannah lifted her hand from Miss Alderson's shoulder to touch her cheek lightly. "Loie," was all she said, but James felt his eyes prickle.

"Come along, Mrs. Park," he said as a gentle reminder, not meaning to separate the sisters, but not ready to cry in front of them, either. "Noah is probably wondering where you are."

"I suppose he is," she replied. She blew a kiss to Miss Alderson, and left the room.

Before he followed, James glanced at Miss Alderson, who had plumped herself down on the bed as though her legs could not hold her. She bowed her head and James watched, amazed and then humbled by the power of forgiveness, as her tears came. He closed the door behind him.

It opened again before they reached the stairs. Miss Alderson was all business now. "Susannah, I have a suggestion," she called after them.

"Yes?"

"If Sir Joseph will agree—and after all, how much trouble is one little boy?—let Noah come tomorrow. He can brush that foul dog some more, and if I have a message to deliver to you or Mr. Trevenen about the festering, decomposing Mr. Higgins, I will send it through him. Noah is quick on his feet and about sixty years younger than anyone Sir Joe would send."

Susannah laughed, and it was a relieved laugh. "I will put the matter to Noah and ask his help."

"Excellent." Miss Alderson went back into the room.

Mrs. Park didn't start to cry until the coachman began the return trip to Alderson House. James did not hesitate to put his arm around her shoulder and pull her close as she sobbed. He handed her his handkerchief and settled them both back against the seat. He inclined his head toward hers, savoring the soft press of her skull against his. She appeared to have forgotten her bonnet. He thought he could have sat that way for hours. It was a simple pleasure, really, not the kind a man would dream of on a deserted island, where all misery was magnified. Just touching another human gave his heart ease.

After too short a time to suit him, Mrs. Park blew her nose and sat up. He would have preferred her to have remained tucked so warm against him, but that wasn't something he could argue about. He only hoped she would not apologize for the familiarity.

She didn't. She leaned closer and kissed his cheek. "I don't know what you did or said, but thank you," she whispered.

He turned his head out of surprise and found his lips right next to hers. He could have groaned out loud when she pulled back.

He knew she was embarrassed, and he did not want to add to her discomfort at her impulsive kiss. He assumed what he hoped was a nonchalant air. "I sailed close to the wind, as I usually do," he told her. "No plan or design."

"It had to be more than that."

"I disagree. After a while, it must be hard for anyone to shoulder all that umbrage." She looked at though she would burst into tears again, so he steered the conversation into different waters. "Tell me what happened at the Pantheon Bazaar."

She smiled. "Lady Pettibone is the silliest of females, but she introduced me to everyone she knew at the Pantheon. No one turned away. No one pulled their skirts aside when I came close."

"Certainly not," he murmured.

"You weren't there when they did, years ago. Perhaps people forget and move on to other topics."

"The kind ones do," he said, and considered Lady Audley briefly, and the long stare she had fixed on him when he left the ship and her dubious company in Cape Town. He had been quite chilled by the loathing on her expressive face. "The kind ones do," he repeated.

"Mr. Trevenen, are you attending?"

Startled, he shook his head.

"You and I and Noah are invited to take Lady Pettibone for a drive on Rotten Row."

"Oh, excellent," he joked. "We can peacock about in good company. I have not a doubt that the horses will bolt, and an elegant gentleman with eyes only for you will save us and then I can fulfill every request of Sir Joseph and return to Cornwall a happy man."

"Have you forgotten? *You* are supposed to marry me."

They both laughed. "My godfather is absurd, I know," she told him. "As long as the man is some sort of gentleman, Sir Joe will not cavil."

"You think *I* am not a gentleman?"

She looked at him, her eyes still bright with laughter. "I *know* you are! But didn't we agree Sir Joe was absurd to meddle?"

"We did," he replied, wondering at his disappointment.

When they got to Alderson House, Noah was sitting on the front steps. Mrs. Park was out of the barouche before James could assist her, hugging Noah. James watched with some envy as the blond woman and red-haired child took such delight in each other.

Dinner at Alderson was a strange event, with Lady Watchmere alternating between a distressing monologue on the fact that Loisa would tend a nobody ("Catching heaven knows how many diseases.") and gloating over the promised carriage ride tomorrow ("It will lead to great things, Susannah. Maybe one of the patronesses of Almack's can be persuaded to procure a voucher for you when the Season begins.").

Lord Watchmere sat half-turned to Miss Alderson's empty chair, describing his day's bird sightings to his absent daughter. When Susannah reminded him that her sister was at Spring Grove, he said "'Pon my word, that is dashed inconvenient," several times, never making clear precisely who was discommoded.

Noah ate happily, asked for seconds and ate those, too. Several times, Mrs. Park glanced James's way. He resisted the urge to put anything from the table into his pockets. Mrs. Park had promised there would be food in his room tonight.

In the sitting room, Noah beat him several times at jackstraws and then let his mama lead him to bed, after the obligatory protest. James remained in the sitting room, listening to Lord Watchmere mumble over his birdwatching journal and watching Lady Watchmere cheat at solitaire, until he could not stand the boredom another moment. Wishing them good-night, he went upstairs.

The door to Noah's room was open, so he knocked, then went inside. Mrs. Park, tucked under the covers with her son, was reading aloud to him. She smiled over the book and paused.

"I'll have that picture of the *Gloriosa* for you when you finish," he told her, then left the room. After taking a good look at the tray of meat and cheese on the bureau top, he flopped onto his own bed and put his hands behind his head, staring at the ceiling until he closed his eyes.

When he opened them again—twenty minutes later or two hours later, he could not tell—someone was sitting in the chair. He gasped and sat up before he realized it was only Mrs. Park. She stared at him, her eyes wide.

"I can come back later," she said, her voice uncertain. She stood up. "I shouldn't even be in here. I wanted to get the sketch but couldn't quite bring myself to disturb you."

"No, no," he told her. "It's no trouble." He got off his bed and went to his bureau. As he slid the treatise from its jacket, he felt his heartbeat slow to its normal rhythm. He slipped out his sketch of the *Gloriosa*, remembering his first encounter with the small creatures in the tidal pool.

"I was so hungry the first time I saw the crabs that I almost caught them and ate them raw," he told her.

"That would have been a loss to science," she teased. "What on earth made you decide to study them?"

He placed the sketch in her lap. As she scrutinized the crude picture he had painted, he perched on the end of his bed so he could be closer to her. "I think that day I was more lonely than hungry. I hunkered down on a rock and just watched them." He smiled at her, feeling foolish. "I was still planning to eat them, but not just then. Do you think I am an idiot?"

"No."

It occurred to him that perhaps it was possible to fall in love in two weeks. She was looking down at his drawing again, tracing her finger across the carapace of the little crab, so he was free for a moment to gaze at her to his heart's content.

He thought how soft she had felt, leaning against him in the barouche as she cried; the pleasant scent of her, not any particular fragrance beyond soap and water; the length of her legs— which he had never seen, of course, but which interested him; the way she had of focusing all her attention upon her son with her hands on his face; the soft rise and fall of her breasts when she sat still; those few tendrils of blond hair that always escaped regimentation low on her neck.

I could live my life and never want another woman, he thought, observing her. He looked away, because the urge to take her in his arms was growing by the moment.

It was all impossible, of course. If she knew what had happened, she would never look at him again in the same way.

Another thought, a new terror, scissored into his brain. Suppose there came a time when all the food in his room at night would not keep away the demon that haunted him. He shuddered and she looked up at him, a question in her eyes.

"James, even if I did lose the wager, I hope you will still tell me the whole story." She spoke softly to him.

"Never," he said, equally quiet. "Never."

Chapter Fourteen

That night, James discovered that even food wouldn't keep the carpenter's mate at bay anymore.

There had been a time right after he'd returned to Cornwall when he had seemed to see the ghoul out of the corner of his eye, as though the specter had just left each room before James entered it. The unease had gone away—he had hoped for good—but the feeling was getting stronger again.

Since the carpenter's mate seemed to prefer sitting in the chair beside the bed, James avoided looking at it. He lay there in the dark, remembering times when he was young and frightened by thunder. He had gone to his parents' room and stood there until his mother pulled back the covers and let him snuggle close to her.

He wondered what Mrs. Park would do if he opened her door and stood there, terrified of his dreams and desperate to lie next to someone who had never seen what he had seen. Would she pull back the covers and let him in? He knew the answer to that.

Only one thought kept him from packing and leaving before anyone except the servants were up. He didn't know if she was aware of it, but Susannah had called him James last night. It was a small matter, but he was willing to grasp at straws.

With a sigh, he stretched out to his full length and put his hands behind his head. His mother had called him Jemmy, but when he went to sea as a small boy, he became Trevenen. Belowdecks in the midshipmen's bleak quarters, and then later on the quarterdeck, his familiars called him Trev, which suited him well enough.

Lady Audley had called him James a time or two on that voyage from Batavia. In fact, his disillusion with her had probably begun when, in the heat of thumping, thrusting passion, she had called him Edward a few times and then Clarence. There had even been a "Leonardo" when he had tried something more experimental he had learned from a whore in Lisbon. Obviously, someone named Leonardo had beaten him to that particular position. By then, he wasn't too surprised.

When he had asked her about Edward, Clarence and Leonardo, she had just laughed. That was probably when his ardor had begun to cool and he had started to wonder whether he might contract a disease from Lady Audley, who apparently knew a lot of men's names and had a bad memory.

As his sleepless night dragged on, he debated what he missed more: coitus or just the fact of someone touching him. I could do with a casual touch, he told himself.

When sunlight finally crept through his curtains, he wondered whether he should go to Spring Grove immediately, or wait for Noah and Susannah. There now. In his mind and heart he would call her Susannah, and wait for permission, if it ever came, to do so aloud.

She probably hadn't meant to call him James. He could wish otherwise all he wanted, but it was unlikely.

He slid a note under Susannah's door before he went downstairs, telling her where he was and assuring her he would see her before the carriage ride that afternoon on Rotten Row, when he would probably have to be Beau Crusoe instead of James Trevenen. Only a few weeks, he reminded himself.

There was no point in dropping in to the breakfast room, because he had taken bread and cheese from the tray on his bureau, that food his butler in Cornwall had suggested he leave to appease the always-hungry specter. He didn't look for his sketch, because he remembered he had given it to Susannah last night.

Thank God he had won the wager with her, considering that he had no plans to ever tell anyone about his years on the island, not even Sir Joseph. Besides, if he had lost, Miss Alderson would still be plaguing Noah.

He strode along the path toward Spring Grove, marveling at the speed of her capitulation. Most people just want to be needed, he thought. Toss us a bone with a little meat on it, and we're scarcely better than Pomeranians.

It was a bad analogy, and one he regretted the moment he had thought of it. He stopped by the row of glass houses and stood in an open space where no one or nothing could stagger out of tropical foliage and surprise him. He waited a moment, until his breathing returned to normal.

The servants were about when he arrived at Spring Grove. The butler offered him breakfast, but he just shook his head and indicated his desire to check on Sam. He knew Sir Joseph and his wife and sister would not be out of bed yet. A maid stood in the hallway, eyeing him expectantly, ready to do anything he should ask for. We are so coddled on this island, he thought. He shook his head and hurried up the stairs.

Careful to walk quietly, he knocked on the door. Miss Alderson was there in an instant with a ferocious expression, as if ready to thrash anyone who made any noise. Sam's in better hands than I would have imagined, James thought as he backed off and raised both hands in surrender.

It had the desired effect. The one-step-closer-and-you-die look left Miss Alderson's face as quickly as it had come. She opened the door but, to his continued amusement, offered no apology for her defense of the man lying within, a man she didn't even know.

James looked at the still form on the bed. "How is he?" he whispered, then impulsively took her hand and tugged her into the corridor. With only one backward look, she let him.

"He is doing well now," she said. He couldn't help but notice the tired lines in her face. "It was a difficult night, though."

"Thank you. I'm sorry I pitchforked you into this."

"I have no regrets," she said. "It's strange. He stares at me and I know he wonders who on earth I am. I tell him, but nothing registers."

"I doubt he remembers any of the events of yesterday. Let me sit with him a while, so you can get some unbroken sleep."

"I suppose I do look a fright," she said, her hand going to her hair.

"Not at all, Miss Alderson," he said, and he meant it. You'll never be mistaken for a beauty, even in a dark room, he thought, but you look fine nonetheless. Maybe compassion is as good a beauty aid as glycerin and rose water.

"I *am* tired," she admitted. "I was afraid to sleep. Thought he might die if I was not watching him. Silly of me."

"No. I appreciate your concern."

"Who is he?"

He shrugged. "I hardly know more than you, really. He was part of a group from the Missionary Society who aimed to Christianize Tonga. It came to nothing, he caught malaria and I was to shepherd him back to London when I took passage on an East India merchant ship in Batavia. He is the son of a farmer from Norfolk."

"The other missionaries?"

"I don't know. One can only hope they didn't try to return to Tonga." He hoped she would not ask much more about that voyage from Batavia, but it was a vain hope.

"How long did it take to get from Batavia to here?"

"Six months. Maybe a little more."

"I wonder you didn't come to know more about him, in such a length of time."

Miss Alderson was the last person with whom he wished to share information about his unfortunate preoccupation with Lady Audley's always wide-spread legs. Just thinking of it made him blush. To his relief, Miss Alderson made no comment. Perhaps the corridor was still dim enough in early morning.

"You go rest," he told her, hoping she wouldn't think he was hurrying her away. "I'll sit with him."

To his relief, she nodded and went to the chamber next to Sam's. "Tap on the door when you are ready to leave, if I am not already awake."

He went into Sam's room and opened the draperies slightly to let in the early morning light. As he stood over the man, he realized the room no longer stank of sweat.

He came closer to Sam and sniffed. Why, you sweet thing, you, he thought. He picked up a bottle by the basin of cool water. Eau de lavender, he read. Miss Alderson had obviously been dabbing him with the fragrance. And Sam was no longer wearing that voluminous nightshirt of Sir Joseph's but a blue-and-white striped shirt more his size.

James sat down in the chair pulled up close to the bed, remembering that voyage from Batavia to Portsmouth, when the other Tonga missionaries had handed off Sam to him almost apologetically. "We expect he won't survive the voyage, but we daren't keep him here," the leader had told him.

Privately, James had agreed with the man. The biggest missionary had carried Sam Higgins in his arms from the dock, slung him over his back for the climb up the rope ladder and deposited him gently on the deck, a skinny, wretched, sweating lump of humanity.

James watched him now. "You weren't even shark chum, friend," he said softly to the sleeping man. "Somehow you survived, and here you are again in my life." He leaned back in the chair, yawned and closed his eyes.

"Lieutenant Trevenen? Did I throw myself on you yesterday?"

James sat up. Sam hadn't changed position, but his eyes were open. The missionary looked sideways at James, as though it was really too much effort to turn his head.

He was still preserving the niceties. Even when James, stark naked, had met the missionaries on the beach and introduced himself, he had always been lieutenant to Sam Higgins. Granted, in ordinary circumstances, they probably moved in far different spheres, but James had wondered who would be so polite in front of a bearded man with not a stitch on. Missionaries, apparently.

James rested the back of his hand against Sam's forehead. He was warm, but not sweating yet. "It's just plain James Trevenen," he said. "I resigned my commission after I dropped you off at Aldergate Street. And yes, you tumbled right on me." He chuckled at yesterday's memory. "Your companions are probably wondering who whisked you away, but pardon me if I doubted their ability to handle the crisis."

"Thank you." Sam closed his eyes again, as the sweats began. James swabbed him with the lavender-scented sponge. Sam gasped for water, but James knew better than to give him a drink from a glass. He had seen more than one fellow officer bleeding from the mouth when he clamped down on a glass during a malarial seizure. Instead, he dribbled water into Sam's mouth, using a clean cloth.

In a few minutes, Sam was quiet again. He opened his eyes. "Where is she?"

"Miss Alderson? She is resting. She was up with you all night."

Sam nodded, barely moving his head. "I never saw…" His eyelids drooped. "…a prettier…" His eyes closed again. "…female."

James gaped at him. *Miss Alderson?* he asked himself, wondering at the potency of Sam's delirium. Not even the world's most generous man could ever accuse Miss Alderson of being pretty.

But James could be somewhat generous, considering all that she was doing for him. "Yes, indeed, she's quite a sight," he said without perjuring himself.

Sam slept. James dreaded to think what would happen when Sam was feeling himself again. The missionary would wonder how on earth he had ever thought Miss Alderson a beauty. True, she did have a remarkable wit, as James had learned yesterday, but that wasn't anything Sam would have discovered yet.

"Amazing," he murmured, and dozed along with Sam.

He was there several hours, enough time for the downstairs maid to bring up a tray with porridge, eggs and bacon on it and toast with marmalade. He ate it all, then wondered guiltily if some of it had been intended for Sam. No matter; the man was sleeping.

He heard people moving about in the corridor. He wanted to find Sir Joseph—if the man was well enough for company—and assure him he had fulfilled the request to "do something about Loisa." However, he didn't leave the room. Some instinct told him that if he did, Miss Alderson, who needed her sleep, would wake in an instant.

Perhaps, Sir Joseph was particularly intuitive. A half hour later, when James had nodded off, Barmley wheeled the old gentleman into the room. James stood up.

Sir Joseph gave him a kind glance over the top of his spectacles, then directed his attention to the sleeping man. "So this is our missionary?" he asked, keeping his voice low. "Do sit down, James."

James didn't mean to stare, but the old baronet looked much more spry this morning.

"Yes, yes, I am doing better," Sir Joseph said, interpreting the look. "Gout is a curious thing, indeed. Some days I could almost—almost, mind you—leap about like a gazelle, and others, not."

James resisted the urge to smile at the image of the rotund Sir Joseph Banks leaping about in any fashion. "Today is more of a…a gazelle day?"

"Indeed. I directed Barmley here to let me have a look at this missionary you have foisted upon this household. I hardly call this a lasting solution, James. What happens to Loisa when he is better?"

"When he is lucid, I intend to entreat Sam to take his time getting better. Perhaps in two weeks I will have time to think of something else."

"I wouldn't doubt it. All right, Barmley, let us go downstairs for breakfast."

"Very well, sir." The footman wheeled him out of the room.

"Barmley," James said, getting out of the chair. The footman came back into the room. "Is that your nightshirt?"

"It is, Mr. Trevenen," Barmley replied. "Miss Alderson requested something that fit him better. Perhaps you know what force she can put behind a request."

"I can well imagine," James replied. "Thank you for what you have done."

"It's nothing, sir. Miss Alderson helped me, and we soon had him reclothed and comfortable."

James winced. "I'm not so certain she is accustomed to seeing a nude male form."

"So I told her," the footman replied, even as he blushed. "She wouldn't listen." He bowed to James and returned to the corridor where Sir Joseph waited.

I must be philosophical about this, James thought as he returned to the chair beside Sam's bed. Miss Alderson is old enough to have some knowledge of the world. He smiled. I hope Sam did not prove to be a disappointment.

After a glance at Sam, James relaxed again, going so far as to remove his shoes and prop his feet on the bed. He tried to stay awake, but he soon slept, too.

He woke as he did at night, half-conscious, but aware someone was in the room besides himself. It is Sam, he thought, even as the hairs on the back of his neck began to rise and prickle. It must be Sam. He heard a whimper, and knew he was making the sound.

The carpenter's mate was on the window ledge this time, one leg swinging to a rhythm only he could hear and the other leg held casually in his hand. He held it out to James, who leaped to his feet and backed up against the door.

"Leave me alone," James pleaded. "Can't you tell it is daytime?"

And then he was gone. James stared at the window. Nothing. It was partially open, and a slight breeze was ruffling the curtains. He slumped into the chair again, closed his eyes, then opened them. I may never sleep again, he told himself.

He looked at Sam, envying his even breathing and deep sleep. He could tell Sam. No, not Sam. He was ill and it would be cruel to burden a sick man with more trouble.

His butler in Cornwall knew some of the story. How could he help but know? Orm had suggested the food on the bureau at night and created some fiction that suited them both about sleeping close by in his dressing room, until the carpenter's mate had seemed to go away.

Orm had been reluctant to see James take the mail coach to London. The butler had known his employer was not ready for the world yet—not if he was seeing dead men on window ledges or telling extravagant lies. Beau Crusoe, indeed. What a sham that was.

He felt himself go hot with the shame of his actions. He had had no business ridding Lord Watchmere of his prized toucans, or even bullying Miss Alderson into watching Sam Higgins. And that nonsense about Sir Percival in the inn. Everything was getting so blown out of proportion, and he felt helpless before it all. He wished Orm were here. No, he needed more than sympathy from a butler. He needed someone would hold him and keep away the dreams.

James got to his feet, unable to sit still another minute. Only one thing would take away some of the terror, and Mrs. Park had it in her possession. If he could just get a look at the *Gloriosa Jubilate*, maybe hold the sketch in his hands, and remember how the little colony of crabs had kept him from madness. He stood a moment looking at Sam. "I'm sorry, old fellow," he whispered. "I hope you feel better soon."

He knocked softly on the next door. Miss Alderson was there in a moment, alert. "I cannot stay here, Miss Alderson," he told her, not caring how desperate he sounded. "I just can't. Please excuse me."

He walked away from her before she could say anything beyond "But, Mr. Trevenen," and hurried down the stairs. He hastened to the front door, which was open in the warmth of a surprisingly languid early October day. He ran then, wondering where Mrs. Park was, hoping to find her and the *Gloriosa*.

He could have cried with relief when he saw Noah coming across the meadow toward him, but his relief lasted only a moment, because the boy's mother was not with him. He had one irrational thought that she had thrown his *Gloriosa* into the fireplace. Calm down, you fool, he told himself. She would never do that. Calm down. You will only frighten Noah.

He forced himself to walk toward the little boy then. Noah

stopped and smiled at him, squinting into the morning sun behind James's back. "Mama told me I was to go to Spring Grove and be a messenger, in case Aunt Loisa wished to communicate with Alderson House."

"It's a big responsibility," James said, amazed how the sight of the child helped to calm him.

The look Noah gave him was dubious, at best. "I told her I didn't think Aunt Loisa would want to see me." He came closer to James. "What do you think? I mean to be brave, but sometimes it isn't easy."

James could have laughed out loud when Noah said that, except he knew his laughter would go on too long and he would frighten the boy. If anyone understood the difficulty of being brave, it was he, James Trevenen, lately of the Royal Navy, and former ruler of a South Seas island that was probably never going to let go of him.

He knelt by Noah. "You needn't worry about your Aunt Loisa. She's quite busy taking care of a friend of mine, and she will be glad to know you are a willing messenger. Things have changed, Noah. They do, sometimes."

"You're certain?"

"Actually, yes," James replied. "Is your mother at Alderson House?"

Noah shook his head, and James felt his heart stop for a moment, until the boy spoke. "She went to the exotic blooms house to see about the right colors for your crab picture. Her paints are there."

My crab picture. Good Lord, I could never be away from it as long as it would take her to paint it, he thought. *What was I thinking? Well, that is one wager she will not have to bother about. I'll take it off her hands right now.* He stood up.

"Very well. You'd…you'd better hurry along now, in case there is a message to deliver."

Noah stood by him another moment. "I will be ready when you and Mama come to get me for the drive in London."

"I had forgotten," James said.

Noah brightened. "Then it is a good thing I reminded you. I am looking forward to it most especially." He started off again, turning around once to wave, and then marched toward Spring Grove, a boy with responsibilities.

James watched him go. Now he would have to make that carriage ride to Rotten Row, because Noah would be disappointed if he were to cancel such a treat for a little boy who probably did not venture out much. I can leave tomorrow, he thought. If I sit up all night because I am afraid to close my eyes, it will do me no real harm. And then what? Perhaps it was time to return to sea.

James didn't run to the glass house, but he didn't waste a moment in getting there. He didn't wish to startle Susannah, so he knocked on the door, then entered. She looked up, curious, probably thinking he was one of the gardeners at first. He felt a little flattered when her eyes lit up as she smiled.

The easel back was facing him, so he could not see the *Gloriosa Jubilate*, but she had returned her gaze to the drawing and his heart slowed to a normal rhythm. She was saying something to him, but there was such a noise in his head that he could not hear her. All he wanted to do was look at the easel and reassure himself.

He came around behind her and sighed with relief. There it was, the little crab all glowing as he remembered it from his first glimpse in the tidal pool, when he had been so hungry he would have scooped it up and eaten it if the colors hadn't fascinated him.

She said nothing when he came forward and picked up the little drawing.

"You don't have to paint it," he said. "I'll just take it with me now."

"I lost the wager," she reminded him. "Besides, I have painted so many flowers that it would be nice to try something different."

"No. Leave it alone." He didn't mean to sound so sharp, but he could tell by the look in her eyes that he had disappointed her, maybe even startled her.

She could have protested, but she did not. Instead, she studied his face as though trying, in her polite way, to understand what he was doing and why. He knew that if he remained much longer in her orbit, she would figure out his terrible secret.

When she cleared her throat and looked him directly in the eye, he knew it was too late. He set the picture back in the easel and looked back at her, doing nothing now to avoid her gaze. She had found him out. He wanted to put his hands over his ears to stop what he knew was coming, but he thought he could at least be as brave as Noah. He waited.

"Dear sir, you're seeing things, aren't you?"

Chapter Fifteen

$\backsim\!\!\sim\!\!\sim$

Now, he was looking beyond her so intently that she turned around.

She saw nothing but two gardeners in the distance. She regarded him again, wishing with all her heart there were some way to erase that expression, a combination of fear and extreme weariness.

Did he see things? During their brief acquaintance, she had come to know Mr. Trevenen was many things—decisive, capable, deceitful, perhaps—but surely not mad. No, if he were insane, she would be afraid of him, and she was not. But then, how does someone recover from years of solitude after a shipwreck?

I have no reputation to speak of, she thought. It won't matter what I do. She put her hand upon his sleeve and pushed down.

He obliged her by kneeling. With a look of utter resignation, he closed his eyes and rested his head in her lap.

She rested her hand on his head. Painting had given her good fingers, so she massaged his head as though he was her son. He did have nice hair, thick and brown with hints of auburn in it.

After a moment of tension at her touch, he relaxed. Her heart went out to him, and she wondered when anyone had last touched Mr. Trevenen. Never mind. She would comfort him the only way she knew how.

His arms went around her, circling her hips and waist. Noah did the same thing, but this embrace was different. She slid forward on her chair, enough to accommodate his arm better behind her back without alarming him.

She closed her eyes against the pleasure of it all. I may be comforting you, Mr. Trevenen, but I am also finding this entirely too agreeable. She opened her eyes with a start. How long has it been since a man touched *me?*

She didn't want to even think about that question. She focused her attention on Mr. Trevenen and continued to caress him, noticing the freckles on his ears, wondering how anyone could survive such an ordeal as he had undergone. I wonder if I could, she thought. Thanks be to God I will never have to find out.

"I'm sorry."

That was all he said for another long time. She continued to smooth his hair.

"Could you do something for me?" he asked eventually.

"That would depend," Susannah replied, knowing she must keep her tone light. "You wouldn't want half my paltry kingdom, and Noah's not for sale."

His face was muffled in her skirt. "Call me James."

She laughed in spite of herself. "I've only known you a short time, sir. How dare I do that?"

"Just do it."

She decided it would not hurt to humor him. In a few weeks he would be back in Cornwall. "Very well. James."

He sat up and looked at her, his face more peaceful. His eyes were moist, and her hand went to her sleeve, where she had tucked a handkerchief. Without a word, she wiped his eyes as though he were no older than her son. "Better, James?" she asked.

He leaned his head against her leg this time, and she could tell from the tilt of it that he was staring at the crab on the drawing board. He seemed to relax further.

He looked at the *Gloriosa Jubilate.* "The *Gloriosa* is a variety of the common fiddler crab. Its scientific name is now *Uca Australuca clarisii.* Sir Joseph said in that letter he sent about the Copley medal that I could name it." He laughed self-consciously. "I named it Clarissa, after my mother."

"I wish she had known," Susannah said.

He couldn't help the long silence. "Perhaps I need to tell you about myself," he said finally.

"Perhaps you just need to talk, Mr. Trev—James."

He made himself comfortable on the floor in front of her, as though sitting there with crossed legs was the normal state of an Englishman. In his case, she supposed it was.

"I hardly know from which end to begin," he said. "I didn't learn of my mother's death until I returned to Cornwall. I suppose that is hardly surprising. I mean, I showed up at Admiralty House and no one was expecting me, naturally. I created no small stir."

She could well imagine. "They believed your story?"

"Of course," he said, surprised. "I had the ship's log, so there was no dispute. Besides, my name was still on the admiralty rolls. I told them what had happened to the *Orion,* the probable latitude and longitude of her sinking and resigned my commission."

"Goodness. You must have been a nine-day wonder in London," she murmured, her eyes on the sketch.

"I wasn't there long enough to be a wonder. I wanted to go home and see my mother and the estate."

She stopped sketching. "You have an estate? Somehow, I never..." She stopped, embarrassed.

"Never pictured me as a man with much in the way of worldly goods?" he teased. "Perhaps it's a good thing Sir Percival has come to my rescue with a tailor. It's a very nice estate, and my cousin managed it quite well while I was dead."

"Don't say that!" she exclaimed.

"I was dead, to them. When I went to visit my mother's grave—she is buried next to my father—I found she had put up a tombstone for me. 'Our dear son, lost at sea,' it read."

She gasped. "You...you pulled it up, of course."

"No, I did not," he replied, his voice serious.

She gave his shoulder a shake. "You must. You're not dead. Far from it."

He put up his hand to keep her own on his shoulder. "Mrs. P, do you ever feel as though part of you isn't there anymore?"

She nodded, her eyes filling with tears, and tightened her grip. "You are very much alive, James." Her thoughts returned to India and that time of cholera. She could hardly trust herself to speak. "No one has wound a sheet around you and taken you to the burning pile."

He looked at her then, his eyes alert. Before she could pull away, he moved his hand and kissed her own on his shoulder. "That's what happened? God, how terrible."

She cried because she couldn't help it. He handed back the handkerchief she had given him and she put it to her eyes, holding it there until she had control of herself. She was barely aware that he was holding on to her skirt.

"There was a bonfire in the courtyard," she told him. "I don't like this time of year at Kew Gardens. What leaves aren't used as mulch around the plants are burned in great heaps."

"Oh, God," he said, the weariness back in his eyes.

"It doesn't smell the same," she assured him, "but I hate to watch the columns of smoke rising. Then I remind myself that India was a long time ago, and I cannot change the past. You can't, either, James."

He released her skirt. From the faint blush on his cheeks, she knew he was embarrassed at his impulsive action. "I wrinkled your skirt."

"In the greater scheme of things, I don't think it matters too much." She touched his face briefly. "Aren't we a pair?"

"We are."

She could tell his mood had lifted, even as her own had. There is something to talking about one's troubles, she thought as she picked up the pencil again. And yet, he hadn't really mentioned his own troubles; she had been the one to speak of David's death. She was little the wiser about Mr. Trevenen's situation. She wanted to dismiss her concerns, but he was looking out the window, his lips tightening. He must be seeing something.

To distract him, she pointed toward the drawing. "The one pincer is so much longer. Are you sure…"

"Positive." He glanced at his own drawing again. "It's a fiddler crab, and I have named it." She could see pride in his eyes. "You see, this makes me more like Adam than Robinson Crusoe, eh?"

She picked up her tin of powdery colors. "Did you name anything else in Eden?"

His face grew serious. "It was never Eden."

"I suppose it was not," she murmured. She hesitated, then leaned closer, pointing to a dab of Prussian blue she had mixed in the little well in the tin box. "Is this close?"

He leaned closer until their heads almost touched. "A little more yellow. When they die, their colors dim almost at once." He pointed toward the crab's midsection. "And a hint of lavender."

"It must have been a little jewel," she said, after she dabbed the blue on the large pincer. "I suppose it will always be the *Gloriosa Jubilate* to you."

"Most certainly."

They were both quiet then. He made no mention of the sketch or himself. With sure strokes, she filled in the pincer. "Is it even close?" she asked finally.

"Close enough. Of course, the colors brighten considerably when the crabs mate."

She couldn't help teasing. "You watched them mate? My blushes, sir."

"I watched them do everything. I swear they even quarreled a time or two. I watched them live and I watched them die. They don't live long." He was silent.

She touched his head again, and her touch seemed to remind him of where he was. "You're not alone now, James," she whispered.

If she thought that would reassure him, she was wrong. He stood up in one smooth motion. "I'm not so sure I was alone then," he told her. He looked out the window. "I'm not alone now."

She felt the faintest chill run from the back of her neck down to the base of her spine, as though skeleton fingers patted each vertebra. She gave a little shudder, then hoped he would not notice.

He did. "I could not harm you," he told her. "I am more of a danger to myself."

"As far as I can see, you have done nothing but good," she

said. "You have exiled the toucans and convinced my sister to help you. What did you say to any of them?"

"Lies," he replied. "My downfall began at the inn, when I allowed Sir Percival to think I had actually saved his silly life. Nothing could have been further from the truth. Now he has embellished the truth and told someone else. My heroism is probably spreading all over London and growing heads like a Hydra. I lied to your sister when I told her that poor Sam lay at death's door. He'll recover in a few days, except that I intend to ask him to prevaricate, as well, and stay a little sicker so she will tend him. Lies, ma'am."

"But you would never lie to me," she said quickly.

"No, but can you ever be sure now?"

They ate luncheon on the lawn, sitting close to each other because he did not seem to want to move far from her side. After a wary look around, which only earned him a friendly wave from the gardeners, he relaxed. He seemed to prefer the outdoors; she wondered how he managed in the winter.

Susannah tried not to watch him eat, but she was curious. Luncheon was only cheese and meat between bread, with a few of her favorite chocolate biscuits thrown in, along with a handful of nuts and dried currants. Someone from the kitchen staff had also put in Noah's favorite boiled eggs.

She hoped she wasn't being obvious, but she was fascinated by the way he left no crumb unconsumed. Even as he talked to her, his eyes would stray to the food in the basket, as though he feared it would disappear. And before he had eaten the last of the sandwich, he had the nuts in front of him and then a handful of currants.

She leaned closer to him, and took his face in both her hands to capture his attention. "James, there is plenty of food on this island. There's so much we waste it. Don't worry."

To her chagrin, his eyes filled with tears. Oh, dear, she asked herself, What am I doing? She tried to remove her hands, but he covered hers with his. They sat that way for several moments, and then he took several deep breaths, letting each out audibly, until he was calm again. He released her.

"I'm sorry," he mumbled. "I didn't think London would be so hard." He stood up in that single, fluid motion she found so beguiling. "I'm going to go back to Cornwall."

She rose, too, but not as gracefully. "It's less than two weeks until you receive the Copley medal."

"They can keep the blamed thing."

She gave him another shake. "No. You earned it. Your treatise is brilliant. They should offer you membership in the Society." She took him by both shoulders. "I don't know what happened on that island, or even if that is where your troubles began. You have a remarkable way of sidestepping questions. But I do know this. You may have been a shipwrecked mariner when you started to study those little *Gloriosas*, but you became a scientist."

The easiest thing in the world happened then. She could only hope that not too many gardeners were watching. Mr. Trevenen walked right into her embrace. She wondered why she had held her arms open to him, but once he was in them, it didn't seem to matter.

He held her close, or maybe she held him close. She could feel the contours of his body, which made her blush, especially when she found herself moving as close as she could. Some part of her brain was clamoring for her to step back from an embrace that left no daylight between the participants, while another part just shrugged.

Mr. Trevenen was not a tall man. She knew if she pulled back, she could almost look directly into his eyes, a convenience she had not experienced with her late husband. She rested her cheek against his shoulder, enjoying the feeling of not having to strain on tiptoe.

In the few seconds before the embrace ended, she had an epiphany. Perhaps it would be best, she told herself, if in future I do not compare other men to my late husband. My memory is not so keen, and it would be unfair of me to inflate the matter.

As she pulled away, Mr. Trevenen watched her, intent and not embarrassed. Oh, dear, she thought. This is a man who studied invertebrates, and now he appears to be studying *me*. I need to turn this around quickly.

"I hope you feel better, Mr. Trevenen," she said, hating the way her words sounded so formal.

His face fell. "I thought I was James to you."

"Maybe it's not such a good idea, sir," she replied. She softened her words by touching his arm again. "I'm sorry. I said I would call you James, didn't I?"

He nodded.

"Then it will be James," she amended, and impulsively took his hand. Poor man, she thought. It has been so long since he must have felt the touch of a woman, to be so tight in that embrace! Are there no suitable ladies in Cornwall?

He stepped close again and grabbed her in a one-armed hug that caught her off guard and made her laugh. Without even thinking, she nudged his hip with hers, then pulled herself away. Less than two weeks now, she told herself.

Chapter Sixteen

James felt foolish for insisting they not leave his rendering of the *Gloriosa* in the exotic blooms house, but to his relief, Susannah made no objection. She tucked it in a pasteboard folder and carried it as they walked to Spring Grove.

Her serenity reminded him of the many calm days on his small island, when the air had almost hummed with peace. Fate had dealt her a terrible hand, but she seemed to manage it so gracefully. She must be poor, because she didn't seem to have much income beyond the shillings Sir Joseph gave her for the drawings. From the looks of things, the Alderson estate wasn't prospering. How could it, with a ninny at its head? She had a tarnished, if unearned, reputation. For now, at least, her sister was busy, but what would happen when Sam was well and Loisa returned to Alderson House? He felt shame that until this moment, he had been think-sing only about smoothing his own passage through the next two weeks. Susannah would have to endure beyond that. And yet, she seemed to bear it all with little complaint.

It occurred to him that nothing would be more pleasant than walking beside this lady for the rest of his life. He wanted to hold her hand as they walked along. Just go where she went, eat what she ate, sleep where she slept. All those years at sea, on his is-land prison, and then his discovery of science in a tidal pool were pale cousins to his feelings about this woman beside him. I will never want another, he told himself.

Something caught his eye then, and he looked toward the line of trees between the meadow and the Thames. And there you are, my life's true companion, he thought—a carpenter's mate. Tim Rowe hopped along at the edge of the trees.

He stopped and grasped Susannah's hand. "Do you see something by the trees?" he asked her.

She looked where he pointed, and shook her head. "No one is there."

You're going to win, aren't you, Tim? he thought miserably. No woman wants to share a bed with two men.

Noah was sitting on the front steps, brushing Neptune. "Oh, dear," Mrs. Park said under her breath. "Perhaps Loisa…"

"He looks happy enough," James whispered back.

Noah stood up. "Mama, I have been delivering messages up and down the stairs for Aunt Loisa!" he declared. "She says I am highly efficient!"

"That sounds like my sister." Susannah's laugh reminded James of the tensions she lived under. His heart lifted at her momentary relief from them.

"Did she send you downstairs for luncheon?" he asked. "Do you know how Mr. Higgins is feeling?"

"I just finished eating. Aunt Loisa said I could play outside."

"And Mr. Higgins?" Susannah asked. "Is he better?"

"He looks awfully pale, Mama, but Aunt Loisa keeps smiling at him anyway."

Susannah looked at James. "Could it be that we are all in your debt, Mr. Trevenen? And for considerably more than toucans?"

Unlikely in the extreme, he thought, as he bowed and declared, "Beau Crusoe at your service, Mrs. P."

James went upstairs and knocked on the door. Loisa opened it while his hand was still raised. He stepped back, hoping she wouldn't be angry at him for disturbing Sam, but she merely put her finger to her lips.

"Is he sleeping?"

She shook her head, but still whispered. "No, he is awake, and I think he is wondering how he got here." She pulled him into the room. "You speak to him for a moment, Mr. Trevenen. I have need of a break."

Her already florid face turned even redder; he knew what she meant. With a backward glance at her charge, Miss Alderson left the room.

James took her place in the chair pulled up to the bed. "Sam, you're faring well," he said.

The missionary turned his head this time. "I feel like my head is full of cotton wadding."

Good sign, James thought. You can joke. "Not yet," he teased in turn. While Sam lay there—clean, sweet-smelling and alert—James explained again how he came to be in a spare bedchamber at Spring Grove.

"Could you send a note to the Society?" he said when James finished.

"I can." James cleared his throat. "I'm also going to tell them you will be here for at least another two weeks."

Sam blinked in surprise. "Mr. Trevenen, I will be better in a day or two."

"Not this time," James contradicted. "You have to keep Miss Alderson occupied for the length of my stay in London. When I arrived here earlier this week, your host, Sir Joseph, asked me to find a way to keep Miss Alderson busy, and you dropped in my lap. I call that divine intervention."

"I don't," Sam replied, amused. "Still, I won't argue with you. She's a charming lady."

"Amazing," James murmured.

"Yes," Sam agreed. "It is hard to find pleasant people in London."

"That wasn't quite what I—" James stopped. No sense in muddying the waters. "You are fortunate to be in the care of such a lady. Will you help me out for two weeks?"

Sam nodded. "I can do that."

Miss Alderson returned to the room. Sam moaned a little. Miss Alderson hurried to Sam's side. "Poor man," she whispered.

"He's wondrously improved, but not out of danger yet," James warned, with a meaningful glance at Sam.

Sam obliged with another groan. James turned away, full to the brim with an urge to laugh. I daren't look at him, he thought. He focused his attention on Miss Alderson, whose eyes seemed to soften as she regarded her charge. And I'm sure I daren't look at her. Time to leave. He went to the door.

He managed a sigh of his own but knew better than to turn around. "It pains me to see him like this, Miss Alderson," he said. "I am forever in your debt."

There was a choking sound from the bed, so he fled the room, only to stand outside the door and spend a moment composing himself. I wonder the Lord doesn't strike me dead. Is there a bigger sinner in the universe than Beau Crusoe?

He came downstairs, still shaking his head at his own folly, to be met by Susannah and Lady Dorothea. "It's time you left for your ride in Hyde Park," said Lady Dorothea.

He took Susannah's arm gladly, tucking her close, but not so close that she would feel inclined to draw away. Noah made room for them in the vehicle. James knew he should probably sit on the facing seat, but he preferred to crowd close to Mrs. Park and watch her with her son. She had gathered Noah in close, her arm resting along the back of the cushion behind her boy.

Sir Percival Pettibone, resplendent in a shiny blue waistcoat with what appeared to be embroidered stars on it, was waiting for them. His mother was equally ornate in a deep purple spencer and matching turban. James thought briefly of toucans. When Lady Pettibone complained that sitting backward to the horses always made her queasy, James obligingly moved and let her sit beside Mrs. Park.

Sir Percival plumped himself down next to James, full of news. "Dear boy, it is all over town that you rescued a dying man from Hyde Park!"

"Nothing of the sort," he replied, striving for patience. "He is someone I knew, but anyone would have done what I did."

Sir Percival shook his head. "Not I, James, not I. Suppose he had wrinkled my neckcloth?"

He seemed to mean it, which startled James. "You mean, even if the poor man had fallen to the ground, you would not have lifted him into a sitting position, at least?"

Sir Percival shook his head. "I would have felt sorry for him, though."

"I suppose that is something," James said, hoping he did not sound quite as disgusted as he felt.

James found much to admire in Hyde Park. Through the trees, he could see the Serpentine, a handsome body of water. He listened idly to Sir Percival's chatter, interjecting a word where required. The baronet rambled on happily, until he seemed to notice his mother was not paying attention to his small orbit.

"Mother, what are you looking at?" he asked.

James swiveled around so he was looking up Rotten Row. "How odd. Someone is shouting up a tree," he reported to Sir Percival.

The noise grew louder. Noah stood up to watch. "It's a man with really blond hair," he reported to the others.

Sir Percival took instant interest. He even went so far as to swivel around himself. "'Pon my word, it is Bartley, Lord Batchley."

James laughed in spite of himself. "Who?"

"I don't laugh at your name," Sir Percival replied pointedly. He looked again, all interest now. "Usually he is the soul of propriety, is Batch." He spoke to the coachman. "Do hurry this conveyance along."

By the time they arrived at the scene, several carriages were parked near the tree. Sir Percival spotted an acquaintance. "I say, Rupert," he called to a man on horseback, "What is this all about?"

Rupert pointed with his whip. "Batch has lost Vixen up a tree."

Sir Percival gasped. "Good God!"

James watched the shouting man. Grossly fat, he stood up in his barouche and waved his cane, shouting, "Have no fear, my pet, Papa will come for you!"

I am in Bedlam, James thought. "Is it a cat?" he asked Sir Percival.

The fop nodded, concern in his eyes. "A black one. Batch usually keeps it on a gold chain."

He means it, James thought in disbelief. "Uh, cats usually come down trees they go up."

Sir Percival peered at him again. "You cannot be so coldhearted."

"Yes, I can," James replied.

He looked back at the man in the carriage, who chose that moment to sink down into the cushions. He's going to have a fit of apoplexy, he told himself. Someone should untie that ridiculously high neckcloth and lower those shirt points. He turned to Susannah. "Mrs. P, we must act."

"I couldn't agree more," she said.

He opened the door. "Certainly, my dear." He stepped down and held out his hand for her. "Coming, too, Noah?"

James took both Parks by the hand and hurried them along. No one else seemed to be doing anything to help…who was it? Benchley, Lord Batchley? Bartley, Lord Bumley? He smiled. Romley, Lord Bromley.

He was pleased how efficiently Susannah took charge. She knelt on the seat beside the man, who was sobbing into his handkerchief now.

"I'm going to remove your neckcloth," Susannah said firmly.

Lord Batchley shrieked. "It took my man an hour to tie that this morning!"

"He can do it again for you tomorrow. Be strong for Vixen," she wheedled.

That was the magic phrase. The old lord let himself go limp.

"I could have told him to save his breath when Mama is determined," Noah whispered to James.

"There now, this will just take a moment." Mrs. Park undid the elaborate neckcloth and then the shirt button underneath. In another moment, Lord Batchley was breathing more regularly.

"My dear, what can we do?" Lord Batchley asked.

Mrs. Park looked at James.

"Cats do come down by themselves," he said, but his argument sounded weak.

"I warned you how she was," Noah said.

The crowd was getting larger, and no one seemed inclined to act. What a slow group, he thought, even as he pulled off his boots. "I climb better barefoot," he said in answer to Mrs. Park's questioning look. "For that matter, I climb better naked, but I don't think London is ready for that."

She blushed but couldn't help herself and laughed. She leaned toward the fat man, who still seemed to be summoning his resources, wherever they were. "Lord Batchley, do you have any advice for Mr. Trevenen? He's going to rescue Vixen."

"Be gentle with him, dear boy! He's confused and frightened."

James unbuttoned his coat. "Does he bite?"

"Only when he's confused and frightened. You should be fine."

James started for the tree, the crowd parting to let him pass. He winced to hear someone whisper "Beau Crusoe" to another standing near by. He grabbed the lowest branch and swung himself up. He pulled himself from branch to branch, until he looked up to see a cat hissing at him.

Good Lord, it must be a sheep, he thought, unaware that cats grew so large. "Here, kittie, kittie, you behemoth," he whispered.

Raising its tail to exhibit its overgrown parts, the cat made its ponderous way farther out on the limb. James slid away until he was leaning against the tree trunk. He removed his coat, spread it open and draped it over the branch just above him.

He made himself comfortable, ignoring the cat. The tree had been warming all day in the sun and felt good against his back. He could see the Serpentine through the leaves. When he started to close his eyes, the branch moved. For one frightening moment, he thought it might be the phantom sailor again, but it was only Vixen, coming toward him.

He knew better than to move. "It can't be too pleasant to be dragged on a golden chain by a fat man," he said, keeping his voice conversational.

Vixen eyed him. James folded his arms across his chest. Then

Vixen was right there, sniffing him. Slowly, James uncrossed his arms and reached for his coat, slipping it quietly off the branch above. Slowly he raised his other arm and, just as slowly, brought the coat down until it rested just above the cat.

Quickly, he dropped the coat around the animal, encircling its neck, but leaving its face free. With a screech, the cat kicked back with its hind legs and nearly toppled them both from the tree. James tightened his legs around the branch and managed to wrap the bundle of ferocity in his coat. Vixen continued to screech, and was answered by sympathetic wails from Brimley, Lord Trimley far below.

I need one more hand, James thought. He leaned over slightly, keeping Vixen's face well away from his arms. "Noah," he called. "Get Lord Broomley's neckcloth and climb up here."

The wails grew louder from below, then all was silent. James smiled. Perhaps Susannah was sitting on the old beauty's windpipe. "Poor kittie, kittie," he crooned, remarkably unsympathetic.

Noah came quickly, the neckcloth around his shoulders. Soon he was on the branch below.

"Excellent, Noah," James declared. "Come here and untie my own neckcloth. I mean to secure it around this beast."

Noah did as he said. He untied James's neckcloth, all the while keeping a close eye on the cat. "I wasn't really planning on an adventure today, Mr. Trevenen," he said.

That is true of everything that has happened to me so far in London, James thought. "Neither was I, Noah," he said. "Sometimes fate decrees otherwise."

When the boy was done, James extended his arms out as far as possible while maintaining his grip on the cat struggling in the coat. "Now, slide yourself down until you're sitting directly in front of me. I want you to start winding my neckcloth where my hands are."

Noah did as he was directed, dropping neatly in front of James. "Like this?"

"Ideal. Cross it under this gut bucket. Excellent. I think I can manage now."

In a few minutes, the cat was tightly trussed into the coat and bound with the neckcloth, its head still exposed.

"Now what?" Noah asked. "He's noisy, isn't he? He doesn't appreciate what we are doing for him."

"Vixen will hate us to the grave and beyond," James said.

"Seems a pity, especially since we are so nice."

Noah held out the old lord's neckcloth to him, so he secured the end to the super-animated bundle and looked down. "Mrs. Park?"

"Yes, Mr. Trevenen?"

"We're belaying an unhappy animal to the ground. Grab Vixen, but be careful."

James sent Vixen on his screeching, frothing way, playing out the neckcloth slowly. He released his hold when he felt a tug on the other end. "That's it, lad. Now it's Lord Brumley's problem."

Noah peered down. "He has your coat."

"He can keep it. I think Vixen committed an indiscretion while he was wearing it."

Noah laughed. "I like it up here," Noah said.

"So do I, but your mother might worry if we stay too long."

"True," Noah said. He looked down. "The carriages are still there. Why don't they leave?" He thought a moment. "Are they waiting for us?"

"I fear so."

"It was just a cat," Noah said. "Do they think we are heroes?"

"Precisely," James replied. "Noah, when we climb out of this tree, we will be famous throughout London."

"*Really?*"

James nodded. "You first." He interpreted Noah's look. "Nothing to it. Just go down the way you came up. Besides, we have no more neckcloths. I cannot lower you."

Noah laughed and climbed down. In a moment, James heard loud applause. My turn, he thought, wishing himself far away from rumors. By tomorrow, I will have rescued two cats, a dog and probably Croomley, Lord Toomley himself.

He arrived on the ground to thunderous applause. He turned around, embarrassed, to face the throng and found himself standing directly in front of Lady Audley, the last person he wanted to see in London.

He stared at her. "What a hero you are, James," she said. He could not read her expression, but then, he could barely bring himself to look at her.

To his horror, she raised his hand high. "Ladies and gentlemen, Beau Crusoe!"

Chapter Seventeen

Watching Lady Audley, Susannah decided London had changed considerably since she was last out in society. Of course, it was possible Lady Audley knew James, but from where, she could not imagine. It was unlikely Lady Audley traveled the shipping lanes.

That she knew him was obvious, especially since the woman was standing so close. For his part, Mr. Trevenen gaped at her with a stricken expression, as though an orangutan had suddenly dropped in front of him, scratching at its armpits.

Susannah did her best not to smile at her mental image. To be fair, she could hardly call Lady Audley an ape, but there was something about her that invited the comparison. She sniffed the air. And such strong perfume, too.

Suzannah had met Lady Audley years ago at a garden party; she doubted the woman remembered. It had been one of Susannah's earliest ventures into society with her mother. She might have been ten years of age then, big-eyed with the wonder of attending a gathering on someone's terrace, and warned to be on her best behavior.

And there Lady Audley was now, standing so close to James. It was then that Susannah knew without doubt Lady Audley must indeed have crossed a shipping lane. No one told her; no one had to. Shame was spreading slowly across James's face, and something close to triumph across Lady Audley's. Susannah knew she could be wrong. Her brief marriage had not made her wise in the ways of the world. Still, people with nothing to hide didn't look as guilty as James did, standing there barefoot in Hyde Park.

Susannah turned to Lord Batchley, who had resumed regular breathing. "Lord Batchley, do excuse me. I am sure you wish to return home with Vixen."

"I do, Mrs. Park," he said. He put a pudgy hand to his bare neck. "You must think me a total fright and devoid of all social graces."

"Quite the contrary," she replied. "I think you've held up remarkably well." One could surely be excused a lie of that nature, she told herself. She had seldom seen a more ridiculous figure than Lord Batchley, wig askew, face red.

She left the carriage and waited for him to depart, but Lord Batchley held up his hand to hold his coachman. He leaned out of the barouche. "Who *is* Beau Crusoe?"

"He is James Trevenen, here to receive the Copley medal from the Royal Society," she said.

"Amazing!" Lord Batchley declared. "A bruising athlete and a brilliant man, as well! He's nearly an Adonis, too." He gazed beyond her. "I say, Mr. Trevenen, do come here."

Mr. Trevenen did as he was bid, moving as though he wished to outdistance Lady Audley. "My lord?" he said.

Lord Batchley grasped Mr. Trevenen's hand. "Dear boy, I am in your debt. How can I ever thank you?"

"Thanks are unnecessary, my lord," Mr. Trevenen said, after a deep breath. "Anyone would have done what I did."

"Unlikely," Lord Batchley said. He glanced around him. "I know these people better than you." He looked at Susannah. "Mr. Trevenen, do bring the charming Mrs. Park around to my house tomorrow for dinner."

She thought James would refuse, but then wariness left his face. He bowed, and she marveled again at how graceful he was, even in his dishevelment.

"With pleasure, sir. Mrs. Park ought to grace many an evening's event during this coming season, don't you think?"

And there it was. James was determined to carry out the final promise her godfather had extracted from him: if not to marry her himself, then to make sure she was seen in polite circles again. Susannah didn't know whether to be exasperated or touched by his intentions.

"Lord Batchley, kindly extend that invitation to me and Lord Audley, as well?" Lady Audley asked, moving into their conversation. She touched James again. "We have an acquaintance to renew."

That is forward, Susannah thought, as Lady Audley came up to stand beside James. To Susannah's gratification, he stepped away.

"Of course you and Lord Audley may come tomorrow," Lord Batchley said, after a slight hesitation. "I know how Lord Audley likes my dinner table."

"We all do, my lord," Lady Audley said. She turned an indulgent smile on Susannah. "Who can resist rich food?" she cooed. "Obviously, you enjoy eating. Mrs. Park, is it?"

Susannah felt her face go red. She glanced at James. Even Lord Batchley seemed puzzled by such a rude statement. The silence seemed to settle in, even though it couldn't have lasted more than a second or two before James spoke.

"Lady Audley, may I present Mrs. Park to you?" he said. "I don't believe you have met."

It was Lady Audley's turn to blush this time, but it was only a thin streak of color across her cheek, leading Susannah to the belief that the woman was beyond blushing. Well done, James, she thought, as she curtsied. How kind of you to point out the indiscretion of a comment before an introduction.

"Lady Audley, we have had the pleasure before. It was some years ago at a garden party. I was ten, and I believe you were newly engaged to Lord Audley. Can it have been fifteen years?"

Susannah said it as sweetly as she could. The color deepened across Lady Audley's cheeks, as though Susannah had said, "Let me see, that would make you thirty-five, if you are a day."

Lady Audley took several deep breaths, which left Susannah with the uneasy feeling that few people came away unscathed from a verbal battle with her.

"I don't remember you at all, Mrs. Park."

"I would be surprised if you did remember me, Lady Audley," she replied with a smile. "I had freckles and sharp elbows. What is more awkward than youth?"

She could tell her reply wasn't what Lady Audley wanted. Susannah held out her hand to Noah. "Come, my dear, let us return to Sir Percival's barouche. Do excuse us."

Susannah had no difficulty leaving James standing there. He was old enough to extricate himself from Lady Audley, if he chose. Where could he possibly have met such a woman? Susannah asked herself as she and Noah seated themselves in the barouche again with Sir Percival and Lady Pettibone.

"I say, Mrs. Park," she exclaimed. "Does Beau Crusoe always attract such large crowds wherever he goes?"

"I don't think he means to," she replied. "He is a man of quick reflexes. If no one else will act, then he feels duty bound."

She didn't want to watch James, but she couldn't help herself. He began to back slowly away from Lady Audley, as though she were a vicious beast. In a moment he was in the barouche, sitting down with a sigh.

Sir Percival put his quizzing glass to his eye. "Mr. Trevenen, you are practically naked!" he declared.

"No, I am not," James contradicted, his voice firm. "I will pull on my boots again, and we will kindly overlook my loss of coat and neckcloth. It's not a catastrophe."

Sir Percival shook his head sadly. "It was supposed to be a simple ride in Hyde Park, to see and be seen."

"I know," James said. "Please don't feel obligated to bring me to London's notice. I wouldn't for the world discomfort you, Sir Percival."

Sir Percival removed the quizzing glass from his eye. "Dear, dear, boy, how could I ever be discomforted by the man who saved me from death?"

To his credit, James tried again. "Sir Percival, I don't wish to cause you embarrassment."

"You're no trouble, Beau."

"I wish you would not call me that!"

Sir Percival only smiled. Poor James, Susannah thought. She put her arm around her son. "Noah, you were particularly handy at helping Mr. Trevenen."

"I was a little frightened," he confessed, leaning against her. "The tree was taller than any I have climbed."

"I never would have known you were afraid," she said.

"Mr. Trevenen wasn't," Noah said. He rose up a little to whisper in her ear. "How is it he always seems to know what to do?"

"Brutal necessity, I think," she whispered back. Brutal necessity can make heroes of us all, she thought, remembering that long week in Bombay after David died, and she had nursed the others without ceasing. She composed her heart and mind. "Maybe it's this way, son—when we have no choice, we may as well be brave."

Not even Sir Percival had much inclination for conversation, although he did bid them *au revoir* with a promise to visit soon, which made James sigh.

As the coachman shut the door, James moved over to sit next to her again. "I'm sorry that happened," he told her.

"If you must rescue cats, then you must, Mr. Trevenen."

"I'm not James now?" he asked. He glanced at Noah. "I meant Lady Audley."

It was on the tip of her tongue to ask him how he had ever met such a piece of work, but she resisted. She knew that no matter what he chose to tell her, it would either be not to her liking, or not the truth. She suddenly wished James had never been so brilliant and won a prize that brought him to London.

But that wasn't true. The toucans were gone and her prickly sister seemed different. Susannah mulled over the matter in silence, happy that James seemed not to wish to converse, either. But she really ought to reply to his last comment, to set him at ease about Lady Audley, whatever his association was with her.

The trouble was, she could think of nothing to say. How could she reassure him about something she didn't understand?

It was all just too much. I have enough to worry about, she thought; James, you are on your own. She let out a small sigh and leaned back against the cushions. She felt his arm against the back of her neck. Mama would be horrified, she told herself. How good that she isn't here.

The tension seemed to go out of James, even as it grew in her. In another moment, he was resting his hand on her shoulder and ever so gently tugging her closer to him. She had been prepared to shift forward if he tried that, but she didn't. Instead, she let him edge her toward him.

She thought he might kiss her, but he did not. He did put his lips close to her ear and say, "I still wish you would at least call me James."

"I forgot," she apologized, trying to imagine how she would feel if, for the past twenty years, no one had ever said her name much. "James," she said finally.

At ease, he leaned his head back and closed his eyes, as though she had given him permission to relax. Or as though he suddenly felt safe. What an odd thought. She turned her head to look at him, surprised to see that he was sound asleep, his hand drooping off her shoulder, his face slack.

Since he was asleep, Susannah allowed herself to move closer, appreciating his warmth in the first chill of a long-delayed fall. Time is passing, she thought. I sketch, paint, earn my shillings and raise my son. I wonder: is there anything else?

As dusk came, Mr. Trevenen—no, James—seemed to draw her closer, until she was nestled right into his shoulder.

She didn't mean for her thoughts to wander, but she couldn't help herself. Almost seven years had passed since her husband had last made love to her. She looked down at James's lap, embarrassing herself as she regarded him. His coat was gone and he hadn't rebuttoned his waistcoat.

It was easy to imagine him naked on his island. I should think a man without clothes would be vulnerable to entanglement in shrubbery, she thought, and nearly laughed out loud at her mental image. Her eyes strayed below his lap and she was unable to prevent herself from comparing him to the late David Park. Mr. Trevenen—best not to think of him as James at moments like this—seemed to come out slightly better, but it had been almost seven years and her memory might be faulty.

This will never do, she told herself, and gently worked her way out of his slack embrace until she was resting against the side of the barouche. She began to breathe a little faster and arched her back slightly. The motion made her breasts feel heavier, as though every part of her wanted to open wide.

I cannot do this, she thought in sudden panic as a liquid feeling spread throughout her lower body. She closed her eyes against her desire, wanting to assuage it. She knew there were things she could do in the solitude of her own bed to relieve the ache, but she knew they were not enough, not now.

She willed herself to think of something besides the man sleeping so peacefully next to her. She tried to distract herself by thinking how poor she was, how improvident her father, how totty-headed her mother, but she came back to James again, marveling that he had convinced her sister to nurse a stranger. How had he done so? She had asked herself that question before; she had no answer.

They arrived at Spring Grove. If she had imagined Loisa would be pining to return to Alderson House after twenty-four hours of constant attendance on an ailing man, Susannah had been wrong. While James and Noah retrieved his precious *Gloriosa* from the sitting room, Susannah went upstairs and knocked on Mr. Higgins's door.

"Come in," Loisa whispered. "He is only just now sleeping again."

Loisa took her hand and pulled her into the room but did not release her, which caused tears of relief to crowd the corners of Susannah's eyes. Her squeeze of her sister's hand brought a similar response.

"How is he?" she asked.

Loisa returned to her seat beside the bed. "He continues to alternate between freezing and sweating, but I think he is better. He is able to talk, at least."

Susannah perched herself on her sister's chair. "And what does he say?" she teased. "Ja…Mr. Trevenen…indicated to me that he was delirious."

Loisa smiled but did not take her eyes from the sleeping man. "He asked me at least five times who I was, but I think we have straightened out the introductions."

She would have said more, but James was in the room now. He sat down on the bed and leaned over Mr. Higgins. Susannah glanced at her sister, who was frowning. You always were possessive, Susannah thought, amused.

"Would you prefer I remained here tonight?" James asked her sister.

"No," came her quick reply. "Sir, you specifically asked me to tend to him."

"I did," James said.

"Then here I shall remain until he is better. Good night, sir. My sister is drooping. I suggest you get her home."

Loisa followed her and James into the corridor. "Mr. Trevenen, we had a visit this afternoon from the missionaries."

James raised his eyebrows. "Do tell. I'm surprised they did not bring along a Bow Street runner to snatch back the man I kidnapped."

"You have an inflated notion of what he is worth to them, sir," Loisa replied.

Her voice shook a little, which startled Susannah. Interested, she watched Loisa's face, unable to dismiss the sudden passion in her voice. Dear me, she thought, I wonder if Loie stood in the doorway and threatened them with a fireplace tool. "They did not want him back?" she asked.

Loisa shook her head. "I hardly know what to think. They sat at his bedside—he was unconscious—and commiserated with each other about what a millstone he is." She seemed close to tears. "There he lay, insensible, and all they could do was harp on his ill-timed relapses." Her face reddened. "I had Barmley eject them both."

"You did what?" James said, startled.

She gave him a long stare. "You heard me, sir. Perhaps I was taking a page from Beau Crusoe's book. I felt obligated to think quickly."

Susannah felt her heart go out to her sister. She put an arm around her, half-expecting her to draw away, but she did not, so she encircled her with both arms. "Good for you, Loie," she whispered.

"You would have done the same thing, Suze."

"I doubt it. I'm not as good as you are at standing up to people," Susannah said. She glanced at James. "That's probably one pagoda I will never climb."

James smiled. "You'll never know until it happens."

He bowed to Loisa. "My congratulations, Miss Alderson. I am certain Sir Joseph will not object to Sam's continued presence here, even if it stretches out a little longer than any of us anticipated."

Loisa gave Susannah another hug and went to the door. "I am counting on you to think of something, Mr. Trevenen, or Beau Crusoe—whichever of you takes an interest in these matters. Good night." She went into the room and closed the door.

James just looked at Susannah. "I feel like the poor man in Indian mythology who grabs hold of a tiger's tail. I don't dare let go."

She tucked her arm through his, and he smiled. "Well, then, James, you had better think of something. Let us take Noah home."

It sounded so intimate, said like that. "You know, back to Alderson House," she corrected.

"It *is* your home, Susannah," he reminded her, not even bothering with the pretence of calling her Mrs. P.

"On sufferance," she replied impulsively.

He shrugged. "Better than no home," he murmured, leaving her to wonder just how lonely life was in Cornwall.

James's new clothes were waiting for him at Alderson House.

"I wouldn't have thought Redfern could work so fast," he said. "Maybe that's what happens when you pay a tailor first." He opened one box, moved aside the tissue paper and pulled out three shirts.

There was a note pinned to the top shirt. James opened it. "Listen to this," he said. "'There is enough here for you to cut a real dash, Mr. Crusoe, although nothing sufficiently apropos for rescuing cats from trees.'"

He groaned. "How fast does news travel in London?"

She looked over his arm at the note. "Oh, I like this: 'There are those of us who wish you had left Vixen up the tree.'"

"You are not supposed to find this so amusing," he warned her with a grin.

"How can I help myself? An ordinary man comes to London to accept an award and finds himself in great demand to rescue a large portion of the population from some crisis or other." She looked him in the eye. "Although you are far from ordinary."

He seemed to be waiting for her to say something else. "Take them upstairs and try them on," she told him. "I will get Noah to bed and then offer you my opinion."

She glanced into the box. "I can see there are no pink waistcoats, so I can almost guarantee you a favorable review."

After a quick meal, Noah offered no protest when she suggested bedtime. He was asleep before she had time to read to him. She returned to her own room and waited for James to knock.

When he did, she opened her door. He stood in the corridor in new leathers, a shirt with the tails out and a waistcoat on. It was dark green and didn't quite button across his stomach. "Would you please retie it in back?" he asked, turning around.

She untied the three bows and told him to button it. He did, and she retied the bows. He turned around. "What do you think?"

She walked around him. "Very smart, sir. I do think the effect will be more successful when you tuck in your shirttails, however and perhaps add a neckcloth, shoes, too. Oh, yes, I recommend shoes."

He unbuttoned his waistcoat again in a casual, one-handed way that looked suddenly so attractive. He had such fine hands. Everything about him seemed capable. She wished he would not smile at her in that pleasant, slow way of his. She wished he would go back to his room, but he seemed in no hurry. She reminded herself that anyone who had lived so long alone would avoid solitude whenever he could. Curtsying to him to indicate that the evening was over seemed far too formal, especially since he stood there in his bare feet. Better just say good-night and shoo him out.

"Good night, sir," she told him. She hadn't meant to sound frosty, and hoped she hadn't, but there was no overlooking the disappointment in his eyes.

He nodded to her. "I promise to wear shoes," he said, then frowned. "Do you think Lord Batchley really means to invite us to his house?"

"We'll see what the morning's post brings," she said.

He lingered in the doorway of her room, then turned away. She didn't want to be rude and close the door immediately, so she watched him cross the corridor. Her heart went out to him then, as he stood facing the door, as though he dreaded to go inside.

As she stood watching, he turned and blew her a kiss. You're a rascal, she thought.

"Good night, dear Mrs. P."

For a moment, he did not feel the tightness in his chest that usually indicated the start of the dream. He had been dreaming of Susannah. The sudden shift to the longboat was so marked it caught him unaware.

The dream began with heat, the copper of a blazing sun boring through his skin and into his vertebrae. The day was no different from any of the other twenty that had passed before. He had kept records meticulously at first, but he wasn't completely sure if he had made his usual *X* that morning. He was too tired now to wonder, or even care, why the others in the boat hadn't trampled over him

to drink that little bit of ink. Since they were able-bodied seamen—
excepting Tim Rowe, the carpenter's mate—and probably illiter-
ate, maybe they hadn't thought of the ink, the only liquid in the boat.

James had thought about drinking it himself, but his sense of
duty had bound him to keep the record, even if not another living
soul ever saw it again. When they were all finally dead, the boat
would eventually capsize.

His pistol lay heavy across his lap. He doubted he had the
energy to raise it and fire when Rowe finally came for him.

Rowe had stashed one body in his kingdom at the other end
of the longboat. He had cracked the bones for the life-giving mar-
row, but even Rowe was tiring. James had not heard him cracking
any bones lately. James was too tired to open his eyes, placing
all reliance on the oars he had crossed at his end of the boat—
his only sentinels—should Rowe seek fresher meat.

They had pulled away from the fast-sinking *Orion* in the only
boat launched before water swallowed the frigate. Over his pro-
tests, the captain had pushed him into the boat and thrown in the
tar-coated packet containing the ship's log. "Look smart, lad,"
was the last thing his skipper said.

He had done that, rowing away to avoid the vortex, then gathering what men he could find; there were but four. He was the
only officer, a longboat his first independent command.

No one said it, but they knew death bobbed with them. James
assigned them what paltry tasks he could think of to keep them
occupied, after first assessing what everyone possessed that could
remotely be called food: a few pieces of hardtack, some wax from
the carpenter's mate, a lump of smelly cheese. It was gone by
the end of the week. They sat motionless in the boat to conserve
energy, baking and waiting to die.

After one week with no food, and no rain beyond a ten-minute
squall, one foretopman went mad. John Weston sat up, his eyes
fixed on something only he could see. He tugged on James's salt-
crusted shirt.

"God be praised, it's Portsmouth harbor," he said in sincere
earnest.

Before James could stop him, the man slipped over the side and started swimming. They shouted to him, but it was no use.

A week later, when Billy Bright, the foretopman, began to hallucinate, and wouldn't even try to drink his own urine anymore, the four of them held a civilized discussion. The foretopman had no objection to being eaten. "Just wait till I'm gone, lieutenant, that's all I ask," he said.

It seemed fair; they waited. One morning, Billy lay there with his eyes wide and staring.

James should have never encouraged Tim Rowe, the carpenter's mate, to carve him up. If he hadn't been so weary with pain and hunger, he would have done it himself. As he watched the man at his work, it occurred to James that Rowe was having too much fun.

James ate his share of the foretopman, Bright, retching after every bite. James and Walter Shepherd both vowed not to eat any more, but Rowe could not be restrained. Over the next few days, they watched in stupefaction as the carpenter's mate consumed the foretopman down to his toenails. James tried to throw the disgusting carcass overboard, but Rowe only snarled at him like a feral dog and hugged the grisly remains.

James tried to stay awake, alternating with Shepherd, but one night they both slept. In the morning, James woke to find the other man dragged to Rowe's end, a knife sunk deep in his chest and the carpenter's mate gnawing on his arm.

Then Rowe did what he always did in every dream: He worked the leg loose from its sorely tried mooring and held it out to James.

James sat up in bed and cried out to see the carpenter's mate in the chair. "I told you food wouldn't keep me away, lieutenant. I told you," Rowe declared in a singsong voice that sounded as though he was underwater. There was that arm again. Would he never consume it?

"Stay away from me," James ordered, raising his voice above the waves slapping against the longboat. "I'll shoot you like the dog you are."

The specter only shook his head and held out the arm bone again, then started to rise.

James screamed.

Chapter Eighteen

Susannah sat up in bed. Noah was a sound sleeper, but every now and then he woke up. She listened intently to a low voice, and felt the hairs rise on her arms. This wasn't Noah.

Uncertain, she got up and opened the connecting door. Her son slept, one leg out of the coverlet. She covered him and stood there, listening.

The voice was louder. It had to be Mr. Trevenen, but whom was he talking to? She closed Noah's door and found her robe, wondering whether she should cross the corridor. She opened her door. Loisa would ordinarily have been in the room next to Mr. Trevenen's, but she was at Spring Grove. Their parents' chambers were at the end of the corridor and Mama had gone to bed earlier with a headache and a tray of potions.

Susannah stood there, barefoot in the dark. The talking stopped finally. She turned to go back to bed, but then she heard Mr. Trevenen crying. He was saying something, too, words she could not quite identify.

Then she understood and darted across the corridor to his room. He was calling for help. She didn't bother to knock, just squared her shoulders and entered.

She stood in the doorway a moment, letting her eyes adjust to the gloom. He hadn't closed the draperies. She had observed that he didn't seem to enjoy confinement.

She couldn't see him, though, and felt that same ripple of hairs along her arms. "Mr. Trevenen?" she whispered. "James? Where are you? You're starting to frighten me."

Silence. "Mr. Trevenen?" she repeated, aware that her voice was quavering now. "Please don't do this."

And then she saw him, curled up on the floor next to the open window. My God, she thought. What is going through his head? Is he mad?

She started to back out of the room, not sure what to do, when he spoke. "Don't leave me, Suzie."

No one called her Suzie. He said it again, no louder than before. Drawn by sympathy, she came into the room. Maybe if she lit a candle and sat down in the chair, he would come to himself again. It must be a bad dream, she thought, one on an unimaginable scale.

She hurried to his bedside table, and struck a lucifer. "There, now," she said. "You were having a dream. I'm going to sit here and—"

As she walked toward the chair, Mr. Trevenen stood up, leaped across the bed and grabbed her around the waist, bearing her back with him to the mattress, where he pushed her down and threw himself on top of her. She tried to object, but he put his hand over her mouth. His lips were close to her ear. "I don't want him to know you're here. He'll have to get to me first before he gets to you. I swear it."

Terrified, she lay in his odd embrace. He was a heavy weight, but as he lay half on, half off her, between her and the chair, she realized he was protecting her. Whatever terrified him held no candle to his desire to keep her safe.

She willed herself to go limp. If she didn't struggle, he might loosen his grip on her. In another moment, he took his hand away.

But how to reason with this man? She said softly, "If you'll let me up, I can show you we are the only people in this room."

He tightened his grip, and she mentally kicked herself.

"You don't know him the way I do, Suzie." He held her tight against him, his hand flat against her stomach. His heart hammered against her back.

She tried another tack. "James, let me help you."

He was silent; she thought he might be considering the matter. She tested the waters again. "I can take care of whatever is in this room. Release me and see if I don't."

"You don't know him," he said again, uncertain now.

"No, I don't," she said simply, "but I know you. You're heavy and I'm having trouble breathing."

"I'm sorry." He moved until he was resting next to her. He wouldn't let go of her, though, so she turned around in his arms until she was facing him.

Her eyes were accustomed to the gloom now and she could see his face. To her surprise, his eyes were closed. What kind of curious state was this, she asked herself. He seemed to be returning to sleep, or at least a level of sleep that took away fear. Hesitantly, she touched his face.

He started, then relaxed again. You're not mad, she thought, as she ran her fingers across his cheek and his nose and down the other side. She repeated the motion over and over until he yawned, released her and rolled over.

She waited another moment until his breathing was regular, then got up. She shut the window and pulled the draperies across the glass so the sun would not wake him in a few hours. She stood by the window, not wanting to look at the chair that seemed to frighten him. You goose, she scolded herself. There are no such things as ghosts.

She approached his bed, not sure she should leave him alone. He seemed to be sleeping peacefully. She kissed his cheek. "Good night, James," she whispered. "Sleep well."

She went to the door and opened it.

"Suzie."

Her hand froze on the knob. She turned around slowly, her heart in her mouth, and looked back. He was asleep.

Morning came with a jolt, when she woke up to find Noah standing beside her bed. She gasped.

"Mama! It is only I!"

Thank God for that, she thought. She pulled back the covers and he climbed in with her.

"Mama, have you seen a ghost?"

"Heavens, no," she said, but what he said struck her. Last night she had thought James was looking at a ghost. But whose? He said he had been alone on the island.

Noah burrowed close, and she was grateful for his warmth, even though it did nothing to temper the sudden chill around her heart. She had never seen a man as wretched as James. She had to know what troubled his dreams.

She thought of Mr. Higgins. Perhaps he knew more than anyone. Hadn't James nursed him to health on the voyage from the Dutch East Indies to England?

Noah slept again. She was tired enough to return to sleep as well, except that her brain was spinning with worry. It was a different kind of worry from her usual care about money, of which she had so little, or her lack of reputation, which probably did not bother her as much as it should have. She could only see James's helplessness against a burden that appeared too heavy to be borne.

If I were a man, I am certain I could get to the bottom of this in no time, she thought. But I am not a man; I am a woman unused to the world outside Papa's door. I am the kind of person Loisa would accuse of not being brave enough to say boo to a goose. And I am presuming to delve into the most intimate part of another person's soul? And a man's, to boot? That would require nerve I do not possess.

She lay there, her arm around her son, and thought of Loisa, longing to tell her what had happened, but hesitant. Now that they were speaking again, she yearned to know her sister's opinion on the matter.

"How will I know if I do not ask?" she murmured, her lips close to her son's hair. Hadn't James said all Loie needed was to be needed? I need her now, Susannah told herself.

Noah woke when she sat up. "I am going to Spring Grove," she told him as she got out of bed. "You may stay here if you wish. I imagine Mr. Trevenen will come looking for me. You can tell him I will be painting in the exotic blooms house, after I visit Spring Grove."

He stretched. "I will come with you, Mama," he said. "We can leave him a note."

"I'm not sure the servants are quite ready for breakfast yet," she cautioned. "We might get hungry."

"Aunt Dorothea always has macaroons," he told her gravely.

"You may have to make do with a baked egg and some bacon," she said, knowing that would not discourage him. She looked forward to his company. "Actually, I need your help, my dear. I wish to talk to Aunt Loisa. You can watch over Mr. Higgins while she and I have a few words."

After she dressed, Susannah wrote a note for James and slid it under his door, then hesitated. Hearing him snoring, she opened the door to check on him—and nearly gasped.

The drapes were pulled back again and the window reopened. The chair by the bed had been turned around until it was facing the wall. *My God, what terror is this?* she asked herself. *He suffered more last night, and I did not know.* She felt tears well in her eyes.

She closed the door quietly, more resolved than ever to figure out what brought such fear to an otherwise rational man. She stood in the corridor rubbing her arms, willing the gooseflesh to subside, until Noah came from his room.

"Is Mr. Trevenen coming with us?" he asked.

"He's asleep, and we won't bother him," she said, hoping she sounded more cheerful than she felt.

They could have stayed for breakfast, but the urge to talk to her sister overrode any hunger Susannah might have felt. She grabbed two muffins from the sideboard for Noah and was starting toward the door with her son when Chumley came into the foyer carrying a large silver tray.

"Mrs. Park," he called. "Is Mr. Trevenen about yet?"

"No," she replied, not even stopping.

"One moment, madam," the butler said. "You should see this."

Susannah stood still. As he came close, she noticed the tray was stacked with letters, all addressed to Beau Crusoe.

"What is this, Chumley?"

"The early morning post, Mrs. Park," he replied. "I do believe these are all invitations. Who would have thought London to be so full of people this time of year?"

"Oh, no," she said under her breath. Beau Crusoe was now officially a nine-day wonder in a city hungry for diversion. "I'm not sure Mr. Trevenen is up to this," she told the butler.

"At least he has the wardrobe for it now," Chumley said.

"What a relief," Susannah said dryly. She glanced at the letters, not wanting to take the time to search through them. "See if you can find one from Lord Batchley. He said yesterday we were to dine with him tonight." *And if you find it, burn it,* she wanted to say, thinking of Lady Audley.

Lady Dorothea and Lady Sophia were just sitting down to breakfast when Susannah burst into the breakfast room, curtsied, and asked if Noah could eat with them while she visited her sister.

"Certainly, my dear," Lady Dorothea said.

Noah gave the sideboard his full attention. "No macaroons," he observed.

Susannah smiled to see her godmother looking as crestfallen as the little boy. "Indeed, no," Lady Dorothea said. "I am desolate, too, but it is hard to convince Cook that macaroons should be served any earlier than three in the afternoon. If he didn't make divine puddings, I would turn him out without a character."

Susannah blew a kiss to the room's inhabitants and took the stairs fast enough to cause the upstairs maid to gawk at her.

Loisa answered her knock promptly and came into the corridor. She put her finger to her lips. "Mr. Higgins is sleeping."

Susannah looked at her sister, who should have been exhausted but seemed to be blooming. She smiled. "Loie, does lack of sleep agree with you?"

"It must," Loisa replied. "We…I mean…he slept well last night. Barmley made up a pallet for me in the dressing room."

"Whatever would Mother say?" Susannah teased.

"I am useful," she replied.

"So you are," Susannah agreed, "and now I am going to burden you further with my troubles. Loie, something is very wrong in Mr. Trevenen's life."

Loisa took her by the arm. "How can this be?" she asked, a little of the old bitterness in her voice. "He is to receive a prestigious award, he's not a homely man and he seems to be creating a stir in London. And if he is not precisely a hero, he is most certainly a survivor. Maybe he has money, too."

"Some, I think," Susannah said. She discovered she was hard put to explain it. "I think he's haunted."

"People aren't haunted, Susannah! Only moldy castles, or perhaps old theaters with too many bad performances!"

"No. He's haunted," Susannah insisted.

"You're serious, aren't you?' Loisa asked. "Tell me more."

Susannah followed her sister into Mr. Higgins's room. There was already one chair by the window, with the beginnings of a tatted border on the seat.

"Lady Dorothea has been here?" Susannah whispered, picking up the tatting.

Loisa shook her head, equally amused. "She thinks I should be useful when I am not tending to Mr. Higgins."

"Whatever does she *do* with this?"

"I haven't the slightest notion." Loisa tiptoed across the room, took such a long look at Mr. Higgins that Susannah smiled and came back with another chair. They sat close together, and Loisa began to tat. "Tell me, my dear," she said.

Keeping her voice low, and glancing now and then at the sleeping Mr. Higgins, Susannah described James's odd way of looking suddenly around a room, as though he saw something no one else could. She took a deep breath and described the frightening events of the night before, while Loisa threw the shuttle faster and faster.

"My goodness," she exclaimed, when Susannah finished. "What could Mr. Trevenen possibly have to fear?"

"I don't know. I wish I did. I'm not sure I can forget that look of terror on his face last night," Susannah said. "Loie, he's seeing ghosts, but whose? And why?"

She waited for her practical sister to chide her and declare ghosts were only figments of an overheated imagination, but Loisa said nothing for a while. She set down her tatting and gazed out the window. "A man is alone on a deserted island. It was deserted?"

"He said it was."

Loisa glanced at the bed. "We could ask Mr. Higgins. After all, they were six months on a ship from the Dutch East Indies to England. Since Mr. Trevenen was tending Mr. Higgins, they must have talked." She looked at the clock on the mantelpiece. "He should be waking soon."

"He'll think I am an idiot," Susannah fretted.

Loisa touched her arm. "No, he won't. Mr. Higgins is a kind man, with only good to say. He…" She stopped, and her face reddened.

Susannah watched her, amazed. "Loie, you're not…" She couldn't even say it, especially since only a few days ago, she and Mr. Trevenen had agreed that people simply didn't fall in love instantly. "Can you possibly be…"

"I don't know," her sister said. She picked up the shuttle again and started tatting faster than before, then sighed and set it down. "I can hardly credit what is going on. I watch over Mr. Higgins, and when he wakes he is so grateful, even if I have not done a thing except keep an eye on him. I read to him. He thanks me, and looks at me as though I am beautiful, and we know that is not the case." She stared out the window, then turned to face Susannah. "Can you imagine anything more unsuitable?"

Susannah didn't even try to hide her smile. "Well, yes, I can. Of all people, I can."

Loisa leaned forward and kissed her cheek. "I wronged you," she said in her practical way. "I am heartily sorry. Will you forgive me for being so beastly?"

Susannah winked back her own tears, even as Loisa's began to flow. "You were forgiven a long time ago, dearest," she said.

"To forgive is divine."

They looked toward the bed. Mr. Higgins had raised himself and was resting on one elbow. Loisa hurried to the bed, scolding him every step of the way, while Susannah put her hand over her mouth so they would not see her smile.

"You're supposed to lie flat and not exert yourself, Mr. Higgins," Loisa ordered, resting the back of her hand against his forehead.

Susannah watched them, touched. Beau Crusoe, she thought, I will call this your greatest triumph, even beyond toucans and rescuing that horrible cat.

She approached the bed, wasting no time with preliminaries. "Mr. Higgins, if you are feeling well enough to talk…"

"Certainly I am," he replied, folding his arms across his chest. He did look better than the day before. "I heard you say something about Mr. Trevenen."

"Mr. Higgins, you may think me the grossest busybody, but I must know. Are you acquainted with Mr. Trevenen's nightmares? I have seen one, and it was of monumental proportions. Do you remember them from your voyage from the Dutch East Indies to England? Do you know their origin?"

Before he answered, Loisa put several pillows behind his head. "I am going to bring up some breakfast for you, Mr. Higgins, and you will eat all of it."

She could have told Loisa that bullying someone she fancied was no way to secure his affections, except that Sam Higgins was looking at his nurse with genuine longing. It appears Loisa does not need any of my paltry advice, she thought with amusement. She nodded to Loisa as her sister left the room, then directed her attention to Mr. Higgins again.

"Please, sir, tell me what you learned from Mr. Trevenen during that voyage from Batavia to England?"

"I really don't remember anything," he said, after a long pause.

You are a dreadful liar, she thought.

"I don't feel so well right now."

That's two in a row. She stood up, heartsick. "I wish you

would tell me something," she said. "Doesn't Mr. Trevenen matter to you?"

He said nothing. She regarded him a moment more, then turned on her heel and left the room without another glance. Am I the only one who cares about James Trevenen? she thought as she descended the stairs. Am I his last chance?

Chapter Nineteen

It began to rain before she reached the exotic blooms house. Mr. Trevenen stood by the door, staring at the ground. He looked so out of place, so foreign, even though he was English. It was as though he belonged to no world except the wooden world of the mariner, bobbing on an endless ocean.

She didn't want to startle him, so she cleared her throat. He looked up, his expression wary, but his gaze softened as he recognized her. The exhaustion in his face made her want to gather him close to her, but she knew better. She opened the door.

"I never thought it might be unlocked," he said, embarrassed, as he followed her inside. "I should have tried it."

"The gardeners always open it early," she said, taking off her sodden shawl.

"Do you paint here the year around?"

"When I can," she said. "There are some days when it is too chilly, even with the stove lit." She smiled at him. "Then we chafe a while and go back to Alderson House."

"Noah is always with you?"

"Nearly. He thought he would help his Aunt Loisa this morning," she told him as she prepared her watercolors, pulling out the tints she had identified yesterday as belonging to the *Gloriosa*. She sat, pulled the small table of colors close to her and indicated the stool beside her. "This was our last summer to-gether, I fear."

He took the *Gloriosa* out of the leather satchel he carried. "School?"

"I am arranging for a tutor to come to Alderson House. That is why I have been painting for these six years."

He set the *Gloriosa* on the smaller easel beside her large one. "I am a nosy fellow, Mrs. P. Cannot your father help you?"

"I want to provide for my son myself, if I can," she replied, sidestepping his query.

Why is this conversation revolving around me, she thought, as she picked up her pencil and finished her outline of the *Gloriosa's* large claw. We are both circling around a much larger issue.

"You're shivering." He retrieved his overcoat, draping it around her shoulders.

She felt his fingers on her neck and she closed her eyes with the pleasure of it. The coat was heavy, but dry on the inside. She outlined the *Gloriosa*, afraid he was not going to mention what had happened last night. She had not the slightest idea how to broach the subject.

Loisa would just ask him, she thought. I wish I had her bold-ness. She looked at the *Gloriosa*. "How big was it?" She indi-cated the drawing with her pencil.

"No more than two inches across, not including the large claw and legs," he said. "You read my treatise."

"I did," she said, and took a large breath, which only brought in the fragrance of his overcoat. "How is it that your coat smells of salt and sand?"

"I go down to the water every day, back in Cornwall," he said. "I can't help myself."

She set down the pencil and dug deep for courage. "James, tell me what happened last night."

He looked away from her. "No." Then, "I did not mean to frighten you."

"You did. I couldn't find you when I opened the door."

He was leaning forward now, the muscles in his legs tensed

as though he wanted to bolt from the bloom house. Don't, she thought. Don't. Talk to me.

He sighed and sat back, not looking at her. "It doesn't happen every night."

"Liar," she said softly, and returned to her sketch. "I think some nights must be worse than others."

"They are. It's nothing I cannot manage."

"Why was the window open, James?" she asked, turning to face him. "Were you going to leap out?"

He looked at her then, and she nearly cried at the bleak depths in his eyes. "I always want an avenue of escape. There *is* no escape at sea."

She touched his face, then cupped it with both her hands. "James, you are a complicated man. Will you keep your window closed and open your door, instead?"

Before she could move her hands, he kissed her palm. "I will. You don't think your family will mind?"

She took her hands away. "I don't care if they do. And do you know, sir, I wish you would trust me with your story."

"I can't," he said, his voice low. "Don't ask me to, or I will leave within the hour."

"Very well, James," she said, unable to hide the disappointment she knew was on her face. "Have it your way. But do not be alarmed if I should come into your room and sit beside you at night."

He regarded her, his expression rueful. "You would have not a shred of reputation."

"I have little now," she reminded him. "Besides, people in my family are sound sleepers, and I know you are the soul of discretion."

He nodded. "I keep my secrets."

Susannah removed his overcoat. The bloom house was quite warm now, even though the rain was coming down more heavily. She returned her attention to the *Gloriosa*. And some wits and philosophers believe females are complicated, she thought. Obviously they've never met James Trevenen.

She heard him rummaging in his leather satchel again and

glanced his way. He pulled out a fistful of letters, the mail that Chumley had showed her when she left Alderson House that morning.

"Invitations, all of them," he said. "All addressed to Beau Crusoe." He pulled out one and put one in her lap. "Perhaps we have to do something about this one."

She picked up the envelope, opening it when he nodded. "Lord Batchley. We are to dine tonight with him." She looked closer at the handsomely calligraphed note. "Dear me, and Vixen, too."

He nodded and picked up another envelope. "We are to attend a balloon ascension tomorrow with…" He held out the invitation. "Sir Wallace Cavanaugh?"

"A leading light in the Royal Society, so you should cultivate him," she said. "He comes to Spring Grove now and again to drink tea with my godfather, and ogle me, I fear."

He leaned back in mock surprise. "Where did I meet this man of supremely good judgment?"

Flattered, she dipped her brush in the pale green. "Either at the inn where you kept Sir Percival from burning alive, in Hyde Park where you rescued Mr. Higgins, at the apothecary's or near the tree by the Serpentine!"

He shook his head. "Amazing. Should we go?"

"Only if you take Noah and not me."

He laughed. "Suzie, you will never catch a husband, if that is your attitude! All men have their faults."

"And all women." She began to paint the large claw.

He picked up another invitation, and another. "We are to drink tea with Lady Featherstone on Saturday, enjoy strawberries al fresco on Sunday with Lord and Lady Walton—does no one go to church in London?—and attend a lecture on metaphysics with Lord Ramsey. Horrors." He let the invitations drop through his fingers to the floor.

"It is entirely your fault, James," she said serenely, dabbing at the inside edge of the large claw. "There now. Is that the proper hue?"

He leaned closer to her. "Very like. I wish you could have seen it, Suzie, and painted it from life."

She wished he would kiss her, this man who had frightened her so badly last night. He did something else that set her nerves humming: gently rubbed his cheek against hers.

It was only a brief touch, as though to reassure her. Then he sat back on the stool, content to watch in silence, alternating between glances at her and at his *Gloriosa*, which was taking shape.

He didn't say anything; she could tell he was miles away. She touched his shoulder, half expecting him to start. He didn't, but when he turned to look at her, his face was troubled.

"You want to go back to your island." It was a statement of fact.

He nodded. Before she could stop him, he took his sketch from the easel beside her painting and left the bloom house.

"Wait! How can I finish this?" she concluded in a softer voice, more worried than irritated. She looked at the partly completed crab and felt tears in her eyes.

Noah joined her after she finished her lunch of bread and meat, bringing macaroons to share with her, and a note from Loisa. Susannah had composed herself by the time her son arrived. She took the note in her color-spackled fingers. It was as blunt as the woman who wrote it:

Sister, we are much the same size. I have a wardrobe full of dresses. There is a pale lavender that ought to impress any of Lord Batchley's dinner guests. A darker-hued shawl is in the press. Mr. Trevenen sat with Sam, then Sir Joseph insisted he take the carriage back to Alderson House for your use tonight. I hardly think it proper, but Mr. Trevenen tells me he will need your help with his neckcloth. Wash your fingers and go home.
Loie

She kissed Noah's head in relief—grateful James had not left—then capped the colors. "My dear, Mr. Trevenen and I are to go to Lord Batchley's house. I hope you won't mind dinner with Chumley below stairs."

He shook his head. "I cannot Mama, I have plans. You and Mr. Trevenen are to drop me back at Spring Grove. Aunt Loisa says she most particularly needs my help tonight, if you can spare me. She promises to read to me and let me sleep on a pallet by Mr. Higgins." He looked at her anxiously then. "That is, if you won't miss me too much."

"You know I will," she replied softly, ruffling his hair. "But that doesn't mean I cannot manage!"

Loisa was right; the lavender dress did fit, even though Susannah found herself staring down at more expanse of her breast than she had become used to showing since her widowhood. "I suppose this is *à la mode*," she murmured as Mama's dresser finished buttoning her up the back.

"Most certainly, Mrs. Park," the woman assured her.

Susannah looked at herself in the mirror and gulped. She had gotten used to stuff gowns of sober hues. What this soft color did to her hair made her smile, in spite of her sudden shyness. She touched the curls the dresser had deftly pinned back around her upswept hair. "I had forgotten," she said simply.

"A lady should never forget," the dresser said. She held out the shawl, and Loisa was right again. The deeper purple was the perfect match.

Noah approved of her transformation. He had been going back and forth across the corridor between her room and Mr. Trevenen's. "Mama," was all he said, but he walked around her twice. Then, "Mama, I almost forgot. Mr. Trevenen most especially asked for your help."

The dresser gathered up her pins and brushes and curtsied.

"Do thank my mother for me," Susannah said. "Or perhaps I should."

The dresser lost none of her dignity, but she did look away and clear her throat. "You'll have to wait to talk to your mama." She cleared her throat again. "Lord Watchmere is visiting her now."

Susannah couldn't hide her smile. "Oh, my," she said, and glanced at the clock on the mantelpiece. "It is only six o' clock."

The dresser lowered her voice so Noah would not hear her. "I was dressing Lady Watchmere for dinner when he tapped on the door and said the toucans had been gone long enough."

Susannah stared at her. "Whatever did he mean?"

"I am sure I do not know, Mrs. Park, but your mother seemed to understand. She told me to tell Cook to delay dinner."

Susannah laughed and then put her hand to her mouth. The dresser left the room. Susannah looked at Noah. "My dear, you say Mr. Trevenen is desperate?"

"He is just holding his neckcloth, Mama."

She crossed the corridor and tapped on the open door. Mr. Trevenen met her, neckcloth in hand, just as Noah had said, dressed in his new evening wear. His waistcoat, a handsome plum color, was draped over the chair.

He bowed to her and her face grew warm to see him look in unabashed admiration at her expanse of naked skin.

"Don't stare at me, James, or I shall call you Mr. Trevenen forevermore!" she threatened.

"My dear Mrs. Park, I am only human," he told her.

"The things I am doing for you," she grumbled. "Hand me that. Sit down."

Susannah straightened James's collar. With a hand practiced from assisting Noah, she fastened his collar button and put the neckcloth where it belonged. As she leaned closer, she knew precisely where his gaze lingered.

"I warned you not to stare."

"I will have to remove my eyes and place them in the back of my head, then, my dear Mrs. Park," he told her. He chuckled. "Of course, my gun crew was always pretty sure I had an extra pair there, too."

"Close them, then!"

"Very well, but what a waste."

She sighed in exasperation. "Stand up, sir," she commanded. "We are much the same height anyway, and I will manage well enough."

He did as she said, looking into her eyes instead, which she found even more unnerving. She looped the cloth twice around his neck, tugging on it once when he started to laugh.

"You'll hang me," he protested mildly.

"Probably someone should have done so years ago," she said. "I am not precisely sure about the knot. Should I summon my father's valet?"

"Lord, no. Have you seen your father lately, when he dresses for the tree blind?"

She laughed in spite of her discomfort and focused her attention on the middle of his throat.

"I saw Grandpapa earlier, going down the corridor to Grandmama's room," Noah said from his perch on James's bed. "I could knock."

Susannah put out her hand to stop him from jumping off the bed. "Oh, no, son, that isn't necessary. I think Grandpapa is occupied."

Her face grew redder. "Mama's dresser said he mentioned something about toucans when he went into Mama's room and then told her to put dinner back a half hour. Sir, I believe you owe me an explanation."

"Not in a million years," he replied, then leaned closer until his lips nearly touched her ear. "Or not until we have deposited Noah at Spring Grove."

She occupied herself with the knot at his neck and tried to ignore his warm breath on her cheek. I cannot ask him not to breathe, she told herself.

"Lift up your chin," she commanded.

He did as she asked, which gained her nothing except a chance to admire his face in profile. She arranged the folds of his neckcloth, wondering how she could ever have thought him ordinary-looking.

"Lower your chin now all the way down," she directed.

He lowered his chin. She stepped back to see the effect. "Excellent, James," she said. "If I ever tire of painting flora and fauna, I do believe I will disguise myself and hire out as a valet."

"I can think of no one on this planet who could look less like a man, even in dim light," he told her, as he reached for his waistcoat. He looked at Noah. "Your mother has strange notions."

"I like her, though," Noah said.

James buttoned his waistcoat. "I do, too," he said. He reached for his coat next and put it on, tugging at the lapels.

"Don't fidget," Susannah told him.

He stood there so elegantly, a far cry from the man yanked from sleep by a nightmare and cowering beside the window in his nightshirt. Poor, dear man, she thought. How you must dread each nightfall. And here you are, gamely going through the business of life.

There was no time to examine her feelings. It was something she had not taken the luxury for in years. "Find your shoes and put them on, sir," she told him. "Even October society—far from sticklers, I should imagine—demands shoes."

"Spoilsport," he grumbled, and Noah giggled.

"You will kindly wear a hat, too."

He knuckled his forehead in imitation of a thousand sailors for probably a thousand years. "Aye, madam, aye." He glanced at Noah, who was watching this exchange with interest. "Does she run roughshod over you like this, lad? I wonder you do not run away."

"I never thought of it," Noah said, plainly puzzled.

"Don't give him ideas," Susannah warned.

Shyness kept her from saying anything to James on the brief ride to Spring Grove. Because it was evening, Sir Joseph had loaned James his small carriage with the crest on the door when he came back from Spring Grove earlier. The three of them sat close together.

Noah kept up a conversation about all he had done for his Aunt Loisa that day. Susannah was suddenly struck by how much he had to say lately. Before Mr. Trevenen had come to town and started to work his strange magic on them all, Noah hadn't talked much. Susannah looked at her own reflection in the glass as dusk came. He had been taking after me, she thought, moving around quietly as I do, trying not to come to anyone's notice.

She made herself relax and soon found herself enjoying the interplay between Mr. Trevenen and her son. You're a born father, Mr. T, she wanted to tell him. Now go home to Cornwall and find a wife.

Nothing is that simple, is it? she asked herself. We could probably give each other good advice until the second coming of Christ and never act upon any of it. This man's life is not my business.

At Spring Grove, when Noah jumped up and let himself out of the carriage, she spoke to James for the first time. "I want to show this dress to my sister," she said.

"I'll come in, too." He smiled in that lazy, confident way of his, the look she was coming to associate with Beau Crusoe. "I would like to hear her opinion of the dress myself."

She could not think when another man had flirted with her in the last seven years, Sir Walter Cavanaugh's clumsy attempts notwithstanding. "You're kind," she said.

"No, I am honest," he replied, then sighed. "Oh, blast, I am the last man in London whose word you would ever believe."

"The very last," she assured him.

Mr. Higgins was sitting up in bed, looking the picture of comfort. Somehow Neptune had found his impressive way into the room, too—perhaps it was the influence of a small boy—and lay on his side by the fireplace. Noah flopped against him and picked up a kaleidoscope. And there was Loisa, sitting beside the bed, tatting. Susannah stood in the doorway, relishing the warmth in the room, and thanking Mr. Trevenen—or was it Beau Crusoe?— for the magic he had worked.

Loisa looked up, blinked, then stood, walking around her sister in the doorway, a smile on her face.

"Oh, Loie, don't," Susannah said, unable to keep the laughter from her voice. "I know this is an indecent amount of skin on view for a widow."

Loisa shrugged. "Can you imagine how frightful that would have looked on me, with my complexion? What was I thinking when I let Mama bully me into approving it? Oh, never mind. Lord

Batchley will probably pop his creaky stays when he sees you." She glanced at James, who was bending over Sam. "Heavens, Susannah, he certainly looks better when a tailor steps in."

"Doesn't he?" Susannah whispered back. But, she wondered, what will happen to him tonight, when he tries to sleep? "Loie, have you seen Sir Joseph about?"

Lois shook her head. "I think he is confined to his room, although his physician has not been here recently. Do you wish to see him? Perhaps you could just knock on his door."

Susannah nodded, put her finger to her lips and left the room. She hurried down the corridor to her godfather's chamber and rapped on the door.

"Come."

She opened the door, prepared for gloom, but the room was fully lit.

"I have not seen much of you, my dear," Sir Joseph said. He reclined on the chaise before the fireplace, his gouty, swollen legs underneath a metal frame that allowed the blanket covering him to cause no more pain than he already felt.

Susannah sat down on a hassock in front of the chaise longue. "Sir Joe, I have so many questions, and Mr. Trevenen sidesteps them all! What should I do?"

"You need to do something about him?" Sir Joseph asked, his voice gentle. "It is less than two weeks now before the Royal Society meeting, and then your duties will be done." He looked at her more closely. "Won't they?"

"I don't know," she said. "I don't…"

He wasn't looking at her, but at the door she had left open. "Mr. Trevenen, did you lose something?"

She turned around to see James Trevenen watching them both. "Yes, as a matter of fact—Mrs. Park. If I am to have any consequence, I had better arrive at events with her, so no one will notice my deficiencies. Lovely, isn't she?"

"Indeed," Sir Joseph replied. "She always was."

"Come, Mrs. Park," he said, extending his hand to her. "Let us mingle in proper society and see how much damage we can do."

She laughed in spite of herself. "Speak for yourself, sir!"

He bowed.

"I'll be with you in a moment," she told him.

He bowed again and in a moment she heard his footsteps in the corridor. She turned back to her godfather. "Sir Joseph, something dreadful is going on with Mr. Trevenen, and I do not understand it."

If she thought her godfather would be startled, she was the one surprised. He only nodded and regarded the dancing flames in the fireplace. "Come alone tomorrow. Perhaps we can figure out this puzzle named Beau Crusoe."

"And if we cannot?"

"Then it will be a loss of tragic proportions to the world of science, my dear." He peered closer. "And maybe even a greater loss to you."

Chapter Twenty

James couldn't say he was comfortable on the ride to Lord Batchley's town house. He should have enjoyed the ride more, since his companion was Mrs. Park, but there was some tension in her eyes he couldn't explain.

He made an attempt. "Mrs. P, what should I know about Lord Batchley? Is he a member of the Royal Society?"

"Yes, actually. Sir Joe tells me he has financed several research vessels: one to Madagascar to study lemurs, and another to the West Indies, although I cannot recall why."

"To analyze the rum?" he teased. "He's too late. It's been done."

She only nodded.

"Susannah, would you advise Beau Crusoe to lean on Lord Batchley, remind him of saving Vixen's life and request a research ship as a reward?" he ventured.

"Stranger things have happened in the last few days, sir."

Indeed they have, and you don't know the half of it, he thought. As he regarded her a moment more, then directed his gaze at the city filling up with night, he knew he was in love. It was a complication he neither welcomed nor encouraged, considering the fool he had made of himself the night before.

She knew too much about him. He couldn't quite remember what he had done the night before, when she found him cowering

beside the open window, but she was quieter today, sadder somehow. He knew last night had not been a shining moment.

There were other problems. He could not avoid thinking of
Lady Audley, who was coming to dine with Lord Batchley as
well, if her vulgar importuning yesterday had succeeded. He did
not doubt it had. The Lady Audleys of the universe generally got
what they wanted.

When he thought of her, he felt disgust boil up from deep inside him, like a pot of reeking bilge left unwatched on Satan's
stove. When they separated so ungraciously at Cape Town, he
had hoped never to see her again.

He had met her in Batavia, when the missionary ship put
into port. The evangels still had not decided whether to return to
England, or to make another attempt to bring Christianity to
South Seas islands more promising than Tonga. He had listened
to them argue long into each night.

For a small coin—a very small one—he would have tossed
all of them over the railing. He had parted company with them
at the docks, conflicted between his gratitude for their rescue and
his weariness with their arguments.

There had been no vessels of the Royal Navy in the harbor,
or he would have boarded one immediately. A fellow officer
would have heard his tale of shipwreck, three weeks adrift, and
five years on a deserted island, and put him into the crew. In
Batavia, there was always room for more seamen because the
port was so prone to fever.

There was only an East India merchant ship bound for Portsmouth, and that was good enough for him. However, his convo-
luted negotiations with a Dutch banker were getting him no closer
to England, until Lady Audley arrived in the banker's office.

She had been returning to England from Macao, where her
husband, Viscount Audley, was engaged in some shady business,
probably opium. Lord Audley was to follow on a later ship.

She wasn't a beauty—her jaw was too large, her eyes too
small—but she commanded his attention the moment he saw her.
Or, as he reflected later, more like the moment she saw him. He

could no more have escaped her grasp than the last macaroon at a garden party.

He did nothing to discourage her overtures, which began in the banker's office. The banker was explaining the difficulty of providing passage to an Englishman with no credit. She looked James over, then signed a draft from her bank to cover his passage. Before he had time to thank her, she left, turning back once to give him a half smile that caused his organ to wake from slumber. Good thing the light was low and the banker myopic from staring at ledgers.

His cabin aboard ship was next to hers. With some funds from her generosity he had purchased a modest wardrobe. It was ready-made and had probably come off the back of a dead man in that port notorious for fever, but it fit relatively well.

Or so Lady Audley's eyes told him as she stood watching him in the narrow passageway. She gestured for him to come closer. Like a sleepwalker, he did. No one else was there. She took him by the neckcloth and gently pulled him closer. When they were nipple to nipple, she began to unbutton his trousers.

Even tonight, riding toward London, he didn't understand why that hadn't surprised him. As his little-used organ grew with remarkable speed inside his trousers, he even helped her.

Then he was inside her small cabin, turning the lock and removing his pants, his heart pounding. He turned to find she had done nothing more than raise her skirts to her waist and settle herself back into the narrow berth, her knees up and spread wide, ready.

As the blood drained from his face and rushed to join the rest of his body fluids just south of his tattoo, she had taken her fingers and delicately spread her lower lips wide. No man could have ignored such a blatant invitation. As he straddled her and rammed his organ home, his last thought was that he didn't even know her first name.

When they finished, he had tried to apologize for his unbecoming conduct. She only grabbed hold of his retreating organ and rubbed it against her slimy bud until she came again. And again, bucking and panting like a dog on a hot day. He had never seen such a performance.

It was repeated over and over as they crossed the Indian Ocean. If there was a position known to Venus that they did not try, he couldn't have named it. Her favorite position was to ride him, lowering herself onto him slowly until he was nearly bug-eyed with anticipation. She would clutch the joist overhead so he could explore her breasts with his fingers, circling her nipples until she started to moan. She liked to be in charge, riding him like a jockey.

There was probably a name for women like Lady Audley, but he didn't know it. All he knew was that when she looked at him, whether they were in the wardroom at dinner or on deck, within fifteen minutes he would be earning his passage to England with his dong.

It would have been an idyllic crossing of a smooth sea—winds from the right quarter and no pirates—but for his obligation to Sam Higgins. When James had staggered back on deck after that first copulation, the missionaries had met him. He had hardly wanted to look at them, certain they could read lasciviousness all over his face—if not smell it around him—but they would not leave him alone.

Guilt-ridden at his recent conduct with Lady Audley, he had agreed to escort Sam Higgins to London. He had them carry the ailing missionary to his cabin and put him into his own berth. He had an able seaman sling a hammock for him in the remaining space. He was used to hammocks from his years at sea, and besides, he planned to spend more time in the next cabin.

As the missionaries departed, leaving a supply of Peruvian bark and a Bible, they told him in return for this service he was rendering to the London Missionary Society and probably God Almighty, they had arranged for his passage through the same Dutch banker in whose office he had met Lady Audley. James had not much faith in the honesty of the Dutch after that.

He kept Sam alive as they crossed the Indian Ocean, feeding him when he would eat, administering Peruvian bark, wiping him down and emptying his pitiful slops.

Sam lived, mainly because he ate steadily, if slowly, and the

Peruvian bark worked. James had experience with malaria, although, thank God, he had never been afflicted with it. He had tended others and knew that the illness made death seem like a long-lost friend.

Sam made few demands on him, which was good, because James was too busy satisfying a woman he knew nothing about, beyond her hypnotic effect on him.

One afternoon when even Lady Audley was satiated and idly fingering the wet hair on his thigh, he decided to tell her about his three weeks in the small boat with his four increasingly desperate companions, then three, then two and then just the carpenter's mate. He had thought on his island that he would never tell anyone, but the story seemed to bubble over inside him. He feared what she would think, but the stopper was out of the bottle.

He couldn't see her face, because she was resting her head on his chest and looking down at the part of him that interested her most. He hoped she would not be too shocked. When he finished, he waited for some reaction.

And waited. With a sinking heart, he realized she was sound asleep.

He never tried to tell her again.

Halfway across the Indian Ocean, Sam began to take an interest in his surroundings. After another week, he told James he really ought to make less noise next door, because every moan and gasp was coming right through the bulkhead.

"Besides," Sam had said one evening when James was taking a break, "isn't she married? You're not helping your immortal soul."

Oh, Lord. The last thing James wanted to think about was his immortal soul, which was soiled in ways the missionary could never fathom, and by far worse crimes than attending to Lady Audley's overactive genitals.

As they neared Cape Town, James decided Sam was right. He knew himself too well to give complete credit to his conscience, obviously not a well-used part of his character. He was weary of Lady Audley calling him by every name except his own, in the heat of her nearly continual passion. For some reason, Dieter, Boris and Ruprecht didn't bother him nearly as much as Pierre, Carlos and Claude. Didn't the woman know Britain had been at war with Spain and France for years now? Had she no patriotism?

The clincher came during a dogwatch in midafternoon. He had been taking solar readings for the captain, but ran belowdeck for his boat cloak when the air turned cold. He heard familiar sounds from Lady Audley's cabin. He opened the door a crack, just enough to see her bare bum as she panted over the purser's puny arousal.

He watched a moment, then closed the door. She could have had me in another two hours, he thought. He returned to deck a wiser man.

She hadn't taken the news well, which made him think he was the first man to reject her. To keep him, she had tried what had always worked before, pulling up her skirts and spreading her legs. He felt himself grow large at the sight—it never failed—but he resisted this time. He grabbed his few possessions strewn about her cabin—his dignity was not in sight—and hurried into his own crowded quarters with Sam.

To his utter relief, when the merchant vessel lowered anchor in Cape Town's magnificent harbor three long days later, there was a British man o' war bobbing on the water. After a brief visit with the captain—who was short a first mate—and the officer's promise to take Sam, too, James Trevenen escaped.

He didn't get away unscathed. After Sam was aboard the *HMS Reconciliation*, James had returned to his cabin for one last look around. When he turned to leave, Lady Audley stood in the hatchway.

He watched her, silent. Even now, as he and Mrs. Park approached Lord Batchley's row house, he felt that same shiver down his spine as in Cape Town's harbor.

"I will not forget this," she had informed him, her tone all the more chilling because it was so matter-of-fact. "You will wish you had not cast me off."

* * *

"You seem to be residing on another planet, Mr. Trev… James."

Startled, he swiveled. "I beg your pardon, Mrs. P. I was thinking of…" Words failed him.

She smiled, looking at the row house. "With any luck, you will not encounter Vixen."

Or Lady Audley, he thought, puzzled all over again as he considered her enthusiasm at seeing him descend from the tree in Hyde Park. "Oh, yes, yes, you are so correct," he stammered. "Hardly anything is as ferocious as an angry…cat." Although the evening was cool, James felt himself begin to perspire in his new evening clothes.

She leaned toward him and he breathed her fragrance. "I wouldn't be so upset, sir," she told him. "It's just a cat."

"Indeed," he murmured. "What can possibly happen?" I'm in London to pick up a damned medal and then I will be gone, he reminded himself. I will take my ghost and *Gloriosa*, and return to Cornwall.

The carriage moved slightly as the servant hopped off the back and came around to open the door. In another few minutes they would be in a crowd of people he either didn't know or had no urge to see again.

He left the carriage and held out his hand for Susannah. He knew she had no way of knowing what he was thinking, but some of his agitation had obviously communicated itself to her. He could have sighed with relief when she tucked her arm through his.

He looked into her eyes and wondered if he could ever tell her about the small boat and its occupants. It was after his unsuccessful attempt to enlist Lady Audley's sympathies that he had begun to see the carpenter's mate, or rather, his ghost. He was just a shadow at first, a feeling that made James whirl around in dark passageways, wondering what he was imagining.

He had thought he could leave the ghoul behind on the merchant ship, but the thing had followed him to the *Reconciliation*, and then traipsed after the mail coach to Cornwall. He sighed. And now it had loped along to London.

Once inside Lord Batchley's home, James almost allowed himself to relax. A quick glance around had revealed no Lady Audley. He began to hope. Maybe she had come down with smallpox and lay near death's door; one could wish.

It was not to be. He smelled her before he saw her. The hairs rose on his neck as he and Mrs. Park stood together in the salon. He took a deep breath and then several shallow ones as he smelled her perfume, a toxic fragrance that reminded him of the rotting floor of a rain forest.

A glance at Mrs. Park told him she had noticed it, too. She frowned and sniffed the air, and then Lady Audley came out of a tight circle of admirers and headed toward them.

Lord, make me invisible, he prayed.

"Dear James," she crowed, holding out both hands to grasp him by his upper arms. "Or should I call you Beau Crusoe, as others do?"

"Mr. Trevenen is even better," he said.

She paused, startled. Her smile seemed to freeze, but only for the smallest second. She turned to Susannah.

"James is such a tease, my dear," she said. "You must invite me to tea so I can tell you how he amused me as we crossed the Indian Ocean."

James could feel the color drain from his face and pool somewhere around his ankles. He thought he could manage a laugh, but to his ears it came out more like a bark. "I would hate to bore Mrs. Park with tales of a tedious ocean passage," he managed.

He hardly dared to look at Mrs. Park, certain she must be staring at him. When he managed the smallest glance, he was amazed at how calm she looked. Perhaps he had not bungled so badly, after all. He wanted to say something else, but he couldn't for the life of him think what. It didn't matter; Lady Audley had directed her attention to Susannah's gown.

"My dear," she purred, "what a lovely color on you. I had no idea lavender was so slimming."

It was Susannah's turn for her smile to freeze in place. James wanted to drag Lady Audley outside by her hair and stuff her in an ash can in payment for the wary look that came into Susannah's eyes. He tried to think how Lady Audley could justify so cruel a cut, eyeing Susannah himself. All he saw was a lovely lady with glowing skin and a generously comfortable bosom. He knew, with an ache in his heart, that she was everything he could want in a wife.

"That must be one of the properties of lavender, Lady Audley," Susannah said after a long pause.

A miracle happened then. A gong sounded. Lord Batchley, resplendent in a gold-threaded waistcoast that would have made even Sir Percival Pettibone wince, separated himself from another circle and gestured them all in to dinner. James latched on to Susannah and led her toward the line that began to form, hoping Lady Audley would not follow.

She didn't, but as they circled the dining room table looking for their place cards, he saw with dismay that some evil genie had seated him next to Lady Audley, with Susannah farther down the table between two older gentlemen. Crushed with disappointment, he saw Susannah to her chair.

Lord Batchley had a reputation as a pinchpurse. There were only seven courses that night. To James, seated beside Lady Audley, each one seemed to last three days. He devoted as much of his time as he could to the elderly lady seated on his left, but she was hard of hearing, and more interested in gumming her duckling à l'orange and dribbling soup. He had no choice but to turn his attention to Lady Audley.

He was too nervous to eat, especially when, under the cover of the table, Lady Audley's fingers began to explore his thigh. As her fingers searched, and then stroked, she leaned toward the man on her right and conversed with him.

Dumbfounded, James inched as far away from her as he could, which wasn't far, considering that the lady on his left was well-stuffed and overflowed her chair. He could only sit there and endure. When he could stand no more, he moved Lady Audley's fingers from his lap and placed them in her own.

That was worse. She grabbed his fingers and held them against her crotch until he unwittingly brought her to orgasm right there at the dinner table. She took it all in stride, setting down her fork and clutching the stem of her wineglass until he feared it might snap.

Desperate now, he wrenched his hand away, which caused Susannah to look in his direction, a question in her eyes. To his unutterable relief, Lady Audley left him alone for the rest of the dinner. James kept his eyes on his plate, miserable beyond belief.

His head began to ache. When the only thing remaining on the table were too many wineglasses, Lord Batchley rose for the usual toasts to king and country.

Relieved to be on his feet because the end was in sight, James joined in. When all were seated again, Lord Batchley called for refills and stood up one more time.

"Ladies and gentlemen," he said, pointing his glass toward James, "I give you Beau Crusoe! I suppose in naval records he is called James Trevenen, but he rescued my dear Vixen yesterday, and from what I hear, has performed other acts…"

"Oh, he has," said Lady Audley quite audibly.

James winced.

"…of daring and bravery. He is also a scientist of great genius and promise." Lord Batchley held up his glass as the others rose. "To Beau Crusoe, who will wear the Copley medal around his neck at the end of next week!"

"Hear! Hear!"

It was painful to his ears. James wanted to leap up and run away, but he nodded and smiled instead. Then he looked beyond the table, where the carpenter's mate held the half-eaten arm high over his head, shaking the ghastly thing toward the table and scattering drops of blood.

James closed his eyes, waiting for the others to begin screaming. Nothing happened. He opened his eyes, seeing again the drops of blood that no one else seemed to notice. Everyone was looking at him and applauding. He could only tear his gaze away from the cavorting apprentice and smile back.

Chapter Twenty-One

Here hated brandy; he never smoked. And there was Tim Rowe leering at him, after the ladies left. Masculine conversation swirled around him. He was glib, he was charming. He wanted to bolt.

Later, in Lord Batchley's impressive salon, he tried to reach Susannah, but the old gentleman himself had offered her his arm, led her to a whist table, and sat her down with the admonition to play well and entertain those appointed to the table.

He turned to James then and took his arm. "Beau, I have a special treat. I know you would like to pay a visit to Vixen. He can show you there are no hard feelings."

"No," James said, startled into incivility, and then embarrassed by the wounded look in his host's eyes. "I mean, I would hate to disturb Vixen again, especially since he feels so ambivalent about me." He looked at Lord Batchley, hoping for some sign of agreement.

"I insist, lad."

Before Lord Batchley could drag him from the room, Lady Audley approached them and took James by the other arm.

"Lord Batchley, I wouldn't have you forced to shepherd the Beau around to the neglect of your other guests," she said. "I will take him to see Vixen. Your duties here are much more important, wouldn't you agree?"

How could he disagree? James felt numb as Lord Batchley bowed and yielded the field.

"You're being silly, James. We'll be only a few minutes," Lady Audley said, tightening her grip on his arm.

He nodded, miserable, wondering what the guests would think if he suddenly bolted from the room. He didn't dare. Imagine how that would set back Susannah's rehabilitation. Wasn't that why he was here?

She led him out of the room toward the stairs, apparently as much at home in Lord Batchley's house as in her own.

He stopped on the stairs. "I do not care to go one step farther with you," he whispered furiously.

She gave him an appraising stare that seemed to suck the blood from his brain. "How suspicious you are," she said. "I assist Lord Batchley, and you think ill of me."

James shook his head. "It was one thing to behave so abominably during dinner…"

"Me?" she asked, her eyes wide with wounded surprise. "Why didn't you *say* something?"

"What could I say?" he retorted.

"Precisely," she told him, and continued to mount the stairs. "Are you coming?"

"I am not."

She shrugged her nearly bare shoulders and started back down the stairs toward him. "Very well, James, if I must." She stood close to him. "Do you want me to return to the drawing room and denounce you as a murderer? Should I tell them what happened on that boat?"

He grabbed her arm, more to hold himself up than to detain her. Her whispered words thundered in his ears. He thought back to that time on the crossing when he had told her everything, only to realize she had fallen asleep before he got to the most damaging part of his wretched story.

"You were not asleep," he said finally.

"Who could sleep through such a recitation?" she asked. Her smile grew until it became almost the most horrible sight he had ever seen. She released herself from his grip. "James, men don't discard me. Truth to tell, you were beginning to bore me. I must admit, I never thought I could actually use your confession until my dear husband informed me you had won the Copley. Imagine my delight."

He followed her. She led him into one of the upstairs chambers, closed the door behind them and turned the key in the lock. Without a word, she took hold of his neckcloth and gave it a sudden yank, undoing Susannah's careful work. She wrapped her arms around him, holding him so close that he could feel the shanks of his own buttons pressing into his chest. He breathed her cloying scent until he wanted to retch.

"Cat got your tongue?" she asked, rubbing herself against him like a baboon in heat he had once observed in a private zoo near Cape Town.

"Don't do this," he pleaded. "Don't. You could barely remember my name on that crossing. What use is this?"

She shrugged again and released him. She went to the bed, raised her skirts and splayed herself before him, naked from the waist down, her knees far apart. She lay there, triumph in her eyes.

He stared at her, furious with himself as his organ began to grow firm, in spite of everything. He felt like a fly drawn into a spider's web, even as his hands went to his buttons.

He was about to climb onto the bed—Lady Audley's eyes were already closed and her mouth open in anticipation—when he stopped. His body was ready—he looked down at himself with disgust—but his mind was not. He rebuttoned himself, sat down on the bed, and gave Lady Audley a push until her knees came together. She opened her eyes in surprise.

"Tell them everything," he said quietly. "I can't do this. It wasn't right then and it isn't right now."

She sat up slowly. She was silent a moment as she put her knees together and rested her chin on them. The look she finally gave him was surprisingly philosophical, but he knew better than to relax. After his moment of wisdom on board the merchant ship, watching her seduce the unfortunate purser, he knew her too well.

"I needn't say anything," she said, pressing her foot gently into his side. "I've already ruined you." She got up, straightened her dress, then went to the mirror to make sure she hadn't disarranged her hair. "You just have to retie that neckcloth and go back downstairs. Amazing how my perfume clings to everything, isn't it?"

His sharp intake of breath told her everything. She turned around, grinning. "Mrs. Park will not speak to you again. You were a fool to follow me here."

She went to the door. "Funny, isn't it? I had planned to denounce you in the drawing room as a murderer and more, and ruin your life." She laughed. "When I saw how Mrs. Park looked at you, I changed my mind. I didn't really expect you to perform for me here. But you're still ruined."

He found his voice, but it wasn't the voice he wanted. "You don't know anything about her," he managed.

"How naive you are! You can't even tell when someone is in love with you." She opened the door, eyeing him with amusement. "She won't say anything to you, because she is a lady. She has no strength of will. She will simply cut you dead." She made a sad face at him. "Poor James. Go back to sea."

She left him alone. James took a deep breath, and another, until he felt light-headed. He leaned against the bedpost until his breathing returned to normal. When his hands stopped shaking, he carried the lamp to the mantelpiece to give himself light enough to retie his neckcloth.

He realized two things, to his deep dismay: It is impossible to retie a neckcloth without looking at one's face, and he didn't care to do that, so disgusted was he with himself. Even worse, he had not the slightest hope of tying his neckcloth to resemble what Susannah had done so competently.

He reeked of Lady Audley's cologne. If, by some divine bit of amnesia, Susannah managed to overlook the inexpert retying of his neckcloth, she would never mistake the odor of Lady Audley all over his clothing. He was well and truly ruined, even more than if he had actually rodgered that foul woman for old times' sake.

He rested his forehead against the mantelpiece, shivering in a room that wasn't cold. He finally looked in the mirror and saw a desperate man staring back at him. And there in the corner of the room, blending into the shadows, was the carpenter's mate.

"I knew you would be there," James said conversationally as he retied his neckcloth in the only style he knew. "I suppose you're enjoying this, too, damn your dead eyes, Timothy. Who knew I would be such a source of entertainment to the living *and* the dead?"

The ghoul said nothing. He wasn't gnawing on an arm this time, but staring at him as if poised to pounce. James turned around, his blood running in chunks. Vixen strolled out of the shadows, waving his great plume of a tail. He jumped on the bed, turned around once, then ignored him.

It was all James could do to force himself back into the drawing room. He couldn't bring himself to look at Susannah, but he didn't have to. Lord Batchley led him to a circle of acquaintances eager to meet Beau Crusoe.

"How did you find Vixen, my dear Beau?" Lord Batchley asked.

At least he could give an honest report. "He ignored me completely," James replied. And so will Susannah, he thought. So will Susannah.

Susannah stared with unseeing eyes at the cards in her hand and heard not a word that her partner was saying, even though his mouth was moving. Put down a card, she thought. Do something.

It hardly mattered. The other two players, an antiquated earl and his equally aged countess, exiled by Lord Batchley to the whist table, were bickering again, each speaking louder and louder to counteract the other's deafness. Lord Audley, her partner, had quit talking now, alternately staring at his cards and at his wife, who had reentered the drawing room by herself.

Susannah glanced at her, then looked away, disquieted by the triumph on the woman's face. Susannah looked at the door again, wondering where James was, then felt her own face grow red as Lady Audley observed her.

She set down all her cards and forced herself to smile at Lord

Audley. "I do not believe there is much point in our continuing this," she told him. "It appears that our partners prefer to argue."

He put down his cards, too, his gaze straying first to his wife, then back to Susannah. He managed a wistful smile. "The game is highly overrated, anyway."

She dug a little deeper, something she was unused to doing. "Lord Audley, it appears that Mr. Trevenen is acquainted with your wife."

He looked at her then, and she saw humiliation on his face. "I believe she met him in the East Indies, when returning from Macao."

"Were you not there, my lord?" It almost seemed heartless to prod, but she had to know.

"I had remained behind in Macao. Business. She wanted to return to England." He glanced across the room. "She has a wide circle of acquaintances," he mumbled.

He didn't need to say any more. Susannah, you are an idiot, she told herself. It was not a comforting observation.

Lord Audley stood up. Their whist partners were quiet now, glaring at each other, but he paid them no mind as he sketched a slight bow to her. "Mrs. Park, do excuse me," he said. "I think I will take my wife home now. She is…well, she is ready to go."

He crossed the room to stand hesitantly beside his wife until she bothered to notice him. Perhaps there are worse things than being a widow, Susannah thought. After all, I could be married.

It was an unpleasant reflection, made not one iota sweeter when she glanced at the door and saw James standing there. He looked more serious than she had ever seen him, but she smiled anyway, or tried to. He nodded to her, then glanced away, as though wishing she had not come.

Before she could decide whether to join him or sink beneath the floorboards, Lord Batchley, all pomp and presence, met James at the door and dragged him into another group. Soon there was laughter and backslapping. Susannah sat where she was, her hands in her lap, wishing herself at Alderson House.

Lord and Lady Audley were among the first to depart; Susannah made a point of not watching them leave. Others followed, and still James—oh, he was Mr. Trevenen again to her—chatted with a small group far away. Several of them were men she recognized from visits to Sir Joseph Banks' estate, so she assumed they were fellows of the Royal Society. Perhaps they were giving Mr. Trevenen tips on the upcoming ceremony, which she knew now could not come a moment too soon for her.

She and Mr. Trevenen were nearly the last to leave. He probably would have remained the night, she thought, if she had not finally stood up, whispered her thanks to Lord Batchley and gone to the door by herself. She could bear the room no longer. Waiting in the carriage would be preferable to sitting by herself.

She glanced back at the nearly empty room. To her dismay, Mr. Trevenen looked at her and appeared to be squaring his shoulders, as if preparing for an ordeal. She wondered what had happened in the course of one evening to render her so distasteful.

Then she knew. As he moved across the room, her eyes went to his neckcloth. The knot wasn't the one she had so carefully arranged earlier that evening. This one was much simpler, the sort of repair work a man would do who was in a hurry.

As he approached, she sniffed the air and glanced around, wondering if Lady Audley had returned. She turned back, eyeing Mr. Trevenen, who refused to meet her gaze.

That was it. Mr. Trevenen reeked of Lady Audley's perfume. It should have given her at least some comfort to realize that he must have been avoiding her out of embarrassment, rather than any shortcoming on her part. I can be philosophical about this, she thought, as she nodded to him. After all, he has no idea I was even for the tiniest moment considering him as a possible successor to my late husband. And by the way, Susannah, she told herself ruthlessly, perhaps you had better continue to measure all men against that fine one.

The journey back to Richmond was so long she would have thought they were traveling from London to the Dover coast. In all that way, she could think of nothing to say to Mr. Trevenen that would not cause her to burst into tears. After they left the city proper, he ventured some remark about the weather. She murmured some reply that left her mind as soon as it left her mouth.

Chumley met them at the door, which caused her some embarrassment because of the lateness of the hour. She hadn't expected him to wait up.

"Mr. Trevenen, I have left some food in your room, in case you are hungry before morning," the butler said.

Mr. Trevenen shrugged. "Thank you, Chumley. It doesn't really seem to make any difference, though."

"Good night, Chumley," she said.

She had hoped Mr. Trevenen would give her some time to go upstairs before coming up himself, but he did not. He was quiet, though. She wouldn't have known he was there, except for the odor of Lady Audley's perfume. She heard him open his door and she glanced back, almost against her will. He was watching her.

"It wasn't what you think," he said, the words quietly spoken.

"That is probably true of everything you have said thus far in London," she told him, unable to keep the hurt from her voice.

He said nothing in his defense. He went into his room but did not close the door. She went into hers and shut the door behind her. Out of habit, she went to Noah's room to check on him, then remembered he was at Spring Grove. She kicked off her shoes and stepped out of her sister's borrowed gown, wishing that Loisa was across the corridor so she could sob her disappointment into a sympathetic ear.

Disappointment about what, pray tell? she asked herself. Mr. Trevenen is obviously not immune to the grossest sort of temptation, even though she could not fathom yielding to it in someone else's house. How long was he upstairs? Twenty minutes?

I'm not going to cry over this, she thought as she undressed for bed. She extinguished her bedside lamp, enjoying that moment when all went dark and she could let her mind travel wherever she chose. Darkness had always been her friend.

Not this night. She lay on her back, thinking about the time she had lost in the last few days enlarging the *Gloriosa*, when she could have kept on with the watercolors that earned her a shilling apiece from the Royal Society.

She closed her eyes, ready to let the dreadful evening wash away like the tide. In the morning, she would insist he find a hotel.

She opened her eyes a few hours later, startled by a sound. She listened, tugging the coverlet higher and drowsily telling herself to retrieve another blanket from the linen closet in the morning.

There it was again. She sat up, pulling her knees close to her chest and hugging them as cold fingers seemed to skitter up and down her spine.

Someone was talking, but she couldn't make out the words. She froze for a moment, wondering if she had locked her door after closing it so decisively on Mr. Trevenen. It was no consolation to remember that she hadn't a clue where any of the keys were to the upstairs chambers.

She listened harder. It had to be Mr. Trevenen. She sat as still as she could, afraid to move. Then the voice stopped, and someone seemed to be breathing close by.

She looked around her room, but saw no one. She held her own breath, trying to locate the sound.

It was someone breathing much faster than she was, the way people gasp when they have been running hard, or living in a place so frightening that every inhalation seemed drawn out, as though it might be the last. She had lived in such a place during the horrible week when cholera killed David and half of the employees in the East India merchants' compound in Bombay.

The voice began again, sounding almost reasonable at first, and then firmer, then commanding in that way she imagined officers of the Royal Navy might speak to their inferiors.

She forced herself to get out of bed and creep across the room. The voice stopped as she reached her door, and the deep breathing began again. She stretched her hand toward the doorknob and then withdrew it, reminding herself of the disgraceful way he had reeked of Lady Audley's foul cologne and had tried to retie his neckcloth after doing heaven-knew-what with her. Mr. Trevenen, you are on your own, she thought, as she returned to bed. If I have to stuff a pillow over my ears tonight, I will.

She could not. She sat on her bed, hands balled into fists at her side, as she listened to Mr. Trevenen. She remembered he had left his door open.

Any minute now, he would probably wake up her parents, who would summon the servants and cause a row. She thought how he had rested his head against her lap in the exotic blooms house, and how he had tried to protect her from nothing she could see during an earlier night.

I can at least close his door, she thought, as she got up again. They won't hear anything then, and perhaps I can wake him up and sit with him until he is sleeping again.

It won't change anything, though. Mr. Trevenen, you are leaving tomorrow morning. We will forget about the balloon ascension you promised Noah and I will make it up to him somehow.

She tiptoed to the door again and opened it a crack. She could see his open door across the corridor. She stood there a moment more, unsure of herself, then opened her door wider and stepped into the corridor.

She gasped and leaped back. Mr. Trevenen sat cross-legged in front of her door, blocking the way.

Chapter Twenty-Two

❦

She stood there, paralyzed.

"Sit down, and the boat will not rock so badly. He will not reach you. Do as I say. We will hear him when he tries to cross the oars."

It was an easy matter to sink down behind him, mainly because she had suddenly discovered that her legs would no longer hold her upright.

"Are you there?"

"Yes, I am," she whispered.

"And you, Timothy, damn you." He stared ahead, as though trying to see through the gloom. "You won't catch me asleep. Not with Mrs. Park here. I will never sleep."

"You poor man," she whispered, forgetting her disgust at his boorish conduct.

She hesitated, then leaned against Mr. Trevenen's back. His heart hammered so hard in his chest she thought it would shake out of his body. She put her arms around his waist, locking them across his stomach. He slowly began to relax.

When she thought he was calm, she shifted to speak into his ear. "I do not wish to startle you, Mr. Trevenen, but I believe you are quite safe."

She hiked up her nightgown, opened her legs and let him lean back against her, her legs on either side of him. With a sigh, he rested one arm on her upraised knee.

There he was, right in her lap. She kissed his head, not caring if he was awake or asleep, then rested her own hand on his chest. To her gratification, his rapid heartbeat began to slow.

Soon it was steady, peaceful.

She couldn't see his face, but she thought he slept. How long do we sit like this? she asked herself. He was not uncomfortable, but he was heavy.

She moved her legs and he paid no mind. She wiggled out from behind him and took him by the arm. He got up obediently, which did surprise her.

She thought about leading him back to his own room, then remembered the open window and the chair turned around. "No, Mr. Trevenen, you need a good night's sleep," she said. "So do I. The important thing will be to get you back to your own room before the 'tween stairs maid shows up."

He seemed to wake up when she climbed into bed and held the cover up for him. He looked around, surprised, then climbed in after her. She wasn't sure he was conscious as he sank back against the pillow.

"It is a comfortable bed, Mr. Trevenen," she murmured. "That is your half; this is mine."

"Suzie," he said, his voice thick. His eyes closed.

"Good night, Mr. Trevenen," she whispered. "Keep your hands to yourself." She rolled over onto her side, more ready to sleep than she would have thought possible, since she was sharing her bed with a man who was either three parts lunatic or just confused. The Society should give *me* that medal, she thought, as she closed her eyes.

She woke up once more closer to morning, because Mr. Trevenen was kneading her breast, his fingers massaging her nipple and then just cupping her breast, his hand slack again.

As Susannah lay there, she felt not so much the protector. She knew how capable he was. Surely something could be done about his terrible dreams. There wasn't anyone else she wanted in her life, not ever again.

She snuggled deeper into her pillow, resolving to wake up and shoo him out before the maid arrived with hot water, but it wasn't necessary. He was gone when she woke. After the maid came and left, Susannah looked to see the door across the corridor, shut tight. She shook her head, not willing to admit how little she knew about Mr. Trevenen.

She woke up again when the sun was high, extraordinarily late for her. She dressed quickly, tying her hair in a quick knot at the back of her neck.

She thought he would be in his room, so she knocked on the door. When no one answered, she peered in. To her dismay, she saw his luggage in the center of the room, as though he had resolved to leave.

She returned to her room and noticed the folded note tacked to her door. "Please, don't tell me you have left," she murmured, "especially now, when I have an inkling what is troubling you."

He wasn't one to waste words, but she knew that from his treatise. "I have gone for a walk. Thank you for last night. I slept well. I'll be leaving. J."

"That's what you think, Mr. Trevenen," she said. She folded the note into small pieces and chucked it into her fireplace. No sense in anyone reading that.

She hoped he might be at Spring Grove, but he was not.

The house was quiet. She peeked in on Noah, reading a book by the fireplace, Neptune as his footstool, but felt disinclined to disturb him. The butler told her that Sir Joseph was in his bookroom and she could have swooned with relief. She hurried down the corridor.

"Come in, my dear. I've been expecting you."

She opened the door. Sir Joseph sat in his wheeled chair, close to the fire, both gouty legs propped on a hassock, but not covered with a wire basket. He nodded to Barmley, who bowed and left the room. She pulled up a stool beside him.

"I'm feeling better," he said.

"I can tell," she replied. She stopped, not sure how to begin, or where.

"He is not a lunatic," he said.

She stared at him, her eyes wide. "I have not told you a thing."

"No, you haven't," Sir Joseph agreed. "Neither has the redoubtable Mr. Trevenen. But Mr. Higgins, who has enough moral fiber for all of us, felt guilty for telling you a real stretcher yesterday."

She jumped to her feet. "I knew he was lying!"

Sir Joseph shrugged and she sat down. "He didn't think it proper to talk about Lady Audley with you. He…"

"That harpy!" she burst out.

He held up his hand. "Susannah, I have not seen you so exercised about *anything* in years!" His expression softened. "I like it. You've been half asleep for seven years, my dearest. Time you woke up, even if he is a cad."

She blushed, but thought it wise not to interrupt again.

"What does Mr. Higgins tell me—Loisa, the mother lioness, had left him alone for a few minutes—but that Mr. Trevenen had fierce nightmares so terrifying that he started to scare the missionaries!"

"Godpapa, he is in the grip of some great terror, and it is going to destroy him."

"I feared as much."

She collected her thoughts, wondering how much to tell her godfather about last night. "I think it had little to do with his island, onerous as that was," she said finally. "I want to know what happened to him after his ship sank."

"So do I," Sir Joseph said.

"He won't say anything." She hesitated, then poured out the events of the last few nights, leaving nothing out. "Think what you will of me, my dear," she said when she finished. "I could not ignore that man's desperation, and knew no other way to give him even a little comfort."

"I will never speak of it," he replied. "You're a sensible woman. Far more sensible than your totty-headed parents." He smiled then. "Who—if I can believe the servants who carry tales from your house to mine—seem to have found some fountain of youth."

"I wish I knew what has happened there!" She laughed and looked away, embarrassed. "I can't help but think Beau Crusoe has

meddled somehow. Everything has been different since he arrived."
She sobered. "What do I do? I don't know where to turn."

"I do," Sir Joseph replied. "We can learn exactly what we want to know."

"When he will not talk?"

"If he was the officer I think he was, he already has, my dear."

She looked at him, startled.

"Remember in his treatise where he wrote that his captain— God rest his soul—threw the ship's log into the small boat?"

"Well, yes. He used the log to write his observations of the *Gloriosa*," she snapped.

He clucked his tongue. "Calm yourself, Susannah! One would think you loved the man, and we know that is not the case. He's a cad."

"Of course he is," she muttered, not willing to look at Sir Joseph.

"I wager he kept a careful record of the proceedings in that small boat."

She stared at him. "Why would he do that?"

"Naval law, my dear, and the custom of the sea," Sir Joseph replied. "In theory, no one commands a lifeboat. In practice, however, he was the ranking officer, and his first duty was to maintain the ship's log." He leaned forward, his expression so loving and troubled at the same time that she felt a catch in her throat. "He had to surrender the ship's log to the Lords of the Admiralty."

She leaped up again, and he made no motion to calm her this time. "How can we read the log?"

He glanced at his desk. "I came in here this morning to write a letter to Sir Richard Bickerton, my old friend." His eyes grew distant. "Would you be surprised to know he was a midshipman on that voyage I took with Captain Cook? There are seven Lords of the Admiralty, and Bickerton is Naval Lord now."

"Nothing would surprise me."

His look was tender then, the look of a parent afraid for his child. "I fear much will surprise you, when you read that log."

"Will Sir Richard let me have it?"

He shook his head. "Not to take. But this note should allow you to read it in Admiralty House."

The butterflies in her stomach seemed to gather into a ball and sink. "You know me, sir. I'm not one to argue, if he decides to ignore your letter."

"He'd better not!" Sir Joseph declared. "I have thought of that, Susannah. As much as I admire you, we cannot pretend you are the bravest soul in company."

"No, we cannot," she agreed.

His face grew serious. "I tremble to think what you will find. I fear I know what it is, because I know something of the sea."

She regarded him in silence, then rose and rested her cheek against his for a moment. "It cannot be worse than watching my husband die, and seeing him thrown onto a funeral pyre."

He flinched at her quiet words. "It might be close, my dear."

She went to his desk and picked up the letter with *Sir Richard Bickerton* scrawled across it. "I wish I were not such a goose."

"I've made arrangements that should see this expedition to Admiralty House arrive at a successful conclusion," he told her.

"You're giving me a frothing hound?" she asked, feeling utterly inadequate.

"Even better," he told her with a smile. "Loisa is going with you."

The frothing hound was more than happy to lend a hand. "I am not as compassionate as you, Susannah," Loisa told her as they started their expedition to Admiralty House in a hackney. "I am a little weary of the sickroom, and frankly, there is nothing wrong with Sam."

"Sam?" Susannah asked.

Loisa didn't even blink. "Yes. He's an excellent fellow with a conscience, as opposed to your Mr. Trevenen."

"He's not my Mr. Trevenen," Susannah said quietly. She looked down at the letter in her lap. "Loie, he's just a rake with bad dreams."

"Why should he concern you, then?"

It was an honest question Susannah chose not to answer. She

looked at her sister with a smile. "So Mr. Hig…Sam is not an advocate of fibs."

"Not really, although I do believe he told you one, regarding Mr. Trevenen."

Susannah nodded. "I think I know why. It probably has to do with some disgraceful amorous activity with Lady Audley."

"Poor little sister," Loisa said, and kissed Susannah's cheek. "He didn't tell me those details, but he did tell me Mr. Trevenen told him to act much sicker than he was, and to keep me occupied for the duration of Mr. Trevenen's stay here."

"It's true, Loie," she said, as the hackney bowled along toward the city. "We can partially blame Sir Joseph, I fear."

"Sir Joseph?"

"Apparently Sir Joe told Mr. Trevenen to do three things: get rid of the toucans and find some way to occupy your time."

Loisa smiled. "Mr. Trevenen already told me. I am no ma-thematician, but I believe that is only two. Confess, Susannah."

Susannah blushed. "Mr. Trevenen told me Sir Joseph expected him to marry me."

Loisa burst into laughter. "He told me that, too. *Why* does Sir Joseph meddle so?"

"Because he loves us," Susannah replied, then started to laugh, as well. "Imagine what trouble we would endure if he disliked us!"

Loisa nodded. She started to speak, then looked away, as if words would draw out more emotion than she was used to showing.

Susannah regarded her sister. "You've changed, Loie. Are you in love?"

Again no words, but another nod.

"Both of you?"

Another nod.

"Well, then, what do you propose to do about it?"

"What can we do?" Loisa burst out.

"You know I am the wrong person to ask. You can do what David and I did. I've already ruined the family, Loie, so what's your fear? Papa has no sense and is ruining the estate by neglecting it for his precious birds. And Mama? She alone will suffer if doors close again."

"I could not," Loisa said finally.

"You could, Loie," she replied. "You're the one in the family with backbone, not I."

"And yet, you left everything behind for love."

"I did, didn't I?" Susannah agreed. "Do I wish things had turned out differently? Of course."

They were both silent as Admiralty House came into view. "What do you know about what happened?" Loisa asked her as they neared the building.

"Very little. I think there is a specter named Timothy he sees in his dreams. Sometimes…sometimes James looks over my shoulder, or peers into a room then clenches his teeth." She shook her head. "Loie, he sees Timothy everywhere."

Loisa shuddered. "That's what Sam fears."

"Perhaps the log will tell us who Timothy is."

"We *will* have that ship's log," Loisa declared, and tapped her reticule. "If all my arguments do not succeed with Sir Richard Bickerton, I have a secret weapon."

"Don't tell me."

"I won't," Loie said as the hackney stopped in front of Admiralty House.

Susannah paid the jehu, and then when he drove off, wished she could summon him back. If there was a more intimidating place in London, she didn't know of it: four massive pillars, with powerful men in gold leaf and fore and aft hats coming and going through the great doors.

It was no better inside. With her artist's eye, she instinctively knew that marble floors in a black-and-white pattern exist only to make petitioners and lowly ensigns feel even more puny than usual. She wanted to grab Loie by the arm and run, but one glance at her sister told her that would never happen.

Loie walked with her head high, ignoring all curious glances. None of the men in the hall spoke to either of them. The two women were as out of place in Admiralty House as visitors from the moon.

"Where are we going?" Loie whispered.

"Sir Joe told me to stop at the high table at the end," Susannah whispered back. "We are to state our wishes and get in line."

"Mention your godfather's name," Loie replied. "Don't forget that."

The man at the table, a glorified porter, peered down at them from a lofty height. "Yes?" he asked in a tone so forbidding the earth seemed to shift on its axis.

Susannah cleared her throat. The room was suddenly silent. She hoped none of the officers present could hear her knees banging together. Oh, God, she thought, the lengths I go to for ill-advised men. "We bring a message from Sir Joseph Banks of the Royal Society and wish an audience with Sir Richard Bickerton."

The porter held out his hand for the letter. Susannah backed away. "It is for his eyes only."

He narrowed his eyes, then waved a hand at the long line before them. "Everyone thinks their petition is important," he challenged.

Susannah swallowed. "I am the widow of Mr. David Park, and I am the daughter of Clarence Alderson, Viscount Watchmere," she told him.

She could tell her words had some effect, but not as much as she had hoped.

"I can tell Sir Richard, but I doubt he will see you." He leaned down from his high perch. "This is a serious place, madam. We are at war, in case you hadn't heard over tea and biscuits."

Some of the officers in the line chuckled. Others shifted their feet in what Susannah hoped was embarrassment, because she felt a fierce need for allies.

She had one in her sister. Loisa stepped forward. She had taken the secret weapon from her reticule. "Sir Joseph anticipated this sort of nonsense," she said, her voice firm and crisp. "If you ignore us, I am to take this letter directly to King George, Sir Joseph's friend." She stepped closer. "If I must do that, you will probably find yourself on a fever boat, bound for a leper colony."

Bravo, Loie, Susannah thought. The porter glared back, but

he knew defeat when he saw it. Mustering all the dignity he could, he climbed down from his elevation and went through the door behind him.

Susannah looked around. "You are a tiger," she whispered. "Let us move to the end of the line. At least we were not tossed out on our rumps."

Loisa took her arm. To Susannah's surprise, she was trembling. "I would not do that on a daily basis," she whispered.

"I thought you were marvelous," Susannah whispered back as she led Loisa to the end of the line where, to her surprise, someone had scrounged up two stools. Her eyes filled with tears. It was a long line of navy men; some leaned on canes, one was even bereft of a leg, and yet one of them had found two stools. She wanted to take the seats to one of the men who obviously struggled, but she knew the sailors wanted her and Loisa to sit. Apparently all navy men are not rascals, she thought, as she nodded to them, curtsied and sat down.

They didn't sit long. The porter returned in less than five minutes, and with him was a man wearing the higher epaulets and gold leaf of a lord of the Admiralty.

She looked around her. The long line had suddenly become much straighter and more orderly. This must be Sir Richard Bickerton himself, she thought, as she stood up, too, Loisa right behind her.

Sir Richard nodded to the porter, who returned to his station, looking more like a mortal this time.

Susannah came forward, pausing for a deep curtsy. "Sir Richard?" she asked.

"The same. Mrs. Park?"

"Yes, sir, and this is my sister, Loisa Alderson."

He nodded to them both, then motioned with his hand. "Follow me."

His office was a curious combination of elegance and utility, with the same intimidating black-and-white marble floor, but also a battered and well-used desk, with plain wooden chairs in front of it, which he indicated.

Before sitting, Susannah handed him the letter from Sir Joseph. The naval lord read it through once, turning the page, then read it again before he looked up and set the missive on his desk.

"I cannot allow this, even if it does come from Sir Joseph Banks," he said finally. "If James Trevenen is of diseased mind, let him report himself to the naval hospital at Greenwich."

"He would never do that. You know he would not," Susannah said quickly, not giving herself time to be more afraid than she already was. "He suffers, Sir Richard, and we do not know why. The information in the log is for his benefit."

He shook his head. "I cannot. A ship's log is classified information."

"The ship *sank*," Susannah reminded him. "All are dead except one, and trust me, he is not speaking. We can be discreet."

Not meeting her eyes, Sir Richard shook his head.

Susannah fought back tears. I will not cry in front of this man, she told herself.

She didn't have to. Loisa stood up slowly, which compelled the naval lord to rise, too. Never taking her eyes from his face, she set her lips tight and pulled the secret weapon from her reticule.

"Sir Joseph Banks feared as much. He told me if you did not honor his wish, my sister and I were to go directly to the king." She held out a letter to Sir Richard, who took it. "You are welcome to read it, if you wish, but I do not think you will like what Sir Joseph has to say of naval lords who do not honor a small request from one who has done so much for his nation, along with Captain James Cook, in the service of science."

Susannah scarcely breathed as Loisa seated herself again, leaving Sir Richard to stare at the envelope with Georgius Rex III written on it. He turned it over in his hands. As she watched his uncertainty, Susannah allowed herself to breathe again.

After a long moment, he handed the letter back to Loisa, then looked at her. "Mrs. Park, I fear the log will shock you."

"We will bear it," she told him, wishing her voice was as firm as Loisa's had been only a moment ago.

"Very well." He reached for a bellpull. "The porter will escort you downstairs." His eyes were steely again. "You will have precisely one hour and no more, and I will hear of no objections, Mrs. Park."

"No…no, sir," she stammered.

He nodded to them both and sat down again. They were dismissed. Loisa took her arm and tugged her toward the door. They were almost there when Sir Richard addressed her again.

"Mrs. Park."

She turned around.

"We mariners are not a bad lot, but we are engaged in a hard service. Bear that in mind when you read."

"I will, Sir Richard," she replied, then smiled at him. "I thank you."

"You won't in a few minutes." He singled out Loisa this time. "Miss Alderson?"

"Yes, Sir Richard?"

"'A fever ship to a leper colony?' My porter was almost afraid to return to his post! Pity the navy will never be able to use you on a quarterdeck."

That was all. He returned his attention to the paperwork before him.

As they waited in the hall for the porter, Loisa suddenly leaned against the wall, as though her legs would not hold her. Alarmed, Susannah tightened her grip on her sister.

"Loisa?"

Loisa couldn't speak. She closed her eyes.

"You were marvelous," Susannah told her. "Who would have thought Sir Joe would have involved our king! I thought they had a falling out a few years ago. Perhaps I was mistaken."

"You were not."

Loisa found her voice, but only barely. With fingers that trembled, she handed Susannah the letter.

She opened it, eager to read what Sir Joseph would have said to his sovereign. Her mouth dropped open in surprise and she leaned against the wall, too. The pages were blank.

"Loie, what did you do?"

"Sir Joe's handwriting isn't so difficult to imitate. I took a chance for you."

Susannah touched her sister's face. "Loie," was all she could say, but it said the world.

Loisa took Susannah by the arm, her fingers steady again, and spoke in her ear. "Make this hour count, dearest."

Chapter Twenty-Three

Staying as far away from Loisa as possible, the porter took them to a low-ceilinged room somewhere in the bowels of the building. He was succeeded by a small man with a wooden leg.

The small man looked at the slip of paper the porter had handed him. "I wondered if someone would ever come for this'un," he said, more to himself than to them.

"Why?" Susannah asked.

"I've read them all, and this is one of the most…interesting. Never thought it would be ladies, though. Do be seated." He indicated a table with two chairs and left them.

"What do you think happened on that boat?" Loisa asked her as they waited.

"I'm pretty sure someone was trying to kill Mr. Trevenen," Susannah replied. "Mr. Trevenen is alive, so…"

"…so he is a murderer," Loisa finished.

"A man is dead, to be sure, but was Mr. Trevenen defending his own life?" She looked around the room. "There is more to it, though, something Mr. Trevenen can almost ignore when he is awake, but not when he sleeps. Or tries to." She leaned closer to her sister. "Loie, tell no one, but I let him into my bed last night."

"Good for you," Loisa said.

"Not like that! It was rather more like comforting a small boy in the grip of a nightmare."

"That is a disappointment," her sister said dryly. It was her turn to look away. "Do you ever have the feeling that life is passing you by? I do."

Susannah covered her sister's hand with her own. "The fault for your disappointment is mine."

"No, it isn't," Loisa said. "It is true that I preferred to blame you, but I know my deficiencies. I owe Beau Crusoe that. His plain speaking only voiced what I knew for myself."

Susannah tightened her grip on her sister's hand. "Now there is Sam?" she asked.

"I believe there is, and I owe the Beau that, as well." She sighed. "It remains to be seen what will come of such ill-advised fondness."

Susannah felt tears gather in her eyes. "I have so many regrets where you are concerned that I—"

Loisa put up a finger to stop her words. "Let us move forward and call ourselves wiser."

It was a magnanimous gesture. Susannah brought Loisa's hand to her lips and kissed it, unable to say anything.

The archivist returned with a tarred bag and an hourglass, which he upended, leaving them in solitude. Susannah grabbed the bag and opened it, wincing against the smell of tar. Loisa pulled the lamp closer. She took a pencil and paper from her reticule. "I will write what you dictate, if there is anything you wish me to record."

Susannah nodded as she turned to the back of the log. "In his treatise, James says he washed ashore on September 4, 1803. Write that, Loisa." She stared at the drawings of crabs in the back of the book, and the way Mr. Trevenen had written in one direction, and then overlaid his text with another, to save space. "He said he transcribed his treatise after leaving Cape Town, while on board the *Reconciliation*."

"Skip it then," Loisa commanded, eyes on the hourglass.

Susannah turned the stiff pages rapidly, finally flipping to the center of the log and scanning the dates and unfamiliar handwriting. "This must be his captain's hand," she murmured. "So ordinary. Watches, sickness, food supplies, the quarter of the wind." She turned faster and then stopped. "Here it is, Loisa." Her voice trembled as she recognized Mr. Trevenen's careful handwriting. "The date is August 9, 1803."

Nearly a month in a small boat, adrift in an empty sea. She read the entry to herself.

> *Orion* sunk. There are coral reefs in this latitude. Damn the first mate. Here we are. James Lawrence Trevenen, age 21, third mate. John Weston, ABS. Bill Bright, ABS. Walter Shepherd, ABS. Timothy Rowe, carpenter's mate. I alone am fully dressed. I was coming up to relieve the first mate when we struck the reef. Split open like a melon. No food in this boat beyond what each of us has in our pockets. This is my first command. God save the king.

Loisa was reading over her shoulder. "Turn the page," she ordered, after writing down the men's names.

Together they scanned each entry, each one with fewer words than the one before. "Loisa, imagine the responsibility," she whispered.

Two weeks into the journal, delirious with thirst, John Weston slipped over the side of the boat after telling Lt. Trevenen he was swimming for help to Portsmouth harbor. No one had the strength to row after him.

Susannah read on, her heart breaking at the awkwardness of James's deteriorating handwriting. She stopped on an entry two days after the foretopman's suicide. "I don't understand," she whispered, and then read out loud. "'Custom of the sea. Bright is next; he is resigned. Can we do this?'"

Then she understood everything. "God," she said, and leaned against Loisa. "I don't want to turn the page."

She knew Loisa hadn't figured it out yet. But then, Loisa had never left England. She had never been on the ocean, so wide and so empty. Susannah remembered the long voyage to India, so taken with her new husband, oblivious to everything else except one thing, something casual once overheard that she had put out of her mind until this moment.

She had come on deck one afternoon by herself and perched on one of the hatches, happy to breathe the cleaner air above deck, especially since the sails were full of wind.

A group of seamen had gathered near the mainmast, squatting on the deck, splicing rope and picking at the endless oakum. They had no idea how well their voices carried in the sea air. She hadn't paid them any mind at first, too preoccupied with her future in India and what she thought was a baby on the way, if the calendar was a reliable indicator.

One of the sailors raised his voice. "And they ate him raw."

She knew better than to stare at the men, but she had been fully alive to their conversation. There had been laughter and jokes about what tasted best, the back of the calf or the fleshy parts of the hip. Another swore he had heard raw was better, because thirst was the biggest demon. Still another insisted that man meat cut into strips and dried lasted longer. Someone else snickered and said the natives of Otaheite called it long pig.

Then someone had glanced in her direction. She noticed him out of the corner of her eye, but continued to act as though she had not heard a word. The sailors returned to their duties, leaving her to digest what she had heard, which she never repeated. Had rarely recalled, until now.

"They have decided to eat Billy Bright. That is the custom of the sea."

Loisa gasped. Susannah took a deep breath and turned the page. "'Bright dead. Tim cut him into strips. I threw head overboard. Tim protested. Cannot bear to look at Bright's face. God help me. Ate his leg raw.'"

Lois turned away, holding her hands over her mouth and leaning forward.

"I must continue," Susannah said in a voice foreign to her own ears. Loisa nodded, but didn't turn around.

She read each spare entry, then stopped at one more horrible than the others, because it helped her understand more fully Mr. Trevenen's night terrors. Timothy Rowe, the carpenter's mate, seemed to have developed a fondness for human flesh. After the first few meals on Bright as their boat drifted on the great currents of the South Pacific, Mr. Trevenen and Walter Shepherd had eaten no more of their former comrade. Nothing had stopped Tim until he finished Billy Bright. Then he began to eye the other two living skeletons.

Loisa, more pale than Susannah had ever seen her, was reading along again now, neither of them speaking, until Loisa murmured, "It cannot get worse, Susannah."

It did. Susannah, in her numbness, thought of Sir Joseph's admonition that morning and Sir Richard's supreme reluctance to allow them access to the log.

With James's handwriting harder and harder to read, Susannah had been following each entry with her finger on the page. She lifted her finger at the next entry, unable even to touch the log again, beyond turning its pages.

When Lt. Trevenen regained consciousness one morning—he wasn't even calling it sleep—Tim was devouring Walter Shepherd, who wasn't quite dead.

"Dear God." Susannah breathed. "Poor man."

She wanted to drop the log and run back to Alderson House, with its totty-headed residents and shabby surroundings. She wanted to be anywhere else, until she reminded herself that with every breath he took, James Trevenen lived with this.

Loisa had left the room and was retching in the corridor. Susannah longed to follow her, but the bottom of the hourglass was rapidly filling. Your ghoul took a liking to human flesh, she thought. I suppose he was growing stronger, and you were getting weaker, my dear man.

There were no more daily entries, except a date and one or two words, enough for Susannah to piece together the story. The two remaining men were seated at opposite ends of the boat, Tim with rotting flesh and bones around him, and James with the oars crossed in front of him and a pistol.

The sand was gone from the glass. Loisa, pale, returned to the room. With a look of fierce defiance on her face, she turned the hourglass over and blocked the door when the archivist tried to enter. He went away, shaking his head and muttered something about "fetching the porter," and "lunatic females."

"Hurry, Susannah," she urged. "They will throw us out."

There wasn't much more to read. August 31st's entry was a question: "How long?" September 1st's entry was briefer: "Land." James had underlined it. She looked closer at the faint writing. There were two or three more words. It looked like "Maybe now," but then the pen dragged off the page, as though the boat had suddenly lurched.

Susannah took a deep breath and let it out slowly. Or perhaps Timothy Rowe, the deranged mate, had finally made his move across the oars, when he thought his lieutenant was busy with his duty of recording all events mundane and monstrous.

That was all. Susannah closed the log. She knew she could not stand up so she did not try, even though she heard footsteps. Loisa was on her feet, ready to do heaven knows what to bar the way, determined to protect her sister.

She also knew, in the second before the door burst open, that she loved James Trevenen: poor, brave genius of a man who owed his sanity to crabs in a peaceful lagoon. He had killed Timothy Rowe, either on the boat or on land. He had survived terrors that would have destroyed most people, taking comfort from studying the *Gloriosa Jubilate*. The very name he had given the little creatures with the large claw said something about the salvation they had provided. He was not insane. He was a survivor.

She stood up as the door opened. "It's all right, Loisa. I am done."

Then she fainted for the first time in her life.

Ammonia under the nose is a wicked thing. Susannah opened her eyes. She was lying on a couch with her head in Loisa's lap. Several men stood around, looking uncomfortable, as she imagined all men would in such a situation.

"I didn't mean to faint," she said.

An officer spoke, and the room cleared out almost by magic. She closed her eyes.

When she opened her eyes again, only Sir Richard Bickerton and Loisa remained in the room. After Loisa helped her sit up, she allowed her a sip of water.

Once the little sparkles of light went away, Susannah felt much better. "I'm sorry, Sir Richard," she said.

He had every right to be indignant, but his eyes were kind, even fatherly. "It's a terrible tale," he said simply. "I should have told it to you, rather than allowed you to read it."

She thought a moment. "He told you the whole thing, didn't he?"

"Of course. All the lords were here for the telling. I would have expected no less of him, and he knew it." He pulled up a chair and sat close to her. He even reached for her hand, then stopped. "Since you know so much, you should hear the rest, the part he did not write."

"Yes. I assume that he killed Timothy Rowe on the boat, or on the island."

"On the boat," Sir Richard began, and then he did take her hand. "Apparently Rowe tried to get at him across those folded oars at about the same time the boat broke up on a coral reef. Lt. Trevenen said there is a gap in the coral that can be seen easily enough."

"Did he kill him, or was he drowned in the wreck?"

Sir Richard patted her hand. "He shot him. We ruled it self-defense."

She saw something more in his eyes, something of doubt. "Truly?"

Sir Richard released her hand then and stood up, as though the chair was suddenly too small. "I must be candid. Even Trevenen isn't sure. At that moment, he was pitched into the water and struggling to stay afloat. I don't know the answer. I'm not certain he does, either, but we are willing to provide considerable latitude to his story. He would never lie."

On the contrary, Susannah thought, he lies all the time. She considered it, hoping he would never lie to the Lords of the Admiralty.

"We expect the truth from men we put to sea in positions of command." Sir Richard folded his hands behind his back. "We did not want to accept the resignation of his commission. The navy needs decisive, quick-acting leaders like Lt. Trevenen."

"He is a better scientist, Sir Richard," she said. "Please attend the ceremony next week when he receives the Copley medal."

"I will be there."

He was at her side as she rose, ready to put his hand under her elbow to sustain her. Susannah found that she could stand on her own, but she did not move away from the comfort of the naval lord. "I am certain you do not wish me to say anything of what I know."

He surprised her. "I leave the matter to you. Tell Sir Joseph Banks, of course." He put his arm around her shoulder and gave her a brief hug, which pleased her.

Sir Richard released her and bowed to Loisa, then administered the same affection. "You are a stern one, Miss Alderson! I repeat what I said about the navy's loss, in your case."

They curtsied and turned to leave, Loisa with a tight grip on Susannah. Sir Richard cleared his throat and they stopped.

"Mrs. Park, be his champion."

Chapter Twenty-Four

Through her tears, Susannah told Sir Joseph and Sam Higgins—both up and about—everything she had learned. When she finished, she picked up the sketch of the *Gloriosa* and propped it on the mantelpiece. Her hands folded in her lap, she regarded the creature in silence as the others occupied themselves with their own thoughts.

Australuca uca clarissii, she thought, not taking her eyes from the sketch. James, how bitter that your mother never knew you were alive and thinking of her. How you wanted to be her child and ended up at sea, instead. How good you are with my son. How desperately you wanted to protect me from that ghoul in your nightmare. How mortal you are, when faced with a whore like Lady Audley. Beau Crusoe, you are frail and flawed as all of us are. I love you with all my heart, though I fear you will be hard to hang on to.

She picked up the sketch as the others watched. "Sir Joseph, James and Noah have gone to a balloon ascension. When they return, I will be in the exotic blooms house. Send them there, please. Loisa, kindly find some excuse to keep Noah here for another night."

"Certainly, dearest," Loisa said. "What are you going to do?"

Susannah looked at her sister, pleased to note that she and Sam

Higgins were holding hands. Loie, you're braver than armies, she thought. Don't be afraid to do what I did.

"I have not the slightest idea," she admitted. "Whatever it is, I do think the smaller the audience, the better."

"What about our parents?" Loisa asked, ever practical.

Susannah felt her face grow warm. "It is the oddest thing. Sir Joseph, Mr. Higgins: do excuse my plain speaking, but our parents seem to have...well...rediscovered each other. He has not been near his bird blind for days now, and the servants tell me that Mama finds excuses to go to her room early each night. I think it has something to do with toucans."

With that, she left the room. "Mull that over," she murmured.

The afternoon had turned chilly. When she arrived at the exotic blooms house, she lit fires in both stoves. Her larger watercolor of the *Gloriosa* rested on the easel where she had left it.

She tied on her apron and prepared the watercolors in their orderly tins. "James, this is for you, even if I never see you again."

She couldn't think beyond that. The pain of never seeing Mr. Trevenen again, should he decide to leave immediately, was so strong it nauseated her even more than reading the ship's log. She wanted to live with him, have his children and tag along around the world, painting what he discovered. She brushed at her tears, then stirred them into the watercolor paint in her lap, blending them into the reds and blues.

She painted quickly, unable, this time, to lose herself in what she was doing. Every dab and stroke felt almost as though she painted her own skin. She hoped the love she felt for the man would come through.

She heard them less than an hour later, as she wiped the brushes clean. She saw them through the wavy glass, Noah running ahead. Mr. Trevenen walked slower, looking around as though he feared Timothy Rowe lurked nearby. Her heart went out to him.

How can I put the carpenter's mate into a grave where he will stay? she asked herself. Perhaps she never could.

"Mama, James and I decided against balloon ascensions. It's too high."

She pulled her son onto her lap, observing with a pang that he was starting to overflow it. "Wise of you," she whispered, but her eyes were on the man who followed him into the glass house.

James looked at her, then away, as though ashamed of what had happened last night. She feared for a moment he was going to leave. Don't, she thought. Please, don't.

"James, are these colors accurate?" she asked.

He took another look behind him, then came down the row of exotic blooms. He stood beside her and Noah, looking past her at the *Gloriosa*.

"Marvelous," he told her.

"But it is accurate?" she persisted.

"As near as can be, considering all things."

Noah stood there, leaning against James as he sometimes leaned against her. The gesture, so unconscious, made her smile. She touched her son's shoulder. "Noah, the head gardener told me that if you would fill that glass jar at the end of the row with dead leaves, he would pay you a farthing. You can save for a sketch book. It's oceans safer than ballooning."

Noah grinned and shot off down the row. When he was out of sight, swallowed up by exotic blooms, she turned her attention to James.

It was a repeat of last night; she wanted him. I hope this isn't a jolt to his equilibrium, she thought, as she stood up, pulled him toward her and kissed him. She hadn't kissed a man in years. She wasn't sure she would remember how, or even if James would return the favor.

He returned the favor. He put his hand gently on her neck to draw her closer and she let him, craving the warmth of his lips, ready with all kinds of suggestions. His hands left her neck and went to her waist. Suddenly he broke off the kiss and backed away, just as Noah came back with a handful of dead leaves.

She glanced at James, horrified to see green paint around his mouth. She brushed her hand with her cheek and green paint came off on her palm.

"Mr. Trevenen, you have green paint on your face," Noah said, as he dumped the dead leaves in her lap. "Are these dead enough?"

"How did that happen?" Mr. Trevenen murmured as he dabbed at his cheek.

"Probably when you were kissing my mother," Noah said prosaically. "She doesn't like it when I do that and get toast crumbs on her."

Mr. Trevenen burst out laughing. "You saw that, did you?"

Noah nodded. He scooped the leaves from Susannah's lap. "I'll put these in the jar and you can show it to the gardener."

"Noah, did you mind that I kissed your mother?" Mr. Trevenen asked.

"Not if she didn't mind." Noah looked up then, as though reminded of something. "Mama, I must return to Spring Grove. Aunt Loisa said she needs me most particularly tonight."

"You may, son."

He watched Noah leave, then put both hands on her neck again and kissed her this time.

She could think of no protest or need for caution, now that Noah was gone, except that Mr. Trevenen stopped, looking over his shoulder. His lips tightened into a firm line.

This time she knew. She stood up, even as he backed away, and pulled him close to her in one fierce motion before releasing him. "There is no one here but us, James," she said, keeping her words precise. "No one."

He tried to pull her with him but she resisted.

"James, Timothy Rowe is not here."

She hated what she was doing to him, especially when his eyes widened and he looked over her shoulder.

"He's right behind you," he said finally, after opening and closing his mouth several times, as though all speech had left his brain. "He's holding Walter Shepherd's arm. Please, come away."

"I'm not moving, James, because no one is here except me. Not John Weston—God rest his soul—or Bill Bright—did you call him Billy?—or poor Walter and especially not Timothy Rowe."

. He looked at her then, with an expression beyond shock or even terror. "You know their names."

"I read the *Orion's* log this afternoon," she said.

The breath went out of him as though someone had punched him hard in the stomach. He moved farther away, and something in his vision cleared, as though the apparition had vanished. "Then you know how cursed I am."

"Please, don't go!" she said, holding out her hand to him. "You're not cursed, my dear. You're just tired."

He stopped. "What did you call me?" he asked, his voice sharp now.

"Exactly what you think I said," she told him. "My dear. Should I call you dearest love, or perhaps beloved? I think I will call you beloved someday, if you aren't too embarrassed."

Her own impetuosity astounded her. Her life with David, though brief, would never dissolve from her heart; she did not expect it to. But this was different. She knew that no matter how much time passed, she would never get over James Trevenen. He was hers forever, whether this moment was the last one they ever shared, or one of many to come.

He left her then, just turned on his heel and walked away.

She did not feel inclined to cry. The toughness of her own mind reassured her. I have Noah, she thought, as she watched James's back. My sister has been restored to me. Sir Joseph will offer solace and Lady Dorothea macaroons.

She wanted more. She continued down the row. "Timothy Rowe, I do wish you would go away," she said in a firm voice. "I cannot blame you for what happened. On any other voyage, you would have been unexceptionable. It is regrettable that you lacked the strength to endure a small boat with desperate men."

Her heart at peace, she looked at both pictures, then picked up the smaller one belonging to Mr. Trevenen. "James, beloved, you will come back because I have the *Gloriosa*. It's that simple." She tucked it under her arm and left the exotic bloom house.

Back at Alderson House, she was not surprised when Chumley handed her a note.

I have gone to White's with Sir Wallace and Sir Percival, who claims he will produce Lord Eberly, whose children— if you will recall—Beau "rescued" from that God- bedamned inn. Don't wait up. I am leaving tomorrow. J.

Oh, you are, are you, she thought, as she folded the note and dismissed Chumley. I might have believed you if you had signed it Trevenen, rather than *J,* which gives both of us some latitude.

Dinner was a silent, curious affair, with Mama and Papa sit- ting close to each other instead of at opposite ends of the table. She could hardly keep from laughing out loud. This was a far cry from the dinner at Lord Batchley's, with James suffering agonies seated next to that vile woman, who had probably been diddling him under the table, for all she knew.

Finally she could manage no more. She put down her fork. "Mama, Papa, we are all adults," she said. Mama frowned when she rested her elbows on the table, but made no comment, be- cause Papa was holding her hand across the rice pudding.

"Papa, what did Mr. Trevenen tell you, to let the toucans go?"

To her amusement, Papa and Mama looked at each other and touched foreheads.

"My blushes, Susannah," he said.

Mama giggled and left the room, but not without a backward glance at her husband that said more than words.

"This is really not for your ears, daughter," he said.

"Papa, I am not a green girl," she reminded him. "I have a son, and I know what is what."

Even though the footmen had left the room and the maid hadn't yet come to remove the dishes, he motioned her closer. "Mr. Trevenen came in the nick of time, daughter. I had no idea, until he told me, that I was poisoning my…ahem…manhood by harboring tropical birds."

She was grateful she was not eating anything, or she would have choked. "Could you explain, Papa, without too much de- tail?" she asked sweetly.

He leaned close to her. "He swears the effluvia from toucans and macaws has a tendency to—how shall I say this—put a man off his usual prowess." Lord Watchmere was beet red now. "He said it would take three or four weeks for any...results. I was to be patient."

Beau Crusoe, you rascal, she thought, struggling to maintain her composure. You knew you would be long gone by then. Yet here was her father, looking more cheerful than she had seen him in years, and all because he believed a lie from a quick-thinking scoundrel.

"Can I gather that you have had—forgive me if I am indelicate, Papa—success sooner than he indicated?"

Lord Watchmere nodded. "You know I am not a patient man, Susannah. Perhaps British men are made of sterner stuff than those Spaniards who live in the tropics."

"Or the equally wretched Portuguese," she teased.

"Certainly." He put the stopper back on the sherry decanter and rose, swaying slightly. She reached out to steady him, and he beamed at her, the soul of satisfaction and complacency. "Susannah, see that the candles are out." He yawned elaborately. "I believe I am going to toddle off to bed."

A napkin to her mouth to stifle her merriment, she watched him leave the dining room, two steps sideways for one step forward, rather like a crab. When he was safely upstairs, she went down the hall to the library, a place little used, since Papa had no head for business.

She cleared the desk off with the napkin she had brought from the dining room. Chumley had followed her, so she turned to him.

"Chumley, do ask a footman to light a fire and bring me some better-trimmed lamps for this desk." She looked in one drawer and then another. "I see plenty of paper, but not a fresh bottle of ink anywhere. See if you can locate one."

"Certainly, Mrs. Park." He hesitated at the door. "Is anything the matter?"

She thought a moment. Everything was the matter, but she was less discouraged than she could have explained.

"No, Chumley. Things are well enough in hand." She took several sheets of paper from the drawer. "About that ink, please?"

He bowed and left. She made herself as comfortable as she

could, because she planned to be at the desk for a while, or at least as long as it took to write in detail everything she had learned that afternoon.

She sharpened a nib, waiting for the butler to return with ink. "Let us write the true story, béloved," she whispered.

Chapter Twenty-Five

She heard him come up the stairs hours later. He passed her door; she thought he even leaned against it. She didn't hear him open his door. To her surprise, he started down the stairs again.

"No, you don't," she said, leaping up.

He sat on the stairs. She sat down beside him, smelling the drink. "Mr. Trevenen, you are positively sodden," she said, by way of greeting.

He nodded, looking at her a bit owl-eyed. "Mr. Trevenen?"

"In this state, yes, indeed."

He groaned. "My brains are washing about."

"I shouldn't wonder."

He clutched her arm then, leaning close so he could whisper in her ear. She wanted to hold her nose.

"Too many people in my room. A whole boatload. They all expect me to do something. Pluck a meal out of the ocean, or summon a vessel. I failed them."

He started to cry. She reckoned they were the boozy tears of a drunk, except for the remorse in his face. He was barely visible in the gloom, but there was enough light to see all that sorrow.

She pulled his head to her breast. "You did everything you could, James. No man could have done more."

"You don't know that," he sobbed into her nightgown. "You weren't there."

"No. It was all on your shoulders," she whispered, cradling his head.

She wished he would say more, but his regular breathing told her he was asleep. She woke him after a few minutes.

"It's time for bed, sir," she said, leaning him against the railing.

"I'm not going to sleep in there," he declared.

"I don't expect you to," she told him. "Come with me."

He didn't argue as she took him by the hand and led him to her room. "You will do better in here," she said as she removed his neckcloth, trying to hold him steady as he swayed.

She lit the lamp so she could see his buttons. "I took the liberty earlier of finding your nightshirt," she said as she removed his waistcoat and then his shirt. He tried to help her with his knee breeches, but appeared sadly baffled when he could not pull them off his legs. She knelt down to unbutton them at his knees, a step he appeared to have forgotten.

He didn't seem embarrassed to stand naked before her, probably because his eyes were half-closed by now and his breathing had become more regular again. "So you will sleep standing up, sir?" she murmured.

She tried to avoid staring at his privates, but his tattoo was hard to ignore. She stared at the arrow, then shook her head in disbelief.

"Not polite to stare, Suzie," he told her. "I would never gawp at your tattoos."

"I don't have any," she assured him. He raised his arms obediently so she could drop down his nightshirt.

She walked him to her bed and pulled back the covers. "Get in."

He did as she said.

"Move over."

"You should probably find your own bed," he told her. "Houses this large should have more than one bed."

"This *is* my bed," she said, patiently. "Move over."

He accepted that as he had everything else, sliding over so she could join him, then resting on his side and putting his arms around her. He rested his cheek against hers, as he had the night before, but without the foul perfume left over from Lady Audley.

She hesitated to move into his warmth, but he solved that reluctance by putting one hand firmly against her stomach and pulling her so close that his organ pressed against her rump. She allowed herself to relax in his embrace, gradually growing used to it. Before she drifted away, she put her cold feet against his shins. He did not even flinch.

It seemed only minutes before he woke her, tossing now, and talking with increasing urgency. His arm was under her head, so she rose up slightly, turned over and rested on her elbow, watching his expressive face in the moonlight. He was shaking his head, and then tugging on her arm. "John, get back in the boat," he said, in that tone of command she had heard before. "Now, man. You cannot swim to Portsmouth from here. Believe me."

He let out a wail. Susannah grabbed him and wrapped herself around him, pushing his face down into her breasts as he cried. "Shh, shh, James," she crooned, sticking to him like a barnacle. "He was delirious. He thought he was helping you."

"It was my first command," he cried.

"It was a small boat, beloved. You were adrift at sea. No man could have done more."

"Beloved?" he asked.

"Yes, beloved," she assured him.

He didn't speak or do anything. He just looked at her face.

"You needn't stare so," she told him. "I'm not going anywhere."

He sighed then and closed his eyes.

He slept again. She knew she should pull away from him, but she did not want to. She stayed where she was, nightgown around her hips, her leg thrown over his, pressed against his privates, wishing suddenly that he would wake up and take her.

He did, toward morning. She offered no objection when he gently placed her on her back and just as gently entered her body, taking his time as though he savored every second, even as she did. It had been so long since David had made love to her that she wanted to ration the moment, even as she began to move beneath him, making no effort to hide her pleasure or stifle her moans.

One of them must have thrown off the coverlet. Nothing hindered her from digging her heels into his rump and rising to meet each motion he made. She came first, shuddering into his shoulder as he kissed her damp hair. He seemed to know precisely what she needed, letting her climax again before he did the same, breathing deep into her ear, and then running his tongue inside it, which only made her come again, as he must have known it would. It had been so long.

Neither of them wanted to move. He raised up on his elbows finally to give her breathing room, tugging at her nipple with his lips and then rooting against the spongy flesh of her breasts until she laughed.

"I could probably stay like this for a year or two," he told her finally. "Someone could feed us through a funnel. Maybe put a blanket over us when the seasons change."

She touched the curling hair on his chest. She lifted her legs off him finally, and tried to stretch, which only arched her hips against his and sparked her desire all over again.

"Sorry," he murmured. "I'm spent."

He rolled off her and began to rub her mound gently, and then thoroughly as her breath came in gasps. When she finished, he left his hand where it was, curving around her wet hair in a proprietary way.

He slept then. When he woke, she was wearing her nightclothes again and looking around for his. He put his hands behind his head to watch her. "I'm not certain who needed that more," he said finally, "you or me."

She propped a chair against her door to keep out the 'tween stairs maid and came back to bed, giving up the search for his nightshirt. As she rested in his arms, he told her everything that had happened between Batavia and Cape Town, confessing his entire doings with Lady Audley.

She told herself not to be shocked, not to berate him in any way. It was not her business to judge him, after all he had endured.

"All those years alone, Suzie," he said. "I couldn't have stopped myself if I had been a eunuch." He kissed her ear, which made her close her eyes and sigh. "Do I regret my dalliance with Lady Audley? More with every day that passes in your company." He took hold of her nightgown, bunching it in his long fingers. "I pray you will forgive that conduct," he said quietly, his eyes on her face and nothing else in the room.

"If you'll forgive mine just now," she said. "We're not married and it wasn't proper."

"Love's proper, dearest. Believe me, I know the difference now." He kissed her forehead.

It was such a chaste gesture that she suddenly felt shy. "I… I've been thinking a lot of you lately," she managed to say.

"Of all my charms?" he teased. "Or just my brilliant mind?"

She felt her face grow warm.

He let humor light his way. "I could be wrong—hardly anyone knows less about females than I—but I could have sworn that your eagerness implied…how do I put this?…little amorous activity since your husband's death."

"You are the first," she assured him.

"I know that. You just saved my life," he told her gently, sitting up, too, and reaching for her.

She let him take her hand. "I did?" she asked. "Then you must do something for me."

"I thought I was," he said with the ghost of a smile. "You've worn me down to a nub."

"Men are so vain," she responded, with a smile of her own. "Last night, when you were carousing, I wrote down everything I learned at Admiralty House yesterday. You must tell me everything that you remember about your island."

"I thought the treatise would be enough." He made no effort to hide the hurt in his voice, sounding remarkably like Noah after some slight.

"It is, for the scientific world," she said, taking his hand and kissing it. He opened his hand then and cupped her face with it. "I want you tell me how Timothy Rowe died, and what you did with his body. You have to."

"I cannot," he said, drawing his hand away.

"You told Sir Richard," she insisted. "You can tell me, too."

He looked at her for a long time. She took some comfort in the steadiness of his gaze, because it told her he saw no one else in the room.

"I told the lords what I thought happened, that I fired at Tim when he tried to climb across the oars."

She waited, watching his face.

"There is a gap in the log," he said finally. "You may have noticed."

She nodded. "Your last entry in the boat is September 1. The log resumes on September 4. What happened?"

"I don't remember."

I don't believe you, she thought, and knew, with a horrible heaviness in her heart, that her thoughts were as plainly plastered across her face as though she had spoken them out loud.

"Can't trust a man who lies so much, eh?" he asked, after a long silence.

He sat up and turned away from her, his feet on the floor. "I've told so many whoppers in the past week, but before God, that is no whopper. I really don't remember. One moment we were on the boat, and that is all until my entry on September 4 that begins the treatise. I remember stuffing the log into the bag, and I remember raising the pistol. It was so heavy I could barely lift it. That is all. Please, believe me."

"Thousands wouldn't," she said with a half smile. "But will you at least tell me about your island? James, there is a key somewhere. I know it."

He considered the matter. When she wondered if he would speak again, he lay back on the bed, his head in her lap.

"My stomach is about to growl," she warned him.

"I don't care." He looked up at her. "Suzie, I have compromised you beyond belief. Now *that* I hadn't intended."

"I thought I seduced *you*."

He considered it, smiled and turned his head to kiss her thigh. "I didn't struggle, did I?"

"I suspect men rarely do." She couldn't help but think of Lady Audley.

He winced, almost as though she had spoken Lady Audley's name aloud. "She tried at Lord Batchley's, but she didn't succeed. Believe me." He tipped his head up to look her directly in the eyes. "As I think of it, I don't believe she cared whether she tupped me or not."

"My blushes, Mr. Trevenen," she murmured.

He laughed. "We've spent half the night spliced together like a seaman's knot and you're worried about my *language?* Women are strange."

He settled back again, making himself comfortable with his head in her lap. "She ripped off my neckcloth and rubbed herself against me in a most appalling way. Then she tried something that used to work rather well."

She should have stopped him, but she was occupied with the growing warmth in her lap where he lay.

"She leaned back on the bed and just raised her skirts." He shook his head. "It didn't work, but she didn't seem to mind. Suzie, I think all she wanted to do was ruin me in your eyes."

"Impossible," Susannah said. "I already thought you were a rascal."

"You looked pretty appalled when I came downstairs."

"I was. You smelled abominable. And did no one ever teach you to tie a neckcloth properly?"

"Yet here I am now."

He didn't speak smugly; there was wonder in his voice. She touched his face, outlining his profile and ending with her fingers on his lips.

"Here you are," she echoed. "I was ruined years ago. Unlike Lady Audley, I have no intention of ruining you." She took a deep breath, and another. "I love you, James."

She hoped he would return the sentiment, but he did not. He gazed into her eyes. "Probably not the wisest thing you ever did."

"I have yet to love any man wisely," she cautioned, even as

she knew with all her heart they were together already, all joking aside.

He was a long time in speaking. "It may be that I can never keep Tim Rowe away," he said slowly. "You might have to share your bedroom with him. I can promise nothing."

"I know. I trust he will eventually get bored and leave."

James smiled. "In that case, perhaps you had better marry me, because I'm quite smitten."

"Is that the same as love?" she asked when he eased his hand under her nightgown.

"I'm beyond love," he said. "The biggest lie I've ever told was that first night when we were returning to Alderson House from Spring Grove. That one when I assured you people don't fall in love in two weeks."

She rested her hand on his chest. "You'd only just seen me."

"Have you no idea what kind of a first impression you make, Mrs. Park?"

"None whatsoever," she told him, amazed.

"Then believe me now. And marry me."

There he was, looking so earnest with his head in her lap. In for a penny, in for a pound, she thought. She tugged her night-gown out from under his head. "Is this what Lady Audley did?"

"The very thing," he told her, amused, even as his breathing came more rapidly. "Maybe if she had said 'please.'"

"Please."

Good God, it was broad daylight. Maybe she really didn't have any shame. She lay back against the pillows and there he was on his stomach now, looking directly at the area between her open legs.

"Have you ever considered a tattoo there?" he teased.

"Never. One is enough for both of us."

She closed her eyes as his lips found her down there. She put her hands on his head, her fingers twining in his hair as he busied himself with the tenderest part of her body. She didn't think she could possibly spread her legs any wider, or arch her back any higher. When she came, it was exquisite. As he mounted her and moved inside her, she was happy to keep his demons away.

He held her in his arms when they were both satisfied.

"Yes. I'll marry you."

He laughed. "If our children ever want to know about our proposal, we will change the subject." He kissed her. "I'll have a license tomorrow, if they can be got that fast."

"I hear they are expensive," she cautioned.

"I can stand the strain for a worthy cause." He played with her nipple idly. "Do you intend to call me Mr. Trevenen? I've noticed you do that, now and then."

She considered it. "I might. I like it, actually. Don't you think it trips off the tongue?"

He sighed. "Midshipmen called me Mr. Trevenen."

"Enough said, James."

While her dear love was dressing, he saw Timothy Rowe again. She could tell, as she sat watching James from the bed she already thought of as theirs, because he stiffened. He backed away and looked over his shoulder at her, as though gauging the distance between the ghoul and the woman he loved.

She was beside him in a minute, her arms tight around his waist, her cheek against his back.

"I wish he would go away, Suzie."

"In time, he will," she replied, hoping she sounded more certain than she felt. "Somehow, we have to put him to rest."

They were both silent then. In a few minutes, he seemed to relax. "Well," he said. He turned around then, and she knew the carpenter's mate was gone. He held out his neckcloth to her. "You're better at this than I am." When she finished, he asked, "Do I look good enough to approach your vicar?"

She nodded. "He will send you to the bishop, who will be relieved I am to be married in an actual church." She got out of bed and went to the clothes press, where she pulled out a folded document with a broken seal.

His hands on her shoulders, he watched as she opened it. "David Park, deceased," he murmured, looking at the certificate. "Bombay. It's a world away, my love. Will you miss his name?"

"A little," she said honestly, "until I get used to yours." She handed it to him. "I can think of nothing else you will need. When are we going to do this deed?"

"Tomorrow?" he asked. "I have a sneaking suspicion I am not going to be particularly welcome in your bed until our antics are a bit more official."

"You would be right," she agreed.

He must have heard the hesitation in her voice, because he turned her around to face him, his hands gentle on her shoulders. "Something is not square with you," he said.

"My sister." She leaned her forehead against him. "I have her love now, and I fear…"

"…she will be left out again. Should we wait?"

"No, but can we say nothing, at least until after the Copley ceremony?"

"What will change between now and then?"

She had no answer. He gathered her close, his arms tight around her. "I'll get this license and we will be married tomorrow morning. I won't say anything, you won't say anything, and we'll hope something magic happens. Suzie, you're a goose."

"I know."

He tipped her chin up and kissed her. "Maybe silence is best. I still feel uneasy about Lady Audley."

"If she thinks her stunt at Lord Batchley's alienated us, she will probably be content."

He kissed the top of her head. "Content is not a word she knows. She would still like to ruin me." He rested his chin on her head. "I wish I knew her game."

She gently separated herself from his embrace and gave him a push toward the door. "I'll be in the exotic blooms house. I must finish the *Gloriosa*."

"I'll see you then." He opened the door. "I was planning to leave the house early this morning and take a room in a hotel. Are you ever amazed how suddenly things can change?"

"No," she told him, her voice quiet. "Neither are you."

Chapter Twenty-Six

They were married the next morning, after a night of peace in each other's arms. He had told her again everything she had read in the log: his uncertainty, the shocking suicide of the foretopman, Tim's voracious appetite. He was shivering when he finished.

She turned slightly in his arms and kissed his cheek. "Go to sleep now."

He had wakened once, murmuring something about crabs. This surprised her, because it did not involve the carpenter's mate this time. She couldn't understand why the crabs would agitate him, because they were so dear to his heart.

They had decided to tell Sir Joseph about their marriage, but no one else. She would return to the exotic blooms house to work on the large *Gloriosa*, and James would stay with Sir Joseph and Sam Higgins. She foresaw no difficulty convincing Loisa to write down what he told them about the island, and how his days were spent. Maybe it was futile, she thought, as her eyes began to close. Maybe nothing would jog his memory about what had actually happened on the small boat. Maybe he had buried the horror of it so deep that Tim Rowe would be his constant companion, as long as they both lived.

This is not a simple thing, she told herself, as James slumbered beside her. I did not swear to live with two men until my death.

* * *

They left the house early in the morning, walking to the parish church, which was only a mile beyond Alderson House, tucked back into trees where the leaves were falling. "Saint James," James said as they came to the entrance. "I'll have no trouble remembering where I was married." He raised her hand to his lips and kissed it. "I'd better not forget the date, either, eh?"

"You had better not," she assured him. "I don't intend to do this again, so give me no excuses to want to."

The vicar hadn't been awake long. Susannah wanted to laugh at the sight of him, with his hair ruffled and his collar not tucked into place. She had known the vicar for years, suffering through many sermons. She braced herself for the homily he was bound to deliver before he actually married them. It was short and to the point, though, and she had James to thank for that.

The vicar had rounded up his wife and a clerk as witnesses, and returned with the Book of Common Prayer. "Mrs. Park, I am pleased to see that you have decided to marry in a proper way this time, even if it is a rush," he greeted her.

James cleared his throat. "Sir, I have spent the vast sum of ten shillings and feel inclined to be married."

That was all. If anyone else had said it, the vicar would have continued with his admonition, she was certain. James never raised his voice, but there was something in the clipped words and set of his jaw that encouraged the vicar to find his place quickly in the book, motion them closer—although he did take a wary step away from James—and begin.

"Dearly beloved, we are gathered together here in the sight of God…"

She glanced at James. His eyes were tired—she knew she could not live on so little unbroken rest—but he smiled, which told her Timothy Rowe was not standing among the witnesses.

After they had both signed the license and it had been duly witnessed, the vicar and his wife left them in the church and the clerk returned to his duties.

"I wish I had a ring for you right now, Mrs. Trevenen—

heavens, how *that* trips off the tongue—but it can wait until I can find the time to buy one. It'll go right there." He kissed her ring finger. "Suzie, don't turn into a watering pot! We just got married. It's not a funeral."

She laughed and wiped her eyes.

He sniffed. "Bacon. It seems to me that for ten shillings, the vicar could have invited us to breakfast." They stepped outside the church. "Of course, it would have cost me a whacking four quid if I had applied for a special license. Did I mention I am frugal?"

The wind had picked up, so she settled her bonnet more firmly on her head and tied the strings. A few leaves were blowing down the street. She looked at her husband to ask him a question, but forgot it the moment she saw his expression. She took his arm. "At least Timothy Rowe had the courtesy to wait for you outside the church," she said.

He shook his head, no less tense, but with a puzzled expression. "He's not here, Suzie. It's something else. I wish I could put my finger on it." He stood still on the windy street, sniffing the air.

"Has it something to do with the sea?" she asked him. "The Thames is through those trees. It can smell noxious, at times."

"No, that's not it," he said. "I don't know. Maybe all that talk last night about the boat reminded me of something." He smiled at her then. "Would you mind terribly if we don't talk so much tonight? I enjoy conversation as much as the next man, Suzie Trevenen, light of my life. However, I did just spend ten shillings and correct me if I misheard, but didn't I say something about 'with my body I thee worship?'"

"If I had a parasol…"

"…which so far I have yet to see you carry…"

"I would beat you with it right now."

He staggered back in mock surprise. "Lord, it doesn't take but a minute for the worm to turn."

If Sir Joseph was surprised by James's quiet words to him in the library at Spring Grove, he recovered quickly. "You'll forgive me for meddling, then, will you?" he asked James. "And you, Susannah?"

She kissed him. "I shouldn't, of course, but I will make an exception in your case, since I am your goddaughter and, hopefully, in your will."

Sir Joseph laughed, then looked at James. "I should have warned you, lad. Once the leg is shackled, you're doomed."

"Sir Joseph, we do appreciate your forbearance in letting us keep our marriage a private matter for a few days, until we find a way to tell Loisa," James said.

"Of course. Now you wish to tell me about your island sojourn?" Sir Joseph asked. "I have been so hoping for that."

"I know you have," James said in a kind voice. "Do you think we can get Sam in here to transcribe what I tell you? Suzie thinks I need this on paper, and I intend to humor her."

"If Sam comes, you will get Loisa, too."

James glanced at Susannah. "I think that two ladies who have read the *Orion's* log are made of stern enough stuff." He took off his coat and loosened his neckcloth. "Suzie, on your way out, please send Barmley for Sam."

"You're not staying?" Sir Joseph asked.

"I have a crab to finish painting," she said. "James would like it done and framed before the Copley ceremony, and set on an easel as he reads his paper."

Sir Joseph nodded. "Excellent. That gives you a few days. Noah is chafing at the bit to see you, and I will send him to the glass house with a supply of macaroons."

"So early?" she teased, and she kissed her husband and opened the door. "I had thought Cook only made macaroons in the afternoon."

"Mrs. Trevenen—my my, how nice that sounds—your son is persuasive."

The wind had abated and the sun had come out by the time she got to the exotic blooms house. The light was precisely right as she seated herself by the windows. She mixed her colors, then glanced outside at the gardeners, who were raking leaves into piles. In a few days they would begin to burn them, and she would have to steel herself against the odor and the smoke.

She picked up her brush, then set it down again and rested her arms in her lap for a moment. David, this was best, she thought. I won't forget you. I couldn't possibly.

She spent the day painting. Noah had joined her to eat macaroons and pick up more dead leaves. She got up several times to stretch and walk around, her hand against the small of her back, and then stepped outside to watch Noah playing.

She hadn't even thought of it until now, but after James received the medal at the end of the week, she and her son would be going with him to Cornwall. She thought of her parents. Mama would be shocked at her hasty marriage, but surely less shocked than by the first one. Papa would eventually return to his bird blind. And Loisa? Susannah did not know. Sam Higgins surely could not keep up the pretence of a malarial relapse much longer, even if it was only for James's benefit now. The London Mission Society did not seem to want him anymore. Perhaps he would go home to farm. Loisa, are we all going to break your heart again? she asked herself as she sat down again to finish the final leg on the left side of the *Gloriosa*. She would do the right side tomorrow, then the antennae, which she had saved until last, because she was not entirely sure of the color. Probably she would have to cajole her framer, since it was short notice.

She smiled. I will tell Mr. Trev…James…to use the ring money to frame the *Gloriosa*. Her smile faded. Timothy Rowe was a carpenter. What a pity he is not useful. "Timothy, can you go away and quit tormenting my husband?" she said.

Nothing. She picked up her brush again.

She spent her wedding night making love quietly with her husband while Noah slept in the next room, back in his own bed again. She loved James so thoroughly she hoped he would be too tired to dream. He dreamed anyway, muttering something again about crabs but not fully rousing himself until he suddenly sat bolt upright in bed, his eyes staring so hard at nothing that she put her hands over them as he shook in terror.

"What is it, beloved?" she whispered. "Can you not tell me?"

He removed her hands from his eyes. He looked around the room, then lay back, his breath ragged.

She lay down again. "Speak to me, James. You just have to."

He turned his face into her breasts and his voice was muffled. "I would if I could, Suzie. In truth, I don't know what it is this time. Something is out there I can't explain."

"Not Timothy Rowe?"

"No, no." His voice was getting drowsy. "He seemed to enjoy his afternoon in the bookroom at Spring Grove, though." He opened his eyes, then closed them again as her heart pounded. "It's something else. Something more."

After such a declaration, she could not sleep. She got up finally, found her nightgown—which had ended up in an armchair, for some reason—and stood by the window. The wind had picked up again, as though trying to blow autumn into winter before any of them were ready.

It was a peaceful sight, and one she always enjoyed. How kind of the Almighty to allow the seasons to change visibly. She glanced back at her husband, who was beginning to move again, agitated by some new demon. Did you have to bring along your friends, Tim? she thought, suddenly angry with a dead man, who, poor soul, had surely never wished any of this on himself.

The next two days were much like the last. James was up early, dressed and at breakfast before Noah woke. It was when he had left the room that she was able to sleep a little longer, curling herself into the warm spot he left, relaxing because she knew her chamber contained no one beyond herself.

She finished the *Gloriosa*. Susannah sat back in her chair, satisfied, and set down the brush. She had painted a light blue wash as a background, which she decided was exactly right. Red, green and gold, with purple stems for the antennae: it was still not a large portrait, because she did not work on great canvases like a Rembrandt or a Raphael, but on paper. Her subjects were flowers and small creatures that skittered around tidal pools in quiet lagoons.

She still had not asked James about their future. If he meant to take her from Richmond, someone else would have to paint the flora that came so regularly from the South Seas and northern latitudes as England's Royal Navy industriously continued to cover the globe. The wars had slowed voyages to southern latitudes but had never entirely stopped those journeys of exploration. There would be plenty of work for a painter.

She picked up the brush again, trying to decide where to place her initials. Maybe it was her particular vanity, even if the much-smaller watercolors were destined only for the British Museum, but she always found a small corner or angle in which to paint *sp*.

"Put it by the third leg on the right."

She looked up, startled, then relaxed. "You were awfully silent," she said, as her husband put his hands on her shoulders.

"You were gazing so intently that a herd of water buffalo could have trooped past," he contradicted.

She poised the brush in the spot he had indicated. "I usually only put *sp*," she told him.

"Continue doing that," he told her.

"You don't mind?"

"No." He kissed the top of her head. "You, of all people, could never accuse me of being jealous of the deceased."

She put the initials in place then set down the brush. "Done," she declared. "What do you think?"

"Beautiful," he said, but he was looking at her.

"The watercolor," she said patiently, even as her cheeks grew warm.

"That, too. Is it dry?"

She nodded. "These aren't done in oil. I will send Barmley with it to Richter's in Regent Street," she told him. "I have already sent a note with the frame dimensions. They will deliver it to Somerset House tomorrow morning. I told them the awards ceremony begins at ten." She rested her hands on top of his. "Was Sir Joseph not feeling quite the thing this morning?"

"He is well enough, but I was using the time to condense my report on the *Gloriosa*. I read it out loud to him."

"Would you read it to me?" she asked.

"No. You can hear it tomorrow morning when I stand up with a medal around my neck and my knees knocking."

"I could never do what you're going to do," she said as she closed the lid on her tin of watercolors.

He straightened up then and took the *Gloriosa* from the easel, holding it out in front of him. "It's my lot to blather on about crabs to the Society. I do hope no one is bored."

As it turned out, no one was.

Intellectual London showed up the next morning, that portion which had not retired to their country estates after the closing of Parliament. The fribbles—Sir Percival Pettibone prominent in his first pink waistcoat of the coming season—turned out in full force, too, eager to see and hear Beau Crusoe.

Sir Joseph had pronounced himself well enough to travel. Barmley and some of the younger footmen on loan from Alderson House lifted him into his carriage. Loisa and Sam Higgins had decided to go in a separate conveyance, which did not surprise Susannah. How many more days could they have together?

James stood patiently while Susannah tied his neckcloth. She could tell he was waiting for her to speak, but she was too occupied to think of anything.

"Really, Suzie," he murmured finally, holding himself quite still. "Isn't this where you are supposed to tell me not to sit down or I will crease my tails, or to make no sudden motions and ruin my neckcloth? I am depending upon you to advise me into perfection."

"I wouldn't dream of it," she said, her eyes on his neckcloth. "If you were Noah's age, I would." She patted the finished product and kissed him. "What a handsome man you are."

He managed a little smile, and she knew from the direction of his glance that Timothy Rowe was in the room, too.

"I trust that Tim is as tidy as it is possible for a ghoul to be?" she asked.

"Don't joke about it," James said, his words clipped, as though he had bitten off the end of each.

She took her hands away from his neck, chastened. "I'm sorry, James," she said. "I just don't know how to deal with him yet."

"Nor I, obviously," he replied, and kissed her quickly. "I didn't mean to be so short with you." He took a deep breath. "I don't often address large crowds, either."

As the coachman pulled up in front of Somerset House, Susannah saw a flotilla of barges and pleasure craft coming to the Thames side of the magnificent building.

"Could we return home that way?" Noah asked.

"No, lad," James said, almost before the boy finished the sentence. "I have no love for small boats."

Susannah held Noah's hand as they joined the crowd of well-dressed gentlemen—a few ladies among them—passing through the stately portico, down the marble corridor and into the largest chamber, with its gilt frames housing the most distinguished former members of the Royal Society: Sir Isaac Newton, Sir Christopher Wren, Samuel Pepys, Robert Boyle.

Noah stared all around. "Mama, what did they do to get painted in here?" he asked, to the amusement of an older lady and gentleman behind him.

"They were very, very good, son."

Standing in the central aisle with her husband beside her, Susannah looked toward the dais, and sighed in relief to see her framed portrait of the *Gloriosa* on an easel. She touched James's shoulder. "My dear, did you ever think when you were observing those little crabs that you would someday be here?"

He shook his head. "I reckoned I would live and die on that island I never named." He looked around at the crowd. "Suzie, I see Sir Percival, with Lord Eberly clinging to him like a winkle. Lord bless me, there is my tailor." The smile left his face. "Timothy Rowe is seated right next to him. I wonder, should I warn him?"

She took his hand and held it for a moment, releasing it when she glanced over a row and saw Lady Audley watching her, a slight smile on her face. "There is Lady Audley," she whispered.

"I know," he whispered back. "I wish I felt easy about this."

He looked down another row and pointed to two chairs. "This is a good place for you and Noah. Sir Joseph said I was to sit in the front row with the Fellows. I'll come for you afterward. I have some ideas about our future, which I think will occupy our return to Richmond." He went to take his place in the front, clutching the portfolio containing his talk.

And then it was ten o'clock. All rose as the secretary of the Royal Society carried in the mace given to the first president by King Charles II himself, and set it on the great carved table in front of the rostrum. Sir Joseph Banks came next, helped along by two senior members of the society. They stood at either side of the rostrum as Sir Joseph banged a gavel once. "Dukes and duchesses, lords and ladies, sirs and gentlewomen—God save the king!"

The audience echoed his last words. He nodded, and motioned to his two Society members to seat themselves. Despite his discomfort, Sir Joseph spoke with the ease of a peer among peers, a man used to command, someone secure in his place.

"We are here for that most happy of duties: to award the Copley medal to one who has brought to our attention the quiet world of a South Pacific lagoon. I give you James Lawrence Trevenen of Cornwall, and formerly of His Majesty's Royal Navy."

James rose and bowed to the audience. He started to seat himself again, but Sir Joseph ushered him forward. He removed his treatise from the portfolio. Susannah smiled to see that he also carried the original *Gloriosa*.

Sir Joseph was speaking again, his hand resting on her husband's shoulder now. "Through a terrible set of circumstances, Lt. Trevenen was cast away onto a deserted island somewhere near that archipelago that my good friend and still-lamented leader, Captain James Cook, allowed me to name after him. Later, Captain Cook named an island farther west for me. That is the happy circumstance of being Adam in a Garden of Eden."

When the laughter died down, Sir Joseph looked at James, who stood solemn and erect. "To entertain himself and maintain some order, Lt. Trevenen began to study a small creature he called the *Gloriosa Jubilate,* because he tells me it was the prettiest name he could think of."

More laughter. "It has a more scientific name now. We will let him tell us that story in a moment. First, though, I think we should weigh him down with some gold jewelry. What say you, Fellows?"

The members of the society rose and applauded.

"Noah, this is something to remember forever," Susannah said, lifting her son onto her lap so he could see better. "Listen!"

Her whole body nearly bursting with pride, she heard shouts of "Hear, hear!" and "Trevenen!" and even "Beau Crusoe!"

As they continued to cheer, and all rose, James lowered his head so Sir Joseph could drape the elegant gold medal with its blue watered silk ribbon around his neck. Susannah smiled to see him look down at the medal, fingering it and lifting it up to read the inscription. Her delight increased as he caught her eye and bowed in her direction.

His own face wreathed in smiles, Sir Joseph held up his hand again for silence and everyone sat down.

Everyone except Lady Audley. She was a tall woman and she was dressed this day in a deep red dress with a high turban.

Susannah felt her face drain of all color as Lady Audley raised her hand and pointed at James, who stared at her, his face pale, too.

The cheers were fading in the room when she spoke.

"You cannot award such an honor to a cannibal, a murderer and a seducer," she said, her voice loud. "You fellows, in the name of all that is decent, I protest. I protest!"

Chapter Twenty-Seven

Men shouted and women screamed. Two seats down from Susannah, a lady slid out of her chair in a dead faint. Noah started to cry. Susannah hugged him to her, her eyes still on her husband, who stared beyond Lady Audley now, as though the audience contained a hundred Timothy Rowes.

For all she knew, it did. "No," she murmured. "Say something, James."

Lady Audley seemed to take it all in with pleasure. She remained on her feet, but lowered her accusing finger. "I dare you to deny any of this," she shouted, loud and brazen enough to be heard above the general tumult.

Say something, James, Susannah thought, as she held her son, sobbing louder now, terrified of the din.

James did nothing but stand there, his expression so stricken that Susannah could hardly bear to watch him. Sir Joseph reached for his gavel and pounded it on the table, but no one paid attention.

All eyes turned to James again. In one simple gesture, he removed the medal and set it on the table. The room fell silent.

"No!"

Susannah looked around in surprise, and realized she had spoken. She was on her feet, after carefully depositing Noah in her chair. She hurried up the aisle to the rostrum where her godfather leaned, so pale now, and where her husband stood silent, head bowed, eyes closed.

She kept her eyes on her husband, even as they filled with tears. She wiped them away. This was no time to cry. There she stood, beside the two men she loved most in the world. She spoke to the two Fellows who had escorted her godfather to the rostrum, who now looked as astonished as rest of the society's august body.

"Help Sir Joseph to his seat again, sirs," she said, in a voice that expected no argument.

They did as she said. She turned to her husband and touched his arm. He was as stiff as a ship's figurehead. Well, never mind. If he would not speak in his own defense, she could, even through her terror. This was not the time to be shy. Beau Crusoe would have acted, if he were there.

"Lady Audley, shame on you," she said, her voice loud in a room suddenly quiet. "This man suffered through an ordeal that would have killed a common man." Her eyes sought out Sir Richard Bickerton. "The Lords of the Admiralty have heard his story in private and have cast no blame. Yes, he ate human flesh. I ask you here present to examine your own souls and decide what you would do to survive."

Even the weeping women were quiet now. With a shaking hand, James picked up the small drawing of the *Gloriosa*. She turned again to face the audience. "Did he murder Timothy Rowe? The Lords have exonerated him. They have called it self-defense against a deranged man. Again I ask: what would you do to survive?"

The audience was as quiet as a nursery full of sleeping children. "And as for the charge of seduction, is there a man in this audience who can imagine anyone *seducing* Lady Audley? I suspect it was rather the opposite." She looked directly at the woman who was still on her feet and scarlet with rage now. "I am continually amazed at the *ton*," Susannah said. "Lady Audley, have you no shame for preying on a lonely man cast away for five years?"

Her words rang out in the silent hall. Susannah knew Lady Audley would have started for her, except that Lord Audley jerked her into her seat again.

Someone else was on his feet. It was the little fellow James had pointed out to her as his tailor when they entered the hall. He pulled himself to his full height. "I don't know about you toffs, but I came to listen to a speech."

There were shouts now of "Hear, hear!"

The tailor wasn't finished. "My name is Thomas Redfern and I am the Beau's tailor. I don't care if he ate half of the Royal Navy. He's the only man in this assembly who ever paid his tailor without whining!"

The audience was shocked into silence again, and then the chuckling began—embarrassed titterings at first from the section where Sir Percival and his minions so elegantly sat in partly paid-for finery, and then hearty laughter from everyone.

When the mirth died down, other voices spoke, all saying the same thing. "Read! Read!"

The treatise lay before her on the rostrum. She turned to her husband. "Would you do the honors now, Mr. Trevenen?"

Maybe it was the formal way she asked him. Maybe he was beyond anything. A stricken look in his eyes, he shook his head, turned on his heel and left the room.

Susannah gasped and watched him go. *I should have called him James,* she thought in horror. *I should have called him James.*

But everyone was demanding the reading. She looked at Sir Joseph. "Please, send someone to stop him," she said in a low voice. "Please."

His face more serious than she had ever seen it, her godfather motioned to two of the Fellows in the front row and spoke to them. They left the room.

She looked down at the manuscript, took a deep breath, willed her hands to stop shaking and turned the title page. The room was silent again. She began.

"'Owing to the workings of Divine Providence and to none of my own puny exertions, since I was far gone, my small boat found a gap in the coral reef surrounding what would become my prison for the next five years, and grounded me on a sandy beach. I alone survived.'"

James had run out the back of Somerset House, which yielded directly onto the Thames. No matter; as terrified as he was of getting into a small boat again, all he wanted was to put London behind him.

It was a simple matter to gesture to a waterman resting at his oars. Reminding himself that no one could be shipwrecked and lost at sea in the Thames, James got in and seated himself. He sighed. Timothy Rowe was already there. At least the ghoul had had the decency to seat himself at the opposite end, in jarring reminder of their last week as shipmates and cannibals in the *Orion's* boat.

"Where, sir?" the waterman asked.

Anywhere, he thought. "The Kew Gardens landing in Richmond."

The waterman nodded and pulled into the stream.

He would take only what clothing he could grab quickly and his money. He could find lodging for the night, and then be on the doorstep of his solicitor's in the morning—not for more money, but to change his will and leave everything to Susannah Trevenen.

She couldn't bring herself to call me James, he thought. Poor Susannah. I forced a shy lady to plead my pitiful case for me. He watched as the waterman steered his craft expertly, not minding the boat as much as he thought he would. Susannah doesn't even know how wealthy I am, he thought. She and Noah will never want for anything again. I hope she likes my estate in Cornwall.

Once he had transferred everything to his wife, he would go to Portsmouth and sign onto the first ship leaving, be it an East India merchantman or a ship of the line off to the blockade. He would sign the roster as Tim Rowe, able-bodied seaman. It was the only work he knew.

The wind picked up and the small craft began to bob. The waterman grimaced in apology, but James only shrugged. "I know small boats," he said. "This isn't anything."

The current took them swiftly to Kew Gardens. He paid the waterman, adding enough extra to allow for Timothy Rowe, too. He started for Alderson House, then stopped. He had enough coins in his pockets for lodging and a change of clothing from a warehouse that supplied the poor with dead men's clothes. He had his original drawing of the *Gloriosa* in the inside pocket of his coat. He needed nothing else.

He wandered idly, and found himself at the pagoda. "I wish you would just wait here, Tim," he called over his shoulder. "I'm tired of your company."

Tim surprised him by staying behind. Maybe I should order him about more, he thought as he climbed to the top of the pagoda. James looked down on the king's lodge and Alderson House through the trees. He was even higher than John Weston. Bill Bright and Walter Shepherd had ever been, those seamen who had shared his life on the *Orion*.

He sobbed out loud, unable to help himself, remembering Weston's determination to swim to that imaginary ship and save them, and Bill Bright's quiet resignation when he told the others, as he lay dying, not to waste him by throwing him overboard, when he was dead.

"How little good I did you all," he said, "and I was your leader."

Exhausted by little sleep, worry, humiliation and despair, he sat down on the top deck and slept.

It was nearly dark when he woke. He couldn't remember where he was at first, but he looked around carefully, hoping Timothy Rowe wasn't seated next to him, waiting to lunge for his throat. He let out his breath slowly when he did not see the ghoul. It figured: Tim was a carpenter's mate; he didn't care much for heights.

James came slowly down, his mind on what he would do next. Some part of him wanted to see Susannah once more before he left, even if only through a window. He doubted she would want to see him again.

He was fully aware of the enormity of what he had done to

her, a quiet woman unused to the public eye because the public eye had turned on her years ago. She had defended him at Somerset House. On his behalf, she had calmed the monster, and he had just stood there like a dolt, unable to do anything except snatch up his *Gloriosa* sketch and run like a guilty man, which he was not. At least, he didn't think he was.

He left the pagoda finally. There was Timothy Rowe, waiting for him. "I wonder, do you mean to claim me?" James asked, exasperated. "Speak up, man. You're beginning to bore me."

Nothing. He looked beyond Tim to the Thames, all sluggish and oily, and felt a sudden longing to be at sea again, where the water was deep and bluish green and the wind…

He stopped walking, suddenly conscious of that other sound he had noticed in front of the church the other day. What *is* that? he asked himself, and why does it matter? He listened a moment longer, then started walking again.

He shook his head. He was an ordinary man, and there was no reason he had survived the sinking of the *Orion* except dumb luck. And the small boat? No reason there, either. True, he had been younger than the others, and he had eaten better food because he sat at the captain's table. Perhaps that had been the boost in his favor, when things were suddenly at their worst in the small boat.

He decided there was nothing to account for it. If there was a God in heaven, and he doubted it, that God never meddled in the puny affairs of men. I am being uncharitable, he thought wryly. Perhaps parting the Red Sea is easier than parting the Pacific Ocean. It was entirely possible that in the great scheme of things, the children of Israel mattered more than a few mariners adrift on a pitiless sea.

He looked back to see Timothy Rowe dogging his footsteps. He shrugged, not sure he even cared anymore. He had fled Somerset House like a coward, leaving Susannah Trevenen— God, his wife!—to face the shame by herself. He didn't dare go to Alderson House. He would probably find his clothes pitched out of the window and her delicate portrait of the *Gloriosa* smoldering in the grate.

The *Gloriosa*. He pulled his smaller sketch from his inside coat pocket as he walked, and stared at it, holding it up to the fading light. It had been his talisman all these years. The colors were fading now. With an ache, he remembered the fetching creatures in the tidal pool he would never see again. Maybe he had even thought his drawing would ward off demons, but he had been wrong.

"You're not much use to me now," he said. He took one last look, then folded the drawing and flung it into the wind. The stiffening breeze caught the *Gloriosa* and boosted it up like a kite. "You protected me from nothing," he called after it. "Good riddance."

Then he heard it, louder and louder now. His heart pounded faster in his chest. That sound! He had not heard it since the island. In one blinding moment, the devil's epiphany, he recognized it. The sound was all around him now. "No. No. Not me this time," he pleaded.

He wanted to run but he forced himself to stand still and look over his shoulder. To his terror, Tim Rowe had turned back, hopping away and shrieking, his hands in the air. In another moment, he had disappeared, leaving James entirely alone to face what he had feared the most.

He shut his eyes as the sound grew louder. He gritted his teeth, hunching his shoulder against what was finally coming after him. As he stood there, half crouching, waiting for his turn, he felt the subtle brushing against his legs, and the noise louder than ever.

He was surrounded; there was nothing more he could do. He opened his eyes, knowing what he would see, but deciding that if quiet Susannah could face all those strangers in his defense, he could at least go to his death with his eyes open.

He looked around. He was standing in the great meadow at Kew. All around him were vast mounds of leaves, blowing here and there. Suzie had said the gardeners gathered them into great piles and burned them.

Leaves. He looked down at his legs, and he saw nothing but

leaves blown along by the wind, making that horrible rustling noise that he had not been able to quite identify until now. It had been the one piece missing from the puzzle of what had happened when the boat broke up as they passed through that jagged coral gap, Tim's fingers at his throat.

"Well, well," he said quietly. The gardeners would be busy tomorrow, when they had to rake all those leaves back into orderly piles. Leaves. He rubbed his arms. The sound was incredibly similar to what had terrified him on the beach when he and Timothy, both alive, had washed ashore.

How simple. Now he knew what had happened to Timothy Rowe, poor man. The sound of rustling leaves had freed his mind to remember. He remembered everything.

He took his watch from his pocket. Good Lord, it was six o'clock. Where would Susannah be, at home in Alderson House, or at Spring Grove?

He decided on Spring Grove, because Sam would be there, and she would want her sister, and Loisa couldn't be pried from Sam's side. Sir Joseph would be there, too, and he most particularly wanted the president of the Royal Society to know that, in truth, he had not tried to award the Copley medal to a murderer.

He was halfway to Spring Grove when he remembered Timothy Rowe. He looked around. There was no one in sight. "Go to sleep, Tim," he said softly. "You've earned a better rest."

He hurried across the terrace, with its French doors opening onto the grand salon. With relief, he saw Susannah inside, walking back and forth in agitation, unlike the Susannah he loved. Sir Joseph sat in his wheeled chair and, thank the Lord, there was Sir Richard Bickerton. This would save him a trip to Admiralty House tomorrow.

The door was unlocked, so he opened it and walked down the corridor where he almost ran into Barmley. The footman gasped and nearly dropped a tray he carried.

"How sits the wind in there?" he whispered to the footman.

Barmley managed to gulp down his surprise. "Mrs. Park is determined to drag the Thames for your body, Mr. Trevenen."

Sir Richard Bickerton saw him first. He tapped Sir Joseph's arm and pointed at the same time that Susannah turned to make another circuit of the room. She stopped in her tracks, her mouth open.

"Suzie," was all he could say.

With a cry she ran across the room and threw herself into his arms, knocking him backward against the sofa, where they sat down together in a sudden heap. She was crying and scolding him at the same time, and then trying to gather all of him into her arms and hold him. He was happy to let her try, easing the matter by enveloping her in his own embrace, so tight she finally had to pull away so she could breathe.

And then she kissed him, holding his face between her hands, then rubbing his forehead with her own, as though she could not get enough of him.

"I was afraid you were going to hate me for what I did to you at Somerset House," he said finally.

"You're an idiot," she told him. She pushed on his chest. "Where have you been?"

"Yes, lad, tell," Sir Joseph said. "Susannah was about to chew the carpet."

"I would hate to think that all Trevenens had peculiar eating practices," he joked, then cupped his hands around her face this time. "You're still willing to be a Trevenen?"

"I told you after the wedding I wasn't going to do that again," she reminded him. "Weren't you listening?"

He glanced at Sir Richard. "Did she tell you?" he asked.

The Sea Lord nodded. "It wasn't hard to figure out, especially when she kept bursting into tears whenever anyone mentioned your name. My congratulations to both of you." He favored James with a long, measuring look. "Lad, you appear to have the weight of the world off your shoulders."

"I have, sir," James said. "I remember what happened to Timothy Rowe now. I didn't murder him. I didn't even shoot him." He raised his arm to gather Susannah closer. "It's a shocking story, my love."

"I'm not leaving."

"I didn't think you would." He took a deep breath and looked at Sir Joseph. "In the few days I have been telling you my story, sir, what is the one creature I have not mentioned at all? Something as common to all Pacific islands as fleas to a hound?"

Sir Joseph thought a moment. When he figured it out, he leaned back in his chair. "Land crabs."

"Precisely." James looked down at Susannah, knowing she would be puzzled. "Not the *Gloriosa*, Suzie. These are big crabs, bluish black. Fifteen to eighteen inches, wouldn't you say, Sir Joseph?"

"At least. They have powerful pincers and they will eat anything."

"They ate Timothy Rowe," James said quietly. "He wasn't even dead and they devoured him."

Susannah gasped and burrowed her face into his shoulder.

He kissed her hair. "I told you it was a terrible thing, Suzie. Obviously, even I didn't want to remember it."

When she could speak, she looked at him, tears in her eyes. "What made you remember?"

"The leaves."

"Leaves?" Sir Richard asked, mystified, and then his expression changed. "I remember that myself. Good Lord, how simple."

"Susannah, when I walked through Kew Gardens——I was going to find a hotel, change my will and leave for Portsmouth—— the wind started blowing those piles of leaves around. You know the sound that many leaves make?"

"Yes, but…"

"That's what hundreds of land crabs sound like when they're on the move," he said, shivering in spite of the fire in the grate.

"They do, indeed," Sir Joseph agreed. "I never would have thought of it, though."

"Nor I," Sir Richard said.

"That's because I doubt you were ever lying on a beach at their mercy," James said. He looked at Sir Richard now. "You saw the log, how the word ran off the page? Timothy started across the oars. By the time I capped the ink and dropped the log into the bag, he was on top of me. I never had a chance to fire the pistol.

I asked myself more than once during those years why I didn't just drop the log and grab the pistol."

"Because you are a well-trained officer," Sir Richard said, his pride unmistakable. "You never lost sight of how important a ship's log is. Bravo, lad. And then?"

"I had noticed the island. I don't know why Tim didn't, except…"

"…he was mad," Sir Joseph finished. "Go on."

"Just as he grabbed me, the boat shot through the gap in the reef and just disemboweled itself. Coral is razor-sharp, Suzie. One moment we were in the boat, and the next we were both floundering about."

He sighed. "I thought I was too weak to hang on to anything, but I got hold of the bow and rode it into the beach." He looked at the fire in the grate for a moment. "Tim was not so lucky. I'm still not totally certain of this in my mind, but I think when the boat broke up, one of the planks went through his chest."

"Poor man," Susannah said, keeping herself tucked close into James's shoulder.

"He was lying about fifteen feet away from me on the beach, bleeding, with that plank sticking through him," James said. He shuddered. "I couldn't reach him. I was so tired from fighting the surf that I couldn't move."

"Understandable," Sir Richard said.

"I fainted then. I think it was the sound of the crabs that roused me." James couldn't help himself. He leaped to his feet. "They were swarming all over the beach. Timothy was screaming, and they were devouring him."

Susannah covered her face with her hands. He knelt in front of her and held her hands. "One of the oars washed ashore and I tried to beat them away from him, but I could barely lift it."

"After what he tried to do to you, a lot of men wouldn't have even made the effort," Sir Richard said finally.

"He was a good carpenter's mate at one time," James said. He sat back on the sofa again. "That is the truth, Sir Richard," he said. "I reckon I did not want to remember it, until the leaves in Kew Gardens forced me."

"I believe you," Sir Richard said. "When you have completed this narrative that Sir Joseph has been telling me about—the whole story now—make a fair copy and I will add it to the ship's log."

"Thank you, Sir Richard," he said. "So many times during those years, I asked myself why I wasn't the one lying dead on the beach. Sometimes I think that nine-tenths of what happens to us is dumb luck."

"Only nine-tenths?" Sir Richard asked dryly.

James looked at Sir Joseph next. "I'm sorry I created such a tumult at Somerset House. Give that medal to next year's winner. I don't feel right about it now."

Sir Joseph stared hard at him. "Damn it, lad, the medal belongs to you!"

James shook his head. "Let this be the year that no one received the Copley." He turned to his wife next. "Susannah, will you forgive me for abandoning you there?"

"I've already forgotten it," she told him. "In case you are interested, your paper was quite well received."

He took her hand. "That's good, but I'm amazed how little it matters, at the moment." He kissed her hand. "Suzie, I'm simply speechless."

She touched his forehead with hers. "I love you," she said softly.

"And I love you," he told her back.

It was then that he noticed she was dressed in traveling clothes. Startled, he looked around. "Where are Sam and Loisa?"

"Guess," Susannah said. She handed him a letter.

He didn't have to look at it. "On their way to Gretna Green?" he asked, without looking at it.

She nodded. "One would think Gretna Green was a family tradition." She rolled her eyes. "I am to retrieve the fleeing couple and talk some sense into them."

He couldn't help but chuckle. "That's a tall order."

She nodded. "Sir Richard was so kindly going to accompany

me on this fool's errand. Since you are here, we will release him to return to his home and you will accompany me."

"To talk some sense into them?"

"Certainly not," she said, standing up. "To congratulate them."

Chapter Twenty-Eight

The coachman of the post chaise Sir Joseph had hired seemed surprised the first stage of their journey to the border meant driving at great speed to the neighboring estate, but his fee had been paid. Why should he quibble?

"This is the test of your love and devotion," Susannah told James as they hurried inside. "The lights tell me Mama and Papa are in the library, of all places. I didn't know my father even remembered where it was. You tell them we are married. I am going to rouse Noah."

"Certainly," he said cheerfully, not bothered at all, apparently, by the onerous chore she had just assigned him.

"Not easy to do," she warned him.

"Dearest, I am Beau Crusoe."

"Tell them the truth!" She turned to start up the stairs, but he took her by the arm and kissed her.

"By my reckoning I need one of those every twenty minutes, so hurry Noah along," he told her. "Take along a few more dresses and things for yourself."

"To the border and back?"

"We're going to Cornwall after we find the happy couple. You need to see your new home."

Noah was easy to rouse. She held a lamp over him, pained to

see tears dried on his cheeks. She held him close, giving him a much-abbreviated and well-purged version of what James had told them at Spring Grove. "We're going to Gretna Green. We'll see Aunt Loisa married, if we are in time, and then we are going to Cornwall for a visit."

He took it all in stride, helping her pack. "Neptune will miss me," he said as they started downstairs.

"I know. We will be back, though."

She handed their luggage to Chumley and hurried down the hall to the bookroom, pausing outside the door to listen first. No hysterics. No shouting. They have either killed him or he has charmed them, she thought.

Mama sat on the sofa, and Papa was actually seated at his desk, the estate ledger, of all things, open before him as James stood looking over his shoulder. When James glanced up and smiled that slow, easy smile, her heart turned over. Please, always look at me like that, she thought.

Noah ran to James, and he scooped up her son, holding him close. "I didn't mean to frighten you at Somerset House," he told the child. "It was a hard time for me, but I am better."

Noah hugged him tighter, doing an amazing imitation of her at Spring Grove, as she had tried to grab all of James at once. Like mother, like son, she thought.

"Noah, you never knew your own father," he said, his voice soft. "Had he lived, he would have loved you greatly."

Noah nodded. "That's what Mama tells me."

"She is right as usual," James said. "I shall love you greatly, too, if you have no objection."

Noah's answer was to burrow closer to him again.

"I must warn you, though, you will probably have little brothers and sisters, and they can be a trial." James patted his back. "Remember this—you are my first mate and always will be."

Susannah wiped her eyes with her fingers, and then her mother held out a handkerchief.

"Susannah, you are so ill-prepared."

"I know, Mama," she said, and blew her nose. "I'm sorry we

did not tell you about our wedding. Events were getting so complicated."

"I should scold you, daughter, but…"

"You've realized I am past remedy?" Susannah teased.

They left Alderson House a few minutes later, Mama waving to them from the front steps, and Papa with his hand on her shoulder. Susannah arranged blankets for Noah on the opposite seat and took her place beside her husband, who put his arm around her.

"Did Noah and I give you enough time to explain the toucans?" she asked him as they started off on the long journey.

"Some things are better left alone."

"Coward."

She could see his smile, even in the dark. "Actually, we were busy with something else. When we get to Cornwall, if my estate manager agrees, I am going to send him to Alderson House. If anyone can work miracles, he can."

She reached up to kiss his cheek. "You are amazing."

"I know."

"But what about your own estate?" she asked, her voice dubious. "I know next to nothing about it."

"And you married me anyway. Susannah, you are a total disgrace to the *ton*."

"I know."

"I don't know if this matters to you, but I have a fine place with lots of land and a magnificent view of the sea…"

"…where I can paint to my heart's content," she finished. She maneuvered herself closer to him. "Drat. I cannot seem to get close enough."

"We can change that when we land ourselves in a bed somewhere. It may be a while, though."

She glanced at Noah.

"He's asleep. I looked." He took her hand. "And you are right. I know next to nothing about estate management, but I have a brilliant idea."

"As Beau or James?" she teased.

"Both. You can congratulate me later, if it proves fruitful. When we meet up with Sam and Loisa, and after they are wed, I intend to ask him to manage my estate."

"I hadn't thought of that."

He kissed her fingers. "After we left Cape Town and Lady Audley, we did find time to talk. Sam's the son of a prosperous farmer in Norfolk. Will this be a comedown for your sister?"

"She won't see it that way, and neither do I. Bless you."

She didn't remember the letter from Sir Joseph until hours later near dawn, when they stopped for an exchange of horses. Noah slept, so they left the coachman to watch him and went inside the inn to eat. Over eggs and bacon, she remembered the letter and pulled it from her reticule.

"This is from Sir Joseph and the Royal Society. He gave it to me before we even knew where you were."

He wiped his mouth on his napkin and looked at it warily. "I can almost hear the scold without breaking the seal. You open it, Susannah. I'm feeling nauseous."

"Then you shouldn't bolt your food. I've been meaning to speak to you about that. One meal does follow another, on this island."

He returned to his bacon as she opened the letter. He looked up, alert, at her soft intake of breath. When she took her napkin off her lap to dab at her eyes, he took the letter from her.

"What a cad I continue to be, making you do my dirty work," he muttered as his eyes scanned the page. The fork clattered to his plate. "Great God in heaven," he said, his meal forgotten. "Suzie! The Society wants to name me First Collector of Kew Gardens!"

She could barely speak. "Have you read the part about the ship?"

"Right here. 'Sir Percival Pettibone and Lord Eberly of Maines have agreed to furnish the expedition, with assistance from the Royal Society.'" He looked up, his eyes bright. "Suzie! We are to return to the South Seas! My word, a man I never saved from fire and another man whose children were never in the slightest danger have changed our lives yet again. How odd."

She swallowed the lump in her throat. "It says nothing about me."

"I wouldn't dream of doing any of this without you and Noah along," he said quietly, dropping the letter in the eggs. "Don't be a goose. I will need a limner. You will be Sydney Parkinson to my Sir Joseph Banks. Susannah love, you can sit cross-legged by the tidal pool and sketch the *Gloriosa*, just as I did. Well?"

"You're serious?"

"Completely. It's a hard life, Suzie." He retrieved the letter and flicked off the eggs. "Look, it says here I can appoint my own staff. Sir Joe knew what I would do. We'll probably be two or three years on the voyage. I'm certain Noah will enjoy it."

He finished the letter. "When we return, we are to have King's Lodge as quarters. Apparently I will be in charge of sending out other ships of exploration. You will paint, as you do now, and I will administer." He smiled at her. "I will grow a double chin, and turn into a bureaucrat."

"Unlikely," she said. "Two or three years?"

"Probably." He finished his bacon and looked toward the door. She watched his face, praying it was not Timothy Rowe.

He gestured with his fork. "The coachman there says he's ready."

She let her breath out slowly. "Let me finish my tea."

He nodded. "Is it yes or no, Susannah? If it is no, I will turn it down. I cannot leave you."

"It is yes," she told him. Her face grew warmer then. "But dearest, there is every likelihood we will find ourselves with child on a voyage of such length."

"I imagine we will," he replied, "if you're not that way already. Suzie, I have every confidence in our ability to deal with anything that comes up. We'll tether our little son or daughter to the mainmast and put the pharmacist's mate in charge."

"James…" she warned.

"Dearest, I am quizzing you!"

The inn was full of people, but she leaned across the table and kissed him over the cold toast. "I say yes most emphatically. I would be unpatriotic, indeed, to permit a lunatic to wander the globe without a keeper."

"All for science, Suzie?" he teased.

She shook her head. "All for love."

* * * * *

Turn the page for a sneak preview of
IF I'D NEVER KNOWN YOUR LOVE
by
Georgia Bockoven

From the brand-new series
Harlequin Everlasting Love
Every great love has a story to tell.™

One year, five months and four days missing

There's no way for you to know this, Evan, but I haven't written to you for a few months. Actually, it's been almost a year. I had a hard time picking up a pen once more after we paid the second ransom and then received a letter saying it wasn't enough. I was so sure you were coming home that I took the kids along to Bogotá so they could fly home with you and me, something I swore I'd never do. I've fallen in love with Colombia and the people who've opened their hearts to me. But fear is a constant companion when I'm there. I won't ever expose our children to that kind of danger again.

I'm at a loss over what to do anymore, Evan. I've begged and pleaded and thrown temper tantrums with every official I can corner both here and at home. They've been incredibly tolerant and understanding, but in the end as ineffectual as the rest of us.

I try to imagine what your life is like now, what you do every day, what you're wearing, what you eat. I want to believe that the people who have you are misguided yet kind, that they treat you well. It's how I survive day to day. To think of you being mistreated hurts too much. If I picture you locked away somewhere and suffering, a weight descends on me that makes it almost impossible to get out of bed in the morning.

Your captors surely know you by now. They have to recognize what a good man you are. I imagine you working with their children, telling them that you have children, too, showing them the pictures you carry in your wallet. Can't the men who have you understand how much your children miss you? How can it not matter to them?

How can they keep you away from us all this time? Over and over, we've done what they asked. Are they oblivious to the depth of their cruelty? What kind of people are they that they don't care?

I used to keep a calendar beside our bed next to the peach rose you picked for me before you left. Every night I marked another day, counting how many you'd been gone. I don't do that any longer. I don't want to be reminded of all the days we'll never get back.

When I can't sleep at night, I tell you about my day. I imagine you hearing me and smiling over the details that make up my life now. I never tell you how defeated I feel at moments or how hard I work to hide it from everyone for fear they will see it as a reason to stop believing you are coming home to us.

And I couldn't tell you about the lump I found in my breast and how difficult it was going through all the tests without you here to lean on. The lump was benign—the process reaching that diagnosis utterly terrifying. I couldn't stop thinking about what would happen to Shelly and Jason if something happened to me.

We need you to come home.

I'm worn down with missing you.

I'm going to read this tomorrow and will probably tear it up or burn it in the fireplace. I don't want you to get the idea I ever doubted what I was doing to free you or thought the work a burden. I would gladly spend the rest of my life at it, even if, in the end, we only had one day together.

You are my life, Evan.

I will love you forever.

* * * * *

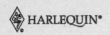

HARLEQUIN® *Romance*®

presents a brand-new trilogy by

PATRICIA THAYER

Rocky Mountain
BRIDES

Three sisters come home to wed.

In April don't miss

Raising the Rancher's Family,

followed by

The Sheriff's Pregnant Wife,

on sale May 2007,

and

A Mother for the Tycoon's Child,

on sale June 2007.

Romantic
SUSPENSE

*Excitement, danger
and passion guaranteed!*

USA TODAY bestselling author
Marie Ferrarella
is back with the second installment
in her popular miniseries,
*The Doctors Pulaski: Medicine
just got more interesting...*
DIAGNOSIS: DANGER is on sale
April 2007 from Silhouette®
Romantic Suspense (formerly
Silhouette Intimate Moments).

*Look for it wherever
you buy books!*
